REVENANT

Also by Kat Richardson

GREYWALKER

POLTERGEIST

UNDERGROUND

VANISHED

LABYRINTH

DOWNPOUR

SEAWITCH

POSSESSION

ANTHOLOGIES

MEAN STREETS

(WITH JIM BUTCHER, SIMON R. GREEN, AND THOMAS E. SNIEGOSKI)

REVENANT

A GREYWALKER NOVEL

KAT RICHARDSON

A ROC BOOK

ROC
Published by the Penguin Group
Penguin Group (USA) LLC, 375 Hudson Street,
New York, New York 10014

USA | Canada | UK | Ireland | Australia | New Zealand | India | South Africa | China
penguin.com
A Penguin Random House Company

First published by Roc, an imprint of New American Library,
a division of Penguin Group (USA) LLC

First Printing, August 2014

 REGISTERED TRADEMARK—MARCA REGISTRADA

LIBRARY OF CONGRESS CATALOGING-IN-PUBLICATION DATA:

Richardson, Kat.
  Revenant: a Greywalker novel/Kat Richardson.
    p. cm—(Greywalker; 9)
  ISBN 978-0-451-46528-3 (hardback)
  1. Blaine, Harper (Fictitious character)—Fiction. 2. Women private investigators—Fiction. 3. Man-woman relationships—Fiction. I. Title.
  PS3618.I3447R48 2014
  813'.6—dc23   2014008562

Printed in the United States of America
10 9 8 7 6 5 4 3 2 1

Set in Adobe Garamond
Designed by Alissa Rose Theodor

This one is for my fans and minions, especially Thea and Eric Maya—
Thing One and Thing Two—with many thanks.

ACKNOWLEDGMENTS

I'd like to thank some people for being awfully good sports: Maggie Griffin; Robin (R. K.) McPherson for notes about Black Ops and bones; the brothers Bara and my first agent, Steve Mancino, for being much nicer than their namesakes here. Colleen Lindsay and Dana Kaye for introducing me to Maggie. Jane Haddam (Orania Papazoglou) for letting me pick her brain about Portugal and the Capela dos Ossos in Évora. Liz Argall as well as trusty friends Elisabeth Shipman and Nancy Durham for beta reading. Laura Anne Gilman, Barbara Ferrer, and Monica Valentinelli for being indefatigable cheerleaders and ass kickers. Wonder agent Sally Harding and the crew at the Cooke Agency. Anne Sowards and the team at Roc—you make me look good! The enormously talented Chris McGrath for the best cover ever! And chief minions Thea and Eric Maya for going through every single volume of the Greywalker saga to find the continuity errors.

Last, but never least, my husband for putting up with me and taking up the slack while I was busy writing this book. I love you.

REVENANT

PROLOGUE

Death doesn't frighten me. We are old friends by now. But just knowing death doesn't mean I seek it. Some people do. Some even reside there, but that's not for me. For me, it's an occupational hazard. I'm a Greywalker. I dance along the high wire between the realms of the living and the dead, in the strange intersection called "the Grey," where ghosts dwell and monsters are real and the fire of magic sings in hot lines of power, gleaming like neon in rain-slicked night that continues all the way to the bottom of the well of the world.

But that's not what my business card says—HAVE GHOST; WILL TRAVEL. No, mine just reads HARPER BLAINE, PRIVATE INVESTIGATOR. I wanted that job and I worked to get it. The other . . . That just happened one day when an angry man beat my head in. It would have happened anyway; he just accelerated the process. I've died and come back three times and each brings me closer to the last, and each time I wake changed. I have no control over it—it just is. I suspect that my next tango with death will be my last.

So I work for ghosts and monsters and sometimes for the people I love. And that's where things get weird. Because a little more than a year ago I wouldn't have expected my lover to leave me within the next six months to pursue his father across Europe, and I wouldn't have expected to get a mysterious message in another eight months summoning me to join him, or that I would bring a vampire along with me when I did.

ONE

I woke in a coffin and knew the rat had died. I'm not normally claustrophobic, but for a moment I hyperventilated and lay there, sweating and quietly freaking out, while wishing I were just in a low-budget horror film rather than in the cargo hold of a transatlantic jet, resting in a cleverly ventilated box with a label on the outside in six languages that read CAUTION: HUMAN REMAINS. HANDLE WITH CARE.

I had no way to know how long I'd been in the box, but I thought it couldn't have been more than a day since I'd received a code-phrase message from my boyfriend, Quinton, summoning me to Europe. There'd been very little information except that he needed me in Lisbon as soon as possible and I was to come without leaving any sign that I was gone or alerting anyone keeping tabs on me that I was exiting the country. I knew from discussions starting a year earlier that it had to appear that I was still in my usual place for as long as possible. Whatever it was Quinton wanted, it involved his father, James McHenry Purlis—spy, manipulator, and all-around villain.

Since I was in a bind, I'd turned to the local vampires for help. They seemed to get around without much harassment from TSA or border patrols, and they owed me a few favors. And there was the matter of Carlos, both vampire and necromancer, who had a personal interest in breaking down Purlis and his mysterious project. If anyone was capable of making me disappear without a trace and reappear elsewhere, it would be him. I'd left messages for him explaining the situation, made discreet arrangements on my own end, and had agreed to meet him. . . .

The location in question was a funeral home. As I walked in through the doors labeled with a tasteful sign—BARRON VIEWING, 7–9 P.M.—it occurred to me that I'd come to trust Seattle's vampires. It had been a slow change and an uncomfortable one, but when I was in a corner, it was most often Cameron and Carlos to whom I turned for help now—a far cry from the relationship I'd had with them when I'd first fallen into the Grey. The situation had changed a lot since I'd met my first vampire, but more than that, I had changed. I wasn't the frightened and defensive loner I had been.

I passed the immaculately dressed funeral director, who stood near an interior door and gave me an inquiring look. I shook my head and murmured, "I have an appointment with Silverstein." He nodded and pointed toward a curtained doorway at the end of the hall. As I passed the open doorway he guarded, I saw that the viewing room was empty. A sad state of affairs for a funeral director: all dressed in black and no one to console.

I gave him a small smile. "I'm sure someone will come soon."

"I doubt it," he replied in a professional, funereal hush. "The man was a child molester. Someone shot him . . . in an appropriate location. I won't mind if no one comes."

I blinked and nodded. "Oh. No. That's fair, I suppose."

He offered me a thin smile. "Thank you." He folded his hands in front of his belt and returned to waiting for no one.

I went to the curtained door and opened it to discover a stair landing and a flight of steps leading down. The walls were a sterile, glossy white that reflected the light from the fixtures on the walls as well as from the room below. I'd been in mortuaries before and the chill and odor told me I was walking down to the prep room—where the dead were made presentable for their grieving families and friends. I was more sure than ever that I wasn't going to like Carlos's transportation methods.

Carlos stood between the embalming tables. A plump, older woman in a black suit stood several feet away, near a cabinet. The woman somehow seemed to fade into the background even in the glare of the lights, but Carlos was indelible. I'd never seen him in a room so well lit. The work lights shining off the high-gloss white walls and poured-cement floor cast illumination into every corner and crevice of the room and every crag of his face. His hair and beard looked blacker than ever as the light bleached color from his skin and chased away the perpetual shadow under his brow. I was shocked to realize that he hadn't been in his forties when he'd died—as I'd long assumed—but in his late twenties or early thirties at the most. I blinked at him, momentarily stunned as I reevaluated what I'd always believed about this particular vampire.

"You act as if you've never seen me before," he said, his voice still as dark and powerful as ever, almost incongruous in a face so suddenly young.

"Maybe I haven't," I said, walking closer. Now I could see the scars, thin as razor cuts, around the edges of his face. They vanished under the thick bristle of his beard and the sweep of his hair, leaving trails like strands of spider silk on his neck and the surface of his forearms, which were revealed by his rolled-up sleeves. I'd seen the marks only once before, fleetingly, and had forgotten them until now. He knew I was staring, but he only raised an eyebrow and let me.

"What caused all this?" I asked.

"Never shy, are you, Blaine?"

"With you? What would be the point?"

He laughed and the sound rolled like thunder, shaking the Grey version of the room. "Perhaps I'll show you the window I was thrown from, if the building still exists."

"Was this—"

"My death? No. I've always been very hard to kill, though several have tried." He raised his chin and touched a patch of skin on his neck where his whiskers grew thin. "That was my mortal wound. Remember this: If you mean to kill a mage, first you silence him and bind his hands behind his back. Better yet, cut them off. Very few can cast by thought alone without killing themselves."

I shuddered and turned my gaze away. "I'm sorry."

"Don't be. If things go badly in Portugal, you'll need every trick you can conjure at your disposal. Luckily, you are also very hard to kill."

"Oh, no. I seem to die all too easily. I just don't stay down. Usually."

I felt his silence as much as heard it.

"There's a limit to everything," I said. "Someday I won't get up again. Maybe soon. Maybe not." I was prevaricating, since I was convinced the next death would be my last. Another Greywalker had told me I would know, but it was like knowing that the earth spun as it orbited the sun, even when you couldn't see or feel it—I just had the feeling that it was true.

Carlos made a low growling sound and closed the distance between us. "Perhaps we shouldn't do this. There is a risk. . . ."

"Living is risky. Driving a car is risky. I'd guess from the setup that we're going to be playing dead—or at least I will—which is only crazy. And you and I, we're pretty good with crazy, by now. So let's just get this over with. I assume whatever transportation you've arranged will be arriving soon."

"Within an hour. Tovah will manage the paperwork and so on." Carlos gestured toward the woman in the corner.

She stepped forward and offered me a handshake, and I could see a tiny dazzle of Grey on her wrist, not much larger than a grain of rice. "It's a pleasure to meet you. I've already filed all the necessary papers with the consulate and completed those that will be traveling with you. All should continue smoothly." She noticed my frown and glanced at her wrist when I didn't reply or shake her hand.

I'm often suspicious of unexplained Grey marks—they're rarely a good sign—and as I knew Purlis's project was aimed at gaining some kind of control of paranormal creatures to use them as spies and engines of terror, it gave me pause. I hated to question it—especially in front of Carlos—but I did. "What is that?"

Tovah shifted her glance to Carlos without turning her head, not at all affronted by my rude behavior.

"Nothing sinister," he said. "All of those who assist us bear a mark, inconspicuous but visible."

I peered at it, giving it a look through the Grey to better see the actual shape. "It looks like a dagger."

"It is mine," he said, as if I should have guessed. Maybe I should have—Carlos has a particular attachment to a knife that once nearly killed him and, being a necromancer, he has an affinity for instruments of death, anyway.

I nodded. "All right. Why haven't I noticed these marks before?"

"You've seen them, but you had no reason to question them. Now you have every reason."

I made a noise of dissatisfaction and turned my attention back to Tovah rather than to the tiny mark on her skin.

"Do you do this often?" I asked.

"Yes," she answered, as if the conversation had never been interrupted. "But not with someone who's still alive. You may find it a bit unsettling—the Portuguese officials require a rather old-fashioned container, which is not as comfortable as a proper casket." She indicated two long wooden boxes that had been arranged on the farthest table.

I had to admit, I'd never considered whether a casket could be called "comfortable." I walked toward them and looked the boxes over. They were built of something like wood chipboard and lined with a dusty-looking metal. Nylon mesh straps formed three loop handles on each long side of the slightly protruding bottom plank and a rubber gasket ran all the way around the open top. Both boxes were the same size and I thought I'd probably be less cramped than Carlos would be, since the box was long enough to accommodate either of us—with a few inches to spare over my five feet ten inches—but rather narrow for the width of his shoulders. Matching lids leaned against the wall nearby, and an electric screw gun and a box of impressively long wood screws stood on the end of the counter.

"They look . . . cozy," I said.

"They're lined with zinc and hermetically sealed," Tovah said. "I hope you have no metal allergies."

"No." I frowned. "So, they're airtight?"

"Usually. Yours is . . . not quite to spec. The consulate does not require an inspection at the arrival destination and the anomaly will be undetectable on X-rays because of the metal lining. All the paperwork is in order, so there should be no reason for anyone to open the boxes anywhere en route. You'll be picked up as soon as customs releases the cases and the Lisbon mortuary will deliver you to your destination. It's all arranged."

"It sounds . . . um . . . fine. Thank you."

She gave me a small smile and stepped back, finished with her recitation and reassurance. She looked at Carlos and he nodded. She left the room through another door that I suspected led to a loading dock or storage area.

"Now what?" I asked him once her door was closed.

"Now . . . I put you to sleep."

"That sounds like the euphemism veterinarians use."

"I assure you, it's not the same. But there is, as I said, a risk."

"And I already said it's acceptable."

"No, you did not. But now you have. Come sit on the table here and remove your boots."

"Why?" I asked even as I moved to do as he directed.

"Because you will be more comfortable without them. And I don't wish to stoop."

"Is your age getting to you?" I teased him.

He closed the distance between us faster than I could see and wrapped his near arm around my waist, pulling me tight to his side. I gagged on the bleakness of his aura and the boiling nausea he brought with him. He put his mouth near my ear and whispered, "There is another way, Blaine."

I had to swallow hard before I could reply. "No. You know the answer will always be the same."

"I cling to hope," he said. Then he laughed, let me go, and took half a step back. "On the table, if you please."

"I feel like a surgical patient, but without the backless gown," I said as I hitched myself up onto the steel embalming table and began taking off my boots.

"No surgery, though there will be some blood."

I rolled my eyes, dropping one boot to the floor. "I should have known."

"And death."

I looked up, trepid and not a little upset. Carlos had his back to me and was reaching into a cupboard near the coffins. He took something down and turned to face me.

It was a rat—a huge rat. "I didn't know they came that size," I said.

"It is very large. It was destined to be dinner for an anaconda at the university, but I borrowed it first."

"And what's it for?"

"This is a spell of similarity. To make you *appear* dead, we'll need another creature that *is* dead. The strands of your life forces will be entangled, and so long as one lies as dead, the other will continue as alive. Currently you're both alive. Someone's state must change, and it's far safer and to our needs that it be the rat and not you."

I felt sick. "No, I can't do that. It's terrible," I said. I don't have any particular soft spot for rats, but it was a healthy, innocent, living creature. It didn't deserve this.

He shrugged. "My power lies in death and within that realm there's only the one other way, which you've already rejected." His voice, though soft, still sent a quivering sensation through my chest.

I stared at the rat. It looked calm, even a bit sleepy, in Carlos's hands. He put it on his shoulder like a pet and picked up two small bottles from the counter nearby. He walked to me, stroking the rat with his knuckles, and held out the bottle in his free hand. "Drink this."

I wanted to cry. I could feel the prickling of tears under my eyelids and the corners of my mouth had turned down so emphatically that it was hard to speak. "Why?"

"It's part of the casting that will bind you together."

I bit my lip and studied the rat. It looked back at me with filmed eyes, the fur along its back grizzled with white. It was an old rat and its lethargy was a natural result, not a magical effect. I supposed that had made it a more attractive lunch than a younger rat that might have injured the snake while fighting for its life. This one looked ready to heave a sigh and give up. "I don't like it," I said.

"I didn't imagine you would. Make up your mind—time is passing and we have very little left."

Unhappy and not at all convinced I was doing the right thing, I took the bottle from Carlos and did my best to swallow the contents around the lump in my throat. He muttered to the rat and fed it from the other bottle as I forced the bitter, burning liquid down my own throat. As I swallowed the last of it, I began to see a narrow strand of green energy that lifted off the rat as if it were a thread in a breeze. Carlos touched one finger to my chest, making me shudder with the cold that came from him, and drew up a similar filament from me, muttering all the while in words that sparked the silvery mist of the Grey in actinic flashes.

He twisted the strands together in his left hand and picked up the rat in his right, still speaking glittering, barbed words that twisted and dug into me and the now-wriggling creature.

He dropped it into my lap. I jerked and the rat bit my leg, its long yellow teeth cutting right through my blue jeans and into my skin. I shouted at the sudden pain and snatched the rat off my lap. A small spot of blood swelled into the fabric of my jeans and a drop of the same hung on the rat's protruding teeth. It licked the blood off with a busy swipe of its tongue and I knew what one of the harsh flavors was in Carlos's brew.

"Oh, you sneaky bastard," I said.

Ignoring my words, Carlos plucked the rat from my grip, rolling and knotting it in the twined coil of our combined lives. Then he put the rat on the table beside me, where it lay without moving, though I could see its sides heaving as it breathed. He held both his hands over it, as if smothering it, and though he didn't touch it, the rat's breathing slowed and the gleam of its life dimmed until it was nearly extinguished.

He wrapped the entangled threads around me now, his lips moving, but the sound so low, I couldn't hear him. I felt dizzy and swayed. Carlos caught me by the shoulders and I could barely feel the piercing cold of his touch as he laid me down on the table beside the dying rat, which he picked up and placed on my chest.

"Poor rat," I murmured, folding my hands over it. I could feel a distant warmth in its still body. "I'm sorry. . . ."

"Breathe," Carlos whispered. "Breathe out. Let your breath go."

Perversely, I sucked in a breath that felt as cold as Arctic snow and had to cough the sharp knife of air out again at once.

The rat squirmed in my hands. My vision dimmed and the last of my breath slid away. I felt the rat push out of my loose grip and trot a step or two down my body before it was lifted off me, squeaking as loudly as a hungry baby.

Darkness and cold that had no real temperature settled on me. My ears rang until the blood slowed down too much to whisper. Something touched my face, brushing my forehead, eyelids, lips, and slid away just as I teetered into the black.

"I'll see you in Lisbon, Blaine."

TWO

I thought I wasn't supposed to wake up yet—surely we hadn't reached Lisbon? My broken sense of time and my helplessness were frustrating and there seemed to be nothing I could do about being awake. I was supposed to be playing dead until after we arrived in Portugal, and I doubted that I was going to pass muster at customs if I was breathing. I slid my hands up, unable to push the box open, feeling an unfamiliar cloth and strapping holding me down as I brushed against my clothes. Or rather, not my clothes. I couldn't see in the dark, but I could tell by the feel that I wasn't wearing the jeans and sweater I'd had on when I lay down on the embalming table.

I shuddered, thinking that someone had changed my clothes and strapped me to the base of the coffin. If that someone was Carlos, I was going to slap him numb, necromancer or not. I chided myself not to get hysterical over such a small point. It was probably Tovah who'd managed it, making me look more corpse-like and appropriately dressed for my funeral, as well as safely tied down. She'd cleaned up the rat bite on my leg as well, for which I was grateful, but not put any more at ease. I plucked at the straps that kept me from rolling and sliding in my casket. No matter how much my clothes made me look like a stiff, I was now breathing and sweating as the silent panic started. I wasn't sure I could be a convincing corpse without Carlos's help and I had no way to get it. It didn't matter if he, too, was wide awake, since neither of us could slither out of our portable graves and have a cozy chat about the problem. Given the state of the world—with terrorism, epidemics, floods, and fires everywhere, and civil war in Syria and Turkey, as well as dozens of other problems leading to unrest and paranoia at home and internationally—if I made one ill-timed sound or rolled in the box as it was being moved, no one was going to simply pass the coffin on without taking a look inside first. That would be a disaster. I schooled myself to be still, still, still, and quiet as my own corpse. I tried sinking down toward the Grey. . . .

My box lurched and I heard the engine downshift and groan. I couldn't concentrate in the jostling box and had to give up my dive for the Grey. But at least it seemed I wasn't in a plane after all. A truck? I hoped it was a truck in Portugal and not a truck crossing the tarmac at whatever transshipment point we'd passed through. I hated the idea of being lost luggage somewhere in Europe.

Wherever I was, something was keeping me from gaining access to—or even a view of—the Grey or its writhing energy grid. It could have been a side effect of the zinc lining in the box, but I wasn't certain. I knew steel and silver both had unusual properties in the Grey, but I wasn't sure if magical interactions were universal to all metals. I would have bet that the problem had something to do with my being inside a metal box inside a metal truck, but there was no way to test the hypothesis at that moment. I wasn't all that interested in trying, anyway. It was always possible I'd sink too far, displace myself, and fall out of the truck at whatever speed we were going in traffic.

After what felt like a couple of hours in my stuffy little coffin as the truck wound up and down some steep hills and swayed around hairpin turns, the vehicle stopped and I was unloaded. I was pretty sure the people moving my box were being careful, but I still got jarred around and collected a couple of bruises from thumping into the side when someone lost their grip. Even through the zinc and wood, I could hear swearing. It wasn't English swearing, but the tone was the same even if I didn't understand the words. I held my breath and didn't swear back, just in case. . . .

Then came the trundling sound of a cart underneath me before another spate of lifting, tilting, jostling, swearing, and finally a ringing thump as the coffin was set down on some hard surface. Eventually, sounds of the box-handlers faded away and the lid was opened.

The dimly lit room I'd been brought to was almost soundless, and the air, while cooler, was only a small relief from the close and overused atmosphere in my box.

A dark-haired woman peered into my container, her expression wary. *"Senhora Blaine?"* The energy around her head was streaked with black and orange like Halloween bunting. She appeared anxious and a little bit dead, but not undead.

I struggled to sit up—which isn't easy after lying still for hours in an unheated cargo hold. I thought every joint in my body had turned to brittle wood that creaked and cracked as I moved. I glanced around, not sure I hadn't somehow ended up in some long-ago place where time had stopped: The stone room was lit with candles in iron sconces near the door and an enchanted silence muffled its natural echo. Deep, dim coils of black and red energy surged along the floor from under the stout wooden door like floodwater slowly rising.

The woman watching me seemed relieved when I was upright. "*Bom*. Come with me," she said. Her accent was one I'd never heard before, something that wasn't quite Spanish and wasn't quite Russian. She straightened up without offering me a hand, but I wasn't entirely surprised. With the exception of Tovah, people who work for vampires aren't the touchy-feely type. Though I tried to look for it, I saw no sign of the sort of mark Tovah had. Apparently some people don't have to be in thrall to be useful.

I clambered out of the coffin, which was resting on the ground, as stiff and awkward as a stick insect as I crawled over the edge and onto the chilly floor, tearing the hem of my black skirt on the steel edge. The entire room seemed to have been carved out of solid stone, but it was definitely a room, not a cavern—it had a flat floor, straight walls, and a symmetrical, vaulted ceiling. Shadows fell into deep folds in the corners away from the door and its nearby candles, and the low gleams of magical energy flowed along the floor toward the darkness, as if seeking a hidden exit bored through the rock. Aside from me, my box, my hostess, and the candles, there seemed to be nothing else in the room. Inside my coffin, I'd been too warm and panicky. In this stone room, dressed like a dead doll in my funeral suit and soft shoes, I was suddenly too cold and my panic had mutated into overactive wariness.

My knees creaked and popped anew, protesting long inaction. The trip, I'd estimated, would be about fourteen hours, but there'd been extra hours in transit to and from airports and through customs and so on, so I was completely out of sync.

"What time is it?" I asked, scraping one bare knee a little on the stone floor as I got to my feet. I felt woozy and wound up at the same time—probably a side effect of what Carlos had done to make me appear dead.

"*Desculpe.* It is"—she paused to pull an old-fashioned watch from a pocket in her skirt, popping the lid open and glancing at it—"twelve minutes past two in the afternoon. Dom Carlos is still asleep."

It was late summertime, so I knew he wouldn't be up and about for another six hours or so, and that was fine. I had things to do that wouldn't require his help, so long as I could get back in time. I assumed I was in Lisbon, though there was always the off chance that something had changed.

"Where is this? I mean, which city?" I asked, just in case. . . .

"Lisboa. This is the family's town house in Alfama," she replied. Alfama meant nothing to me, but at least I knew I was in the right city.

Now I had to find Quinton and discover why he'd needed me here now. If the rendezvous didn't work out, I'd have to find an Internet café and see whether I could make contact again, since he didn't know where I was any more than I knew where he was. The codes he'd sent implied a situation that couldn't wait, so I hoped I'd find him the first time.

"Am I free to come and go?" I asked, not sure what the situation was in which I found myself. Was this some kind of vampire chapter house or something else? It certainly wasn't the usual B and B, and I wasn't sure whose "family" she meant when she talked about the house, since vampires over a certain age generally have no close mortal kin. I'm not sure they think of one another as "family," either, unless it's in the context of dangerous siblings that they may need to kill later.

"You are a guest. The doors will open for you—you may come and go as you please, though Dom Carlos will expect you when he wakes."

"How do you know that?"

She gave a shrug that was as much a change of expression as an actual movement of head and shoulders. "Avó said so. I will await Dom Carlos's instructions. If you must go out, return by sundown."

I had no intention of running away, but this business couldn't wait on Carlos. My lingering panic had transferred to finding Quinton.

The woman nodded, as if she understood my train of thought, and she turned, leading me out of the room. "There is a suite for you upstairs. I will show you the way."

We went along a windowless, stone-walled corridor in the company of ghosts, past several heavy wooden doors with ancient-looking iron hinges and handles, all lit by candles. A draft of cooler air, smelling of stone and earth, passed along the hallway with us and rose up the stairs at the end as we ascended. My guide put her candle down on a table at the head of the stairs and opened a door, leaning down to blow out the flame as a mixture of sun and electric light flooded the landing. We emerged into a wider hallway with a floor of colorful, fitted stone tiles and walls of pale yellow plaster, and passed through a narrow but impressive Moorish entry hall. Decorative ironwork grilles hung over the windows on one side and matching iron railings edged the staircase and the gallery that looked down from above. Grey energy hung down the walls like gleaming draperies of ragged gold and red with twisting threads of black and white tangling through them and creeping down the walls like cracks in the plaster. The room wept quietly in the Grey with a sound like a distant viola accompanying a melancholy guitar. A grand staircase curved around the sides and back of the room. A pair of ghosts dressed in some kind of medieval clothes glided up the stairs and vanished around the gallery on the updraft of air from the cellars. I got the impression the house hadn't been occupied in a while and was trying to shed the collected heat and stale air of many summers. It made the elegant little entry oppressive. It was a very old house and it had seen hundreds of summers.

The entry may have been stuffy and hot, but a breeze was fighting its way up the staircase from the cooler cellars below and the house seemed to breathe more easily as we ascended yet another staircase. The woman finally unlocked a door and led me into a tiny room with a few items of furniture, a bed not among them. Beyond a small sofa and a desk lay another door, which she opened and stood beside, holding the large old-fashioned key.

"This bedroom is at the front of the house. It is not as grand as some, but it has a better breeze from the river. The back of the house is quieter, but it faces the castle and the air is not so cool."

"Castle?" I asked, startled at the idea of being close enough to one that it blocked the breeze. It was either a very large castle or very close. . . . Either way, being an American, I tended to find the very idea of castles intriguing, let alone the idea of one in the backyard.

"*Sim. Castelo de São Jorge.*" She pointed toward the back of the house. "It is just up the hill. You can see it from the roof and rear windows on this floor. The tourists enjoy it in the mornings and at sunset. Otherwise, it is much too hot to wander the grounds at midday until late October." She offered me the room key. "If you would like to bathe and change before you go out, the bath is through the next door. There are clothes in the wardrobe and you are to treat the house as your own. It is still very warm this season and you may wish to do your business in lighter clothes. Even here on the hill, the afternoons are hot. I will be downstairs if you have any other requirements."

I took the heavy old key and she glided out of the room before I had a chance to ask her name. She made no sound as she crossed the polished wooden floor and for a fleeting instant I wondered whether she was an apparition. I felt like I'd landed in a Gothic novel and expected to hear that there was an insane relative locked in the attic.

I wanted to rush out but knew I needed to change out of my torn skirt and wash my face at the very least. Tovah must have applied a layer of thick makeup to make me look more corpse-like, and I could feel it cracking with every movement of my face. I looked around as I started for the bathroom.

The rooms were small by American standards, but at least the ceilings were high. All of the doorways and windows were arched— not a square frame to be seen—and all of the floors were old, dark wood, rippled with age. The first room we'd passed through appeared to be a sort of sitting room or personal office and the inner room was the bedroom. Nothing was built in—no closet, no shelves. The furniture just sat up against the dusty cream plaster walls. The various pieces all looked as old as the house—which I was guessing at six hundred years or more from the ghosts and the general style.

I wasn't holding out a lot of hope about the bath being much more modern, but I was wrong. The toilet was distinctly old-fashioned and the taps might have been a hundred years old, but they worked. The hot water was nearly scalding, whereas the cold water seemed to have been drawn through the rocky foundations of the house, so it was icy and tasted mineral and sharp. The tub was a large built-in basin, covered in tiny, painted tiles, long and deep enough that even I could probably submerge myself in it without significant body parts sticking out. Tiled pillars rose from the corners of the bath to support the ceiling above, which was also covered in tiles that made a mosaic of the night sky. A modern handheld shower thing had been attached to the plumbing, somewhat ruining the palatial effect. The room smelled of bleach and orange peels.

A door on the other side of the bathroom led to another bedroom and sitting room, the mirror image of the suite I'd been assigned. Curious, I walked through it, past furniture shrouded by covers, to the tall windows at the back, and I pushed them open. The hinges of the windows squealed and the air stirred up a draft of old dust. The scent of oranges and lemons came from a small walled garden at the back of the house. A steep slope beyond put the first floor of the next house up the hill almost on a level with the bedroom I was standing in. Tilting my head back, I looked farther up the slope.

Stone walls with square crenellated tops rose beyond the next house and a fringe of palm trees. I couldn't make out more of the castle looking up, but from this position there was no other building as far as I could see from side to side, just castle walls checkered with quarried stones of white, gray, and butter yellow as they caught the sunlight over the housetops. Even in the shade at the back of the house, it was warm.

I returned to my bedroom and hunted for the change of clothes my hostess had mentioned. I hadn't been able to pack my own clothes and I was surprised to find the wardrobe half full with blouses and skirts that all appeared to be my size, though I'd never seen any of them before. My own sweater and jeans from the night I'd gone to sleep looked scruffy hanging next to them. Someone had gone to a lot of trouble, and I supposed I should be grateful, though at that moment, I felt a little creeped out.

The whole reason I'd slipped illegally into the country in the guise of a corpse was to remain below certain people's radar by letting them think I was still in Seattle, doing what I usually do. Staying off anyone's scope meant blending into the background, which was going to be difficult enough as an American who spoke no Portuguese. But it would be easier if I didn't look like an American tourist. So I was grateful to Carlos—or to whomever he'd had pick up the clothes in my size—because they were lightly used and appeared to be of local or at least southern European manufacture. If I kept my mouth shut and my head down, I would at least be slightly less conspicuous and seem slightly less American. My height would be a problem, though, and there was nothing I could do about that but try to stay out of places where I'd stand out.

I didn't have time to take a full bath, but I did wash the makeup off and put on what I hoped was a boring outfit of blouse, skirt, and flat shoes. I didn't have my usual shoulder bag full of useful stuff— including my gun, which was locked in a safe-deposit box at my bank in Seattle. I did need some kind of purse or shopping bag to put a few items in, since the skirt—which would have been midcalf on many women but barely covered my knees—had only two shallow pockets and the blouse had none. It was much too hot to wear a jacket. I started downstairs feeling a bit naked, since I rarely wear skirts or any shoes of a lighter construction than sneakers since I gave up professional dance. I'm much more at home in jeans and boots.

On the second floor just before the head of the stairs, a ghost stood in my way and stared intently at me. She looked like the medieval woman I'd seen ascending the staircase earlier, but it was hard to be sure since I hadn't had a good look at her before. I stopped and gazed back at her. A mist swirled and ran around her feet like a whirlpool, expanding outward and rising slowly, as if she were being swallowed up in the maelstrom. She was very young, a teenager, really, in an age before that concept existed. Her face was long and serious. Long dark hair that fell to her hips was swept back from her high forehead with a band of cloth. She studied me, saying nothing and pursing her mouth as if she couldn't make up her mind.

I took a step toward her and put out my hand, palm up. "My name is Harper. I won't be staying very long."

She cocked her head as if straining to hear me. Then she turned her head aside sharply, disrupting her rising tide of mist so it blew outward and swirled away, dissolving into empty air. I walked to the stair rail and looked down, but she wasn't on the stairs. My mysterious hostess stepped out from one of the arches along the side of the entry and glanced up at me.

"Are you all right, *senhora*?"

"I'm fine. Did you see her?"

"The ghost? I see them sometimes. They don't care to show themselves to me often. Where are you going?"

"I'm not sure . . . someplace where sick toys go to get well?" The only open part of the message had used the phrase "where sick toys get well."

She frowned for a moment as if she had to translate the phrase. "Ah. O Hospital de Bonecas. The doll hospital. It is in the Baixa— the lower town—on Praça da Figueira. It will be faster to walk than take the tram. I will draw you a map."

I followed her back into the tiled hallway to a kitchen, which was probably of the same vintage as the bathroom upstairs but not as luxuriously appointed. The sink and counters looked to have been carved from granite and there was still a cooking hearth on one side of the room, though it had clearly not been used in a century or so. She took a pad of paper and a jasmine-scented pencil from the worktable and drew quickly. I watched her. Her hands were bony and thin, but not like an old woman's, and they moved swift as birds, drawing little sketches of the landmarks she thought I'd need to navigate by. It was a remarkable piece of work for something done so casually. When she was finished, she tore the page off and handed it to me. I took it, blinking at her in surprise.

"Thank you. What is your name, by the way?"

She puzzled that question for a moment, then gave a small smile that vanished as quickly as it arrived. *"Meu nome é Rafa."*

"Thank you, Rafa." I looked at her map again. "This is very kind of you."

She blushed, which seemed to take her by surprise, and she put her hands to her cheeks. *"De nada.* And you look very nice." She reached up and touched my hair. "But you should wear a scarf or a hat. You are very pale."

Even at the end of an unusually dry summer, I hadn't gotten much of a tan in Seattle, though I wouldn't have said I was pale. Compared to Rafa, though, I looked as white as the ghost on the staircase. "I don't have a hat. Or a purse for that matter."

"I will find a purse and a hat for you." She scurried out and, although I followed her as quickly as I could through the cluttered kitchen, she'd vanished by the time I came to the hall. I stopped where I was, rather than wander off and get lost. In a moment, Rafa returned with a wide-brimmed straw hat, a blue silk scarf, and a sort of purse made of the same soft, woven straw as the hat. Giving me no time to object, she gathered my hair back and tied it with the scarf, then put the hat on my head and looped the purse over my arm. "You look perfect now."

Apparently I was doomed to be dressed by strangers whether I liked it or not.

She walked me to the front door and handed me another key. "This is for the front gates. Be back before sundown and don't lose the key."

She stood behind the door when she opened it, keeping to the shadow, and shooed me out.

THREE

I was in a tiny courtyard facing iron gates across an expanse of cobbles. A car no bigger than a shoe was parked on the cobbles to my left next to a small fountain in the shape of a leonine face mounted to the tiled wall of the courtyard. The fountain looked slightly surprised to see me as water dribbled out of its oval mouth into the small basin of carved stone beneath it. I waved at it and walked over to unlatch the gates and let myself into the street. I used the key to lock the gates behind me—the ironwork looked like the vines of Sleeping Beauty's castle, closing out the world from a secret realm within. I took note of the number carved into the stone above the gateway and started down the steep, stone-paved street. I tried to tuck my things into my skirt pockets, but the keys were too large to stay securely in the shallow spaces. I put them into the purse and folded Rafa's map into my pocket instead.

At a bend in the street, I paused to read the street's name off a tiled plaque on a wall. I checked the map, turned to continue on my way, and found myself looking out at a sea of red-tiled roofs and hidden courtyards, tumbling in a maze of streets down the slope toward a wide band of glittering water that must have been the Tagus River. For a moment I just stood there and stared at it. The hill was so steep that the houses were almost like terraces in a photo of Asian rice paddies, each little bastion bounded by its own short sweep of walls that fell sharp and straight down to the next. The angles were all higgledy-piggledy and random, like the honeycomb of disturbed bees. And they were old . . . so old that the narrow, twisted streets thronged with more of the dead than the living—the dead of centuries stretching back so far, I couldn't even guess the eras. They climbed, ran, strolled, and urged their beasts of burden through the stone-paved passages, between tall houses real and ghostly, their collective voices twining into the noise of the Grid as a song both beautiful and sad that coiled through the twisted streets like fog. The houses they passed, current and not, were mostly plastered in cream, red, blue, and yellow, the colors faded and peeling from the unremitting sun. The rest were covered in tiles glazed with repeating geometric patterns that crazed the eye, broken by symmetrical ranks of windows with small iron balconies strung with drying laundry, or piled with flower boxes drooping red and purple blossoms over their filigreed metal sides. Here and there, the ghost of an older house or a terraced Moorish garden of tiled fountains and orange trees hung over another, but the overlay of phantom buildings was rare—at least from the outside.

I couldn't afford to stand and stare, but it was a hard sight to turn from, so unlike anything American. I had to keep an eye on my feet as I continued down the road, the twisting slope so long and precipitous that it made the Counterbalance up Queen Anne Avenue North in Seattle look like a speed bump. I was glad it wasn't raining, as it would have been at home. The dust in the road was dry and tamped down too much to make the sidewalks of laid flat stones slippery with grit. All stone and plaster, wood and iron, Alfama was old the way things in the Americas never are.

I wended my way down until I passed through an arch in a wall and out into a sort of arrow-shaped intersection of two narrow streets shaded with trees. A sign on the wall to my left gave information about the Castelo de São Jorge, which now lay behind me. I could no longer see the river and I wasn't sure which direction I was facing. I looked at Rafa's map and recognized the switchback hard on my right where the pedestrian path doubled back on itself, past a row of shops, and downward to a flatter bit of road. My shins and knees ached from the activity after so many hours of lying still.

I rounded the corner and the river reappeared as an aqua ribbon that seemed to float above the end of the street as if the paving rolled down into it. It didn't. The street turned abruptly after a block—though "block" was a complete misnomer here—and I turned to my right with it and continued.

The route was necessarily twisted and longer than the distance point to point, but with a few more turns and a walk past a small triangular plaza created by the high, pink-painted embankments that held up the streets, I was into much flatter streets that first went down and then rose gently upward again, turning away from the river. The architecture changed from the close-packed old houses of Alfama and its yellow stone walls to broader, younger buildings with flat fronts and stone pediments—a sort of plain-Jane version of Baroque.

The road was covered in tarmac now instead of cobbles, but the sidewalks were still paved in small squares of pale stone. The farther I walked, the wider the doors and windows of the buildings became, evolving slowly toward the eighteenth century and away from the medieval maze of the castle's hill. This road was mostly shops at street level. Ground-floor frontages were more frequently of dressed stone than painted plaster, though the tiling continued in fits. One front I passed had a vibrantly glazed tile mural of fish and seaweed. Signs from the simple to the slick hung over doorways, businesses as divergent as a sleek contemporary furniture retailer side by side with hole-in-the-wall taverns and shops selling medicines and herbs.

I tired to puzzle out some of the words as I passed, some like the Spanish I had grown up with in Southern California, but many more utterly meaningless. English words stood out in odd places, "snack bar" and "seaside" jostling with words like *"malhas."* I wondered what a *"mundo das malhas"* was. "World of Sweaters," judging by the window display—an item I wasn't feeling much use for at that moment, even on the shady side street that was busy with the cold spirits of merchants and farmers driving goods to some long-gone marketplace.

An old-fashioned-looking yellow tram clanged its bell and rattled along the tracks in the street past me as I stepped out into a large public square shrouded in the memory of several past buildings that had disappeared long ago to leave the acre or so in the middle nearly empty. One of these buildings was a Victorian monstrosity that reminded me a little, in kind more than style, of London's Smithfield Market. Another was a much older building I couldn't peg. A bronze statue of someone I took to be a soldier or a statesman was riding his bronze horse on a huge white stone plinth beside a tree off to the side of the square's central expanse of white and gray stone tiles. There was no tarmac or road paint here. Every street and sidewalk surface was paved in the black or white stone squares, right down to the lane markers and pedestrian crossing lines. I turned right and paused, looking in the window of the World of . . . whatever, sweating a little from the change of exertion and the heat rising in the nearly shadeless square. The buildings facing the square were much more formal than the areas I'd already walked through, the shops giving off a higher-class sheen. This was saying quite a bit, since the last few blocks had been increasingly swanky in the modern era, in spite of being more working-class in the lingering past.

A sign placed high on the wall at the corner told me I was at Praça da Figueira. I looked at Rafa's map again, having almost missed my destination because she'd drawn a tiny picture of the statue, but not the square it was standing in. The drawing was very good and even caught the way the plume on the rider's head seemed to be flowing in the wind of his movement. The address I wanted was number seven. According to the map, it was somewhere on the long expanse of Baroque buildings facing the horse's backside, but there wasn't anything that instantly stood out to my sight as likely to be a doll hospital.

The openness of the square made me a little nervous about meeting Quinton here. There was no way to approach any of the shops, restaurants, or hotels without being in the open, and while the businesses on the square were moderately busy and traffic was heavy enough to qualify as the run-up to what passed for rush hour in Lisbon, it wasn't exactly New York or Los Angeles busy. The cars, buses, and trams were more of a problem than the people, since the sidewalks had little raised curb to speak of and pedestrians were separated from the vehicular traffic by upright metal posts about hip high, placed every five feet or so along the white sidewalk edge.

As I stood at the corner, I saw a small car swoop around a bus by hiking its two closest wheels up on the edge of the curb where there weren't any uprights and drive half up on the sidewalk, honking its horn like a frustrated goose before bolting back into traffic to a cacophony of other horns and outraged curses from some of the pedestrians. Not all the pedestrians seemed upset or even surprised, however, even as they scattered away from the pushy little car. Two older women wearing black dresses simply stepped aside, watched the disturbance, and shook their heads. Then they shrugged, and walked on, their shopping bags hanging limply off their arms as they chattered to each other, heads turned inward.

I went into the sweater shop, buying time and hoping to get a better look at the area without being too conspicuous. The air-conditioning was on and I shivered in the sudden cool. An attractive middle-aged woman wished me *bom dia* and seemed to be offering assistance, but I wasn't sure. She might have been asking if I liked cashmere socks for all I knew. I apologized for my lack of Portuguese, and she replied in unhalting English in the same not-quite-Spanish accent Rafa had.

"Oh, are you American?"

"I'm from Connecticut," I replied, picking a state at random.

She seemed puzzled. "That is in the United States?"

"It's on the East Coast, near New York."

"Oh! Yes, I know New York. You will have beautiful autumn leaves soon. Perhaps you'll want a warm shawl to take home," she said, turning her hand gracefully toward a rack hung with folded lengths of knitted silk and wool, some so intricate and fine that they looked like lace.

"They're lovely, but, in fact, I'm lost."

She seemed disappointed but rallied a smile anyhow. "Perhaps I can help you with that. What place were you looking for?"

"The doll hospital."

Her smile broadened, showing teeth that were clean and white, but more crooked than most Americans'—I'd noticed that our dental fetish doesn't extend much past Canada. "Ah! O Hospital de

Bonecas! It is on the north side, near the Nestlé kiosk—the blue ice-cream bar." She walked me outside and pointed up the square to the small blue lump of a prefab vendor's booth with a yellow post sticking out of its roof at an angle. I'd thought it was a newsstand, but I could just make out the word NESTLÉ on the post—which I supposed to be the stick of a blue-wrapped frozen dessert. The bright little building sat just inside the pedestrian bollards, almost daring cars or buses to swipe it. "The hospital's door is just behind the kiosk," the clerk said, "past A Coutada—the hunting shop—and next to the jeweler in the building with the tiles."

"Thank you," I said, giving her a smile since I had nothing else.

She returned a smile and a slight shrug. "*De nada*. I hope you enjoy it."

I thanked her and walked up the arcade in the general direction she'd pointed, since it would have been suicidal to try to cross the street diagonally with the current traffic. In the empty center I could see the black shade of the now-gone market building hanging over the large shape of the older building, which seemed to heave and fall apart like a time-lapse film, over and over, accompanied by the rumbling and shrieking of destruction and the sobbing of mourners. Having grown up in Southern California, I knew the sound of an earthquake when I heard it, even at accelerated speed. I remembered Carlos saying that Lisbon had experienced a devastating quake in the mid-eighteenth century and it had been partially his doing. If this shadowy disaster film was part of that, it was far worse than what my imagination had originally conjured. The ancient building collapsed into rubble in minutes, crushing people inside and tumbling stones into the street to kill still more. Then great waves of seawater rolled over the wreckage and away again, leaving everything that remained to be engulfed in sudden flames that turned the water to steam. The conflagration spread from other buildings up the road, sprouting from broken gas lamps. The dead and their shattered homes burned while more people screamed and ran and died, until the horror faded into smoke and the loop of disaster began again, spinning forward the history of devastation in minutes before my appalled gaze. I shook myself and kept walking—it wouldn't do to call attention by gawking at nothing. I hoped we wouldn't be staying long in Lisbon.

I turned at the corner and crossed the road to the north arcade, keeping my sight on the shop fronts to my right, away from the continuous loop of phantom disaster. I glanced in the window of a restaurant, which only reminded me how long it had been since I'd eaten. The hunting and fishing store was just past the restaurant and several signs for the Pensão Praça da Figueira—which advertised ROOMS! in English, so I assumed it was some kind of hotel.

I overshot the door with the green sign hand-painted on the inside of the glass above that read HOSPITAL DE BONECAS 1830 ERVANÁRIA PORTUGUESA. An old woman dressed in black sat in a chair outside, stitching the neck of a cloth doll together where it had torn at the shoulder and was spitting forth buds of wooly stuffing. She was little more than a shadow under the canvas awning, but to me she was as obvious as if she were still alive. *"Você certamente levou muito tempo para chegar aqui,"* she muttered, her voice coming slow and creaking. In my head I heard the sentiment, roughly translated as "You took your time getting here."

I didn't dare drop toward the Grey to talk to her more easily, but strolled a step backward to look into the window of the jewelry shop next door. "And why do you care?" I muttered in reply. I saw something black and glimmering, far away above the buildings, that soared into the sky and fell back toward earth, leaving trails of Grey like cirrus clouds.

"Much to mend, much to fix. Little time," the old ghost replied, still watching the fabric between her fingers as she set tiny stitches into the doll's neck. *"Os Magos do Osso."*

I turned my head to give her a more-direct stare, letting my curiosity about the black thing in the sky go. Her words had a ring of memory in them that chimed on words Carlos had used, even though the two phrases sounded nothing alike. "Kostní Mágové," I said. Bone Mages.

She nodded, not looking up, and faded away.

I took that as my cue to go inside.

The space was narrow and made more so by a large floor-to-ceiling glass case filled with old dolls, miniatures, and toys that seemed to watch me as I entered. Not far back from the door lay a staircase. Signs reading MUSEU and OFICINA PARA RESTAUROS pointed up the stairs. There wasn't enough room on the ground floor to hide a potted plant in, much less Quinton, so I went up the stairs.

The first room was mostly a shop, with displays of dollhouse miniatures, doll clothes, and a plethora of accessories. It was all high quality—no cheap plastic, mass-produced junk—and a lot of it looked handmade. Layer on layer of ghostly children wandered through the displays. Behind a counter at the back were ceiling-high niches in which sat dozens of dolls and stuffed toys of every description and age, from near-new Barbies to ancient teddy bears and porcelain-headed ladies in fancy dresses. Most of them watched me with phantom eyes.

I walked up another flight of stairs to the hospital itself, where dolls and toys were taken in with loving care by the white-coated staff, who marked a number on the bottoms of their feet or tied a paper tag to the leg to identify them later and then carried them off to be "operated" on at white tables. Glass-fronted drawers held disembodied doll parts: heads, legs, arms, eyes. . . . It gave me the willies.

I was unnerved enough by the dismembered dolls that I jumped when Quinton spoke into my ear. "It's a little disturbing, isn't it?"

I whirled to glare at him. He caught me by the shoulders, saying, "God, I missed you," and kissed me. It was a long, hard kiss that made my already wobbly knees go weak. Quinton had to haul me tight against his body so I wouldn't slither to the floor and that was not at all disagreeable. Nearby a small child made a sound of disgust, which is the same in any language: "Eww . . ." We both gave the child—a little girl with a mop of short, dark curls—a stern look. She turned away to chase after her mother, saying something in Portuguese that was probably, "Those people are kissing!" because her mother laughed and shot us a curious glance.

Quinton stiffened in my arms, staring for a second at the little girl as she grabbed onto her mother's hand.

"What's wrong?" I asked, taking a small step back from him.

Quinton shook himself. "She looks so much like Soraia. . . ."

"Who?"

"My niece. My sister's daughter. My father kidnapped her."

"What?" I asked, appalled.

"That was my reaction. I'll tell you as we go."

Even angry and a bit shaken, he looked good to me. I hadn't seen him in months. He'd cut his hair again, so it didn't quite hit his shoulders, and had trimmed his beard much smaller and narrower, so he managed to look both shaggy and fashionable at the same time. His clothes were a little more fashion-conscious also, but not enough to stand out in a crowd of Europeans. He was carrying a small-brimmed black hat and a smaller version of his usual backpack that looked more like a portfolio or messenger bag.

We went downstairs together and Quinton paused to put on his hat as I slipped outside in the Grey to take a look around. I didn't see a sign of anything immediately threatening, although the constant replay of Lisbon's earthquake left me feeling disquieted.

FOUR

We walked out of the doll hospital and along the sidewalk toward a wide opening between the buildings on the west side of the square, making an effort to be casual when we both felt bleak and worried.

"Why did you pick that place to meet?" I asked. He was tense even while he did a pretty good imitation of a man in no hurry.

He paused to adjust his hat, cocking the brim down a little farther so his face was less exposed to the cameras dotted here and there throughout the public square. "About ninety percent of the agents working for my dad are male. They'd have been pretty easy to spot in there and I had been watching out the windows for anyone I recognized working the square. "Why did you go into the knitwear shop?"

"Is that what it was?" I replied. "I thought it was World of Sweaters."

He gave a strained laugh, the darkness around us lightening for only a moment. "'*Malhas*' means 'knits.' So you were close."

"I didn't know you spoke Portuguese."

"Only a little tourist pidgin. I looked it up. Why did you go into the shop?"

"I wanted to get a better look and more information without wandering aimlessly around a haunted plaza."

"Haunted?"

"Yes. There was an earthquake here, remember? It killed thousands of people and knocked down most of downtown Lisbon at the time. The building that was here then is stuck in a loop, and I could see it falling, burning, and being swamped with water over and over. It's very unpleasant."

Quinton looked more unhappy than ever. "We'd better wrap up our business in Lisbon quickly, then."

"I'd appreciate that."

"How did you get here, if you don't mind my asking? I mean, I didn't give you any helpful hints on that, I know, and I'm sorry."

"It wasn't a problem. I went to Carlos."

"I can't say I'm surprised. I assume he came along."

"He did. Now, tell me what's going on."

He ignored my request, giving a tiny shake of the head. "I'm not sure how happy I am about Carlos's involvement. . . ."

I sighed. "He has a vested interest in the mages behind this business. I think he'll be invaluable, even if he's a bit obsessive and scarier than usual. Kind of like you're being right now. Not that I blame you."

"What did you tell him?"

"Only that I'd heard from you and needed to get here. He didn't give me an option about his accompanying me and I wasn't going to argue. He does have an interest in your father's project and his focus on the Kostní Mágové is absolute."

The previous year, Quinton had nearly died trying to stop his father's mysterious project. James Purlis had persuaded someone in the black depths of the espionage community to fund what he called "the Ghost Division"—some kind of dreadful research that involved, among other things, capturing paranormals and vivisecting them to see how they ticked and if any of their abilities were useful to Papa Purlis's plans. He wanted to see whether they could be made to work for him, or even if the source of their abilities could somehow be applied to someone already under his control. In the mess he'd left behind when Quinton shut down the Seattle end, Carlos was able to discover that Purlis wasn't working this angle alone: He'd enlisted the help of an ancient cabal of bone mages who probably had their own agenda. Carlos had also said these Kostní Mágové were extremely dangerous and that he'd known them since he'd lived in Lisbon before the earthquake. It was apparent, now, that Purlis had either learned a few tricks from his captured paranormals since last July or worked out a much more advantageous arrangement with the Kostní Mágové. I'd already picked up a bit from Carlos about them, but I wanted more. I hadn't pressed for it, knowing it was likely to come out once Quinton and I were able to talk to him in person.

Quinton made a noise in his throat. "I haven't been able to keep as close track of my dad as I'd have liked," he admitted, his expression growing tortured. "He gave me the slip a while ago and I haven't seen him in the flesh since—I've just been following his spoor, so to speak. He's been busy—he's got small units all over Europe and the Near East and he's traveled through all of them. He's spread his resources thin, but it's effective. I don't think there's any coincidence that when he arrives, shit happens—political unrest, riots, outbreaks of weird diseases. He was in Turkey right before the suicide bombings, in Greece just ahead of a series of financial riots, in Paris before a rash of anti-Semitic violence, just ahead of an outbreak of Avian flu in northern Germany, and on and on, more of the same with me always one step too far behind, trying to stop him or at least minimize his effect. I can't believe I missed this business with Soraia. I should have been here sooner."

I'd been holding his hand and now I put my arm around him, pulling him closer. "You can't be on watch every minute—you're just one man. Your father is a slippery scumbag who's been in the business a lot longer than you and has a lot more resources."

"He's always been willing to put others in danger."

"I doubt it was quite as extreme as this in the past—kidnapping his own granddaughter is a bit out there. He must be deteriorating, mentally, over time. He bailed you out a few years ago. He let your mother and your sister get away."

"My mother didn't exactly escape him."

I turned a curious look on him, but he shook his head. "Not now. I can barely manage my rage over what he's done to my sister and her kids. If I start talking about Mom, I'll lose it."

I would have asked him to try, but as we stepped out from between the buildings and into the plaza beyond, I was struck dumb: The square ahead of us was huge, open, and flat, about three times the size of the square the doll hospital faced. It was anchored at each end by a large, tiered bronze fountain. Right in the middle, straight ahead, stood a soaring marble column with a bronze statue on top. Poking up above the buildings beyond the column was what looked like the ruins of a medieval cathedral, dripping blackness and fiery red streamers of Grey, and all the way around the square were Baroque and later buildings much more ornate than those in the Praça da Figueira. One end of the square was dominated full width by a three-story stone building with a neoclassical front, complete with columns and a pediment. At the other end was a bright yellow facade, pierced by a large stone archway leading to another smaller road, smack in the middle of a row of ornate buildings. At the end of the avenue on our side, far down the road, another impressive arch, standing at least three stories tall, spanned the whole boulevard. The entire open court had been tiled in the ubiquitous black and white stones to create a geometric wave pattern that played on my eyes so the surface seemed to be under a thin sheet of clear water, rippled by the wind. Trees lined the long boulevards that ran north to south the length of the square. Near the great white stone building on the north end, another phantom horror movie played out, but this one predated the earthquake.

Quinton noticed my horrified stare. "What is it?"

"I'm not sure. . . . Did Portugal have an Inquisition, like Spain?"

"It's a Catholic country. I'm pretty sure it did."

I closed my eyes and turned my head away. "At the north end of the square where the big white building is now, there used to be another building. In front of that is where they had the public trials, the penance, and the executions. They're piled up there—the images— like overlapping film." My knees wobbled and I swayed a little.

Quinton steadied me, putting one arm around my waist, mirroring my hold on him. "That bad?"

"It's pretty bad."

"Let me get you out of here. We need to catch a train anyway."

He steered me away from the scene of burnings and beatings, to a wide staircase leading down to a subway station. "Keep hold of your purse at all times," he warned. "This area's famous for its pickpockets."

"I don't have anything but a map and two keys," I replied. "No money, no ID . . . nothing."

"I'll take care of that later. For now, stick close to me. Oh—keep your head down near cameras. Portugal doesn't use an on-the-fly facial recognition system, but if any of Dad's creeps have access to the feed, they may start looking for us in the tapes later."

"All right," I replied, adjusting my hat. "I was planning on sticking close to you anyhow." I was disturbed by his lack of response. Even in the Grey, he was not quite himself, distracted from me, but focused on other things, and the energy surrounding him was dark, bleak, streaked with orange anxiety and red anger.

He paused and looked around. "I'd better tell you the rest once we're on the train—we have too much moving around to do here. I'm barely keeping my thoughts together and this gets complicated."

"The metro or the story?"

"Both."

"Can you tell me where we're going, at least?"

"First we have to get to the train station, and then I'll tell you."

I frowned at him and he saw it. "Lisbon was full of spies during the Second World War. I don't know why, but the place makes me feel like I'm being watched, like those old, dead spies are still around, doing their work. And with what my dad does, I'm not sure they aren't. Humor me."

It wasn't hard to do so—Lisbon fairly crawled with ghosts. I nodded and followed him past a sign that identified the station as Rossio.

FIVE

s best I could tell, the metro station took up a large part of the space under the central square with a complex of stairs and concourses leading downward. As with the streets above, the tile work was distractingly beautiful: One bit of floor had an old-style compass rose of tiny mosaic squares. A wall had a long panel of painted tiles running at shoulder height of a woman in a voluminous coat walking along with us, rendered in delicate blue brushwork on white. A staircase descended past a mural of abstracted leaves and flowers in squares of green and gold. It was like walking through a museum collection. I was surprised that most of the people in the station paid it no attention, flowing along in their colorful streams of busy energy to destinations I couldn't guess, accompanied by the ghosts of commuters past.

"What's with the tile?" I asked as we continued toward our platform. Determined not to force him to discuss the case, I was still hungry to talk after the long silence of eight months apart.

"I'm not really sure," he said, still distracted though making an effort, "but much of Portugal was controlled by the Moors for quite a while and I would guess it's some kind of artistic holdover of their influence. You saw the tiles on the doll hospital building and others, I'm sure. Even the street signs in most places are plaques of painted tiles mounted on the walls. It's not as common to see the sort of signboards you and I grew up with. On the highways, yes, and in a few very modern 'designed' communities, but otherwise, it's mostly the tiles."

It was still early for rush hour, but the station was busy and we got a little turned around finding our train and buying tickets. Once we were on the metro, the ride was only a few minutes long. It almost seemed ridiculous not to have walked it, but we did have the advantage of being in a crowd and therefore harder to spot.

We exited the metro outside the Cais do Sodré rail station, which had another breathtaking view of the river—when you could see it past the trains and the people. I was momentarily disoriented by finding myself walking through the ghostly hull of an ancient wooden ship instead of the halls of a modern train station.

"I'd guess this used to be a shipyard," I said.

Quinton shrugged. "I'm not sure, but it would make sense. Right here where the river widens before joining the sea would be ideal and Portugal was, once, the greatest maritime nation in the Western Hemisphere. That required a lot of ships. You know—Vasco da Gama, Henry the Navigator, and guys like that sailing off and discovering India and Japan and a quarter of Africa, and so on. I've never really been able to figure out how they went from being the masters of the seas—the greatest navigators in the world—to this."

"What do you mean . . . 'this'?" I asked.

"*Saudade*—which roughly translates as 'yearning.' Maybe you haven't been here long enough to notice, but there's a sort of sadness to the Portuguese—especially the Lisboans. Sometime after the earthquake and the loss of Brazil and before the Great Depression, they began to look backward instead of forward. Terrible things happened and although they rebuilt, they didn't spring back. There are still ruins of the earthquake here in Lisbon—like that church you saw from Rossio. Two hundred and fifty years later, the shells of buildings, the arch of a church doorway . . . They're still as they were, not cleared away but not really memorialized, either. If you didn't know what you were looking at, you might think they were just urban blight—people paint graffiti on the walls as if they were the remains of burned-out tenements in South Central L.A."

"No wonder all the history I see replaying here is of the gruesome variety."

"But the Portuguese are mostly friendly folks. They're the sort of people who fix broken dolls for kids and make pencils that smell like orange blossoms and sing sad songs about loss and yearning in tiny bars on the beach where the liquor will kick your legs out from under you. At the same time, some believe there's a 'Sleeping King' who'll come back to make things right some day, and old women crawl a tenth of a mile on their knees to reach the shrine of Our Lady of Fátima. They're an odd mix, modern and medieval and generous and sad."

"I wonder what your father has in mind for them."

"He may not have much in mind at all aside from snatching Soraia. I haven't been able to figure out his larger plan beyond 'sow chaos and reap destruction.' I haven't seen much sign of the paranormal, even though I know it's a big part of whatever he's up to. I think we may have destroyed a lot of his progress in that respect back in Seattle, but he's been successful with the ghost boxes at least enough to plant one in most of his units. The way he manages to get information and set people up is uncanny, and I can't think of any other way he could be doing it."

"You mean like the box that Sergeyev was stored in—imprisoned ghosts who act as spies and agitators?"

"Yeah. But I can't see ghosts like you can and it's one of the things I need you for." He seemed frustrated at acknowledging that he needed anything, and furious with himself. "I'm missing something—missing too much, obviously, if I missed his taking Soraia."

I was on the point of telling him to stop blaming himself when he turned to me sharply and started for the train station, saying, "We need the train to Cascais."

"We do?"

"We won't be going that far. Sam lives in Carcavelos. It's on the coast before you get all the way out to the famous parts around Estoril—that area is full of fancy resorts for the wealthy for the most part and always has been. Carcavelos is more famous for its surf. The Tagus River still has an effect at that location, so the waves are a lot more defined. And it used to be a British communication depot, so there are still a lot more English speakers there than in most small towns in Portugal. Come on," he added, urging me into the building.

The station was sleek and modern inside, all cement and steel, but there were still bits of art here and there, like a row of giant anthropomorphized rabbits in blue suits rushing across the platform walls from the metro to the train station. It took a while to figure out which train we needed since there were several types of service. Quinton found a clerk who spoke excellent English and who explained the various trains running on the Cascais line and which one would get us to Carcavelos quickest. Then we had to purchase passes from a vending machine and go through various turnstiles and validate the pass, find our track . . . and miss our train by seconds. The next would leave in twenty minutes.

We doubled back to a small food vendor selling a sort of spicy pork sandwich called a *bifana*. The smell reminded me that I hadn't eaten since Seattle. I didn't appear to be the only one who was ravenous: The area was busy and we were jostled by hurrying commuters and hungry customers. Several men with ominous clouds of Grey energy around them passed as well. I tried to watch them and figure out what they were up to or who they were, but I couldn't guess. We received our sandwiches wrapped to go—which had caused some sighing as if there was no understanding the silly ideas of tourists—and I asked Quinton what he thought of one of the men and if any were familiar.

"Haven't seen them before specifically," he said, "but they remind me of the guys from one of the units I didn't work with at a certain agency. Mostly young agents from the KGB and Stasi, who suddenly didn't have a job when the wall came down in Berlin. They were at loose ends, not particularly idealistic, but well trained and resentful of being unemployed. Most of them were willing to work for the highest bidder or the government most likely to let them emigrate. By the time I met any, they were middle-aged, cynical, and mean as snakes."

"Sounds familiar."

"If you mean they remind you of my dad, I'd say these guys were less charming and had limits even they wouldn't exceed—which is not something I can say about Dad anymore. Not after this business. Who kidnaps his own granddaughter . . . ?"

I had worked on parental kidnapping cases and I knew that there were plenty of people in the world who didn't find the idea of snatching their own child, grandchild, niece, or nephew to be out of the question. Some did it for what they thought were altruistic reasons, like getting a child out of a bad situation when the law hadn't. But most did it for selfish and often crazy reasons, like getting back at an ex-spouse, or believing that their methods or motives for raising the child would be better. Some of their reasons were less sane and far more terrible—which I hoped wasn't going to be the case with Papa Purlis.

"So, what would men like that be doing here?"

"Europe's in upheaval—at least partly thanks to Dad, but also just the circumstances he's taking advantage of. Most of it seems fairly normal most of the time, but it's a complex problem that's widespread. There've been a lot of economic problems and those have bred a lot of social and political unrest—not just things like Ukraine, but smaller and surprisingly vicious. Guys like that always show up where the opportunity for violence or political or economic advantage is high. Right now, there are a lot of those opportunities. The Portuguese people haven't been pleased with their government's austerity measures—which seem to hit the taxpayers a lot harder than the politicians and government bureaucrats. They almost broke out in riots near the first of the year. That was avoided, but there's still a lot of discomfort about the situation and that means there are people who are ready to use that turmoil and discomfort to their advantage—people who'd pay to have others make the situation worse in strategic ways. That's what those guys are—the hired guns."

"Do you think any of them work for your father?"

"Probably, but they don't know who we are. At least not yet. There's no way of knowing which of these guys, if any, are in Dad's employ, though, so we need to avoid them if we can. Just play tourist for now. They aren't looking for a nice couple on their way to the beach."

I frowned, thinking as I ate my *bifana*. As a fanatic—and he was—James Purlis was willing to do whatever he thought necessary to achieve his goals. He hadn't caviled at trying to trap and manipulate Quinton, nor had he been unwilling to harm—or possibly kill—his son when Quinton had refused to play along. Quinton had been monkey-wrenching his plans for a while and it sounded as if he might have managed to stop a few of Papa Purlis's attempts at economic and social disruption. That would make Quinton a thorn in his side worth plucking out, but whatever Purlis was planning to do with Soraia was probably a lot bigger and more horrible than just using his grandchild as short-term leverage against his son.

The sandwich stuck in my throat and I felt a lump of fear harden in my chest. It weighed on me for the entire trip, making it hard to appreciate the beauty of much of our route along the riverbank and out to the edge of the sea.

The rails wove in and out of the riverside fringes of Lisbon, past developments dated by their architecture, including an area of swooping cement buildings that looked a little like leftovers from a world's fair. We passed a stretch of churning water where the river clearly met the surging sea, creating a choppy band of waves even in the mild weather. A square tower of the same butter-colored stone as the castle above Alfama stuck out of the sea nearby. Our yellow-faced train rushed on, clacking and spitting sparks from the overhead wires.

Once we were ensconced in seats as isolated as we could manage on the train, I prompted Quinton to restart the story he'd dropped in Lisbon.

"So, tell me what happened. Your dad snatched your niece. . . ."

Quinton let out a heavy sigh, the colors of his aura dimming and flashing red for a moment. "Soraia. Yes. Three days ago I picked up a message from Sam—that's my sister. Her name is Samantha. Samantha Elizabeth Rebelo. She doesn't use 'Purlis' or 'Quinn.'"

"I'm following you," I said.

"Sam married a Portuguese guy. Well, he's half Dutch, but that doesn't matter. Piet Rebelo. His dad was with the diplomatic corps and they met while she was taking care of our grandparents in Rhode Island and he was visiting some of his family that lived there—lots of Portuguese in Rhode Island. Piet is kind of like me—went into the family business in a manner of speaking. He works with one of the ever-changing EU trade-negotiation groups. Travels in fits. So . . . he's currently out of town on business and Sam didn't want to get the local cops involved in this because, while the Portuguese authorities are pretty serious about crimes involving children, she was worried about Dad's government contacts hearing about it. She was afraid he'd find out through them if she'd reported it and maybe do something to her or Piet or the baby."

"Baby?"

"She has a baby boy—Martim. He's almost two and Sam was thinking about going back to work part-time. Soraia's six, so she's in school a lot of the time now and that makes it easier on Sam, but taking care of kids is a big job and Sam fears that if she calls attention to herself, Dad will find a way to spin it so she looks like a negligent parent instead of a victim. Neither of us thinks it's a coincidence that Dad took Soraia right after Piet left town, so even if Sam had called him and he'd turned right around to come home, it would have been a day or more before Piet got here, and that's extra time to Dad's advantage."

"So your sister didn't call her husband? That's kind of strange."

"Not for Sam. She's the supercompetent one. She rarely calls for help and she couldn't even reach Piet initially. By the time I got in touch with her, she'd decided she didn't want to let him know because he'd insist on getting the government and police involved. Sam believes that would play into Dad's hands in a worst-case scenario and put her in a position of being unable to do anything herself. She doesn't want to think the worst, but she does. Dad is up to something terrible."

I felt a little odd about the situation. On the one hand, Purlis was dangerous and crazy enough to do everything his children feared. On the other, going after him alone and without any help from the police was going to be rough. But this wasn't a typical kidnapping, so Sam might have been right in feeling that the police would be more of a hindrance than a help. The most important thing was that there was a six-year-old girl in the hands of a man I thought wasn't safe or stable.

I nodded. "I wouldn't put anything past your father."

"Me, neither. But the thing that worries me is that I haven't been seeing much sign of the paranormal side of his project and I'm afraid Soraia may be why."

I frowned at him. "In what way?"

"I have a bad feeling that whatever he's up to is just waiting on some triggering event, and the timing of this makes me think Soraia is meant to be part of that."

I felt ill and fell silent, thinking about all the horrible things magic could make of a six-year-old girl. . . .

I t was nearly five o'clock when we disembarked in Carcavelos.
The houses were mostly plastered and painted in soft colors
like smaller versions of the grand Baroque buildings I'd seen
in Lisbon, but the town reminded me of Manhattan Beach,
an upper-middle-class beach suburb of Los Angeles. The architecture and the light were totally different, but the laid-back surfer
kids, the well-heeled family houses in yards filled with shaggy palm
trees behind stuccoed walls covered in purple bougainvillea, and a
practical but recent-model car in the driveway were entirely familiar.
The sidewalks were stone tile here, too, and, as Quinton had said, the
street signs were mostly plaques mounted on the corners of buildings
at the intersections. Only a few major streets with no convenient
location for such signs had the kind of signboards I was more familiar with. I also found it strange that the stop signs read STOP and not
some other word.

Quinton watched me puzzle over them. "It's the universal traffic
sign—everyone uses it."

I felt quite provincial for not knowing that and I think I blushed, but it was hard to be sure since although it was cooler on the ocean coast than it had been in downtown Lisbon, I could no longer kid myself that the air was less than warm. I'd been too long in the cool, moist air of the Pacific Northwest and had lost my California-girl tolerance of the heat.

We walked around for a while, trying to figure out where Sam's house was, since neither of us had been there and we didn't have the convenience of a cell phone with GPS navigation. We found a shop that sold trinkets and books for tourists to read on the beach, bought a local map, and asked the way to the international school, which Quinton knew was quite close to Sam's house. The clerk directed us to Saint Julian's with a lot of hand gestures and English that wasn't quite as good as his speed of spitting it out.

We walked down the tree-lined Avenida Jorge V, past a long stretch of empty land on one side and houses on the other. An old stone wall painted with fading graffiti separated the pedestrian walk-way from the vacant acreage that rolled lower than the street level. The area beyond the wall wasn't cultivated or maintained except in a very basic way, so it didn't seem to be a park. The tourist map iden-tified the area as a former *quinta*—an estate in this case that had once been the vineyard and country home of a Portuguese noble-man. The school was housed in the old manor house, according to the tourist guide, so we were heading in the right direction. The slightly overgrown area and the trees made for a pleasant walk in the gently weeping music of the Grey—a gentler version of the sound in Lisbon—though I'm not sure either of us appreciated it. The magical energy of the area was less busy, swirling like currents in a lazy stream and sparking light greens, clear blue, and lemon yellow, which was a relief after so much horror lining the streets of downtown Lisbon. The area was mostly ghostless, but I supposed that a place that had been used only for agriculture for a few hundred years hadn't acquired the depth of life and death that towns and cities do.

After a very long block, we turned and crossed the street to follow a smaller road into the residential area. The houses were all different from one another in size and grandeur. Some were huge, two-storied cubes with balconies that sat in the middle of massive walled yards, while others were narrow at the front and ran deep into a small yard like a shoe box. The only thing the houses had in common was plaster. Every house—even the few that were obviously built of stone—was covered in a coat of painted plaster under a red clay tile roof. One impressively large house and its surrounding wall were painted the same bright magenta as the bougainvillea that flowered in the yard next door, but most were painted in softer colors. Not every house had a wall, but it was common enough that those without were the noticeable exception.

Sam's house had a wall and palm trees, but I couldn't tell anything more about the place from the distance at which we had paused. I sank a bit into the Grey, while Quinton kept an eye on the area in the normal world. The illuminated corona of Sam's house was spiked with jagged red bolts of anger that seemed at odds with the gleaming bands of bright blue that curled around the house and yard and drifted up over the edges of the wall like a cloud. Streaks of black and white that looked like old barbed wire made paths around the outside of the wall, cutting through the blue only at the front gate in thin traces.

I eased back. "I don't see any sign of watchers—paranormal or otherwise—but there's a remnant of something I'd like to get a closer look at. Do you see anything?"

"No. Dad must be very confident."

"That's not reassuring."

"No, it really isn't. I hope Sam's all right. It's been a couple of days. . . ."

"The house looks otherwise normal, but we'll know more up close," I said.

We walked down the street toward the house, hand in hand like a couple of lovers out for a stroll. Nothing was interested in us, except a cat that sat on the top of a wall and watched us with a show of indifference. We crossed the street toward Sam's house but leaving enough room to approach at an angle without going straight through the front gate. I stopped again to drop into the Grey and look more closely at the tracks of magic someone had left behind.

Correction: two someones. The two strands of energy residue weren't identical, though they were very similar. I hadn't seen magical signatures quite like them before. They weren't a spell, but the residue itself was shaped into knotted and jagged lines that resembled gouges in wax or clay more than calligraphy—they seemed incised on the surface of the Grey, though they didn't react magically to my inspection or prodding in any way. It almost seemed as if the people who'd caused them trod more heavily on the Grey than other creatures of magic, whose usually thin and fluid tracks faded swiftly. The black threads felt cold and smooth, but with an edge of grit to them, the twining white more angular and brittle. I closed my hand around one and pulled a little. It snapped and crumbled away, leaving a fading dust on the silvery surface of the mist world. Once broken, the rest of the line began to fade as well. I touched the other one, finding it a little warmer to the touch and rougher on the surface, though it was equally fragile when crushed in my hand.

I stepped back from the Grey and leaned my shoulder against the wall outside Sam's house for a moment, thinking as Quinton watched me.

"So . . . ?"

"I can't figure it. Two magical people have been here and they walked around the house like they were casing it, but the traces they left seem to be magically inert and fragile. And those traces are weird in their own right, being two colors that twine together—black and a creamy white color I'm not familiar with. Compound energy rarely remains in such distinct strands—it tends to blend. But these are more like . . . threads of disparate energy twisted together. Really odd."

"Sam said our father had two other people with him—a man and a woman—whom she didn't feel good about and who didn't speak or come close," Quinton said. "I'd assume the marks belong to them."

"I can buy that—I never saw anything like this from your dad, but I can't figure out these people's intention or what they may have done."

"These traces don't seem to be a trap or a spell or anything like that?"

I took off my hat and paused to smooth my hair back into the scarf tied at my nape as I thought about it. Then I shook my head. "No, they don't feel like anything active or even lying in wait. They shatter easily, too, and I don't feel any movement of magical energy when I break them, as I would with a spell, ward, or trap of any kind. It's like snapping a burned twig and getting a bit of charcoal on your hand, but nothing more."

"That sounds a lot creepier than you may think."

I had to shrug. I'm no longer sure what's creepy to someone more normal than me. "I think it's some sort of deliberate residue—like graffiti—but it can't be meant for us, since neither of us recognizes it. But I don't believe there's anything here to cause us concern. Let's go in and talk to your sister."

Deciding we had nothing to lose, we went to the front gate and pressed a button on a call box mounted to the faded stone wall. Through the iron gate I could see a small slice of the front of the house, which was built of the same material as the wall. The upper story was plastered, but the lower was not and the tawny stone had the mellow, soft look of rock that's been in the weather a long time.

I heard something mechanical move and looked up to see a small camera in a steel housing turn our way from the top of the gatepost, sheltered by palm fronds. The gate buzzed and fell open a half inch. We glanced at each other and walked into the yard, closing the gate behind us.

The front yard had been cultivated into a neat lawn bounded by the palms and a close-growing row of prickly pink rosebushes that hugged the wall. The perfume of jasmine drifted on a breeze from the sea that snuck over the wall behind the house. We got only a few steps up the laid-stone path before the front door opened and a young brunette stepped out with a baby in her arms.

"Jay!" she shouted, running toward us as fast as the jiggling weight of the baby would allow. I had to remind myself that only I and my lover's underground friends called him "Quinton"; to most of the rest of world he was either James Jason Purlis, deceased, or Reggie McCrea Lassiter, depending on whom you asked.

Sam was slim and short—her head wouldn't have come up to my cheek. I stood still and watched her in silence as she closed the distance to her brother, and I thought that they looked more alike than I would have expected even of siblings. She moved awkwardly, as if her knees and ankles didn't work quite right, and yet her demeanor was confident, the energy around her predominantly cool and calm with only threads and occasional sparks of orange anxiety and scarlet anger.

"Hey, short-stuff!" Quinton replied, removing his hat, his face alight at seeing her even in these circumstances.

She stopped short in front of him and raised her eyebrows—the expression was exactly like one of her brother's. "'Short-stuff'? Just for that, you get to hold Martim—he's wet. You have spectacularly bad timing, big brother."

"At least it's some kind of spectacular," he said, returning the hat to his head and accepting the squirming bundle of baby, who began to wail the moment he was no longer in his mother's arms. "Oh boy, you weren't kidding. He *is* wet," Quinton said, holding the baby out in front of him.

Sam gave him a hard look and scooped Martim back onto her hip. "That's not how you hold a baby."

Quinton grinned at her. "I know, but now I'm not the one holding him."

"Sneaky, big brother. Very sneaky. Come on inside and we'll change him."

"We?"

"Yes. It's your penance." She looked at me. "You must be Harper."

I nodded. "I am. And I'm terrible at changing babies, unless you mean in some existential kind of way."

Sam forced a laugh, her aura jumping a little. She was trying very hard to make the scene look good for the neighbors, but playing nice with a stranger was difficult under the circumstances. "You don't have to change anything. You look exactly as I knew you would."

She turned to lead us inside before I could ask what that was.

The house was old—European old, not American old—and had a thin, clinging film of history that wasn't particularly dramatic. Sam noticed me looking around the wood-and-stone interior.

"It's mostly restored to the original—or as close as we could get and still be practical," she said. "It used to be the vineyard manager's house when the estate was still producing wine."

"It's lovely," I said. I really did like it—I have a taste for old things and not much appreciation for things sleek and modern—and the house was warm and cozy. It hadn't been a perfectly happy place all of its existence, judging from the energetic colors and the ghosts, but it was now. Or it had been until a few days ago.

Quinton left our hats and bags by the door and followed Sam into another room off to the left of the main entry. The siblings fell into some chitchat while Sam changed the baby. I could hear them murmuring through the open doorway as I continued to look around the main room. It was a lofty space that rose to the roof beams on one side and opened into a dining area and kitchen toward the back. The baby-changing room and probably a couple more rooms were hidden off to the left of the doorway and a wooden staircase with chunky wooden rails marched up one interior wall to the bedrooms above. A modest fireplace anchored the end of the main room while views of the yards at the front and back could be glimpsed through the tall, narrow windows on each side of the living room and dining area. It was a more-modern design than the house itself, but it suited the building's current use better than the smaller, closed rooms it must have had originally. The soft yellow stone had been left bare on the fireplace and staircase walls, but it had been plastered and probably insulated on the longer exterior walls. The rear windows that faced south had been left open to the ocean breeze that came in with the scent of brine, jasmine, and lemons. One of the vineyard managers had lingered around the fireplace, pacing in perpetuity. While Quinton and Sam were still busy with Martim, I walked over to see if he was a repeater or a more-aware spirit.

The pacing ghost didn't notice me until he walked through me.

Then he stopped, startled, and looked around until he spotted me. *"Eh? O que é isso? Quem está aí?"*

I didn't need a translator to get the gist of what he'd said. I sank a bit closer to the Grey, edging toward the fluttering cold current of his temporacline, but not entering the layer of time. I didn't want to vanish from the normal world; I only wanted to chat.

"I didn't mean to startle you," I said, hoping he understood at least my tone, if not my words. "I'm . . . an investigator—a seeker of lost things."

He peered at my shadowy form. *"Inglês?* What do you want, spirit?" His English was rough and stumbling, but not inaccessible.

I worked a hunch. "Have you been bothered by a pair of mages recently?" Willful spirits and those with some awareness of their surroundings usually notice things like mages and magic in their vicinity the way normal people notice small earthquakes.

"What? *Bruxos! Sim,*" he added, nodding. "Two that want the little girl. They watch her until the mother took her away. I have not seen her again. What happens?"

"They may have taken her."

The phantom man looked angry. "You will get her back? The house is happy with her here—with her family here. They do not bother me."

"Can you tell me anything about the mages?"

"Me? What would I know?"

"What sort of magic did they use? Could you feel it?"

"Feel . . . ? The air was colder when they were near. It made my bones ache. And the smell . . . like the vineyard when the rain comes too late and rots the grapes. But magic? I know nothing."

It was still more than I'd had before. "Was there anything around them like old burned wood, like charcoal? Brittle, black, or white . . . ?"

He shook his head. I guessed he didn't experience the magic the same way as I had felt its residue, but it had been worth a shot. "Thank you," I said.

"I did not help you," he said, puzzled.

"Yes, you did. I'll be able to recognize them, now, when I smell rot and feel cold where it's warm and clean."

His craggy face lit. "*Bom.* Bring her home. She makes us smile."

"I will," I promised, backing out of the Grey.

Quinton and Sam were watching me from the kitchen archway. Sam was startled and pale, her eyes wide while small, sharp sparks jumped from her aura. Quinton still looked a little tense, but he gave me a tiny smile and turned to his sister. "She does that a lot."

Sam cut her eyes from me to him. "Do you get used to it?"

"Not really."

She gave a nod and pulled her discomfort and fear back, smothering the sparks in her energy corona. She turned back to me. "What did you see?"

I always feel a bit strange telling people their homes are haunted. Some freak out, others think I'm lying, and some claim it's cool until something goes wrong. I studied her, the way she stood oddly poised on both feet without leaning toward me or away, the serious expression on her face, even the way she had shifted slightly toward Quinton and her son in his arms. She was a little bit afraid or wary of what I was going to say, but she wanted to hear it anyway.

"You have a significant ghost. Not a haunting, per se, just one ghost who's at least a little aware of your presence in the house. Don't worry, though—he likes your family."

She looked uncomfortable and grew a little paler. "He?"

"One of the vineyard managers, I would guess, or a winemaker . . . I'm not sure which. He's an older man and very concerned about the vines and the weather and the house. I didn't get his name and I couldn't tell you what time period he's from—his clothes aren't distinctive in that way. He doesn't have a full manifestation. He's more of a moving shadow I happened to be able to catch and talk to."

She was taken aback and blinked at me. "You're some kind of psychic, then."

Quinton and I both shook our heads and Sam frowned. "No, I'm not a psychic," I said. "At least not as you use the term. I go to them—they don't come to me."

Her frown told me she didn't quite get the distinction, but it wasn't worth trying to explain further. "Anyhow," I continued, "he wasn't much help, but he did give me a description that could come in handy."

"Of one of Dad's friends? But I could have given you that."

"Not what they looked like, but more . . . the effect they had on things. It wouldn't be useful to most people, but most people don't talk to ghosts, either."

She made a small dismissive gesture with her hands. "The only thing that matters to me is if it will help get my daughter back. Will it?"

"Possibly. It will help me identify the people who took her. You said a man and a woman were with your father just before Soraia disappeared."

Sam nodded and started walking into the living room. "Yes, but I'm sorry, I really need to sit. My knees are kind of a mess." She sat down on a sofa that faced the empty fireplace, then held her arms up to Quinton who handed her the baby he'd been carrying. "OK, so, yes. A man and a woman were with him, but as I said, they kept their distance and said nothing."

"What did they look like?"

Sam bounced the baby in her lap as she spoke. "He was old—I'd guess about seventy—and Portuguese, wavy hair with a lot of gray, though I think it was originally black. He had blue eyes—very disconcerting."

"How do you know he was Portuguese and not, say, Spanish or French?"

She stopped and blinked rapidly, her gaze turning inward as she thought about it. "I think because he was so dour. He had a sort of stern face with a prominent nose—very eagle-like. It gave him an austere look. The woman was American or English, very pale skinned with straight blond hair that was a bit faded, but not really gray. I think she was in her late fifties, but it's hard to say. At first I thought she was friendly—she had this little smile that kept sneaking out—but then I began to change my mind. They both had a disquieting way of looking at me as if they were studying an insect they intended to kill and mount on a pin, and I thought she was smiling about adding another bug to her collection. It's a very uncomfortable feeling."

Martim whined in protest and Sam began bouncing him again. He giggled, spewing happy gold sparks into the Grey mist of the room.

Quinton asked a question of his own now, his demeanor much more focused and grim than it had been in the yard. "Did Dad introduce them? Say anything about them?"

"No," Sam replied. Then she looked at me. "That's not odd for our father. He never says anything more than he has to, so I assumed the people with him were associates and not concerned with whatever brought him to my home."

"Do you see him often? Or was this a bit of a surprise?" I asked.

"Oh, it wasn't quite a surprise—I knew he was coming since he'd called and said so. I was almost not home, but he claimed he wanted to bring the kids some birthday presents, since he'd missed so many of those events. I should have told him to ship them. What was a surprise was his calling in the first place. I have done everything I can to stay off his radar. Our father isn't a nice man and I don't want my family mixed up in the things he does. I thought I had made that clear to him. This was the one time I had a moment of weakness over the possibility that Dad might have a paternal bone in his body—I'm an idiot to have imagined he'd be less of a son of a bitch after all this time. Now Soraia and the rest of us are paying for my bad judgment."

She didn't sound bitter; it was just a statement. Sam was the most collected, calm woman I'd ever met who wasn't some sort of gruesome magic user. It was strange, especially when coupled with her painful gait.

"The leg made me think he'd lost his edge and might be feeling his mortality a bit," she continued, "wanting to mend some fences now that he was disabled."

Quinton rolled his eyes. "Playing it up, was he? Leave it to our father to pull the sympathy card for knee surgery."

Samantha frowned and blinked at Quinton, confused. "I'm not sure what you mean. His left leg is missing from the knee down. He had a temporary prosthesis that didn't fit very well, so his limp was quite pronounced. Worse than mine."

Quinton was startled and stared at her, shaking his head. "No. . . . He was fine when I saw him last. The knee surgery was ten months ago and he was a model patient. He needed a cane to steady his stride on that side, but he was otherwise perfect. What happened to his leg?"

Sam shrugged. "I don't know. He didn't offer much of an explanation—just said he'd had an injury in the field. He acted as if it were nothing and just went on with the rest of what he'd come to say."

Quinton couldn't seem to get a grip on the idea of his father's missing leg. "You're sure it was a prosthetic? He wasn't just limping from some other problem with the knee?"

Sam rolled her eyes and gave him an exasperated look. "I did actually finish my medical degree, Jay. I know a cheap prosthetic when I see one."

"I just don't get it. . . . It was fine when I saw him last."

"When was that?" I asked.

He bit his lip and frowned at the floor, thinking. "Must be four or five months ago, about the time he was in Turkey. I lost track of him there, but I was able to stay on top of his assistants and follow his trail."

"Maybe it was a false trail," I suggested. "He may have known you—or someone else—was watching him and created another series of events to follow while he did something that redamaged the leg."

"It's possible. . . . I just . . . What did he do?"

I shrugged and Samantha mirrored me. "You said he'd had surgery on his knee," Sam started. "Dozens of things can happen to a knee if the patient isn't careful with it early on. And our father is certainly the sort of man who plunges into things without too much worry about the potential damage."

Quinton was disturbed. "I suppose. I'm still a bit thrown by it, though. I have a bad feeling. . . ."

I'd had a bad feeling about James Purlis for a long time and this was only increasing my alarm with the situation. "This particular line of inquiry isn't helping us find Soraia," I said. "While it may be relevant—your father rarely does anything that's not part of a larger plan—we can't get any closer to him with only this information. We need something else." My words sparked an idea in my head. "Did he leave anything? You said he brought presents for the kids. There could be a clue there."

Sam handed Martim to Quinton and got clumsily to her feet again. "I'll get them. I thought it wasn't appropriate to let the children open them without their father around, since we weren't near either of their birthdays and it's still three months to Christmas. Dad didn't seem to like that, but I didn't give him a choice about it. By that time I was starting to be very uncomfortable with his presence—and that of his friends. I asked him to leave a few minutes later and then I took Soraia to school. . . ." Her eyes reddened as she said it, getting misty with tears, but she sniffed, rubbed at her eyes with the back of her hand, and turned to fetch the packages. "This will only take a minute. . . ."

The ghosts seemed to swirl around her as she left the room as if they all felt her passage and turned to look. It was an odd reaction, especially since she was oblivious to them and they didn't actually turn toward her. She had some kind of weight in the Grey that was unusual.

I glanced at Quinton and found him watching me. "What do you think?"

"I think your sister is the calmest woman I've ever met. I'd be throwing a screaming fit if someone had kidnapped my daughter."

"No, you wouldn't. You would be thinking about how to hunt them down and kill them."

"Like you are?" I asked, but I had to concede that point. "All right. I probably would."

"Are you thinking that things didn't go as she says?"

"No. I think they went exactly as she described them. I'm just surprised to see her so collected. It's been three—or is it four days—and she apparently hasn't heard any more about her missing daughter, but she's sitting here, talking calmly to us about it."

"That's just how Sam is. She took care of our grandparents—Mom's folks—when they were . . . declining. And she finished her medical degree at the same time. Sam is what the English would call 'a brick.' She's totally unflappable."

"And what happened to her legs?" I asked, uncomfortable but unwilling to let it slide.

"She was in a bus accident when we were kids. Crushed her legs, did a bunch of damage to her spine, but she survived and the damage was rehabilitated up to a point. It just didn't come back quite as well as everyone hoped. Sam got to a stage of exasperation where she called a halt to the surgeries and experiments and said she'd just live with it. And she does, but that's partially a credit to our grandparents for supporting her and looking after her when our mom and dad weren't able to. That's why she spent so much time taking care of them, later—it was like . . . coming full circle."

"I still don't understand what happened to your mother. She's still alive, isn't she?"

"She is, but—"

Quinton cut himself off when Sam came back into the room with an armload of wrapped boxes. "Good God, it *is* Christmas!" he said.

"Three for each of them—two Christmas and one birthday," Sam said. "You can tell by the wrapping."

"I think we'd better unwrap them and see what Dad left."

"Agreed," said Sam, putting the gifts down on the slab of unstained wood that served as a coffee table. "I'll put them back together later if they prove to be genuine presents and not something . . . else."

With three of us, it took less than two minutes to open all the packages. The gifts for Martim were generic baby things—a stuffed animal we decided was a platypus, a clattering box with doors that opened and closed to reveal various bells and rattles, and a package of baby-sized T-shirts—but Soraia's gifts were a bit creepy. There was a very old china-headed doll whose face bore a watchful expression, a large smoky quartz crystal run through with black shards that hung from an ornate silver cap and chain, and a small flute-like instrument made of a smooth white material with an air hole on the top that looked like someone had taken a bite of it.

Quinton had unwrapped that one and he started to hand it to me. I leaned away from it as the jagged, black-and-white energy that writhed around it surged toward me. "No. I don't want to touch that with my bare hands. Not until I can get Carlos to take a look at it."

"Why?" Sam asked.

"It's magical and whatever type of magic it has is all too eager to attach itself to me. That's a bad sign, since it has no interest in either of you or the baby, so my best guess is that what it's after is a person with a touch of the Grey. I'm guessing Soraia is a little . . . unusual. Is she prone to seeing things that you can't see? Does she have imaginary friends?" I asked.

Sam nodded. "She does, but I thought that was just the sort of thing all little girls do when they suddenly have a little brother to compete with."

"I didn't do that," said Quinton.

"I'm not a little brother," Sam replied. "Besides, you had all those fun camping and hunting trips with Dad. You didn't need an imaginary friend."

"Do I hear some resentment there?"

"No. It's simply a fact that your every waking hour that wasn't spent in school or in front of some bit of technology was spent on what were, in essence, training missions with our father. If you had time for an imaginary friend, it would have been at night, in your sleeping bag, while you devised ways to escape from Camp Purlis."

Quinton's face looked as if she'd punched him in the gut. "Sam . . . I'm sorry."

She closed her eyes and took a long breath before opening them again. "Don't be. I was mad sometimes, when we were kids, but, really, I got the better deal. Just look at our lives. Look at us. I am so much better off. I have a family I love and can be with every day, in the open, like a normal person. I have a wonderful job—when I'm not chasing toddlers—a wonderful husband who works normal hours when he's home, and a wonderful house whose front door isn't camouflaged to blend into the landscape. It's taken you years to find Harper and be together, and you still have to sneak and hide and live in the shadows. It may be a life you like, but not me."

"I don't like it. And I don't want it. But until this business with Dad is over—"

"I know. But will this be the end of it? What are you going to do once you find him and Soraia? Kill him?"

"No!" Quinton was aghast.

Sam shook her head, her eyes once again suspiciously red and wet. Her aura jumped with sudden scarlet sparks. "Then it will never be over. Dad will stop plotting and maneuvering and manipulating when he's in his grave and not one minute before."

"You think I should . . . ?"

"I'm not saying you should kill him. But I'm not saying you shouldn't, either. He's a monster. He took my child. He tried to give her that thing your girlfriend won't even touch. He used you, and when you resisted, he almost killed you. He had our mom locked up in a psychiatric hospital. He is not a person who should be running loose in the world, but you can't lock him up and be sure he'd stay there. The only other choice is to keep hiding. How do you want to live, Jay? That's the only thing I'm saying." I took note of everything she said, but I didn't interrupt—this wasn't my conversation.

Quinton put the flute on the table and rubbed one of his hands over his face and into his brown hair. "There has to be some other solution. I almost shot him in Seattle—I did shoot him, but I mean I almost shot him dead and Harper stopped me. I don't want to be a murderer, no matter how terrible he is. I just . . . It was something I couldn't live with at the NSA and I won't bring that back down on myself. I don't want to kill people, not even by remote control, through blinds and cutouts and a dozen layers of protocol that turned an elegant little programming problem into a weapon. I don't want . . . that. That is no better a life than hiding and skulking. I don't want to start a new life waist-deep in blood—anyone's blood and especially not my father's. He's a villain, but killing him would not make me a hero."

Sam threw her arms around him, catching Martim as well in her embrace. "Oh, Jay! I'm sorry, that's not what I mean at all. I don't want that, either. I am so sorry. I am . . . I'm. . . . I just want it to end! I want my daughter back. I just . . . want her back so much. . . ." It was as close to a breakdown as I had seen from Sam, although still very contained, and I wondered if being "a brick" was really a good thing for the brick. The baby didn't seem to care for it, either, making squeals of protest at being squashed between the two adults.

Quinton clung to Sam with his free arm, saying, "I know. I know . . ." over and over.

I noted that Sam had avoided any further discussion of the idea that her daughter might be in touch with the Grey and I shifted my own focus to something productive. I used the stuffed toy to shove the flute back into its box and then put the lid on it while the siblings cried on each other's shoulders. It wasn't that I wasn't affected by the scene and had no stake in it—I had a big one—but there was nothing I could do or say. It was their moment, and interrupting it to say, "Your daughter is probably psychic or some kind of magic user" wasn't appropriate. I found the horrible flute increasingly disturbing, so I dealt with that, instead. I felt better once the flute was back in its box, and Quinton and Sam both sat back, looking a little relieved themselves.

As I put the package on the table, a tapping came on the front window. We all looked toward it, but only I saw the old vineyard manager standing on the other side, waving for me to come out to the yard. I stood up. "I think there's something that the resident ghost wants us to see."

SEVEN

Brother and sister followed me out of the house, Sam carrying Martim on her hip as he gurgled happily about going outdoors. I walked around to a shaded spot next to the wall where the ghost was waiting. He pointed to the ground. "Can you hear the noise?" he asked.

I concentrated on listening and, in the somber song of the Grey, I could hear an odd thread of melody, thin and high. Like a bird or a piccolo.

I stooped and looked around in the Grey, trying to locate the sound. I closed my eyes and moved my head until I heard the sound more clearly. Then I opened my eyes. The wall was directly in front of me. I humphed in surprise. How could a wall make sound?

The ghost knelt down next to me and pointed to the bottom of the wall, obscured in the prickly canes of the rosebushes. "There. It doesn't belong here."

I had to lie down to see the chink in the wall. It passed all the way through the wall and was wide enough for me to slide my forefinger into with plenty of room to spare. A current of magic jolted me like an electric shock, but rather than knocking me back, it seemed to pull me forward. I yanked my hand away, pushing myself violently out of the edge of the Grey.

I knocked into Quinton's legs. He reached to pull me back to my feet, giving me a quick once-over. "You all right?"

I nodded, brushing soil and grass off the front of my blouse and skirt. "Just shocked. There's something in a chink in the wall down there, but I can't get it—it's very powerful."

"Could I try?"

"I'm not sure that's wise. . . ."

But he had knelt down and was already stretching himself out on the ground. "I see it. Just a sec . . ." he said, pulling a tool from his pocket and unfolding it into a pair of narrow pliers. Even in much nicer clothes than his usual jeans, T-shirt, and coat, he still had pockets full of useful things.

In a moment, Quinton got to his feet and held up another small white cylinder. "It's the twin to the one Dad gave Soraia."

He held the tiny flute out, clasped in the pliers' jaws. It was very similar but not actually a twin. The mouthpiece was a little different and the tone holes were not in quite the same placement. I thought the slight bend in the tube went the opposite way, but without opening the box, I couldn't be sure. I'd not only left the box in the living room; I had no intention of opening it again without Carlos around. This flute was also dirty, and it was the dark, rubbed-in soil that made the difference, revealing a grain I hadn't seen on the clean specimen.

"It's a bone flute," I said. "They both are. From nearly identical bones, I think."

"What a terrible gift for a child," said the ghost.

Just behind him, Sam said the same thing.

I peered at the ghost. "Why? I can tell it's a bad object, but why specifically a bad gift for a child?"

"They call Coca. They bring bad luck upon the child so it will be carried off by monsters."

"What's Coca?" I asked.

But it was Sam who answered. "Coca? It's a dragon—a sort of Portuguese boogeyman. I sing the song to Martim sometimes when he's being really difficult. *Dorme, menino,*" she began singing, "*dorme agora, ou o Coca vem te comer.* Basically it's 'Be quiet, little one, go to sleep, or the Coca will come and get you.'"

"Oh, that's a lovely sentiment," I said.

"About as nice as any fairy tale with girls in glass coffins and witches who eat kids," Sam shot back in an unusual flash of temper. She calmed herself and continued. "The legend says Saint George killed Coca, but it's really a fertility thing—every year there's a festival where the knight is supposed to kill the dragon, and if he doesn't, the crops will fail. What does that have to do with my daughter?"

"The ghost says this flute calls Coca to take children away—though in this case I think it was the other way around," I said.

The old man ghost looked away, as if he were about to cry. "The poor girl. You must find her quickly. *Bruxos* who make such things, they cannot have any good in mind for her."

"I'm inclined to agree." I looked at the ground, noticing that a bit of the black-and-white residue left by Purlis's companions had been pulled through the hole with the flute. I addressed the ghost. "I know who put it there. But did they make it, also?"

The ghost shrugged. "I cannot say. The ways of *bruxos* . . ."

I nodded. "Thank you. Again."

He nodded himself away.

Quinton was waiting patiently for me to return my attention to the living. Sam was eyeing me a bit askance. I guessed that my tendency to talk to what looked like empty air disconcerted her. But she was more worried by the flute Quinton was holding.

"Another one? Who put it there and why would they do that?"

"Is there a gate near this location?" I asked.

Sam nodded. "The alley gate is just beyond the roses."

"Then my guess would be that your father's creepy companions put it here. It makes a noise in the Grey that was probably supposed to lure Soraia out to this part of the garden so they could snatch her. It turned out they didn't have to, but they couldn't come back for it and risk meeting you again after they'd taken her, so they left it behind. They probably thought you'd never find it. I'm willing to bet it's unique in some way we can try to track down."

"And we'll probably need Carlos for that, I'm betting," Quinton said.

"Well, he is the local expert on bits of dead things." I turned to Sam. "We need to take both of these with us and show them to a friend who might be able to tell us where they came from or who made them. And that may help us find Soraia."

"May?"

"It's not a certainty. It seems likely, but I'll admit, I am making an educated guess here."

Sam chewed on that thought for a moment, shifting the baby on her hip without conscious thought. Obviously, I still wasn't quite a sure thing for her. She loved and believed her brother, but it's a little hard to take seriously a woman who throws herself down on the ground to talk to ghosts, I suppose.

"It'll be all right," Quinton assured her. "I know all this sounds a bit crazy, but I told you about Harper and you know I wouldn't lie to you. She knows what she's doing."

Sam looked at him. "I know. I know and I trust you, but it is somewhat hard to swallow. . . ."

"You didn't have any problem with what Dad may be up to, but you choke on the idea of a woman who talks to ghosts? Sam . . ." Quinton was disappointed and shook his head.

She looked down. "It is a bit . . . strange to see someone talking to the air. . . ."

"You haven't seen the *really* strange stuff yet."

"I hope I won't."

I interrupted. "It won't matter if we don't get this investigation back on track." I fixed my gaze on Sam. "Earlier I asked you if Soraia claims to see things you don't see or if she has imaginary friends. You indicated she did. So, tell me more about what seems to be going on with her and how long that's been the case. Your father didn't take her because she was a convenient child he had access to. He took her for some specific reason, which appears to be something about Soraia herself, not just leverage to draw Qu—" I had to stop myself and remember to use the name she did. "I mean Jay—back into his web. What does she see, or say, or do . . . ?"

Sam shifted from foot to foot, juggling Martim in a preoccupied manner. "She told me about the man near the fireplace—the same one you described and . . . talked to. I was very startled when you said the same thing. And she said there are fairies in the yard—which is exactly what all little girls think, isn't it?"

"Not me. I never saw a fairy in my life except in toe shoes and a tutu—and only because they made me wear the tutu."

"Oh. Well . . . sometimes she seems to know things she really shouldn't. . . . I mean that she has no way of knowing them, not that they're the sort of things little girls shouldn't know about. Where are Daddy's missing keys or does Mommy's patient have cancer. . . . Sometimes things happen near her that are . . . just extraordinary. She was swarmed by honeybees once, and not a single one stung her. They just flew up to her like she was a queen and buzzed around for a while, then flew away. And there's a green woodpecker she says talks to her—she calls it Tio Pássaro," she added, giving Quinton a significant look that was lost on me. "I think it's one of the fairies. I've seen the bird in the lemon tree in the backyard, although I know they're not tree-borers. Once in a while, Soraia wishes for things to happen and they do—which is where the woodpecker came from. We were having lunch outside one day, and she wished aloud for the bird to fly down from the tree so she could give it a bit of her bread, and the woodpecker flew down and landed on the tabletop beside her, though it wasn't very interested in the bread. It's been around ever since, though . . . I haven't seen the bird since she was taken."

"And none of these things gave you an idea that there was something unusual about your daughter."

"They didn't happen all in a rush. It was one odd incident at the time. Then some other time another odd incident, but they never seemed threatening—except for the bees and they didn't harm her, so I thought it was just a fluke. They never seemed to have a pattern. My daughter is not a freak, just a gifted little girl."

I chose not to take up the gauntlet of "freak," but that didn't mean I wasn't a little pissed off by it. "These sorts of things aren't really the usual little-girl thing," I said. "Fairies and make-believe and invisible friends, yes. Seeing ghosts, magical wishes, talking birds, and knowing the answers to questions she can't even formulate, no. The bee thing—definitely way out of the norm, but that could, as you say, have been a fluke of nature. But fluke or not, your daughter is a very special girl. And I don't mean in that usual Auntie-says-so kind of way. She has a touch of something that goes well beyond the normal and I think that's why your father took her. Unfortunately, that means that whatever he's up to is pretty strong magic. This project of his has taken some gruesome turns, but everything he touches—and destroys or subverts—is either paranormal or closely connected to the paranormal. Governments have done paranormal research in the past—there's always someone thinking the freaks might be the answer to some political problem—but what your father is up to goes well beyond bending spoons, trying to read cards that are in another room, or staring at goats until they faint."

Sam was mad, which was interesting to see, her aura all streaked in red and sparking like a Tesla coil. "And your point . . . ?" she asked, glaring at me and bouncing the baby so rapidly that he began hiccuping.

"Point is: Put a lid on your disbelief. And when we get her back, get your scientific brain set on helping her and nurturing her talent so it doesn't twist itself into something dangerous. It could be a tiny little talent that doesn't go any further than charming birds, but if it's a big talent, denying it and trying to make it go away will be the worst thing you can do."

Sam ground her teeth and breathed through her nose in noisy gusts. Quinton reached over and slid Martim out of her grip as the baby started making distressed noises. She glared at her brother.

"Hey, you're scaring him and giving him some nice bruises," Quinton said. "Harper is right, whether you like it or not. When we get Soraia back, she's going to need a lot of help and understanding. Just on the normal things, like why her grandfather kidnapped her. That is not going to be easy for her to get over. You're going to have to be open to the idea that she's more than you imagined and can be hurt in ways you never thought of. As to the rest, if you can't help her, it's just like parents who deny their kids were molested. The hurt won't stop—it'll just turn into something worse. Have an open mind, Dr. Rebelo."

Her bottom lip trembled, but she didn't cry. She took a few deep breaths, swallowed her upset, and put her arms out. "May I have my son back, please?"

Quinton handed the baby over and Sam hugged Martim to her chest, kissing the top of his head and holding him close. "All right. I will . . . have an open mind. Because I want my kids to have a better life than we had. I'm not sure about all of this yet, but . . . I'll work with it. What do we do now?"

"For now, we take the flutes to my friend in Lisbon and see what he has to say," I replied.

"I'll get Martim's things."

"At this stage, it's better if you stay here and wait until we have information to proceed on. If your husband or your father tries to contact you, they'll expect you to be here. It's the hardest job of all— waiting. But it's necessary so we don't miss anything."

She looked combative, but she nodded and pressed her face against the top of the baby's head. "I understand. But once you have information, I want to be in the loop."

Quinton gave her upper arm a squeeze. "You will be."

It was hard to leave, taking all of Soraia's gifts with us—just in case. Sam was fighting the urge to throw caution to the wind and come with us, which must have caused her considerable mental tur-moil, judging by the agitated colors of her energy corona. Quinton was uncomfortable abandoning her to the mind-killing tedium of waiting, but since the only safe base of operations we had at the moment was the house in Lisbon, neither of us thought it wise to bring her along until after we'd discussed it with Carlos. It's rude to bring a guest for dinner if there's a chance she might end up as the main course.

EIGHT

We talked less than I would have liked on the trip back to Lisbon, but we each had things we didn't really want to say. Finally Quinton stopped playing with the brim of his hat and asked, "What do you think about the bone flutes?"

"I'm not sure what they're for, but I keep getting directed to those bone mages Carlos mentioned last year—the Kostní Mágové. The flutes seem like something that might be connected to them. Given his reaction to said mages, that worries me."

"You were a little . . . hard on Sam."

"She was being stubborn and hardheaded about the idea of anything paranormal, and I don't want some little girl—and especially not your niece—to go through the sort of horrors my father went through because other people didn't believe what he experienced."

"Do you really think she's . . . Grey?"

"It sounds like it. But I'm more convinced by your father's gifts and his taking her at what appears to be a period of increasing activity for him. It makes no sense for him to kidnap his own granddaughter unless she's useful to him in a specific way. Otherwise, he'd find some other child—some poor immigrant kid no one is watching out for or some drug addict's kid, or any of hundreds of children he could find a way to grab without having to go all the way to Carcavelos and take a member of his own family. It's got to be significant." I shook my head in frustration. "I wish Mara were here. She'd have a much better idea of what might be going on with your niece. I really miss Mara."

Quinton frowned. "Because she could be useful." He hated that I leaned on my friends for help that often got them hurt. I'd made myself break that habit, but the memory of it was still there and it rankled that he thought I might fall back into that pattern.

"No. Not because she's a witch," I said. "Because she's a mother. I'm not. I know I bullied Sam a little back there. I am not proud of that. I just don't know any other way to talk to professionals except to give it to them straight. I treated your sister like a doctor who wasn't reading the whole chart. Because I'm not any good at being gentle to a mother's feelings about her kids. I'm a moose in a mouse factory where that sort of thing is concerned. Mara would have done much better. And she would have had a reasonable idea of what Soraia's talents are and why your father might have snatched her. And that's why I wish Mara were here. That and I miss her—I haven't seen any of the Danzigers in, what . . . four years? Brian must be in school by now."

"He's Soraia's age."

I peered sideways at him. "Oh really?"

He nodded, blushing. "They're in Spain. I saw them once, from a distance a few months ago."

"No wonder you quit the spy game—you're sentimental!"

"No. I'm just . . . concerned about my friends when they might be in the way of trouble."

"And are they?"

"As it happens, no. Mara and Ben seem to have good instincts for when they should move on. But . . . they are just over the border about a hundred miles."

"Which is nothing to an American, the way a hundred years is nothing to a European. Are you suggesting we call them into this?"

"No. Or not yet. But as you say, you're not a mother and Mara is, so maybe when we're closer to getting Soraia back, it would be a good idea to get the Danzigers in on the act. Sam and the kids will need a safer place to stay until this is all over—with someone who can protect them from the paranormal as well as the usual threats— and I don't think that getting Soraia back from Dad is going to put his plans on hold for very long."

"Unless he's dead."

Quinton shuddered. "I can't—"

"I'm not asking you to. But your sister was right about that, and you know it. He won't stop. So yeah, even if we get Soraia back, he's going to have a plan B and he'll put it in motion as soon as he can. You know we're going to have to find some permanent way to neutralize him or this is never going to be over."

Quinton sighed and leaned his head against the back of the seat. "I know. God, I know."

We both fell silent and looked out the window until we reached the Cais do Sodré again. It was a little after six in the evening and Quinton asked to walk instead of taking the metro back to Rossio station where we'd started. He seemed to need to move, to burn off the red anger that had been building around him since we'd left Carcavelos. We had more than an hour until Carlos would wake up, so I agreed. He put his hat on and kept his head down as he went, shadowing his face. I did the same, just in case.

We walked a zigzag track through the straight streets of Lisbon's downtown—the Pombaline downtown, Quinton called it, named for the Portuguese nobleman responsible for the rebuilding after the earthquake of 1755. The ruler-straight roads and rows of aesthetically similar buildings reminded me a little of Seattle's downtown core that had been forced to be flat and geometrically pleasing by tearing the hills down and throwing the dirt into the gaping hole that was now South Downtown. It didn't look the same, but the shadows of what had been before were as persistent. We passed through misty walls as easily as ghosts and the specters of the long-dead stepped suddenly in front of us, running from destruction on roads that had vanished two centuries before. I tried to think more about the resurrection of the city than its destruction, and that seemed to help with the feelings of pain and panic that threatened to overwhelm me in the presence of the endless repetition of Lisbon's collapse.

We wove and turned until I wasn't sure where we were or what direction we faced. Then Quinton turned through a doorway into a bookshop. It was small and smelled dusty, but it was well-ordered and the strange, warm light of Lisbon fell through the windowpanes to touch the books with gold. I wandered among the stacks while Quinton went to talk to the proprietor. Passing the occasional ghostly customer, I was relieved at the insulation that the shop seemed to have from the worst of the memories outside. Old Possum's—my friend Phoebe's used bookstore at home—had a similar effect. I wondered whether books somehow collected the intellectual joy of their readers and let it back out, subtly, when they were gathered in a critical mass. The idea charmed me, even if it wasn't likely to be right.

Most of the books were in Portuguese, but there was also a section of books in English. I was poking through an aging hardcover edition of Daphne Du Maurier's *The House on the Strand*—and feeling entirely in sympathy with the discomfort and distress of the time-traveling hero—when Quinton came back to find me.

"I have a present for you," he said, holding out a package wrapped in a loose bit of green cloth.

I took it, curious, and flipped the cloth open to find a set of ID—including a British passport and driver's license in the name of Helena Robinson-Smith. I thought the name sounded far too posh, but the photos were of me, nonetheless. Under the cards was a small pile of money in euros.

"Oh, you shouldn't have," I said in mock surprise.

"Well, you can't go around with no ID and no cash." He held up his own ID, which was in the name of Christopher Marlowe Smith.

I raised an eyebrow. "Really."

"It's not my fault the guy's parents had a queer literary bent. Honestly, that's the name that came up—I had nothing to do with it. I will only admit that I didn't say no to being Kit Marlowe for a while."

"So long as you don't get killed in a tavern brawl or decide your taste suddenly runs to men, I guess I can live with it."

"Unlikely on both counts. You should put those away in your purse before we go outside. Remember the pickpockets."

"Are they really that bad?" I asked as I tucked the ID and cash into my little straw bag. As my hand brushed the bottom, I felt only one key.

My heart lurched and I knelt down to turn the purse out onto the floor. The ID and cash were there, of course, but only one key, and it didn't look like the big, old iron house key Rafa had given me. "Oh . . . Damn it! The house keys are gone!" I picked up the remaining key—a boring modern door key in appearance—and it weighed far too much. I stared at it, cocking my head to the side to look through the edges of the Grey.

The key looked as it had inside the house—a large, old skeleton-type key that would fit the lock on my suite door, but not the larger lock on the gate. "What the hell?" I puzzled with it for a moment as Quinton knelt down beside me.

"What happened?"

"Well, someone did pick my pocket, but all they got was the gate key. And it won't look like much to them, so with luck I can get the housekeeper's attention and get in without it. I still have the key to my room." I held it up.

"Doesn't look like much, but I take it from the way you're staring at it, that there's more to it than that."

I nodded. "When she handed it to me, it was a big old-fashioned key, like something from a castle dungeon. It still feels the same weight, but I can only see the real shape of the key in the Grey. There's something very interesting about that house. . . ."

"I'll bet. Do you have any idea where the key was taken from you?"

"No. Could have been at the train station or in Rossio Square, or on the metro. . . . I was jostled a lot. If I were guessing, I'd say the train station on the way out to your sister's place, but that's only a guess."

"I don't think we're going to find it, but we can walk back to the station and ask. . . ."

I shook my head, replacing the contents of the bag and getting to my feet with a sigh. "No, there's no point. I could identify it only if they show me the key, since it would look like this nondescript one to anyone who couldn't see it in the Grey. Somewhere there's a very confused pickpocket—he grabbed something that felt big and heavy and impressive and got what appears to be an overweight house key. He probably threw it away in disgust."

"I hope this isn't going to cause you problems."

"I hope not, too, but I'll deal with that if it happens."

"Ah, that's my Helena. So pragmatic as well as beautiful."

"Helena? Oh," I said, remembering the name on my new ID.

He gave me a silly grin and said, "You remember. 'Was this the face that launched a thousand ships, and burnt the topless towers of Ilium? Sweet Helen, make me immortal with a kiss.'"

I gave him a sour look instead. "More likely I'll make you immortal by introducing you to the wrong vampire. I think Kit Marlowe has gone to your head."

He gave a very small, strained laugh. "Well, so long as there's some kissing in there somewhere, I guess I'll be OK with it. It has been quite a while. . . ."

I laughed at him and gave him a fast kiss. And then a longer one. "You are a very odd man."

"At least I make you laugh when things get terrible."

"You do," I conceded, knowing that at least part of the laughter was a sham on both our parts. "But, eww! Vampire kisses!" I gave a mock shudder.

"Some people obviously like them."

I thought of the mark on Tovah's wrist and the way she'd deferred to Carlos. "I would never volunteer to be a vampire snack," I said.

"Why not?" Quinton asked, taking my book and looking it over, keeping his face turned from mine.

"How can you ask that?"

He looked up, still holding the book in one hand, and took my arm, turning me so we could make our way out of the store. "Because I want to understand it. While I know you never would, I'm not actually sure why." As we passed the elderly man at the front counter, Quinton tipped his hat with one hand and held up the book in the other. *"Obrigado, Doutor Barros."*

"De nada, Senhor Smith," the man replied, nodding and smiling as if we weren't stealing his book.

Outside, Quinton continued to steer me along the streets, his expression serious as he kept his eyes on anything but me, and repeated his question in a soft voice. "Why would you not? I just want to understand what makes you certain you wouldn't give in—I mean that is kind of their stock-in-trade."

I replied in a low voice, feeling confused by his choice of topic. "Because they're dead and they're power mongers. Their glamour doesn't affect me, so as far as I'm concerned, all vampires are just upright corpses with terrible habits. And they smell bad. Also, Carlos and Cameron have let it slip once or twice that there's more to blood in the vampire community than just cells and plasma. I don't want to give up a little chunk of my life or be under anyone's control—no matter how slight, distant, or seemingly useful—regardless of the upside. Bitten by a walking corpse . . . ? Does that sound like a good thing to you?"

"No. But my own ideas about why turn out not to be the same as yours."

"Oh? What was your idea?"

"I'd rather not discuss it," he replied, blushing.

I frowned at him, thinking. "Oh. Yuck! I wouldn't do *that* with a vampire, either!"

Quinton laughed. "I didn't think so."

"Oh, you did, too. You might not have believed it, but you thought it."

"I blame popular fiction."

I made a face. "When do you read pop fiction? I thought you were a politics and sciences guy."

"I've spent a lot of time on trains and lurking around in public places. Having a book in front of your nose excuses a lot of just sitting around. But you have to pick a title no one is likely to ask you about. Oddly enough, few people want to pick the brains of men who read fantasy novels. Except those by George R. R. Martin— everyone wants to ask if you've seen the TV show."

"And have you?"

"No. I'm more of a *Doctor Who* guy."

I made a disbelieving noise in the back of my throat and let the conversation die.

I was managing the upheaval of the earthquake better now, but it was difficult until I let the sound weave into it, rather than trying to separate vision from hearing. I'd been a dancer longer than I'd been an investigator, and though I can't sing, feeling the relationship of music to image and movement had once been a habit. The sad song of Lisbon's magical Grid seemed to transform the events of 1755 into tragedy, instead of nightmare, drawing across the strands of my own energetic core like a bow over the strings of a violin. It urged me to slow down, to move with drooping, dolorous gestures, letting tears rise to the edge of my lashes until I had to stop and lean against a building to wipe them away.

Quinton paused and turned back to me. "Are you all right?"

"It's this place—it makes me cry."

"Earlier, it made you ache. Is this an improvement?"

"No. Pain I can work through. Anger I can use. Sorrow is difficult to turn into positive energy."

"What can I do?"

"Just . . . be you."

"I'm usually good at that, though I've been so many other people in the past eight months, I may be out of practice," he replied, making his best effort not to slide back into his anger.

"Let's keep going. I can manage better if you hold my hand while we walk."

He smiled—imperfect and still worried, but still an expression that lifted my heart. "That will be a pleasure. It's not as good as kissing you, but I can settle."

I laughed a little, as he'd no doubt hoped, and put my hand in his.

NINE

We meandered toward Alfama by a slightly different route than I'd used coming down the hill. It wasn't a long walk either way, though we now had only an hour to kill thanks to our stop at the bookstore. I almost wished we had more time. It had been so long since I'd seen Quinton; I wanted to linger with him before the situation grew grimmer, as it certainly would.

We walked up a rising, gently curving road and passed a small rococo church, which Quinton identified as Santo António. It stood right in front of a cathedral with Romanesque front towers and a rose window. The cathedral had been pieced back together with bits of other styles over time and after the earthquake—a bit of Gothic here, a bit of Baroque there. The stonework was now mismatched colors and textures from centuries of construction and repair. I was almost tempted to go inside and look at it, but the shuddering of the temporaclines around it was more than I could take and we hurried farther along the road. We passed several shops with signs that read ANTIGUIDADES—"antiques" I guessed by the displays—and an increasing number of small cafés and restaurants, walls tagged with ubiquitous graffiti. I noticed no one had had the heretical temerity to tag the cathedral or chapel.

I was sure we weren't in the right place and would never get back to the house, but we passed a directional sign reading ALFAMA with an arrow pointing ahead, and we kept going up a tiled road cut by trolley tracks. Two men in clerical collars—one in a black suit and the other in a brown cassock—passed us coming downhill, talking together with serious expressions as they walked. They were an odd pair being of the same vocation, yet drastically different from each other—one in his suit with an aura a curious shade of ivory threaded with dark blue, the other more traditional in his clerical robes and an energy corona of sky blue that sparked with bright white bolts as they talked. I wondered if the conversation was contentious in some way. They nodded as we made room for them on the sidewalk, but they didn't interrupt their chat even as they met up with another, older man who seemed to have been waiting for them in the plaza in front of one of the many antique stores. In spite of his smile, the man's aura—a fit of black, white, and red spikes—gave me the creeps. The dampened violence of it seemed incongruous for a man of his vocation.

I hadn't passed so many religious buildings or their residents anywhere else in the city and wondered if the strange trio was heading for the cathedral. Even with the presence of servants of the Catholic Almighty, I was still a bit paranoid; having lost one key, I now carried my purse in front of me. I felt less foolish about it when one of the priests spun around and shouted, *"Gatuno!"* He then hiked up his cassock and ran after a skinny young man who had passed us earlier in a buzzing cloud of pea green energy jagged with white sparks. The pickpocket zipped up the road much faster than his middle-aged mark, jinked under an arch in the wall, and seemed to vanish completely. His victim tried to follow, but gave up, panting, and turned back to his companions, gesturing and talking in a dismayed manner.

"I could catch him," I said to Quinton. "His aura is so agitated, he left a trail like a comet in the Grey."

"Would it be worth it?" He kept his hat brim down and pointed discreetly to cameras mounted on a pole at the corner ahead. "I'm pretty sure the local cops record everything and they'd certainly take note of a bystander suddenly finding a thief who did a disappearing act. I'm not saying it's not a nice thing to do, but it's got a risk factor. This is a popular tourist area, so it's got a lot of criminal and police traffic as well."

It galled me to walk away from something I could fix. After a few steps up the hill, I stopped under the pole on which the cameras hung. I took off my hat and my purse and handed them to Quinton. "Hold on to these. I'll be right back."

I threw myself into the Grey, searching for a temporacline in which there had been no cameras, but the buildings were still the same. I found one and slid into it, shivering at the sudden, intense chill after so much heat.

In the silvery world of the Grey past, I walked back to the arch in the wall and stepped through, and then I stepped back out of the Grey, into the normal. The arch led to a narrow covered walkway that opened into a courtyard. The contrast in light made the walkway seem dark as the inside of a dog, but I could see the sickly green glimmer of the pickpocket's aura as he huddled in a niche, waiting until he thought the coast was clear to emerge. I walked up to his hiding spot and tapped him on the shoulder.

He jerked around to face me, catching one of his bony elbows on the hard stone edge of the niche. *"O que você quer? Foda-se!"* His whole skinny body seemed to quiver.

"Give me the wallet."

"Wallet? What are you talking about, bitch?" His manners were horrid, but at least his English was excellent.

I rolled my eyes and held out my hand. "Wallet. Now. Or I scream for the cops."

He launched forward, tucking his head down to hit me in the face with the top of his skull, but I stepped aside and gave him a shove, using his own momentum to send him across the narrow alley headfirst, into the opposite wall. He hit hard enough to bounce and stagger back before he sat down, shaking his head at the same time he tried to cradle it in his hands. "Ow!"

I bent down. "You're a lucky guy—usually a blow like that knocks you out or cracks your skull. You must have a head like a rock."

He made a weak attempt to hit me and I batted his hand aside. "Give me the wallet, or do you want me to go through your pockets myself?"

He muttered something I suspected was both derogatory and physically impossible, but he dug the stolen wallet from his pocket and handed it to me. "I need it more than you do."

"This isn't for me. It's for your soul—robbing a priest? Do you really think that's a good idea?"

He glared up at me, shaking. "I need the money. You think I'd rob a priest for nothing? I had to do it. I need the money!" I almost had to admire his skill: It must have been tricky lifting the guy's wallet through the side slits in the cassock and clothes beneath, but now the pickpocket was shaking so hard, I was surprised he'd managed it.

"You didn't have to choose a priest."

"Those priests, they aren't so pure. Look, I just . . . You don't know what it's like. You—what do you want? You want to help somebody? Give me the damned wallet!"

I studied him for a moment. He was shivering now, sweat oozing off his bruised forehead and his nose running. He was in a bad way and what did it really matter to me, in the end? He hadn't done anyone physical harm and unless the priest was carrying something unusual in his wallet, he wasn't going to be as badly off as this guy.

I looked into the wallet and saw a few euros, two slips of paper with notes in Portuguese, and some ID cards—nothing that seemed significant and nothing that gleamed with threads of Grey.

I sighed. "I'm going to regret this. . . ." I scooped the money—which wasn't much—from the wallet, but retained the rest and handed the cash to the skinny, quivering thief. "Here. Now, find another part of town to work for a while. And see a doctor about your head—you hit the wall hard enough to break something."

He clutched the thin stack of bills to his chest and squirmed against the wall as I left, making no move to follow me. I eased back into the temporacline, shivering, and made my way to the corner.

Quinton didn't jump when I reemerged into the normal world, but he did raise his eyebrows at me as I reclaimed my things. I put on the hat, tucked the wallet into my purse, and started walking up the hill toward a white building that I could see on the right-hand side of the road. It had a Roman cross on the roof and a Maltese cross carved into the pediment below it, as if the builder had wanted to be sure to cover his bases. Quinton caught up in a step or two.

"How's the thief?"

"Has a headache, may have given himself a concussion, but considering how perfectly his language centers were working, I think he'll be OK."

"'Given *himself* a concussion'?"

I nodded. "Ran headfirst into a wall. All I did was direct the course. He's one messed-up little addict."

"Addict? How can you tell?"

"Aura color, too thin, has the shakes—I'm surprised he could lift the wallet at all with the way his hands were trembling."

Quinton made a speculative noise. "Huh . . . That's odd. . . . Addiction and teen usage rates are down since Portugal decriminalized personal use."

"Down doesn't mean none. This guy is one of those who fell through the cracks."

"Well, they don't have much in terms of prevention and rehab programs right now because of the austerity measures. They had to cut them."

"Makes it hard to get on your feet when there's no one to help you up. I let him keep the money. I hope I didn't do the wrong thing, but the guy was so pathetic that I figured it was better to let him go."

Quinton shook his head. "For him, I think nothing's ever going to get better. But for a lot of others, it might if there was money and hope. The lack of economic support for education, rehab, and other programs leaves a hole in the social structure that is too easily exploited by the fearmongering of people like my father."

I thought about it as we walked on.

On our right, the road opened out into a large terraced garden that hung at the top of a cliff overlooking another part of Alfama and the river beyond. The view as the sun dipped lower in the west was breathtaking, gilded and burnished with red and gold and delineated by purple shadows. At the top of the rise on the terraced side stood the small white church—Santa Luzia—with the Roman cross gleaming on the roof in the golden light of the westering sun and beaming in its own time-built corona of pale blue—very much like the aura of the priest who'd been robbed.

I walked through the heaving memory of the earthquake and what seemed like endless fire to the doors of the church and slipped inside with Quinton in my wake.

It was a very traditional little Catholic church and it had a collection box for donations to the needy. I put the priest's wallet into the box, sure it would be found soon and hoping that I hadn't made a big mistake.

Twilight was descending rapidly on this side of the hill when we left the church to find our way back to the house. I could see shadows lengthening in the narrow streets ahead, taking on strange shapes as a whistling sound wound down the road. Something black rose up into the sky, thinning to nearly invisible once it climbed into the dying light of the sun above the hill. I followed its flight over the castle and Quinton looked up with me.

"What is it? I can barely see. . . ."

"It's familiar, but I don't know. I think I saw something like it earlier in the day, but that one was a lot farther off. It's something Grey, but that you can see it, too, is worrisome."

"Something of Dad's?"

"I hope not."

The shape that now looked more like a ripple in the wind than something solid turned on an updraft and began back toward us. The light seemed to tear it into pieces as we watched and things began falling from it. In a moment, nothing remained but falling debris.

A few people ran out from the street ahead, looking back at the pale objects falling from the sky, chattering and nervous. We both began running toward the spot not far away where the falling bits had disappeared behind stucco walls. We came out from the throat of a narrow road where the Grey began to sing high, shrieking discords, into sudden, ancient devastation. Directly before us stood the graffiti-adorned ruins of perhaps half a dozen old houses knocked down by the earthquake of 1755. Windows had been bricked up to hold back the hillside, weeds and flowers grew over the remains of tiled floors, and a couple of cars had been parked among the crumbling walls near one of the rebuilt sections that was painted a slapdash white, allowing the ghosts of graffiti past to peep through. Pale green things, like sticks, lay scattered all over the abandoned foundations, smoking a little as if they were hot or burning with acid.

Before I could think of what they reminded me of, my knees buckled and I felt as if someone had punched me in the chest. Quinton caught me as the unexpected blow of remembered anguish and death made me stumble and fall. He swore and pulled me up, hitching his arm around my waist to haul me to his side and run for an archway that pierced the whitewashed wall ahead. As I wound my arm around his back, I felt something hard in his pack that wasn't a laptop, but I had no breath with which to ask him about it.

We dove into another narrow, roofed passage between tall plastered buildings. Every step away from the untouched ruins brought relief from the keening pain of the skeletal buildings and their song of death and loss. I was able to unbend and walk more upright, but the ache of death was still with me and my lungs felt like they were too heavy to fill. I gasped short breaths as we went forward. We stepped out into a luxuriously tiled courtyard where expensive cars had been parked on this side of a gateway. Ignoring suspicious glances, we hurried through the tiny square and out into the street.

On our right, where the road turned the corner toward us, was an outdoor urinal that gave me a shudder of another sort, both funny and repulsive with its fancy iron sign that read URINOL and a steel silhouette of a young boy pissing off the top of the sign against the thousand-year-old stone wall. Steel privacy screens ended two feet above the tiled road. The smell was unmistakable.

Catching my breath at last, I muttered, "Out of the frying pan . . ."

"And into the *pissoir*," Quinton added.

But ahead I could see the freestanding arch I'd walked under as I came down the steep road from the castle. "I know where we are," I said.

"Oh, good, because I'm lost."

TEN

I put my hand over Quinton's bag and rubbed the surface, pressing just hard enough to feel the rough shapes of the objects within. Most were rectangular, flat, or tubular. One wasn't. He watched me with a wary look.

"So," I said, leaving my hand over the odd shape, "is that a gun in your bag or are you just happy to see me?"

Quinton's expression grew more tense. "Better to have it and not need it, than need it and not have it. At least with my dad and his creeps in town. Does it bother you?"

"No. I'm just not sure how helpful it'll be. And they're a liability here, aren't they?"

He shook his head. "Not really. Unless someone searches me, then I might be in trouble."

I was still out of breath, so I took a step away from him and leaned against the wall, far enough away from the outdoor urinal to avoid anything that might have splashed, but still too close to avoid the smell. It did bother me a little—usually I'm the one carrying while Quinton relies on his brains and ability to adapt. I wasn't sure the reversal was comfortable, but there was no reason to object that I could see. "We'll burn that bridge when we come to it."

"OK. My turn: You have any better idea what that thing was that fell from the sky?" he asked.

"No. It's familiar, but I'm not sure about it. Another thing to discuss with Carlos. He should be up by the time we reach the house."

Quinton nodded and I walked to him to put my arm back around his waist and start up the hill.

Even without Rafa's map, I remembered the route back to the house below the castle and we made it up the steep, twisty streets in the swiftly falling dusk with no further trouble. The problem arose when I didn't have the gate key. There was no light, camera, or intercom box and the gate was locked, but there was a very old-fashioned bellpull of the sort that looks like an ornate handle on a stiff iron rod. I yanked on it, leaving Quinton to stand peering in through the iron vines of the gate.

"I think someone's coming," he said after my third try.

In a few minutes, a man with a flashlight approached the gate and shone his beam on us. *"Boa tarde. O que é que você quer aqui?"*

"Rafa?" I asked. "Is Rafa here? I lost my key."

"Rafa? The old housekeeper?" The man scowled. "She retired in 1992 and died in 2000. She was eighty-five. When did you receive a key from her?"

"Will you think I'm crazy if I say this morning?"

He seemed to consider it, but decided I wasn't. "Is your name Harper?"

I nodded, disturbed and frowning.

"Then, you had better come in."

I looked at Quinton, knowing he'd heard the conversation.

He shook his head. "I'm not much help if it's a ghost thing and I don't get along with that timey-wimey stuff if it's not. It's better if I wait here until you're done."

"All right," I said, feeling reluctant to walk away from him but sure I didn't have a lot of choice. I put my hand into my purse and held on to the other key, knowing how it must work and hoping it would help me find the right temporacline through which to reach Rafa or Carlos. I followed the man with the flashlight toward the house.

"I was concerned when your box was empty," he said.

"Rafa helped me out."

He grunted. "I've never heard of the ghosts doing much here before. They break things once in a while, but otherwise, you'd never know the place was haunted." He gave me an odd, sideways glance and amended, "Well, you might." Apparently someone had told him more than my name.

The female ghost I'd seen on the stairs that afternoon rushed me as I stepped into the entry. It was much darker now, and only a small lamp near the stairs was lit, so I hadn't seen her before she was on me. She shoved me backward and then dragged me forward again, leaving my guide to stand, openmouthed, at the doorway as the ghost whisked me up to the gallery. She pulled me up the stairs and I could hear the man coming along behind us, shouting, "Where are you going?"

The ghostly woman dragged me up the last flight, to the door of my room. I put the key in the lock and twisted. . . .

The sound of the man behind me ceased and the formerly dark hallway was illuminated with dim bulbs in distant lamps from another decade. Rafa came down the hall toward me from the back of the house. She didn't look like a ghost, but they never do when seen in their native temporacline.

"I feared you were lost."

"I was. My gate key was stolen and I couldn't get back in the right way."

"But you have found another. Dom Carlos will be asking for you in a few minutes, I think."

"I have a friend downstairs at the gate. He needs to come in, too."

"Oh. I shall have to find more keys," Rafa said, and turned to go to the stairs and walk down.

She left me at my door without another word. I stared after her, then turned my head to see the ghost who had dragged me upstairs still standing by my side. She had a thin face framed in elaborate dark braids and curls, and her clothes were easier to see now—something like an elegant nightgown with a wide, scooped neck that barely covered the hard line of a long corset, and a voluminous silk robe thrown loosely over it all. She looked grave and pale, even for a ghost, as she studied me.

"Who are you?" I asked. "What do you want from me?"

"Amélia. I do not forget," came her thoughts into my head, not really words, but the meaning as clear as if spoken. She vanished like a blown-out candle, leaving only a curl of mist to mark her place.

"Damned capricious spooks," I muttered. I relocked the door and the illumination instantly flickered down to just two dim night lamps. The man who'd let me in turned around from where he'd been standing farther down the hall, looking startled, and walked toward me, flipping a wall switch as he came, which turned on a newer, brighter set of bulbs in antique-styled sconces along the walls.

In the light, I could see he was an older man, in good health and with excellent posture that had made him seem younger in the dimmer illumination. He was puzzled by me, but not scared. "There you are!"

"I'm sorry to have vanished like that."

"I guess I'll get used to it. I just can't keep up on those stairs. What are you doing up at this room?"

"I have the key—another one Rafa gave me that I didn't lose."

"Funny . . . It's not the room we made up for you, but all your things disappeared out of the room downstairs. This is the room guests never stay in—and the room in the tower."

"Guests?"

"Usually the house is leased to travelers—business people or long-term visitors. It's been empty a lot recently with the economy and the EU problems. We never tell people not to use this room, but for some reason, they just don't. The tower is locked, though. We don't even mention it exists most of the time, since the stair is hidden. You can see it outside, but most people aren't curious enough to try to find the way up. They assume it's a false front, I think. We don't lease to people with kids—they're much too curious and destructive."

"I see. Who else works here? You keep saying 'we.'"

"Oh, no one really works here. I'm Gonçalo, the caretaker and handyman, and I come by every week. Everyone else works for the management company. They come when needed."

I nodded. "And who else is expected in this party?"

"Just Senhor Ataíde. His note said he'd arrive tonight, but he didn't say when."

I nodded. "The man who came with me to the gate will also be staying, but I can take care of that arrangement. There was another box delivered with mine, wasn't there?"

He nodded. "It's still downstairs. I unbolted it, as instructed, but I didn't lift the lid. Do you want to see it?"

"I do. I think I can find my way down, if you'll go fetch my fiancé from the gate."

Gonçalo grinned. "Oh! I see! Yes, I will do that." He walked past me to the stairs and I followed him. He chuckled to himself all the way down to the entry.

I stopped him at the foot of the stairs. "I'll go to the basement from here. Take Kit upstairs and I'll catch up to him there." I'd almost said, "Quinton," but so long as I wasn't sure who Gonçalo really worked for, I thought it better to keep up the fiction of Kit Smith.

Gonçalo was still chuckling as he headed to the front door, saying, "I will. I will."

I dashed for the basement door I'd used with Rafa and clattered down the stone steps as fast as I could without falling. There were several big iron-bound doors, but only one stood slightly ajar. I pushed hard on the heavy door and walked in.

The room boiled with black and red energy, churning up the mist of the Grey like a storm at sea. Carlos was standing just in front of his shipping box. He was disheveled, unusually pale, and glowering. "I am not at my best when I wake, Blaine."

"I guessed that. Which is why I sent the caretaker to let Quinton in instead of coming down here for dinner."

Carlos growled at me and the sound resonated in my chest through the Grey. "I am not without restraint or resources."

"I thought not, but there's a lot we need to discuss as quickly as possible. I figured it would be better if I spoke to you now, rather than wait. The situation is pressing. And we saw something Grey in the sky today. We weren't the only ones, either. I wasn't sure, but the bits it left behind reminded me of that dragon-thing we encountered in the lab last year."

He cocked his head and peered at me sideways, the same way I study things through the edge of the Grey. I wondered if he did something similar, trying to see what ghostly telltales might have attached themselves to me. "It will have to wait until I come back. My hunger should be of greater concern to you at this moment than drachen and the machinations of your beloved's father—however dire. So, unless you've decided to offer yourself, I suggest you step out of the path between me and the door." He made an impatient flicking gesture with one hand.

I stepped aside. He started to pass, but he stopped for just a second beside me, closing his eyes, before casting me a curious glance and going out the door. I followed as far as the hallway, but he had gone toward the back of the cellar, rather than heading for the stairs. He didn't turn, but said, "I will see you soon, Blaine. Go up to the tower and wait for me there. Both of you."

"The tower is locked and the stairs are hidden," I said.

"Not anymore." He opened one of the other doors onto profound darkness that the candlelight couldn't penetrate, and stepped into it, closing the door behind himself. I heard the bolt snick into place and then there was silence.

Having no choice, I went back upstairs and started for the upper floors. I met the caretaker on his way down from the second floor.

"Senhor Smith is upstairs. If you don't need anything else, I'll go now."

"You don't need to wait for Senhor Ataíde?"

"Oh no. I was waiting for you. Here," he added, taking a ring of keys from his jacket pocket and handing them to me, "these are all the house keys, including the tower key—it's the large one—and I've left the staircase door open at the end of the top-floor corridor. If you need anything, the management company's number is in the kitchen by the phone. You may want to lock the gate behind me when I drive out—unless you think Senhor Ataíde will be here soon. The area can be a bit rough at night."

"I expect he'll be here within the hour and he's not afraid of rough neighborhoods."

Gonçalo nodded. "*Bom*. It's good to have a member of the family here again."

He started to go and I stopped him. "Wait. What family?"

"The Ataídes. The family has a tragic history and there are very few of them left. Centuries ago, they were the House of Atouguia—the Counts of Atouguia—but that title became extinct." He took my hand and gave it a gentle squeeze instead of a shake. "I hope your business here will be better fated than theirs, *senhorina*."

"So do I."

I walked out to close and lock the gates behind him and then returned to the house—Carlos's house. I headed upstairs to what I thought of as my room despite its being assigned by a ghost with unknown motives. I couldn't help thinking how little I really knew about Carlos and his past.

Quinton was waiting for me on the small sofa in the sitting room. He looked over my shoulder as I entered. "Where's the Guest of Honor?"

"Out to dinner," I said, finally remembering to remove my hat, "but I suspect it'll be fast food. He said he'd be back soon and we should meet him in the tower." I untied my hair and shook it loose.

Quinton perked up and his aura sparkled with interest. "This place has a tower?"

"And secret passages, apparently, as well as cellars carved into the bedrock, and some resident ghosts who like to play games and are getting on my nerves."

Quinton raised his eyebrows. "Oh?"

"Yes. Rafa, the woman I met when I first got here, was the house-keeper until 1992, but she died fourteen years ago. I'm not sure, but the keys she gave me appear to lock a temporacline in place within the house, so the room or the house itself reverts to that time period and the ghosts in it become manifest and solid. They look and act just like normal people. What's strange is, it's Carlos's house, but I don't think he knows about her, because he sent instructions to Gonçalo to get the house ready for us and to wait for me here. I can't imagine he'd do that if he knew Rafa was capable of managing it for him."

"I assume Gonçalo's not a ghost, since I also saw him."

I shook my head. "Not a ghost. But we might be if we don't get up to the tower. Carlos was not in a good mood."

A smell like asphalt and orange blossoms on a hot day wafted into the room and an object thumped to the floor in front of the desk. Two more objects followed in close order. I walked over to look at them.

"House keys like the one Rafa gave me. We must not be in her temporacline now, because she apported them, rather than coming in and handing them to us, so it is most likely these keys that operate the time phenomenon. For some reason she wants to be sure we can get to her."

"Control fiend?"

"Too early to speculate, not to mention she can probably hear us. Let's go to the tower. I suspect we'll have more privacy there. Until Carlos gets back." I glanced around the room, trying to get a fix on where Rafa's presence might be and directed my attention to a thin column of silvery mist near the hall door. "Thank you, Rafa. I'll leave them for now, but I'll pick them up before we go out."

The mist shimmered and faded away.

Leaving the keys where they lay, I took my purse with Soraia's gifts in it and started for the door. Quinton followed and we went down the hall to the formerly hidden door at the end.

It wasn't so much a secret door, as a why-bother-to-look-at-it door. A section of the tiled wall at the back end of the corridor stood agape from floor to ceiling. Anyone seriously looking would have found the cracks, the keyhole, and the small handle in the tiles without much effort, but the busy design of the blue-and-white tiles made it a frustrating exercise if you didn't know what to look for. In the Grey, I could see shreds of an old spell that had broken and faded long ago, leaving only a cobweb remnant of the original energy and form laid over the tiles. I pulled the door farther open, and we went up the narrow staircase concealed in the wall in single file, me in front because I didn't give Quinton a chance to go first.

The stairs ended in another door—thick, iron-bound wooden planks carved around the edges with symbols that gleamed black to my Grey sight. I moved my hand toward the twisted bronze handle and the ward stretched toward me, rising into a tangled web, twisted with sharp black barbs dripping a shining illusion of blood. I pulled back, feeling queasy and weak even without having touched the door. I took the ring of keys Gonçalo had given me out of my shallow skirt pocket and flicked through until I found the largest of them. It was almost hot to the touch and impossible to miss even in the gloom of the unlighted staircase. I held up the key and pushed it toward the lock.

"No. Don't touch it," Carlos said from below us, his unexpected voice making me jump.

The ward pulled back, sinking into the wood. The door swung open and illumination by fire and candle flooded out of the room beyond, drowning the thin light in the staircase behind us.

I whirled on the landing and looked back down the stairs to where Carlos stood at the bottom. "My apologies," he said, walking up to meet us. "I had forgotten about the ward. The key alone won't open the door safely, though I'm surprised to find my safeguard intact after so much time and change."

"What would have happened if I'd touched it?" I asked.

Carlos brushed past both of us to enter the room. "To you? Probably only passing illness and incapacity. To our friend, here . . . ? Something unpleasant and debilitating, but not fatal. Come in and sit. We have much to discuss."

ELEVEN

Carlos looked his usual self—no sign of the disordered and hungry state I'd found him in less than an hour ago. He strode to the window and glanced down, then turned aside and found a bit of naked stone wall to lean against. He crossed his arms over his chest and glared around the room in annoyance. "A shambles," he muttered. "What a state my house has fallen into."

The tower room wasn't round, but rectangular, narrower at the front and rear where the windows broke the wall with tiny mullions of thick, wavy glass in lead and iron frames. A tiled mantelpiece took up the center of the left wall and surrounded a deep fireplace that currently flickered with an eerie yellow light that gave off no heat. A large map of Lisbon as it had been before the earthquake hung above the mantel. Candles in sconces and many-armed candelabra added a more-normal firelight to the room. The flames swayed in the currents of air we made as we moved to a long wooden bench set in front of a table opposite the fire. There were two heavy chairs next to the hearth, but I had no desire to sit in either of them, tangled as they were with remnant threads of red and black energy. There was not a single ghost to be seen and the temporaclines lay in cold, compacted strata against the floor, shimmering like ice, shot through by a hot pillar of dark red energy that rose straight from the floor and spread a network of smaller lines like blood vessels across the ceiling and walls.

The fireplace was large and had a pot hook, but no pot, hanging over it, though there were several dusty, cobwebbed iron vessels piled near it on one side. Half of the walls were covered in bookshelves laden with moldering books, their leather spines cracked with age or eaten away by beetles. A carved, dark wood desk stood among the shelves, also scattered with tomes, dust, and spiderwebs. Old, dark stains the color of dried blood marred the pages of one open book. Stains of a similar color crossed the floor and vanished under the moth-eaten carpet. I closed my eyes a moment and concentrated, feeling the slightest tremor of lingering magic and death beneath my feet. A row of skulls occupied the top of one of the bookshelves, their empty eye sockets and grinning teeth unpleasantly white and gleaming, as if the former residents still hovered near their bones in forms of transient light. The right side of the room was mostly occupied with worktables, cabinets, and equipment I couldn't—and didn't want to—name. An odor hung in the air, a blend of melting beeswax, crumbling books, and dire experiments.

Beside me on the bench, Quinton hunched his shoulders and leaned a bit forward, unconsciously keeping his back from touching the worktable behind us.

"I hadn't thought I'd be gone so long," Carlos said, "or I would have worked a different ward over this place. It kept people out, perhaps too well, but had no effect on filth or vermin. I had expected the house to have changed in two hundred and fifty years, but I foolishly left this room exactly as it was. And thus . . . it is exactly as it is." He made a sound of disgust and gestured at the hearth, wiping out the illusion of a fire and dimming the room enough to induce shadows in the corners and under the tables. He plucked a bit of blackness from a shadow and whispered to it, *"Venhais, minhas sombras,"* spinning it between his fingers and then crushing it into his fist, which he then flicked open underhand, scattering the glittering dust of shadow into the murk beneath the chairs and tables. Something black crept there, where there had been nothing before.

I had rarely seen him work magic so casually and I wondered if it was the place—in spite of his discontent with it—that made it easy, or something else. I thought the creeping thing beneath the table was one of the nevoacria I'd seen at Carlos's Seattle house—shadow creatures that skulked along the ground of the former graveyard. I knew that calling them any great distance would have been wasteful and difficult, so I assumed this one was created on the spot, as easily as most men button their cuffs. Neither summoning nor creating is a simple cantrip, so I was impressed and a little disturbed by his trick. As I stared at it, the nevoacria seemed to grow, like the darkness of rising night, deepening until there was no light to show any feature, only the strange, slithering movement of the shadow-thing as it multiplied and spread in the gloom.

Carlos turned his gaze back to us and leaned against the wall. "What developed while I slept?"

I started with, "James Purlis has kidnapped his granddaughter—Quinton's niece—and I believe I saw some kind of drachen today. Quinton saw one of them as well, just down the hill from here."

"In the daylight?" Carlos asked, scowling.

"Yes, though it was sunset. Others saw it, too. It didn't last long or seem to do anything but fall apart, but I don't think it's a coincidence that we saw something like this at Purlis's Seattle lab more than a year ago and again here when he's obviously in town and up to no good."

"Hmm," Carlos rumbled, the resonance of his voice making the old house shiver. "It's unlikely to be coincidence and it could be a different creature entirely, but it may mean more once I've heard the rest. Go on."

Between us, Quinton and I told him about Soraia's abduction by her grandfather and those who'd been with him. When I told him I suspected she had a touch of Grey to her, Carlos stopped me with an upraised hand.

"How old is this child?"

"Six."

"That is quite young to display a talent."

"I don't think she's manifested a particular talent yet—she might not ever. But she sees ghosts, claims to see fairies in the garden, knows the answers to questions she has no reason to know, experiences strange events without any idea that they're unusual, and charms birds. There is also the rather odd collection of presents Purlis and his two companions left for her."

I got the gifts from my purse, handling them with care so I didn't touch anything but the boxes and wrappers containing them. I laid them on the nearest table and stepped away to let Carlos examine them. "The white box contains both of the bone flutes. I get a sort of shock when I touch them, so you'll have to open the box yourself."

"Bone flutes are hardly an oddity on their own account," Carlos said. "The bones of birds and cattle or deer shins have been used in musical instruments for eons."

"These gave me the impression of human bones."

Quinton stood beside me and we watched Carlos unwrap and study the objects. He picked each up, muttering, looking it over, then closing his eyes and cocking his head slightly as if listening to each in turn.

Carlos set the flutes aside with a delicate touch as if they might shatter in an instant. Then he picked up the crystal on its chain in one hand and the doll in the other.

"Quinton, were you a Boy Scout?"

"I was a Purlis scout. Why?"

"The wood is very old, but I hope you can build a fire with it."

Quinton eyed the dusty, cobwebbed chunks of wood beside the fireplace. "They might burn a little fast if the bugs have gotten to them, but, yeah, I can make a fire with those."

"Do so. Please."

I made a face as Quinton busied himself with the logs. "I wasn't a Girl Scout, but I do know how to make a fire."

"I have no doubt, Blaine, but I need you to hold this," Carlos said, handing me the chain. "Let the crystal dangle without swaying and take care not to touch it."

I did as he instructed, letting the smoky, black-stabbed quartz hang straight from my fist with the excess length of chain wrapped around my hand. It was an uncomfortable object, making my hand prickle with cold as if it had fallen asleep.

Kneeling at the hearth, Quinton struck a spark from a small metal object with the back of his pocketknife, and the fire caught immediately on the dry tinder he'd placed under the wood. As soon as the fire had begun to consume the logs, Carlos told him to stand aside. Quinton, looking nervous, retreated to the corner of the desk.

Carlos drew his arm back and flung the doll into the fireplace with sufficient force to shatter its porcelain head. A vile black shape like a spider with too many legs fell from the broken doll and burst into flame with a shriek. The necromancer stepped closer to the fire, muttering rapidly and reaching forward as if to catch the black smoke that curled from the burning thing. The wisp of darkness bowed toward him, flowing against the natural current of air, which should have gone up the chimney but bent, instead, into Carlos's hand. *"Mostre-me onde ela é,"* he said, sweeping the smoke toward me.

The black fume curled and flowed toward the crystal, then into it, swirling through the network of rutile that cut through the quartz. The crystal twitched and swung in a circle, then jerked north, the pendant wavering between two points for a moment until the crystal cracked with a harsh sound. A sudden rush of black smoke poured from the crystal in two directions until all the darkness had fled the room, leaving a nauseating stench like burning creosote in the air.

Carlos opened the window at the front while Quinton hurried to do the same at the rear of the room, letting the night's cool wind sweep the stink away on the weeping song of Lisbon. I stood still with the broken crystal dangling from my hand, not sure what Carlos wanted me to do with the thing.

In a moment he crossed the room to face me, putting out his hand and narrowing his eyes as if he were thinking difficult thoughts. "That I did not expect."

"What? The swinging or the breaking?" I asked, handing over the shattered pendant, glad to release it and feel warmth rush back into my hand.

Carlos took the crystal and chain with care and laid them on the table. "The inability to pick a direction. Unless the child is moving back and forth, there must be more than one 'she' that this device cleaved to."

"If one is my niece, then, could the other be the mage who made this nasty bit of work?" Quinton asked, casting a disgusted glance at the wreck of the doll and its passenger, still burning in the grate.

"One of Dad's companions was female and Sam said she made an unpleasant impression."

Carlos raised an eyebrow. "There were no female bone mages in my day—as there were no female priests, either—but there well could be now. It would explain a great deal. Let us see what else we can discover."

"I'd be willing to bet the man with her was of the same party," I added.

"Young or old?" Carlos asked.

"Seventy or so, Sam said, and she thought he was Portuguese, but I assume appearances can be deceiving in this case. She said he had blue eyes—she found it striking."

He grunted, thinking, and asked, "What of the other?"

"Sam said the woman looked to be in her fifties, blond, probably American or English."

Carlos looked intrigued and thoughtful as he turned back to the table where the two bone flutes lay. He picked up each one in turn and studied them. "An interesting pair. Made from matching bones and very similar, but not carved by the same mage."

"I thought they looked like the same bone from different . . . um . . . donors," I said.

"No. These came from the same human body. They are two arm bones—the radii—from the same person. Together they are a pair left and right, but not identical." He held up the darker of the two flutes. "This was created by the master some time ago, a man I knew when *he* was but an apprentice"—he held up the other, cleaner flute—"and this recently by the current apprentice. Her name is Maggie Griffin, though that means nothing to me. It is strange, however, that the lesser instrument has the more difficult mouth-piece. . . ."

Quinton and I exchanged looks. "What do you mean?" I asked.

"The older instrument has a fipple—like the mouth of a recorder or tin whistle. They make sound easily. But the apprentice's instrument is end-blown, like a *quena*, and has only an elliptical notch that is much harder to use. There's no need for such difficulty, so it must be vanity. . . ."

"Vanity can be very useful from our perspective," I said.

"Yes. In this, I think the apprentice made a mistake that will help us find her all the faster."

"Do you think the apprentice is the woman who came to Sam's house?" Quinton asked, scowling.

"Without a doubt. Even if her companion was the master, he would still insist on her placing the instruments herself. It was a test. The doll and crystal were lesser attempts, simpler, but less sophisticated. That there was a redundant method for luring your niece away speaks of ongoing training, though it is increasingly advanced. Perhaps not an apprentice but a journeyman, still within her master's house, which could be why she chose the difficult mouthpiece—to show him her skill at small details."

"To show off," Quinton corrected.

Carlos gave him a small nod. "Perhaps. Certainly it would explain the vanity of such a piece. She has pride, which may be her undoing."

"We can hope," Quinton added.

"Before we can undo her, we must find her more precisely. . . ." Carlos began looking through the various equipment around the room, searching the cabinets, lifting up the pans piled beside the fireplace, and raising dust into the air. He put a few items, including the shattered crystal, on the worktable Quinton and I had been leaning against and where the bone flutes now rested. Then he went to the hearth and stooped to scoop some of the bright red coals out of the fire and into a three-footed iron bowl—some sort of small brazier, I guessed. The bowl smoked a little as the coals burned away the remnants of dust and cobwebs. Holding the smoking bowl in his bare hand, Carlos brought it back to the table and set it down, then arranged the flutes on either side of it, the mouthpieces facing the bowl of coals.

"Snuff most of the candles, being careful not to raise the dust. Leave a scattering of them alight," Carlos ordered, scribing a circle around the brazier in the tabletop's dust. Once closed, the circle gleamed gold.

Quinton and I scrambled to extinguish as many of the candles as we could, leaving four burning in various locations throughout the room. The light was just enough to see the room by and no brighter. Carlos dropped dried matter and powders onto the bright red coals in the brazier. Then he put his open hand palm up on the bench where shadows now gathered. Two of the nevoacria crept into it, making his hand disappear in their darkness. He lifted them to the table and they crept to huddle in the shade of the bowl.

The bowl emitted the smell of sandalwood and graveyard dust, white smoke curling upward from the embers.

"Quinton, I require a drop of your blood."

"Mine? Why?" he asked, but still started forward.

"The familial tie should strengthen our connection to your missing niece and the woman who took her. My own blood won't do, and I fear to think what would happen if I fed this spell a drop of a Greywalker's blood."

Quinton finished crossing the room faster and stopped beside Carlos. He put out his hand, looking determined, though his fingers trembled. "If that's what it takes."

Carlos must have noticed Quinton's fear and discomfort, but he said nothing, picked up a measuring compass from the tabletop outside the circle, and pricked the smallest finger on Quinton's hand with one of the points. Quinton flinched but made no sound as a single large, bright drop of blood fell onto the smoking coals. Quinton yanked his hand back as if it had been scalded.

The smoke billowed into a cloud that expanded only as far as the edges of the circle, but rose upward in a confined column. Carlos put the compass down. "Step away from the table."

Quinton did as he was told, watching the smoking brazier with suspicion.

Carlos snatched both the nevoacria from their hiding place under the hot bowl and threw them into the brazier, one on each side. The shadow creatures squealed and writhed in the heat, but they didn't burn or dissolve. Carlos muttered while making a pulling-apart motion with both hands over the squirming things. They stretched from the bowl until they had touched the flutes, their bodies of shade and gloom forming conduits through which I could see the smoke begin to flow.

The candles flickered and burned low. Carlos continued to speak in a low, rapid voice that seemed to rob the world of sound rather than add to it—until the flutes began to sing.

The smoke from the brazier gave voices to the bone flutes and they played a long, high chord of melancholy and pain. Carlos snatched at the smoke as it rose from the flutes and muttered into his fisted hands, "Show me where the child is. Show me Soraia Rebelo," before he blew the smoke away.

The keening smoke coiled and seemed to resist for a minute. Then it turned, swirling trails of white vapor in the air, and moved toward the map pinned to the wall above the mantel. It wove back and forth a moment, then plunged into the map on the north wall, spinning against the dusty surface and raising a smell of burning.

In a few moments the smoke had vanished as the flutes burned to ash, leaving only a smudge and a stink of singed parchment. Carlos put a lid over the brazier, smothering the coals and the screaming nevoacria. Then he smeared his hand over the edge of the circle, wiping a clean swath in the dust all the way to the edge of the table. The light of the remaining candles flared up brighter, chasing away the closed feeling and silencing the crying sound of the city below.

Quinton and Carlos looked at the map while I stood a bit behind them. "It points to nothing, just north again. That's more than we had, but not much," Quinton said.

Carlos frowned at the map. "The stain lies beyond the city's edge. . . ."

"Only when that map was accurate," I said. "I'd be willing to bet there's something there now. We need a modern map the same scale as that one. We can overlay the location and find out what's there now."

Quinton gave a harsh laugh. "We don't need to go to that much trouble. I have a computer. All we need is to measure the distance and direction from here and then enter the two sets of coordinates into the right type of mapping program. I just need that compass from the table and I can get to work."

Quinton was relieved to finally have something to do, rather than just marching through the collection of data and waiting through the arcana of spell casting, and he went at it with a grim determination. Once Carlos had handed him the compass, he set it against the distance scale on the edge of the map and prepared to stab one of the measuring points into the parchment. "Where are we on this map, Carlos?"

Carlos touched a small brown square on the lower section of the map. "Here."

Quinton set one of the compass points on the square and used the spine of a book to guide him as he measured the distance, muttering to himself, before asking for something with which to write the information down. When he was satisfied, we closed the windows and extinguished the candles before we left the tower and returned to my rooms.

Quinton fetched his small laptop from his messenger bag and opened it on the tiny desk. "It's a good thing the management company installed a data line a few years ago or we'd be screwed," he said. He fiddled and typed for a while, entered some data, typed some more. . . .

"Carlos, tell me if I've got the right house."

The vampire looked over his shoulder. "You do."

Quinton grunted. He typed some more numbers and then hit RETURN.

We waited a few minutes and the map appeared with two red pins on it. Quinton zoomed the view in to the point he calculated the smoke had touched on the other map. It looked like a huge empty field about a half mile from the nearest major road, with only a single crooked block of shanty buildings sitting in the middle of nothing at the end of a dirt road called Alta da Eira.

"What is that?" I asked.

"The area is called Penha de França and that in particular looks like a car repair shop in an abandoned commercial development. I think the area's scheduled for urban renewal, but until the bulldozers come and the building starts, it's pretty depressed and there aren't a lot of people there. A perfect place to hide a little girl for a few days."

Carlos continued to look at the screen for a while without speaking. At last he said, "It was a pastoral hill and fields for miles in every direction around the Rock of France and its small church. Shepherds and cowherds grazed flocks under the trees. Now there are no trees, no flocks, no church. Only the emptiness of progress."

"The church is still there," Quinton said, tapping the screen with his fingertip on a tiny building packed tightly into a block of other buildings.

"That is not the church I recall."

"It may have been rebuilt."

"I have no doubt." Carlos's tone closed that avenue of the conversation like a tomb.

The silence lingered and weighed upon us until Quinton broke its hold. "Carlos . . . What do you think these bone mages want my niece for?"

The necromancer turned his bowed head, studying Quinton with narrowed eyes and an unpleasant curl to his lips. "For her bones, boy. What else?"

"They'll kill her for them?"

"Yes, but not casually or quickly. They are frugal and it will be done by rite and ceremony they may have had no time to prepare yet. And they may have other uses for her before she dies."

Quinton paled, but in cold fury, not fear. "You probably shouldn't tell me what other 'uses' they might have."

Carlos scoffed. "Nothing so profane as you're imagining. They're aesthetes, priests of the bones. They'd have little interest in defiling her in such a manner."

"That isn't much of a relief. Who would murder a six-year-old girl for her bones? What kind of monsters can do that?"

One corner of Carlos's mouth quirked up in an ironic expression.

Quinton saw it and shook his head. "No. You wouldn't."

"I have. And much worse." Carlos glanced at me and back to Quinton, adding, "But I am not what I was."

"Yes, but . . . what do they want her bones for? What is my father up to?"

"Your father may know nothing of their purpose, or he may have convinced himself that such a sacrifice is necessary for a greater good. Either way, the Kostní Mágové are not known for subtlety. If they require the bones of a young child of the family as their price for whatever agreement they have with your father, their goal is nothing short of catastrophic. They will build something of those bones, something of magic and horrors. I don't yet know what, though the appearance of drachen may be telling. Whatever it is, it shall be devastating."

"How are we going to get her back and stop them?"

"Those are two separate goals. In depriving them of your niece, we will only redirect their plans, but it will buy us time to discover what they intend."

"But how?" Quinton yelled, pounding one fist into the top of the delicate antique desk so hard it creaked under the blow.

"We attack the weakest link—we confront Maggie Griffin."

"It's not going to be that easy to get Soraia back."

"No, but Griffin has the child and we have no other choices. The sooner we find your niece, the better the chance that she'll be alive. As I presume that is your preference, we must move tonight."

Over his shoulder, for only a moment, Amélia appeared and vanished again.

TWELVE

I t was nearly midnight when we reached the head of Alta da Eira. Carlos had been busy in his tower while Quinton and I had eaten a desultory supper, done research, and talked about the problem of what to do once we'd recovered Soraia. Just sending her back home with Sam wasn't safe. Sam and her kids would have to be hidden until this was over and with that in mind, I had called the Danzigers.

Mara answered the phone, and it took a minute or so of excited exclamations and inquiries before I could talk to her about the situation.

"So," she said, "you're wanting Ben and Brian and me to drive to Lisbon immediately and help you hide a little girl and her mother from a band of villains? It sounds like old times!"

"I know," I said, "and I'm sorry about that. I didn't want to put you in the middle again, but we both thought you would understand this better than most people. Sam isn't very comfortable with the magic angle, but she and the kids are going to need to be in hiding until the danger's past or Purlis will just snatch them all."

Mara gave a short, harsh laugh. "Oh, he won't be doing that—I'll make sure of it. And don't tear yourself down over asking for help— we're pleased as anything to do it. And it'll be good to see you both again."

"We are working with Carlos . . ." I added.

She made a speculative sound. "I might even be glad to see *him*, if the child's all right."

"She'd better be," I replied in a grim voice.

I made the arrangements and told them where we'd meet them to hand over Soraia, Martim, and Sam for safekeeping. Then Quinton had called Sam and went through much the same thing with her. There would be a lag between the time Sam and Martim arrived and whenever the Danzigers got here, but that couldn't be helped. We'd have to be vigilant during that period, but once the Danzigers took charge of Sam's family, I felt reasonably sure they'd be safe. All of them.

We had borrowed a car from the house management company to drive up to Penha de França and now left it at the bend of the road among a lot of other cars parked on the streets around the blocks of apartments that dominated the area, crowded together like convicts in a prison movie. I'd reclaimed my jeans for this job, since they seemed more practical than a skirt, and now we three, dressed in dark clothes, stood in the shadows, facing a long stretch of open nothing between the end of the road and the beginning of the L-shaped group of buildings that housed the car repair. We moved forward with great care, certain that there would be guards, alarms, or charms to keep us at bay. There was a strange, low sound in the air, as of some dread music heard from a great distance.

The sound seemed to attract a pack of dogs that loped toward us from the hillside, cutting off the most direct path to the buildings.

There was nothing paranormal about the dogs, but their presence was threatening enough by itself. They barked and yipped when they spotted us, then fell silent as they spread out in an attempt to herd us into a good position for an attack, the ones on the center snarling and yipping to draw our attention away from those moving toward our flanks.

As the dogs spread out, a bright beam of light fell from the lone, square building that stood facing the crook of the L, but no one emerged.

"Motion sensor," Quinton whispered as the light extinguished again. "They aren't very worried about scaring off anything more troublesome than a dog. Either the locals know better than to come up here, or there's something pretty terrible inside."

I was tempted to drop into the Grey to see what I could spot, but that would take me away from the steadily encroaching dogs. I reminded myself that I didn't need to go anywhere with Carlos nearby, since he could detect auras of the living or undead as well as I could without withdrawing from the normal world. "How many people in the buildings?" I asked.

"Five," Carlos replied, puzzled. "I see one with no touch of magic, and the rest are much brighter. There are other things within, however, not living, but not precisely undead. Constructs."

"Are they all in that little building?"

"Yes. The rest are empty of life, though there may be other things there that aren't alive."

"It's not going to be as easy to approach as it looks. There must be perimeter or door alarms at least. No matter how badass they are, they wouldn't want anyone just walking in," Quinton said, watching the dogs as they edged closer. "Once we're past these dogs, we may have no margin of time to make a surprise entrance."

Carlos chuckled. "It's not so difficult if we don't care that they see us coming."

"Don't we? What if they hurt Soraia?"

"They cannot risk doing her any serious harm outside the ceremonial circle—it would taint the bones with fear and pain. If they wished for that, they'd have started already and we'd have heard her screaming by now."

Quinton shuddered. "You're just a bundle of joy, aren't you, Carlos?"

"Not since I was an infant, and likely not then, either."

"You two can stop now, and do something about these dogs," I said.

The dogs were only a body length away in front of us, the dog on each side even closer, poised to lunge. The obvious pack leader crouched just a few inches ahead of the rest, teeth bared and a low snarl issuing from its mouth. None of us wanted to resort to Quinton's gun and the unmistakable noise it would make, but that left us with no other weapons.

Carlos knelt and bowed his head, murmuring and putting his hands near the ground. For a moment, the dogs seemed confused and then the leader leapt.

Carlos spat a word and slammed his palms against the earth. A flame front roared up around us in a flash of light and rushed outward. The dogs yelped and howled, turning and running from the fire that was already dying out.

Carlos rose again to his feet as Quinton muttered, "I think we blew our chance to do this stealthily."

The door of the little square building in the crook of the L opened and a figure in dark clothes was silhouetted against eerie, flickering light from indoors for just a moment before closing the door and stepping into darkness.

I looked sideways through the Grey to see the man's energy corona, but there was nothing to see beyond tangles of darkness. "Don't bother with the gun—whatever that was, it's not alive."

"Rush it," Quinton said.

We all ran forward, separated by no more than an arm's length. I could see the black tangle of energy that hung on whatever the thing was, moving upright like a man, but making no sound. At first, it seemed not to see us; then it turned and a stray beam of starlight fell across the gleam of white bone where a face should have been. I ran harder and was the first to crash into it, throwing my shoulder into the construct of bone and magic. It dug into me, remnant muscle holding bone together and allowing it to push back. I heard its teeth clack above my head.

"Go, go! I got this one!" I yelled, enveloped in the odor of its rot.

Neither of the men paused, but kept running forward as I fought with the animated skeleton. It had no remains of a soul or life, only the brittle black-and-white magic that held it together, and though it was fierce, it was fragile. I plunged my hand through the arch of its ribs and laid hold of the ice-cold core of the spell that bound it together.

The thing raked at me with its defleshed hands. I ducked my head, losing my grip on the frozen bit of magic that held the thing in form. It brought the memory of its weight with it, and I had to crouch and roll it over my hip as it lunged to grapple with me. It flipped over and hit the ground. I threw myself onto it and clutched through the gap of its ribs, ripping out the icy blackness that animated the thing. It subsided to the ground, parts falling aside as it reverted to death. I winced as the small shred of its demise passed through me like a narrow blade. Whatever had killed the person who used to own these bones, it had been recent, the remnant thread of its dying caught in the tangle of reanimation.

I scrambled to my feet in a moment and ran for the door through which Quinton and Carlos had already disappeared. I stepped into the room and stopped short, my ears filled with an eerie whispering and wailing that wound through a rising and falling chant, bringing a giddy nausea much like what I experienced near Carlos. The people in the room ignored my entrance, continuing with their strange work. I wasn't sure why they didn't seem to have seen me.

I looked around. The edges and corners of the room fell into shadow that was thickened by barbed coils of magic. All light came from the center of the room, but stopped abruptly at the edge of the black shroud of energy that seemed to creep like the nevoacria, slowly surrounding the people at the center. At first, the room was so dark outside the circle on my side that I couldn't see. I tilted my vision toward the Grey and glimpsed Carlos moving around the edge of the room clockwise as Quinton prowled in the other direction beneath the mantle of shadow I was sure Carlos had conjured—it had the feel of his magic to it. Their advance was a slow agony when my own thoughts urged me to run forward, disrupt the scene by force, and take Soraia back immediately. But no matter how it galled, I knew there was a purpose in this careful progress. I crouched to take the moment's measure. When my hands touched the ground, I felt the chill of death in the rounded shapes of bones rubbed smooth by time.

The single large room of the building seemed to float in light the color of tarnished silver. It appeared to be some kind of bizarre chapel built of skeletal remains. The room was cold and reeked of rot, the weight of vile magic hanging in the air as a choking ivory fog. The walls and floor were covered in carved and painted bones, but the bones were not merely lying or stacked like cordwood; they were assembled into patterns and objects, as if in a gruesome parody of a church. Murals built of skeletal corpses seemed frozen in the midst of some action or another. Massive columns and candelabra of bones and skulls rose from the floor—even the altar and the cross above it were constructed from the bones of the dead. Perhaps a dozen narrow wooden boxes stood against the walls of the room, each no more than eighteen inches tall, wreathed in Grey mist and knotted spells, the polished surfaces reflecting strange illumination.

The light in the room seemed to come partially from the candelabra in which stood macabre tapers of fingers and bones only partially flensed of flesh and dipped in wax. The flesh and fat of the dead burned with a sickening stink and added to the strange silver glow. The floor was a mosaic of stars, crosses, and circles created in tiny bones that ranged from the palest cream, through every shade of brown, to flame-darkened gray and black, all set in white mortar and worn smooth over time. The rest of the uncanny light rose from the largest circle, beaming upward from the floor like cold footlights on a stage in hell.

At the center of the floor, where the shapes of cross, star, and circle overlapped, sat an old man dressed in black, his back to me as he levitated a few feet from the surface on a column of mist reflecting the silvery green light of the circle. His energy corona showed bonewhite amid a storm of black and rising spikes of bloody red. I knew I'd seen it before, but I had no focus to spend on remembering where. The mist seemed to hold him in a bubble of moving light that passed through him and made a path from him to the altar and from his right to his left. My eyes followed the illumination.

To his left lay a pile of human bones and on his right sat a cage built of bone and silver metal that took on an oily, iridescent glow when viewed through the Grey. A little girl with black curls looked out through the cage bars. She lay flat with one arm sticking out of her prison as if pointing through the man to the pile of bones on his other side. Her hand lay palm up, exposing the pale, tender skin on the underside. Shallow parallel cuts ran from her elbow to her wrist, weeping blood onto the bone-covered floor. The light seemed to lap at her blood and carry it away in droplets of red that moved toward the floating man.

The little girl whimpered, watching me, then shifted her eyes away to the altar at the front of the room, along the moving path of light. I felt breathless as my own horror tangled with the reflection of Quinton's rage and anxiety, twisting the paranormal connection between us. The girl must have been Soraia. I fought the desire to run to her, fearing that a wrong move would kill her. I wanted to scream in frustration and anger.

What was Quinton doing about it? I looked to my right, toward the movement I'd detected there when I entered. Quinton had crouched down to the floor in his covering of darkness just a few feet from another man who wore black robes and stood by the three-o'clock position of the circle, holding a large black candle burning in his hand. Both men were perfectly still, looking toward the altar. Quinton was poised for some action while the other man, oblivious to him, seemed mesmerized by the ceremony going on. Quinton glanced toward me as if he knew I was ready to leap, and shook his head with an angry grimace. He didn't like it any better than I did. Carlos must have told him to wait for something, and we would do so, but I could feel his frustration mixing with my own.

At the front of the room, a tall, slim woman in a narrow black dress and black high heels stood in front of the altar. Her blond hair was streaked with silvery gray, and the lines at the corners of her eyes said she had already seen fifty, but everything else said otherwise. She had picked up an ornate cup from the altar and held it in front of her while murmuring words that twined into the strange sound that occupied the room like another living being. A man, dressed just like the one at the edge of the circle, walked from the shadows and poured red liquid from a matching pitcher into the cup. The gold-colored lining of the cup turned black, and a dark vapor boiled over the rim, swirling into the air in an expanding spiral that wound toward the edges of the room.

As the dark mist touched the carved bones on the walls, they began to sing and wail, the smoke twisting through holes carved in the hollow shafts of arm and leg bones, around the curves of ribs, and through the gaping eye sockets of human skulls.

The woman said something that was drowned in the rising wail of the bone flutes. The greater volume of blood that ran from Soraia's arm lifted from the floor and flowed swiftly now toward the floating man at the middle of the circle, following the path of light like water in a pipe. As it touched his outstretched right hand, the blood turned to mist that spread over his arm and side, vanishing in the black cloth. The spell moved through him as if he were some kind of conductor. Bones from the pile on his left rose into the air in the moving light, assembling themselves into a skeleton that gained the momentary shape of its former owner.

Sharp memories of death enveloped me in pain as the ghost seemed to fight and resist, spinning in the light, and was then crushed with a screech back into a bundle of white that tumbled across the room to fall into one of the polished wooden boxes on the right side of the circle. The man with the candle walked to the box, closed the lid over the clattering bones, and fastened the latch. Then he murmured over it as he dripped the black wax over the latch until the metal was covered. He pressed a small object against the wax and the remains fell silent.

The song of the bones faded to what it had been before. I caught my breath at the same moment that the woman at the altar seemed to draw hers for the first time in minutes. Her shoulders slumped a little as if they'd been doing this all night. "Now the girl," she said.

The man with the candle began to walk counterclockwise around the circle as if he were going to change sides. Quinton lunged forward, shedding his cloak of darkness, and wrapped his arms around the man's shoulders and head, then twisted, using his momentum to add power to the motion.

I didn't hear the man's neck break, but the shock of his death knocked me to the ground with a gasp and I fell across the edge of the illuminated circle. The woman screamed in rage. Quinton buckled to the floor with me, caught in the lashing pain by our paranormal connection.

The light from the circle's edge seemed to burn through me for a moment before it flashed and vanished with a stink of burning hair. I struggled to regain my feet, just inside the circle this time, aching and breathing as raggedly as if I'd been punched in the stomach. I turned to lurch toward Soraia from my knees; however, as the one to break the circle, I was subject to the effect of the bone magic now that I was outside the cloak of Carlos's protection. The presence of the ghastly bones with all their death hummed in the lingering cloud of power that the mage had raised. The strange magic seemed to stab at my own skeleton with hooked blades, slowing me and pulling me downward.

Carlos had darted across the broken circle, revealed from the shadows, and was reaching for the floating man who was moving as though dazed in his bubble of light. The woman shouted some words and upended the cup on the altar, red liquid flowing in bloody rivulets over the white bones. She snatched the hand of her assistant and drove a knife through it, pinning him to the base of the cup as he screamed in shock. Blood ran down the cup and into the intricate carvings on the altar bones, burning them red.

The floating man plunged to the floor in a clatter of bones and an icy pall of mist enclosed him, seeming to bear him to the floor and hold him there. Carlos smashed his fist against the opaque white shape the steam and bones had taken. His hand rebounded as if the dome had hardened. He roared in anger and turned toward the woman as Quinton ran several steps ahead of me, heading for the cage that held his niece.

The woman spoke rapidly and made a flinging motion in Quinton's direction. A whirling ivory chain of bone caught him around the legs and upper body, flipping him to the floor with a crash that shook dust from the columns of skulls nearby. He tried to ignore the spell and squirmed toward Soraia's cage, but he could move only a few inches. He gasped, his face going pale, and he fought to move forward, the labor of his breathing mixing with his niece's weak sobs and the panting of the man whose hand was transfixed by a dagger.

The woman made another gesture, as if lofting something into the air, and four of the bony figures from the walls began to detach and walk toward us. The first reached me in a moment and snatched for my head with its skeletal hands. I ducked, wincing, and swiped at it, yanking a bone loose from its lower leg and rolling aside. The bone melded to the floor as the walking skeleton fell over me. Its bones rattled against the mosaic of smaller bones, sticking and forming a partial cage around me. Kicking and yanking, I thrashed, breaking the bones as I tried to get back to my feet. The next skeleton didn't even try to grab me, but threw itself on top of the other, its bones sliding straight down like spears.

I yanked the edge of the Grey and tugged it over me like a shield, isolating myself in the folds as the bones pierced through, shoved aside by the Grey where they hadn't yet encountered another bone. Then they sealed themselves to the floor or to other bones when they touched at last. The cage was tight and without the edge of the Grey over me, the plunging bones would have gone right through me. I had no desire to see what would happen if they had pushed through my flesh to my own bones. But the bones were brittle with age and I continued to kick and beat at them, making my way out.

The third skeleton crushed itself over Quinton as he crept toward Soraia's prison, but Quinton rolled, knocking more of the bones aside than I had been able to. The scattered bones hit the floor and made a small obstacle. Quinton was still barely moving, squirming forward by inches, borne down by the spell that enclosed him. I fought to get back to my feet, but it felt like the floor was drawing my own bones down to it and rising was more difficult than it should have been.

The woman took a step away from the altar, satisfied that Quinton and I were no threat now. She picked up a small white object and left her minion still pinned without a single glance of concern. Her expression narrowed and she focused on Carlos, who stood just to the left of the room's center in a rising shimmer of obsidian light that climbed up his body and wove around him like a dancing chorus of deadly vines. He seemed gigantic, enfolded in the shroud of his power, and the last of the bone constructs sparkled into dust as it touched him. Sparks snapped in the air around him as if he stood at the eye of an electric storm. The woman seemed unfazed, though she did keep her distance from him.

"Well done, Maggie Griffin," Carlos said. "You saved your master from my wrath. For now."

She tried to restrain a wince at his knowledge of her name, but if I saw it, Carlos had, too. Instead of replying, she spread her arms and the room shook as the rest of the bony figures on the walls pulled themselves loose from the plaster and stepped onto the floor, animated and enraged. They turned toward Carlos and me, clicking as they began to walk toward us, ignoring Quinton and Soraia. I was barely up when the nearest skeleton swung its arms, clawing at me. I dropped and swept its feet out from under it, but I was sweating with the effort, pulling against the hungry grip of the floor.

The bones scattered, not sticking this time, but now other bone constructs were close enough to grab at me. As I tried to manage the increasing number of fragile assailants, the skeleton I'd just broken began drawing back together. I would have cursed, but I was already breathing too hard to want to waste my breath.

Griffin laughed. "Which of your friends will you save? You can't possibly manage them both before the bones collect them."

Carlos crouched on the floor, his hands rising, drawing black tendrils from the ground. Blood ran through the interstices of the bone mosaic, drawn toward him from the altar and from the place Soraia had bled onto the floor. Carlos slammed his palms onto the floor with the same gesture he'd used to frighten the dogs. The room shook and the skeletons shattered, bones tumbling to the ground.

Griffin narrowed her eyes and walked closer to me. I dodged to the side, running as best I could toward Quinton. A bone candelabrum tumbled to the ground, knocking me down and blocking the direct route to my lover and his niece. I shot a glance over my shoulder. Griffin smirked at me and made a clawing, clutching gesture. The floor beneath me heaved, knocking over more of the reeking candelabra. I was enclosed in a ring of fire and burning bones. It wasn't as much of a barrier to me as it would have been to some, but it looked intimidating and I could feel the floor reaching for me again, tiny ivory spurs cutting through my thin shoes and skin, reaching for my bones. I danced aside, coming perilously close to the flames. I snatched another cold edge of the Grey between myself and the grasping bones, but it meant bending down, which put my face uncomfortably close to them. I could hear the whispers of their song as my Grey shield cut through them.

Carlos rose back to his full height. "Your ideas could not begin to encompass what I can 'manage.'" He made another gesture, a small thing limned in blackness. The bones of the altar bent, bristling and snatching at her.

Griffin darted forward, startled, as the bones grabbed hold of the man pinned to the altar. He screeched as they touched him and began to pierce his flesh. He yanked his hand back from the cup, dislodging the knife a little as he tried to escape.

The dome of bone around Griffin's master shivered on the floor. Carlos smiled.

Griffin spun around, snatched the pitcher from the altar, and bashed it against her minion's head with killing force, splattering the walls with crimson liquid that stank of sour wine and curdled blood. His skull smashed against the bristling altar and I was on my knees, choking and gasping as his death hit me. She never noticed, her attention focused on the bone shield at the center of the room.

Carlos made another small gesture, empowered by the presence of death as much as I was debilitated by it. The dome around Griffin's master cracked and shivered.

Griffin put her hand on the bloodied skull of her dying companion and lifted a piece of it away, holding it tight enough to crush in her fist as she muttered under her breath. Hard shafts of white energy bolted upward and then plunged to the floor. For a moment, a black pit yawned around the dome of white in the center of the room, and the bone chapel shook, causing loose finger bones, skulls, and ribs to drop from the ceiling and fall into the hole until the blackness vanished again. Griffin smiled, an unpleasant, cold expression.

She turned and, as the man beside her died, she shoved the knife back down through his hand, repinning the spell to the cup and altar, and the white dome hardened again. But the floor had ceased to grasp for me and, with his passing, the man's death no longer held me down.

"You are remarkably loyal in spite of your other flaws," Carlos said, drawing Griffin's attention back to him as I rolled through the spreading ring of fire and crawled to Quinton and Soraia.

"But this is a waste of effort. You cannot stand against me. Release the girl and I will not dine upon your soul tonight."

"You really are sure of yourself, aren't you, Mysterious Stranger?" Griffin replied, but her bravado was a sham, her voice rough as the coruscation of power around her fluttered. She'd burned through a lot of energy, but she wasn't backing down.

Carlos laughed at her. "You already see that I can send you forth 'to shoreless space, to wander its limitless solitudes without friend or comrade forever. . . .'" Carlos pulled the broken crystal pendant from his pocket and held it up in the strange light of the room. "Even your master, swaddled in his shroud of bones, isn't safe from me."

Griffin twitched. "You threaten us with that?" she said, faking a laugh as she pointed at the pendant, moving her other hand to the side and out of his view. "It's broken. You know that you'll never get that little girl out of there without my say-so—which I won't give if you harm him. And if you kill me, she'll remain locked in that cage forever with your friends dead beside her, just more bones for our temple."

There wasn't going to be much of a temple left, I thought, as the flames continued spreading.

THIRTEEN

I reached Quinton and Soraia as a coil of white mist rose from the bones behind Carlos and the crystal began to sway in his grip. The mist started solidifying into a shape that seemed disturbingly familiar, like a small beast with scales and wings and a mouth full of vicious fangs. The blood and blackness of Carlos's own power touched and wove into the shape as it came together faster, fleshing the skeleton of the Night Dragon. The silver chain of the pendant began to smoke.

Carlos dropped the crystal as the spectral dragon swooped.

Griffin laughed and sprang forward, more confident in spite of her flagging power. She'd obviously been working all night and, in spite of the venue, she was running out of steam. But she was laughing and it filled me with dread.

Carlos stepped aside, turning, and swiped through the dragon with a gleam of blackness as he crushed the crystal underfoot. I wound my hands into the white mass of Griffin's spell that held Quinton to the floor and felt for the cold particle that held it in shape. My fingers burned as if I'd touched dry ice and I closed my aching hand around the linchpin of misery, removing it with a long, smooth pull. The spell crumbled into white dust around us and Quinton sucked in a lungful of air tainted with the increasing stench of burning flesh and bone.

As Quinton caught his breath, the nightmare thing that Griffin had unleashed wove through the air, but the blackness Carlos wielded cut its wing and it crashed to the ground, the bones—not pale green like the ones I'd seen before, but black and smoking—rebounding off the floor like hailstones as its borrowed darkness swarmed back to Carlos.

One of the wooden boxes burst into flame and the bones around the room began howling and singing as the heat and smoke rose. The box burned like a fuse and then collapsed. A screaming phantom shot up from the ruined box, arcing toward the ceiling to vanish through the roof. I could hear the distant chime and rattle of scales over silvery bones and feel the cold sweep of the Guardian Beast nearby, collecting the escaped revenant.

Griffin let out a moan, twisting and bending where she stood as if the broken illusions bore her down with them. The threads that linked her to the fallen Night Dragon dragged her to the floor, her burned energy weighing on her now. She raised her arms, and a fragile scaffold of bones arched over her.

I looked at Carlos, who had stooped to sweep up the rods of rutile that had scattered from the crushed crystal. He did not pause to see what had become of us, but gathered to him the fleeing darkness of the Night Dragon and its lines of control that connected it to Griffin, drawing the black shards of enchanted crystal into the baleful energy as if he were spinning yarn. The strand of his spell lengthened in his fingers, writhing around his hands like a snake looking for a place to strike. He caught it and wove it between his fingers like a cat's cradle, twisting it as he murmured into the void between the filaments of death.

He pulled the intricate weave tighter, and Griffin crumpled with a strangled scream, her shield of bones collapsing and dissolving into the floor. The last of the uncanny light winked out, leaving only the stinking reek of the spreading fire from the fallen bone candles and the bleak glow of Carlos's power to illuminate the room.

Carlos strode to the altar and yanked the knife from the dead man's hand. The corpse slumped to the floor in a spill of blood and brains. The white dome at the center of the room dissolved, but of the man who had occupied it there was no sign—only broken bones and dust that fell away into a hole in the floor where the dark void had been. Growling, Carlos returned to stand over Griffin, the trailing pearls of death and darkness thinning and disappearing behind him. "Release the girl and I will let you live. Today. Otherwise . . ." he added, and pulled harder on the filaments woven between his hands so the shape thinned and strained.

Griffin writhed and blanched, gasping. She made a gesture while choking out a few words, and the cage of bones and silver shivered. She clenched her teeth in useless fury.

As Soraia's wretched prison shuddered, Quinton yanked one side open. It fell apart around her and she let out a thin cry, throwing herself into her uncle's arms. The blood from her forearm smeared over his back.

As I helped Quinton to his feet, Carlos dropped the fabric of his working onto Griffin's body and stepped back as she lay like a corpse beneath it. He walked away from her to look down at the remains of the bony tomb that had protected the floating man but now showed only a gaping pit in the floor. "Your aegis of bone allowed him to escape. He was blind to what happened here—which will obscure your failure for now, but Rui will not be pleased when he returns. He shouldn't have let the beauty of the finish blind him to the essentially shoddy quality of your work, nor to your need to borrow a spell from someone else to hold me at bay. Were I you, I'd be gone before he returned. Not that running will save you. . . ."

"Bastard," Griffin spat.

Another of the ghost receptacles cracked open in the heat, sending its shrieking, burning ghost into the air in a shock of ethereal cold that made me wince and shudder. Everyone else ignored it. Quinton continued to the door, skirting the flames as he carried Soraia. He was moving more heavily than I had ever seen him.

Carlos bowed to Griffin. "Indeed. If you're still here when he returns, tell Rui you did your best but failed nonetheless because he's become as lazy a master as he was a student. He'll tell you that you never stood a chance against me."

"Against whom? Who are you that I should accept this . . . humiliation like a good little sport?"

"My name is Carlos, but it will do you no good against me when we meet again—as we will."

Carlos turned from her and walked toward the door, apparently unconcerned for the fire that I knew could easily destroy him. He never looked to see whether we were behind him. I helped Quinton and Soraia to the door as if I didn't want to run, screaming, from the place as fast as possible.

Carlos paused at the threshold without turning back, letting us pass him, and then muttered a few words, pushing his hands out to the side in a sweeping gesture. The remaining candelabra exploded in flames, and the dry bones began to burn in the sudden, intense heat. He walked out of the building, allowing the door to swing closed behind him. The sparking, gleaming black energy drained away, fading as he stepped through the doorway to the outside.

Quinton, holding Soraia in his arms, was leaning against the wall of the building, his posture revealing his exhaustion. He stumbled toward me and Carlos, then stopped to set the little girl on the ground. He knelt down, saying, "Can you walk with us, Soraia? We need to go to the car." He looked ill and unsteady, and I hoped whatever spell Griffin had cast over him had no lingering effects.

The girl nodded, huge-eyed and pale, but I stepped to his side and knelt down. "I can take her," I said. I held out my arms and the small blood-smeared girl crept into them.

I felt the sickening presence of Carlos beside us and Soraia recoiled in my arms, making a frightened, keening noise in her throat. I patted her back and stood up with her in my arms as he said, "We should go as quickly as possible. The fire will bring attention."

"This girl is going to need some attention, too. She's still bleeding." Soraia continued to hold herself as far from Carlos as she could. "And something's not right with Quinton, either."

"I will assist him. Carry the girl to the car—her bleeding is slowing and we must go swiftly. I promise that neither of them will die before we reach safety."

I jogged as well as I could with forty-five pounds of cringing child in my arms and turned back only once to glance up, watching the flames leap as the misty forms of ghosts flooded the air above the building. Amid the smoke and ghostlight, I could see the twining, sinuous form of the Guardian Beast as it gathered up the stolen souls and herded the spirits back into the Grey.

I turned back and continued to the car, feeling some dark and heavy thing dragging on me through my connection to Quinton.

The distance to the car was grueling. I finally put Soraia down in the backseat as Carlos placed Quinton beside her from the other side. Soraia was shivering and I was shaking a bit myself. She looked more like a ghost than a girl.

"May I see your arm?" I asked.

She nodded, staring at me with very wide eyes. *"Você é um anjo esquisito,"* she whispered as I inspected the long, weeping tracks of the cuts on her arm.

I felt Carlos behind me. "She believes you're an angel," he said.

I didn't look up. "It must be the aura. No angel here, just you and me." I looked back to her slashed skin. The cuts were bleeding less after being pressed to the cloth of first Quinton's shirt and then mine, but they were starting again. I looked up at her. "We're going to take you to your mother, all right?"

She nodded.

"We have to do something about this first, though. Can you be very brave just a little longer?"

Quinton put his arm around her from his side of the car and hugged her. "I know you can, Little Fairy."

Carlos knelt down beside the open door. She cringed away from him, squirming back against Quinton and gasping in fear while drawing her arms in.

"It's all right, Soraia," Quinton said, kissing the top of her head as he held her close to his side. "He's not going to hurt you. I won't let him."

Carlos asked her a question in Portuguese, and I could feel an unusual, warm swell of his glamour enfolding her, sparks of golden light shimmering between them. She still looked frightened, but she nodded, holding out her bleeding arm and shivering. He didn't smile or attempt to soothe her any further. He only put one of his hands over her arm and bent very low over it, as if he were going to kiss her wrist.

Quinton started to pull Soraia away, but I caught his eye and shook my head. Carlos had done too much to get her back alive to harm her now. He was a vampire—blood and death were his specialties and though we were all pushed to the limit, I wasn't going to second-guess him.

Soraia blinked sleepily, her head drooping, as Carlos crouched over her. After a minute, he stood, running his fingers up her arm, and stepped away from her, the golden gleam of his glamour extinguished like a candle. He looked even more fatigued than before, but there was no sign of blood on him and her arm, though still marked, was no longer bleeding.

Carlos asked Soraia another question. She nodded drowsily, muttering something and trying to curl up to sleep against Quinton while drawing her arm in against her body. Quinton pulled her into his embrace and she nuzzled his chest, her eyes closing. Carlos and I folded ourselves into the front seats and talked in low voices while I drove.

As I took the little car down the road, I could see the fire and the storm of ghosts above it. "All those dead . . ." I murmured. "I suspect some of them weren't just spirits they had harvested from somewhere, but ghosts they made themselves."

"If I'd had more power to draw from, there would have been four more. Perhaps I should have let your spouse-in-soul shoot them. . . . Even with the deaths of two of his acolytes at my disposal, I was at a disadvantage and couldn't have killed them all in his own temple. Rui will realize that, once he's back in the world. We couldn't have fooled him with such a charade, but since Griffin did us the favor of locking him—and his power—away, I was able to convince her I could have destroyed her and her master within their own bastion. She wouldn't have let the girl go otherwise, and next time, she'll know better."

"You faked all that?"

"No. But it was not so overwhelming as it may have appeared. We were lucky that she was only a student. Her master chose to channel the ritual through his own body to control it if she should make a mistake. If he'd had more confidence in her and chosen to take part directly, we would have had to deal with him on his own ground rather than with his cocksure apprentice whose first concern was protecting him. Her shield kept him from turning the tide of this skirmish, and only the deaths of the two lesser priests gave me power enough to make such a show."

I wanted to curse at him, but I put my attention on more important things. "Priests . . . ?" I thought about the robed men and the perversion of a church they'd died in; I thought about the man in the clerical collar with a strange, violent aura who'd stood in the little plaza below the small white church on the hill. I shuddered, sickened to the core.

He nodded. "Most of the Kostní Mágové are priests, nuns, monks. . . . They are religious fanatics who believe in the allegory of the bones—death in life, the transience of worldly power—but only as a conduit for their own. I am sorry for the pain their deaths caused you, but it was a necessary risk."

I resisted the urge to punch him for putting me through the agony of their passing—and nearly that of Quinton as well. He gave me a measuring look. "What do you plan to do with the child? It won't be safe for her to return to her mother."

"We've made arrangements. Quinton and I can handle it from there—if Quinton is still able, that is."

"I will look after him as well."

"I'm not sure about your variety of care, Carlos."

"Without it, he will die."

I pulled my eyes from the road only long enough to glare at him.

"Griffin's spell allowed the bones of the dead to draw life from him," he explained. "I can remove that connection before it kills him. It touched you also, but you'll heal yourself of it—being what you are. His niece's injuries can be cured by medicine, but his cannot. We must return to the house."

"So long as we get everyone into your house without any interference from the ghosts, you can save him?"

Carlos interrupted his nod to frown at me. "The ghosts have caused you a problem?"

It was hard to turn my mind back to the topic of the ghosts in Carlos's house as I continued to think about Quinton and Soraia, bones and priests, and ghosts imprisoned in boxes the way my first Grey client had been. I shook my scrambled thoughts off and concentrated on the matter of the spirits that haunted Carlos's house.

"Not a problem so much as a . . . conundrum. When I arrived, I was let out of the box by a woman named Rafa, who used to be the housekeeper until she retired in 1992. She died in 2000. I don't know why she's been interfering, but she gave me keys that unlock not just the house, but a particular time frame of the house's past—Rafa's time frame. I lost one of the keys and had to get in the old-fashioned way—by knocking—or I never would have been sure what was going on. I haven't seen her since I relocked the temporacline."

"I never knew her. . . ."

"Which is kind of weird, because she seemed to know you. She called you 'Dom Carlos,' and talked about 'the family' as if there were others around, but the only other ghost I've had any contact with is another woman—she seems to want something, but I haven't been able to ask her what. She said 'I don't forget,' but I have no idea what she was referring to. Her name was Amélia. Ring any bells?"

Carlos raised an eyebrow and leaned away from me. He seemed stunned—an emotion I'd never seen on him before.

"Amélia was my wife."

FOURTEEN

Now it was my turn to be stunned. "Your wife? You were married?" I couldn't imagine it. "I thought your preferences ran in another direction."

Carlos chuckled, seeming relieved I'd pick that topic rather than Amélia herself to start with. "My preferences are broader than you know."

"I'm having a hard time imagining you married to anyone."

"I was sixteen when we wed. Amélia was thirteen. It was common for the children of important houses to marry young by arrangement."

"I know the history of marriage in Europe, Carlos," I said. "I didn't know you came from an influential family until today."

"They are no longer." He glanced back at Soraia, who was asleep in her uncle's arms as we drew closer to Alfama. "Perhaps we should continue this discussion another time. . . ."

"Is this in the same category as showing me the window you were thrown out of?" I asked.

"It is."

I humphed, but honored his desire to let the subject lie for now.

When we arrived at the house and drove the tiny car into the courtyard for safekeeping, we found Sam waiting in her own small car just outside the gates. She ran to scoop up her daughter the moment the girl stumbled, half asleep, from the car.

"Soraia! Are you all right?"

Soraia nodded, looking frightened, sleepy, and overwhelmed.

Sam was panicky. "*Anjinho*, say something. I've been so worried about you. I just want to hear your voice."

"*Estou bem, Mamãe,*" she whispered, then looked ready to cry. "Oh . . . English. I'm sorry," the little girl said, hanging her head and breaking into sobs.

"Oh, little angel, it's all right. I don't care if you speak *Russian* right now. I'm so glad to see you!"

"Where's Martim?" Soraia asked, her voice still so low I could barely hear her. "I don't want Avô to hurt him, too. . . ."

"What? Your grandfather hurt you?" Sam said, her eyes huge with fear. She held her daughter and looked back at her car, not knowing what to do first. "Oh God! I left Martim in the car seat!"

Quinton walked to Sam's car and extracted his whimpering nephew with unsteady hands. I caught up to him as he carried the baby back to Sam and Soraia. He was shaking as he held Martim out for his sister to take into her arms.

Sam stood, accepting Martim while Soraia clung to her leg. "Thank you! I was so worried about Soraia, I forgot Martim!"

"He's just anxious," Quinton said, taking a step back. Sam frowned, knowing something was wrong, but too distracted with concern for her children to fix on it yet.

I started to put my arm around Quinton, but he closed his eyes and shook his head. "Not now, Harper," he muttered, his aura flickering tight to his body, as if he were exerting considerable effort to remain upright and any touch would break him. I let my arm drop but stayed close, whether he liked it or not.

His sister had already turned her attention back to her kids, holding Martim close and bending down again to look at her daughter. "What happened, *fadinha*? Avô hurt you? Where?"

Soraia held out her arm, still scratched and red but no longer bleeding. She pointed at Carlos. "He fixed it."

For a moment, Sam was relieved it was just the little girl's arm; then she whipped her head around to stare at Carlos, but he was already walking toward the house. She turned her gaze up to Quinton and then me. "What is she talking about? What happened?"

"I think we should have this discussion indoors," I said.

Quinton, moving a little unsteadily, knelt down and peeled Soraia off her mother's leg. "Come on, Fairy Princess. Let's go in."

Soraia bit her lip and frowned at the house, then dug her heels in, shaking her head.

"Are you afraid to go inside?" Quinton asked.

She nodded.

"This is Senhor Carlos's house. He won't hurt you."

Soraia's mouth turned down and her lip trembled. "He's a bad man, like the old man from the bone house," she whispered. "Black."

Sam cast a confused look between her brother and me.

"I think she means he's wearing black, like one of the men who hurt her," I said, but I didn't believe it. If Soraia had a touch of power to her, it wasn't unlikely that she could see his death-black aura and thought it resembled the energy of the bone mages.

Quinton put his arm around her. "I know he seems scary, but he's not like that man. He made your arm better. He doesn't want to hurt you."

She still wasn't convinced, hanging back.

"Not everything that's frightening is hurtful."

"Will you keep the ghosts away?"

Quinton hugged her tight. "Yes, we will, Fairy Princess. Me and Harper and your mother and even Carlos will keep you safe. I promise."

Soraia chewed on her lips for a moment. Then she turned to face the house, putting her hand in Quinton's, and nodded.

We all filed in through the open door; I was in the rear with some of the family luggage. Carlos was waiting for me in the entry and put out an arm, restraining me from following the rest of the party.

When they were gone, he gave me a dark look from the side and said, "You understand that without Quinton's niece, the Kostní Mágové will have to seek the bones of another suitable child."

"I suppose that's true. You'll forgive me if I was more worried about rescuing my almost-niece from being flayed than about what would happen if she wasn't."

He turned all the way to face me, blocking my way in and my view of anyone inside. "I do not question your motives, Blaine. But what we've done won't stop them. It will only infuriate them and redirect their efforts."

"Are you suggesting that they would come after some other member of the family?"

"Without knowing precisely what they intend to conjure, I can't know what change they will have to make or who their victim will be in exchange. If the Night Dragon that Griffin produced had been her own work, I would know what they intend. But it wasn't a true drache, and without the bones, informed guesses are the best I can do at the moment—though it pains me to say so."

"There were bones."

"Not drachen bones."

"Not at the church. That's what I think fell from the sky when the dragon Quinton and I saw earlier broke down. They looked like sticks, but I didn't see them well. They were pale green and they smoked where they touched the ground—like the ones we saw in Seattle last year."

Carlos scowled and I felt a stab of cold. "That bodes ill. There's much yet for me to do before dawn, so I must rely on you to communicate the appropriate information—or withhold it as you see fit. I may be able to discover more tomorrow night, but it will be risky and I must prepare in what time remains tonight. There is also the matter of your spouse-in-soul."

"You're tired. I'll help you."

"You cannot. Your presence would be a liability for both of us."

"Then what are you asking of me?"

"Look after him and search for news of bones—of anything bizarre or unusual that has happened recently in Europe—especially in the more superstitious corners. And make sure that the children are truly safe. If you have to take them yourself, do it. We cannot risk any of the family falling into the wrong hands. The girl's mother cannot comprehend and your beloved is not, at the moment, clearheaded enough. I can trust only you to know the real dangers of this."

His focus on me was intense and I found myself wincing and drawing my shoulders in defensively as if his stare had physical weight. He seemed to realize it and stepped back, cutting his gaze to the side. "My apologies."

I let out a breathless chuckle. "You've apologized to me more in the past twenty-four hours than in our entire acquaintance up to this point."

"Have I?"

"Yes. I might start to think you're growing a conscience."

"Never that." He growled and turned his back so he could walk into the house.

I followed him, once I had conquered my urge to laugh.

There was no sign of Carlos when I cleared the door, but Quinton was waiting for me near the stairs. He looked horrible even in the subdued light of the room.

"There was a message on the answering machine—I didn't know people still had those," he said. "The Danzigers' car died, so we'll have to get Sam and the kids to Spain ourselves." We'd known the Danzigers wouldn't be here too soon, but I hadn't expected this complication—it was almost as if Carlos had known it was going to happen. . . .

I looked at Quinton and saw that the color of his flickering aura was a sick olive drab with thin threads of black wound through it. "I'll do it. I don't know my way around as well as you, but Sam can help me. You need some rest and I have an assignment from Carlos that you'll be much better at than I could be."

"I'm not feeling too well and I—I am disturbed by what I did. I killed a man. . . ."

"You did it to save your niece. You didn't have much choice."

"It hurt you and I didn't have to . . . kill him. I could have disabled him, left him alive. . . ."

"I'm not sure you could have. You had no idea what he was capable of, and if it had become a fight, or if he'd gotten back up in a few minutes, the advantage would have been lost. We would have lost."

He hung his head. "I don't know. And I don't feel right about sending you off—"

"I know you don't, but I can see that you're sick and I'm sure Sam will understand."

"Do you think we did the right thing . . . ?"

"Of course we did. Why do you ask that?"

"I'm not stupid. Dad—or these mages—will be looking for a substitute for Soraia."

"Yes. But you can't worry about that now. You need to rest and I'll deal with the other stuff. Where are Sam and the kids?"

"They're in the kitchen. There's a clean bedroom on the second floor I figured they can have."

"Good idea. Go join them and I'll be right back."

"Where are you going?" His voice was breathy and unsteady.

"To dump the luggage and risk the wrath of Carlos before he gets too involved in whatever else he needs to do. He thinks he can find out to-morrow night what the Kostní Mágové are trying to make, but he's got to do something first. I want to intrude before he gets too immersed."

"All right. But if you're not back down in fifteen minutes, I'm coming to get you."

I was afraid he might not be able to, but I smiled and hugged him. He felt stiff, slick with sweat, and too warm. "Go get Dr. Rebelo to look at you," I said as I let him go.

He picked up one of the bags—which had Sam's initials on it. "She'll never let me live this down," he muttered, trudging toward the kitchen.

I ran up the first set of stairs and dropped the remaining bags without ceremony in the hall on my way past, then up the last flights of steps to the tower and knocked on the door, panting a little from the steepness of the final risers.

Carlos opened the door a few inches and held out a small paper packet. I could smell something vile cooking in the room beyond. "Make him drink this in some warm liquid. He'll sleep heavily, but he'll live. Go, and don't disturb me again before tomorrow at sunset."

I took the folded paper. "What is it?" I asked, but he had already shut the door. I sighed. "Thank you, I guess," I said, and started back down the stairs, hoping the cure wasn't going to be worse than the disease.

Without a doubt, I'd only known a paler version of Carlos up until now. Even though he was near exhaustion, there was something more to his powers here in Lisbon than at home in Seattle. But then, this *was* his home and it wasn't far-fetched to imagine that a vampire who was also a mage had a special connection to the place where he'd been born, died, and been reborn. It didn't seem to be true for me, but I'm not a magic-user or a vampire.

I walked back down to the kitchen and joined the family. A kettle was simmering on the stove and there were mugs of something sitting around, untouched by anyone. Soraia was seated at the table with Martim, who'd fallen asleep with his head in her lap and his rump on the neighboring chair. Soraia had wrapped her arms around him as if she feared someone would snatch him away. Sam was examining her brother with one of those annoying light things doctors use to look down your throat. Quinton, seated at the end of the table, appeared to be at death's door, pale and shivering as if he had a virulent case of the flu and not protesting his sister's prodding. Soraia started when I came in, even though she looked barely awake, herself.

"Tio Pássaro is sick," she said, her voice shaking more than it had on her own behalf. "The bad woman hurt him."

"I can see that, honey," I said, catching her shoulder and turning her back to address her steaming cup. I could feel Sam's gaze on me, uncomfortable, no doubt, with what her daughter had probably been telling her and now worried about her brother as well as her kids. "Senhor Carlos gave me some medicine for him, so we'll have to see how he feels after he takes it."

"He doesn't need some kind of folk remedy," Sam snapped, distressed beyond her ability to remain composed. "He's ill and I don't know why. Fever, sweats, difficulty breathing, his eyes are discolored. . . . It's not the flu—it came on too quickly. I'd say it's some kind of poisoning, but he needs tests, a hospital. . . ."

"We don't have that luxury," I said. "Your father's friends will be looking for us, and if they know he's sick, any hospital won't be safe."

I held out the packet to Quinton who blinked at it as if unable to see it clearly. He wasn't arguing—not a good sign. I started to open the folded paper and pour the powder inside into an untouched mug, but Sam snatched the package from me.

"What is it?"

"I don't know," I said, "but Carlos says it'll cure him and I believe that."

"You trust your friend with Jay's life?"

I was still struggling to remember to call Quinton "Jay," but I replied, "He's trusted Jay with his."

Sam sniffed at the packet. "It smells like . . . mint. Or catnip."

It didn't smell like either to me, but it also didn't look completely benign in my sight, either—the glow around the package was as black as the poison that had dripped from Carlos's wards, but I knew he didn't need to go to this kind of trouble if he wanted any of us dead. And I did trust him.

"Dr. Rebelo," I started, "if you can suggest anything better at this stage, I'm game to try it, but Jay isn't improving while we argue."

With poor grace, she handed the folded paper back to me. "All right. But I don't like this. Your friend is a bit high-handed."

"You get used to it after a few years."

Sam bit her lip and her gaze darted around the room as she stuffed her fear and temper back down. With an effort, she sat next to her children and put her hand on Soraia's head, smoothing the curls compulsively. "Just what the hell happened in that place?"

"It's not a story we need to go over right now." I filled a mug with hot water from the kettle and dumped the powder into it, then sat down next to Quinton and put my arm around his back. "Dr. Carlos says you have to drink this while it's still warm." His skin was hotter than before, but he was shivering and his muscles were stiff.

Quinton lifted the cup in a shaking hand. His face was the color of unfired porcelain. "It smells vile. . . . Will it turn me into a newt?"

"Yes, but you'll get better." At least he still had a sense of humor. . . .

He grumbled and slurped the liquid. "Tastes like dirt."

"Could be worse," I said, thinking of all the other things it could have tasted like, given its origin. "I think you're supposed to drink the whole thing."

He made a disgusted sound but drank the rest. "I don't feel any better." He squeezed his eyes shut, then opened them, horrified. "Oh God . . ."

He dove for the sink and vomited. I dashed to hold him up when he swayed and started to heave again.

Soraia huddled against her mother crying, pressing her face to Sam's chest, and though it was clear Sam wanted to get up and help her brother, she stayed seated and comforted her daughter, instead. "It's all right, little angel, Uncle Jay will be all right. Shhh, shhh. . . . It's all right. . . ."

I kept close to Quinton when he was done and gave him a glass of water to rinse his mouth with before he staggered back to his chair. He didn't say anything for a few minutes, and I washed the mug and the sink out hastily before Sam could act all doctor-y and want to examine the contents. What Quinton had thrown up looked like a tarantula and it smoked at the touch of the water I'd used to rinse his mug. White spines like broken bits of bone and bile the color of squid ink swirled around the drain before they disappeared.

"I think I need to go to bed," Quinton croaked.

Soraia pulled away from her mother and threw herself on him, clutching him as if she would hold on until the world ended. Her frightened crying blowing up to hysterical sobbing, tears streaking her face, she said, "No! No! You can't sleep! You'll die! I don't want you to die, Tio! Nooo . . ."

Sam was startled and tried to pull her daughter back, which only made Soraia act more like a limpet. The noise and motion startled drowsy Martim into fussing and crying as well. Sam let go of Soraia and tried to hush the baby while I took over the panicking-child duty.

In spite of Soraia's hysteria, Quinton did look slightly better. He wasn't shivering as hard and his color wasn't so much like raw clay. The black threads had vanished from his aura as well, and although it was still weak and an unhealthy shade of green, it was shifting as I watched. I put my hand on Soraia's back and said, "He'll be OK. See—he's getting better already. You have to look at him from far-ther back. See?"

I encouraged her to lean back so her view was broader. If she re-ally had a touch of Grey to her, she might be able to see some of what I saw while I was touching her. It was a long shot, but worth the trouble.

Soraia pulled back with reluctance and studied her uncle with a serious expression. She gestured at her own face. "Not all black any-more." She leaned forward again and hugged Quinton so hard he squeaked. "I love you, Tio. Don't die."

"I love you, too, Soraia," he said, his voice rough and cracking. "I love you too much to die."

"*Promete?*"

"Yes, I promise."

"Come on, now, *anjinho*," Sam said, bundling the baby against her chest as she stood up. "Let your uncle go to bed. You know sick people need to rest. And so do little girls who've had scary adventures."

Soraia looked at each of us as if sizing up who was most likely to tell her the truth. She picked me, turning a baleful silence and piercing stare on me as if to say she'd hold me personally responsible if anything went south.

"I'll take care of him," I said. "I promise. He'll be fine and in the morning I'm going to take you guys to meet some friends of mine." I'm terrible around children—I never know what I'm supposed to say or do, and I was, as always, sure I was getting it wrong.

Soraia shivered and appeared on the verge of tears. I had to bend down to put a hand on her shoulder. "It's all right. They're very nice. They'll keep all the bad people away from you. And they have a son who's about your age," I added, hoping to distract her from the horror and morbid thoughts that seemed to occupy her mind. "His name is Brian and he's a lot like your uncle Jay, only smaller." I hoped I was guessing right about Brian, since I hadn't seen him in years, but I couldn't imagine the Danzigers' son being a serious problem—Mara would have turned him into a toad a long time ago if he misbehaved. "Now, let's all go upstairs and go to bed. OK? We have to get up very early."

Soraia stood, scowling with serious thoughts and trying not to fall asleep on her feet. She reached for her mother's hand while I helped Quinton to his feet. "I'll protect you and Martim from the ghosts, Mamãe," she quavered.

"Ghosts?" Sam asked, hefting the sleeping toddler onto her shoulder to rebalance her uneven stride. "Are you sure they aren't fairies?"

Soraia's face remained serious as she shook her head. She was tired, scared, and had barely escaped from a terrifying ordeal. Talking seemed to drain her.

We made our way out of the kitchen and up the stairs in a ragged parade with Quinton and me in front only because we knew where the bedrooms were. Soraia, Sam, and Martim came behind as one lumpy unit moving steadily slower and slower.

There was only one bed made up in the room that the caretaker had arranged for me originally, but it was a large one and Sam assured us that they'd be able to manage just fine. I suspected that they'd all have ended up in one bed to ward off the terrors anyhow. Sam looked worn to a thread, but we didn't linger to see if she needed anything more. She was capable of letting us know if she wanted help—and I doubted she needed anything more than to hug her children in privacy.

Quinton barely had the energy to make it through a bath and into bed. I would have skipped the bath, but the stink of rot and burning clinging to us was unbearable and our clothes were probably a loss. I thought I might have to drag him to the bed, but he made it on his own and I fell in next to him.

"I feel like I unswallowed a porcupine," he muttered as I curled up next to him and pulled him close. "What was that thing I chucked up?"

"I'd say it was a physical manifestation of whatever spell residue remained on you after you got out from under Griffin's work."

"She wasn't incompetent."

"What?"

"Carlos made her mad, teasing her about being a crummy mage, but she wasn't. He was messing with her head to make her screw up."

"Yeah, well . . . He thought that spell would have killed you, given time."

He nodded, barely awake. "What was that stuff you gave me?"

"Sort of a magical emetic, I'd guess, but it seems to work."

He made a sleepy noise of assent. Now his body didn't feel warm enough, so I snuggled closer to him.

"Sorry," he whispered.

"Why?"

"Too tired to do anything but sleep. Been months . . . dreaming of getting you into bed . . ."

"I've been dreaming of you, too. I love you and it's enough to just be like this. Go to sleep, superhero."

He made a noise, but it turned into a gentle snore and the tension in his limbs drained away. I was tired enough to fall asleep, too, but I couldn't, and as I lay beside him, his snoring died away. After a while, he seemed to grow colder, his skin feeling like wet newspaper and his breathing so shallow that I had a moment's panic until I forced myself to look at him through the Grey before jumping to any conclusions. He seemed barely alive and any normal person might not have realized he wasn't dead, except for the rapid movement of his eyes beneath closed lids. I considered going to Carlos again, but I doubted he would appreciate the intrusion. So long as I could see Quinton was still alive, I didn't want to leave him alone.

In a few hours, his body began to warm again and his sleep became more normal. Relieved, I must have fallen asleep myself, because Soraia woke me at six a.m.

FIFTEEN

There was a presence looming at the bedside. I opened my gummy, gritty eyes and looked up. Soraia offered a trembling smile.

Children have such piercing voices, especially when I've had only two hours of sleep. I had to say something before she could stab me with her fluting tones. "I'm awake now, Soraia, but your uncle Jay isn't. He's still sick."

She replied in a serious whisper, "Will he be all right?" Soraia was hesitant and I had the impression that wasn't normal for her. Everything about her seemed withdrawn, unnaturally restrained—even the energetic colors around her lay tighter to her body than they should have and there were none of the vagrant sparks or bubbles I usually saw around kids. She was shutting herself down and I wanted to inflict an equal measure of brutality on Purlis and his bone mages for that. Children shouldn't be terrified and used like commodities.

Soraia shied a little and I struggled to push my anger aside. I offered her a small smile and said, "I think so—when he's had some more sleep. We're going to meet my friends today." I started to get out of bed but thought better of flashing the six-year-old. "Um . . . sweetie, could you go downstairs and wait for me in the kitchen or something? I need to get dressed."

Soraia gave me a big-eyed stare and started to run out of the room. Then she turned back around and looked at me from under her eyebrows, shaking with effort. "Thank you for coming to save me, Auntie Harper. And Uncle Jay and Senhor Carlos, too."

I didn't laugh. She was deadly serious and still frightened. I respected the effort her gratitude required. "You are very welcome."

I waited in the bed for her to leave, but she didn't. She stood, trembling, halfway between the bed and the door. Then she blurted, "What's an 'odd duck'?"

"Excuse me?" I asked.

"Mamãe says you're an odd duck. Why are you a duck?"

Now I laughed. "I'm not a duck. She just means I'm hard for her to understand. I'm strange."

"Oh," she said, her left hand fluttering up to touch her chest and then dropping back to her side.

"What are you thinking?" I asked.

"I—I'm strange, too."

"Oh, honey. A lot of people are strange and hard to understand. But they're like anyone else—some of them are nice and some of them aren't, and being strange isn't what makes them that way."

She looked thoughtful and the energy around her began to brighten through several shades of blue with a tiny eruption of gold sparks. "Your strange . . . is different from Senhor Carlos's strange? And from the bad wizards'?"

"A lot different."

"Why isn't Uncle Jay strange, too?"

"He is, but it's not the same kind of strange. And that's all right."

She chewed on her lips and considered. "Will I—will I be like them?"

Uh-oh . . . Looking at her, it was pretty obvious she wasn't an ordinary little girl. Aside from being smart and articulate for a six-year-old and coming through a terrible situation, she displayed all the energetic markers of someone in touch with the Grey. It was a weak and rough attachment right now that could have been destroyed without much effort by the wrong sort of people, but it was there. "Soraia," I started, "some things are complex and hard to explain. You're special—"

She made a face.

"Yes, I know . . . People say that when they mean that you're weird or you frighten them. Well, in this case, I'm going to say the same thing for a different reason. Sometimes it's not a good idea to tell people about the things you can see or the ghosts and fairies you can talk to. They don't understand and it scares them."

She shivered. "Even Mamãe."

"Yeah, even your mother. But it's not because she's afraid or doesn't love you. She doesn't mean to upset you. She's not as strange as you and sometimes she doesn't know what to do for you, but she loves you very much and she doesn't want other people to hurt you."

"You mean . . . like the bad wizards . . . ?"

"Not the same way—not usually—but other ways, little ways, mean ways. You shouldn't stop being strange or special because of those people, but sometimes you might want to let them think you're . . . not an odd duck."

Soraia's serious look curled up into a small, uncertain smile. "I don't want to be a duck. I want to be all white and sparkly, like you."

"Oh," I started, uncomfortable and not sure what to say, "I don't know. I don't think so. . . ."

Soraia looked crushed.

I felt terribly constrained by being stuck in the bed. I turned my hands up, imploring her to listen. "Sweetheart, sometimes we don't get to choose. It just happens the way it happens."

"The bad wizards are bad because they are . . . bad? What if they want to be good? Senhor Carlos is bad, but he was good." She started crying. "I don't want to be bad. . . ."

"Oh no! That's not what I mean. I mean . . . um. . . . OK, so . . . the kind of strange you have is just what you have, like being a girl or having curly hair. What you do with it is what you choose. You could do bad things or you could do good things, but it's up to you." I hoped that made more sense to Soraia than it did to me, because I was sure I was babbling like a moron.

She puzzled it over for a while. "Like Max."

"Max?"

"From the book. From *The Wild Things*."

"Oh, *Where the Wild Things Are*. Yes, like Max."

Soraia nodded, serious again but no longer crying, the bright sparks dampening in her aura. "So . . . even if I have a bad strange, I won't be . . . like them?"

"Not unless you decide to be. But I think you're going to grow up to be a beautiful, nice person who does beautiful things. Because you know what the alternative is like."

"What's 'alternative'?"

"It means 'the other choice,'" I said.

"Oh." She hesitated. "Are you a wizard?"

"Nope. I just see ghosts and magic, things like that. The lady we're going to meet today is a witch," I offered.

Soraia shrank away.

Quickly I continued. "Oh no, sweetheart. Not a bad witch. She's a good witch—she's all green and gold and has beautiful red hair. I just mean that there are a lot of ways to be strange like us without being the same as someone else."

Soraia nodded and kept nodding, thinking, as she left the room.

I breathed a sigh and got out of bed as soon as the door was closed. I made sure it was properly locked this time—though I thought I'd locked it earlier. Then I checked on Quinton, relieved to find him sleeping heavily, but like a normal human. His skin was still a little pale and there were violet smudges around his eyes, but his breathing was normal and his pulse was strong. I kissed his cheek and left him to sleep while I got dressed and went downstairs for breakfast with Sam and the kids.

Both Soraia and the baby were well behaved, and Sam had discovered supplies in the fridge and cupboards to make a quick, cold meal of buttered bread with ham that was more like prosciutto than the moist, pink American kind. It was an odd breakfast to me, but there were no complaints.

Sam took one look at me and pointed to the stove. "There's espresso on. It's very hot, so use the cloth when you pick it up."

"Thank you," I said. "Do I have a sign over my head that says 'coffee junkie'?"

"You don't need one—you're a classic case. And you look like you hardly slept."

"I had some difficulty. . . ."

"How's Jay?"

"Doing much better, but he's still out. He'll have to stay here and rest while I drive. But that'll work out all right, since there's some research that needs to be done and Jay's extraordinary at digging up information."

"I know. He used to get in trouble for that when we were kids—he was a hacker before it was a dirty word. So." She studied me in silence for a while as I made my best efforts at sipping the coffee without scalding myself. "I don't suppose anyone is going to tell me what happened last night. Jay didn't and Soraia's version is a bit garbled."

"Probably not as garbled as you think. Short version: Carlos—the big scary guy who owns this house—recognized the workmanship on the 'gifts' your father left for Soraia. He was able to ID the woman who made them and we found out where she was—we think she's the woman you saw with your father and her name is Maggie Griffin. We went to confront her and found Soraia there. Griffin and Carlos had a discussion, she lost her temper, put up a fight, and he slapped her down. We got Soraia and brought her back here. Pretty much all the news that's fit to print."

"What about the injury to her arm and this 'old man' she keeps talking about? And what happened to this Maggie Griffin? Was she arrested?"

"No. As you pointed out, that would only give your father more information about what we know. Your father wasn't there, so he won't know what happened for a while, even though the 'old man' escaped. We think he's the man who was with Griffin and your father. As to what happened to Soraia's arm, it looks like this is a sort of fanatical cult and they had some idea of using her bones for something very unsavory, the details of which you don't want to know. Right now, we have some lead time and a rough idea of their plans, but we have to move before your father knows what we're doing about it."

"What *are* you doing? All I cared about was getting Soraia back, but there's obviously more to this."

"Well, your father's up to something nasty and it looks like he was, basically, giving your daughter to some unpleasant people as a payment for other services."

Sam's mouth dropped open. "He wouldn't. . . ."

"He did. We just got there before the next step could be taken."

"Dear God . . ."

"You're surprised he's that much of a monster? Because I'm not. What he did in Seattle was horrific and it was just an overture to whatever he has in mind here. We still have a lot to do if we're going to stop that plan, but before we can move ahead, you and the kids have to be taken to safety. I suppose Jay told you about the Danzigers?"

"A little. He was too sick to make a lot of sense."

"Ben and Mara Danziger. They're old friends of ours from Seattle—university professors. He's a linguistics and languages scholar and works in comparative religions, folklore, mythology, and that sort of thing. She teaches geology. They have a son named Brian and he's about Soraia's age. He's a lot like a miniature version of Jay."

"Lord have mercy on us," Sam replied.

I laughed. "I think you'll all get along very well, but the thing that you're going to have a hard time with is that Mara's a witch."

Sam narrowed her eyes, but she didn't say anything.

"Anyhow, the reason we thought of them is not only are they reliable people who are also parents, but they understand the complications of this sort of situation. Mara's the best protection you could have from anything paranormal that your father and his friends could throw at you." I put up my hand to stop the objection forming on her lips. "I know you don't swallow the creepy, woo-woo angle of this case, but it is a factor. If it makes you feel better, you can think of them as some kind of fanatical terrorists. Their ideas sound crazy to you, but they're willing to act on those ideas, which makes them dangerous, and having an expert in their brand of crazy on your side will make you a lot safer."

"I'll accept that. I'm not sure about the witch thing. . . ."

"She'll either convince you herself, or she won't, but that's up to you."

"How is it that you happen to have friends here, so conveniently?"

"I rather suspect your brother had a hand in that. Unless you believe in fate, which I assume you don't."

Sam shook her head and I managed to gulp down enough of my coffee to feel less like I was operating by remote control.

"Anyhow, they're on sabbatical and Ben was doing some research into European folklore for a book. Ben was offered a publishing contract, so the research got extended and they've been traveling around for about two years now. So, my guess is that Jay got in touch with them to get some other information, but he also got their itinerary and probably asked them if they could manage to be in the general vicinity, in case he needed backup before I got here. They're the best people in the world. Ben's one of those guys who'll jump in without a second thought if he thinks he's going to see or learn something rare in his field or if a friend needs his help. He's full of enthusiasm. Mara's the levelheaded one."

"The witch." Sam was biting her lip—a nervous habit her brother also had on rare occasion and one her daughter had picked up already, too.

I nodded. "That's her. She's also a geologist and a teacher and while her personal vocation may be a little unusual, she's methodical, well educated, and very smart. I think you'll like her. Ben's more the absentminded, bookworm scholar. He also speaks seven or eight languages, but I don't know if Portuguese is one of them."

"And what about our host, Carlos? What's he?"

Soraia looked up at me with the same hard question in her eyes. "Carlos . . . That's harder to explain." I think it's a mistake to lie to friends and allies if I can avoid it, and lying to kids in particular seems to backfire a lot. Obfuscating, on the other hand, is probably the only viable option when the whole truth is not acceptable. Soraia would probably be thrilled if I told the truth, but I wasn't going to, since it wasn't mine to tell. "You could say he's an expert on anything dead, so the bone flutes were right up his alley. Aside from that, you'd have to ask him."

Soraia got her thoughtful expression, but her mother continued. "It doesn't look like I'll have that chance. He hasn't come down yet. I should thank him for helping us, though he is a little . . ."

"Creepy?" I suggested. Even people with little magical sensitivity get weirded out around Carlos when he hasn't affected a glamour to charm them, and he rarely bothers with more than the minimum of psychic camouflage. He is, by nature and necessity, a killer, even more so than most vampires.

Sam hesitated, then said, "Brusque."

"That's a word for it."

"Is he always like that?"

"Pretty much."

"I hope he's not ill, like Jay. . . . Maybe I should go up and see. . . ."

"No," I said, putting up my hand to stop her rising from the table. "He's fine. Trust me, you really don't want to see Carlos when he's just gotten up."

"Is he a vampire?" Soraia asked.

Her mother was shocked. "Soraia!"

The little girl's eyes widened and her lip trembled.

I caught her eye and shook my head. It was a very small gesture, but she saw it and shut up. "As I said, that's something you'd have to ask him and now would not be appropriate."

Soraia swallowed her fear, nodded, and said nothing.

I ate a few bites of my breakfast and finished my coffee before making another ham sandwich and putting it on a plate to take to Quinton. I excused myself and said we'd leave as soon as I got back downstairs. Then I returned to my room to wake the sleeper, but I didn't get quite the reception I'd expected.

Amélia's ghost was hovering over Quinton, whispering into his ears as he tossed restlessly. He looked paler than he had when I'd left him less than an hour earlier and it appeared that she was doing something to make him so.

I dropped the plate and threw myself across the room through the Grey to snatch at her.

Her energetic form was thin and cold, but she caught in my fingers like a tangle of hair. I yanked her away from Quinton as she screeched.

"Get away from him!" I shouted, flinging her energy at the misty shadow of the wall.

The house was unusually present and solid in the Grey, having been here for many years and filled with the constant flux of magic. Deep in the Grid I could see a nexus beneath, adding strength and permanence to all magical workings above it.

Amélia crashed into the ghostly wall as if it were solid and rebounded, broken into shards of herself like the reflection in a shattered mirror. She put up her hands and hid her face, her voice like the sobbing of mourning doves. *"Tenha misericórdia! Fiz tudo isso para você!"*

I wasn't sure I got the gist, but I spat back in words that cut the mist in heat and barbed red anger, "When I want a favor from you, I'll ask for it! Get out! Or I'll rip you into shreds and feed you to the Guardian Beast! Get out!"

She vanished in a cry. The mist sank where she had been, drawn downward as she left the room.

My chest was heaving and the cold mist of the Grey made me feel frozen through. I backed from the mist world into the normal, keeping an eye peeled for her return and fell over the bed.

Quinton stirred and rolled to the side with a grunt of discomfort.

"Hey," I said as he opened one bleary eye.

"Hey." He sounded like he'd been gargling with glass.

"I brought you a sandwich, but I dropped it. I'm sorry."

"Don't need a sandwich," he muttered, trying to draw me down into the bed with him.

I traded some dopey kisses with him for a moment, warming myself in his affection. Reluctantly, I pulled away in a minute.

He made a disappointed-puppy noise but didn't fight it.

"None of that," I said. "I feel guilty enough as it is. I'm about to leave with your sister."

"I'll get up—"

I pushed him back down as he tried it and it wasn't hard to do. "No, you won't. You need more sleep and I need you to do some research for Carlos while I'm gone."

"What kind?"

"Online. He wants to know about any recent incidents concerning bones or bodies being disinterred, disturbed, or stolen or anything bizarre connected to bones or relics. Anywhere in Europe. He's looking for information that could tell us what the Kostní Mágové are building out of these bones and what they'll have to do now that we've denied them Soraia."

"Oh. All right." He slumped back into his pillow. "I feel wretched."

"I think the term you're after is 'like death warmed over.'"

"Twice."

I started to go but turned back. "Be careful of the ghosts around here. I know you can't see them like I can, but if you have an eerie feeling, heed it."

"Why? What's wrong?"

"Nothing, but some of them have their own agendas and I don't want you sucked into them."

"Oh. OK." He closed his eyes, sleep trying to drown him once again.

I returned to the bed and kissed him one more time. "I love you, my superhero."

"Love you, too," he murmured, sinking into sleep as I watched.

I didn't feel quite so bad about leaving once I knew he was asleep again. I only hoped I'd scared Amélia off badly enough to keep her from repeating whatever she'd been doing. Quinton was still too close to his brush with death to be immune to the machinations of ghosts. I was going on faith that he'd been awake enough to remember what I'd told him.

I picked up the scattered remains of the sandwich and took them back downstairs.

SIXTEEN

I don't remember the trip to Spain. I slept through most of it in the backseat with the baby. Apparently, I managed to miss a minor temper tantrum, two lost "binkies," and a diaper change without so much as wrinkling my nose. Soraia decided this was my superpower and I was anointed—in my sleep—as the coolest aunt in the world. And I'd thought it was because I walked through walls—shows what I know about how to impress six-year-olds. We arrived in a modest city called Valverde del Camino after five hours on the road. We'd hit several patches of bad traffic getting out of Lisbon, then had to take a detour around some road work, which had added time to what I'd expected to be a three-hour drive.

The oldest parts of Valverde looked a lot like the nice parts of Mexico City, while the industrial bits looked exactly what they were. As far as I could tell from the places we passed—including a fenced yard filled with wooden chairs piled two stories high—the area produced a lot of furniture, olives, and leather goods. We searched for the Danzigers' address for forty minutes and found it in a pleasant public square, above an old-fashioned cobbler's shop in a building with a front of bright yellow tile.

Sam found a parking space for the tiny management company car—we'd decided it was better to leave hers in a long-term car park near the Lisbon airport, where tracing the plate would do no one any good. As we walked up to knock on the Danzigers' door, Martim began fussing. Such is my lack of charm for toddlers—though it might have been that Mara's wards around the building woke him up. The curling, vine-like magic wasn't identical to the protections around their house in Seattle, but it was still recognizably hers in my Grey sight.

The black door ahead of us swung open and Mara stepped out onto the landing. "Oh my! Is it past time for lunch?" she asked, looking at the baby. "Oh, there's a hungry lad, aren't you? Better come in, then. I'm so glad I thought to make extra. What's this little one's name, then?"

Sam gazed up at the tall, redheaded woman as if she'd never seen a more welcome sight. "Martim. And I'm Samantha—Sam Rebelo. This is my daughter, Soraia."

"It's a pleasure to meet you all. I'm Mara Danziger and you're welcome to stay as long as you like." Mara held out her arms and offered to take Martim off Sam's hands, which earned her a smile of a radiance fit to blind angels. Mara wiggled her fingers at the baby, letting tiny blue stars sparkle off her fingertips as she cooed what sounded like nonsense. He quieted down at once and watched her with complete fascination.

The apartment seemed to glow with soothing golden light, just as their house had, and I felt the brush of Mara's magic, as warmly reassuring as a fireside after a night in the cold. I could see the tension and paranoia dropping away from Sam as she walked inside.

Soraia also watched Mara and my friend noticed her as we straggled through the doorway.

"Hello, there, my little love," Mara said.

Wavering, Soraia murmured, "Hello, Miss Witch."

Mara laughed her whooping, infectious laugh. "My! You're a polite one. Welcome to my home, little witchling."

Soraia almost smiled. "I'm not a witch."

"Oh, but you might be. It's never wise to assume otherwise." Mara winked at her and Soraia finally smiled.

Sam didn't even seem upset by the exchange, though she did look a bit puzzled.

Mara turned her gaze on me and graced me with the same beaming grin. "And you! Harper! I feared you'd never cross my threshold again. I'm that pleased to see you!" She threw her free arm around me and pulled me into a hug. "I hope you've not been spreading yourself too thin as usual," she whispered in my ear. "You look done in."

"I'm better than I look." I backed away far enough to see her whole face, rather than just an ear. "Rough night, that's all."

"So I gathered. Oh, Ben's in the study with Brian. They'll be out in a bit." She turned her attention to Sam and Soraia. "Let's go to the kitchen. The best parties always happen there. The lads'll be along in a moment and I've got fresh flan, if you care for it. Brian's decided it's the best food in the world, so I've been making it by the busload!"

Like most boys, Brian seemed to have a well-honed radar for food, and he came scrambling into the kitchen a few minutes later with Ben in tow, chattering with glee.

"I saw one this time! I swear I did!" Brian had grown leggy and gangly like his father, his dark hair falling in his face and a sparkle of mischief in his eyes that was pure Mara. He looked older than

Soraia, but it could have been his unusual height as much as an actual point of age. "We'll catch one next time, Da!"

He saw all of us and stopped dead at the edge of the large painted table Mara had ushered us to. She was busy putting Martim into a wooden high chair and looked up at Sam to introduce them. "These beasts are my son, Brian, and my husband, Ben. You'll excuse the lack of manners—they've been off down the alleys hunting snarks, I suspect."

Brian rushed forward, ignoring his mother completely, and threw his arms around my hips to give me a hug that almost knocked me down, while he shouted, "Harper!"

"Wow," I said, giving him a half hug from my constrained position mostly above him. "I didn't think you'd recognize me, Brian."

"I would always rec'anize you, Harper. You're all glowy. I missed you!"

Mara barely turned her head to chide her offspring, "I'm sure she was after missing you, too, y'little hellion. And did you wash your hands, or will I have to dump you in the sink and scrub you like an oyster again?"

"I washed!" Brian objected, letting go of me. "Da made me."

Mara laughed and turned around, having secured the baby to her satisfaction. "Brian, say hello to the rest of our guests. This is Mrs. Rebelo and her children, Soraia and Martim. They're going to stay with us for a few days." Sam and Soraia both looked stunned. Martim just laughed and pounded on the high chair's tray.

"Hello," Brian said, nodding at Sam and Martim. Then he looked to Soraia. "Do you like flan? My mother makes the best flan in Spain."

Soraia nodded, biting her lip and Brian abandoned me to go stand closer to her and discuss important things, like food, instead of how much soap he'd saved.

Mara looked at Ben who was standing where Brian had been a few seconds earlier. "And you?" she asked. "Was this one-sided washing?"

"You can't tell from the water stains?" Ben, tall, stooped, and still looking more like an escapee from a road show production of *Yentl* than he did like an esteemed scholar of things religious, linguistic, and paranormal, was wet all down the front of his shirt and his black hair hung in damp curls around his face.

"Ah! That should have been a giveaway. You're soaked through!"

Ben looked at Sam and started to offer his hand, then thought better of it. "It's a pleasure to meet you. Please excuse my drips. Brian thought he saw a nixie, so we had to chase it. I say it was pipe leak, but I've been wrong before."

Mara scoffed. "Well then, dry off and sit down before our guests die of hunger."

Martim made a fussy gurgle as demonstration. Ben darted out of the room and returned with a towel around his shoulders, but not much drier. He looked over the kitchen full of guests and his face lit as he saw me. "Harper! You made it! Where's Quinton? Is he coming?"

I shook my head. "No, he's ill. I tied him to the bed and made him stay in it to get some sleep or he'd have been here, too."

Ben strode around the table and gave me a hug even more exuberant than his wife's or son's had been. I had to gasp for breath before he put me back down—Ben being one of the few men I know who's substantially taller than I am.

"It's so good to see you! I want to hear about every creature you've met in the past three years—any really good monsters? Didn't you have a run-in with some merfolk and *dobhr chú* a while back? I'd have loved to see them!"

"I'm sure you would, but you'd have been a lot more wet than you are now," I said, shooting a glance at Sam to see how she was taking all this.

Sam still seemed utterly confounded, her mouth slightly open and her eyes blinking. I wasn't the only one to notice.

"Oh, Ben," Mara said. "Don't be pestering the woman already. There're children starving in Spain, you know."

He looked at her and tried to appear contrite. "Are there? Are any of them black-haired nixie-chasers?"

"No!" Brian shouted back, dragging up a blue chair next to Soraia's red one. "I'm not starving. But Soraia and Martim are. C'mon, Da. We want to eat!"

Sam fell into her chair as if she were giving up all attempts at rationalizing any of the conversation so far. Ben helped Brian into the blue chair and made sure Sam and Soraia were comfortable while I helped Mara put the food on the table.

"She's managing fairly well," Mara whispered to me as she handed me a bowl.

"Who? Sam or Soraia?"

"Well, I was thinking of the little girl, but her mother does seem a bit dazed by it all."

"She's not too comfortable with the magic angle. And the kidnapping . . ."

Mara pursed her mouth and made a speculative sound. "True," she said, and went back to getting the meal on the table. I wondered what she was thinking, but I couldn't ask.

I should have realized that meals with the Danzigers wouldn't have changed except to become more noisy as Brian got older.

Mara surveyed the room from her position at the foot of the table and nodded. "Well, if we're to get any peace from nixies, we'll have to set an example ourselves. Brian?"

Brian became still and nodded. "Yes, ma'am." He fell silent and put his hands in his lap, waiting for her approval, but not fool enough to take his attention completely off the food. In a moment, everyone but Mara had followed Brian's lead—even the baby—and a calm fell over the group. I couldn't see Mara doing anything, but somehow the lull in the noise and activity made the room seem cooler and everyone in it more serene, less worried, and less stressed.

Mara sat down and looked us all over. She picked up her glass, which Ben had filled with water, and said, "May the hinges of our friendship never grow rusty." Everyone but Martim got the hint and took a sip from their own glass. Then Mara took a long, slow breath and let it back out again with a satisfied sound. "Well, then. Every-one start a dish."

We each turned our attention to the nearest dish of food and all sense of decorum and silence died.

Lunch was magnificent, the sort of huge, languorous meal Americans eat on holidays and at formal dinners, but in the Danziger household it was served without the stuffy manners and polite service. As I'd hoped, the kids got along like old friends and Soraia was ready to go investigate Brian's room as soon as they'd finished eating, but Mara insisted they stay until the adults were ready to settle into postprandial conversation.

When we finally got up from the table, Brian and Soraia took some cookies and repaired to Brian's room. Sam went to clean up Martim and tuck him under a blanket on the sofa for a nap while I helped the Danzigers clear the table.

"What have you been up to?" Ben asked while we washed dishes.

"The usual—working for ghosts and fighting monsters in between pretrials and background searches."

"I'm serious. You seem different."

"Less annoying?"

"Less annoyed."

"Well, I wouldn't know. I've never been good at analyzing myself."

"You're more calm," Mara offered.

"Me? At the moment I'm only calm because I'm tired."

"I wasn't meaning that," Mara said, putting leftovers into the
fridge. "I meant your magical state seems more settled, stronger.
You're doing very well in that respect, yes?"

"I guess I am. Not much comes completely out of the blue anymore, and I generally know what I'm doing—or I can make an educated guess. No more unintentional slipping sideways through the
Grey, less flying by the seat of my paranormal pants."

"Good. So, what's the situation with the Rebelos?"

"I don't know about the husband—I haven't met him, so his per-
sonality is a blank—but Sam's another hardhead like I used to be.
She's a doctor and she isn't as open-minded about the paranormal as
she tried to be when we met yesterday. It's been rough on her, trying
to take in so much and make the necessary mental adjustment to
what her father's done and what it's connected to. So she's going to
need help on her own end as well as needing to help her daughter.

"The biggest complication is that Soraia sees things. She talks to
ghosts and claims to see fairies, and she's guessed that Carlos is a
vampire. We had a little chat about 'being strange' and how it's not
a bad thing, but she's still confused about what she's experiencing in
paranormal terms. She's got no context or background to help her
understand this stuff in the best situation and now her situation is

far from the best. She's very tough, but I suspect this shy, calm appearance is unusual for her. What she experienced last night alone was pretty terrible and we haven't yet discovered what she may have been through in the three days she was missing. A couple of bone mages were planning to cut her up for spare parts after they let her bleed to death so they could make something Carlos hasn't figured out yet. In addition, we saw these mages imprisoning revenants last night in the same sort of boxes Sergeyev was stuck in."

Mara stopped me and asked, "So there are likely to be more willful spirits in boxes somewhere?"

"Yes," I said. "And like Sergeyev, they're probably aware of their state—dead, but imprisoned and being used like slaves and spies, moved wherever Purlis and the bone mages want them—and we don't know exactly how they mean to use them, but you know what happened with Sergeyev. The boxes on the site last night burned and the ghosts escaped—the Guardian rounded them up—but that doesn't mean there aren't more of them elsewhere. Quinton believes there are some already in place throughout Europe."

Mara and Ben both looked sickened at the thought. They'd been in at the beginning of the Sergeyev case, though we'd barely gotten acquainted by then, and knew very well what sort of nightmares it brought to adults, much less little girls. "I am afraid of what's going to happen as soon as Soraia has the luxury of slowing down," I continued, "and Sam isn't prepared to help her. That was the real reason I wanted you two to take them in. Sam's a doctor, so she understands trauma, but she doesn't have the mental preparation or any magical ability to help her daughter with the paranormal aspects of this, and if she doesn't get help . . . you know how badly that can turn out."

Mara covered her mouth in shock for a moment—a gesture I had rarely seen her make even when we'd faced things more monstrous than vampires. "Oh . . . bloody hell. She's a lovely child—poor thing. I'd have to test her—which won't be appropriate now—but I suspect she may be a witch herself. And not a hedge witch like me, but something much more unusual."

"Like what?"

"I'd rather not be saying until I'm sure."

"Is it a good thing?"

"It can be. It can also be terrible if twisted by bad teachers and evil circumstances."

"Then you're going to have to find some way to talk to her without her mother going off the deep end. Soraia knows she's what we're calling 'strange,' but she's terrified that she's going to be evil, as if it's something she can't avoid after seeing what she saw."

"I'll find a way. . . . I'm glad you brought them to us. I think there's a touch of something unusual in the baby as well. I'd like to meet their father. . . ."

"You'll have to hold off until Carlos and Quinton and I can put a stop to whatever *his* father is up to. It's not going to be safe for Sam to contact Piet—that's her husband—or go home until this situation is completely dismantled with no hope of a rebuild."

"I can see that. I only wish I'd be having a hand in serving up some just deserts to a man who'd do this to his own grandchild. The vile bastard. I'll work it out with Sam, then, shall I?"

"I think you should."

I told them the rest of the background as we finished up and then went into the more recent points once we were all seated in what Mara laughingly called "El Salón," since the main part of the apartment was mostly one large room broken up by the placement of furniture to indicate what each area was used for. Sam was less comfortable than ever with the details Ben and Mara dragged out of me.

"So these Kostní Mágové are another type of necromancer?" Mara asked.

"I'd say they're more like a subclass. They don't seem to have any affinity for death in general, only for bones. Carlos said it's related to a more mainstream religious thing taken to a bizarre extreme. It's pretty odd."

"It's rather medieval," Ben put in. "The cult of bones goes back a long way in the Catholic Church, and it's still active in pockets throughout the Christian world. A lot of the belief turns on the principle that we are only shadows walking toward death and our heavenly reward. Our earthly lives are toil and suffering, so we shouldn't be overly proud, materialistic, or live an ungodly life regardless of our social station, because we're all going to be food for worms eventually. It was very common up through the plagues and later abominations like the Inquisition—the mortification of the flesh is a great excuse for all sorts of torments in the name of God. It's one of the reasons you find these medieval ossuaries all over Europe."

"Ossuaries. Those are collections of bones, right?" I asked, thinking of the unholy church in which we'd found Soraia.

"Yeah, but it's more than that. They're often the bones of the religious community that served the local church—the godly—and of the long-dead parishioners, buried in consecrated ground until the bones were stripped of all flesh. Then the bones are gathered into a chapel or a catacomb to make more room in the graveyard and to remind the people that in life they are in the presence and shadow of death. It's where the danse macabre tradition comes from. In the case of ossuaries, the bones aren't just gathered. They're arranged or piled with great care, not so often as individual people and whole skeletons, but as parts—piles of femurs or skulls in one room, ribs in another . . . that sort of thing. Or they use the bones themselves to decorate the chapel they rest in—that's fairly rare, but there are some spectacular examples of it around. The ossuaries of Rome, Milan, and Paris are famous, and there's a well-known chapel in Évora, and a really amazing display in Sedlec, outside Prague. Oh, and one in Czermna, Poland, I really want to see. The chapel is built—walls, ceiling, and floors—from the bones of victims of plagues and wars that have ravaged the area for generations. The interesting thing about that one is that it was built recently—relatively speaking—in the late eighteenth and into the early nineteenth centuries by a single priest. Modern ossuaries are so rare!"

Mara fixed her husband with a quelling look. "Ben, we're not in the lecture hall today."

"But it's fascinating and I'd think that magic users who channel their powers through bones would be attracted to such places. Have any of the problems been associated with ossuaries?"

"Not that I know of—not known ossuaries at least," I replied. "I'll have to check into it when I get back." I looked at my watch. It was past three o'clock and I wasn't sure how it had gotten so late. "And I need to get back before much later or I won't get enough done before Carlos wants my attention."

Sam was looking appalled, her eyes wide as she cuddled Martim on her lap. The boy wriggled until she reluctantly let him go to toddle around the room. "What is it he was planning?" Sam asked.

"I wish I knew," I said. "He didn't tell me last night because he wanted to get to work as quickly as possible."

"No. Not . . . your friend. I mean my father. Why would he do this?"

"I don't know. He has some plan about destabilizing Europe, though how this fits, is beyond me."

"His own granddaughter . . ." The horror was starting to hit her.

"He gave her to those people. . . . They cut her arm. What were they doing to her?"

"What did she tell you?"

Sam was pale and her voice was a little shaky. "It didn't make sense. She's . . . She's always been such a happy girl and now she's obsessed with death and skeletons and ghosts—she talked all night in her sleep, tossing around and crying. . . ."

"What did she tell you?" I repeated, not wanting to plant any false ideas by speaking of what I knew Soraia had seen.

"She said . . . She said there were dead people—corpses. She said they walked around. She said the bad people—that's what she called them—bad people. She said they boiled them. . . ." Sam's voice broke. "She said they took the bones out of a boy who was still alive! Oh my God, oh my God . . ." She began crying, her voice coming in hiccuping gulps. "It can't be true! Oh God . . ."

Martim sat down hard on the floor and started screaming, his hysteria matching his mother's. Sam made no move to go to him but stared into empty space, shaking. Ben got up to comfort Martim. Mara and I leaned forward to help Sam, but Sam shook us off with a sharp cry and turned aside, starting to rock and fold in on herself.

"I didn't take care of her! I didn't protect her! I let that bastard come near her and—and—and he took her and it's my fault! He gave her to those people! Oh my God, oh my God . . . Soraia!"

As she screamed for her daughter, both the baby and Soraia—off in Brian's room—screamed, too.

Brian ran out and skidded to a stop, his eyes wide. "She's hurt! I think—"

Behind him came Soraia, screaming, eyes wide as she ran toward her mother. She threw herself at Sam, wrapping her arms around her, screeching in spasms of distress, *Mamãe! Mamãe!*

Mara was off the couch in an instant, kneeling in front of Sam. She shot Brian a look over her shoulder. "It's not you, Brian, love. Go back to your room. Ben, bring me the baby."

Brian began to retreat, but he only went as far as the hall to the bedrooms, standing in the shadow to watch, quivering, wide-eyed. Ben strode across the floor with Martim clutched to his chest and bent down next to his wife. The chorus of screams rose in volume. Mara scooped Martim from her husband's arms and held him against Sam's rocking body, until the baby had wrapped his arms around her, too. But although the character of their screaming changed, it didn't stop.

"Ben," Mara said without raising her head, "I need a burdock root, anise, and a sprig of rosemary. Harper, I need you, too. And Brian, if you're not going to leave the room, be useful and get the damned salt bowl off my worktable. And a match. Now!"

Ben and Brian ran as I stood next to Mara.

"What should I do?" I asked.

"There's a knot that needs unpicking. Sam's guilt is affecting Soraia and things are becoming a tangle. The girl thinks she's to blame. The mother thinks the same of herself. The poor baby's in the middle and just adding to the feedback. I need you to get hold of the loop between Soraia and Sam, find the knot, and pick it loose when I say so."

Ben and Brian came pounding back into the salon, handing over their objects as quickly as Mara would take them. Mara set the copper bowl of salt on the floor in front of Sam and lit the dry, wizened burdock root on fire, dropping the vile, smoking thing into the salt dish.

"Harper, time for you," she said, and I dropped into the Grey, letting the icy mist swallow me as Mara began twining the rosemary and anise together in her fingers and whispering to the herbs as she did.

In the silvery world I could see the anxious orange sparks around Ben and Brian while Mara remained a calm gold and green, her whispers coiling into the burdock smoke and wafting toward the tangled, knotted ball of red and olive green that was Sam and her children. Their screaming shook the world. I didn't have time to examine much as boiling mist swirled around them, threatening to choke me in a sea of half-formed faces. Random lightning struck around me, growing worse with every moment.

I pushed my hand into the edge of the intertwined auras, sliding along the burning strands until I hit a bump, a knot. I started to pick at it with my fingertips and wished I had the pheasant feather an old Salish woman had given me to help ease the knot apart. Usually I had little trouble with energy strands these days, but the knot of this hysteria was writhing and tying itself tighter with every shriek. I pushed my arm deep into the mess, working blindly, by feel alone. "Come on . . ." I muttered. "Come on, Soraia, let go." But when I thought she wasn't going to give me any slack, the knot moved. I shoved my fingers into the slightly open loop and wedged it wider, grabbing the strand that ran through the open bend and pulling it back toward me.

For a moment, the boiling Grey mist pressed itself into a shape with wide eyes under a mop of curls and I was sure I was looking into Soraia's face, somehow.

"Let go," I said, still tugging on the burning strand of energy in my hand. "Please."

The mist sank down and the knot flowed open with the cool slither of silk, falling away.

I pushed back up to the normal world, into panting silence.

The burning burdock root still stank and Mara had torn the rose-mary and anise into shreds, but the little family on the couch was no longer screaming. Their postures had softened, slumped, so the chil-dren were merely leaning on their mother, one on each side, while Sam sat with her face in her hands, trying to catch her breath. Ben and Brian had both retreated a few steps and Ben was holding his son as the boy hugged him, shivering. Soraia lifted her head and stared at me.

"I'm sorry," she whispered.

"For what?" I asked.

"I hurt Mamãe."

Before I could say it, Sam had put one arm around her daughter and said, "No, you didn't. I'm so sorry, *anjinho*. I'm sorry I let those horrible things happen to you."

"You didn't . . . hurt me, Mamãe."

"But I let your grandfather take you away."

Soraia just shook her head, adamant. "No."

Sam cuddled both of her children closer. She put her head down against Soraia's hair, crying softly now.

Mara picked up her bowl and got to her feet. She backed away from the sofa and motioned to me to follow her to the kitchen. Ben and Brian were a few steps behind us.

"They'll be all right," Mara whispered as she put the salt bowl on the drain board. "At least in time. There are some awful things in that poor little girl's head and her mother's almost as haunted."

"Are you sure they'll be OK?" I asked.

"It may be a long road, but yes. Eventually." She smiled at me, a tired, troubled smile. "Well done, Harper."

"I didn't do much," I said.

"Oh no. I'm the one who didn't do much—I just calmed them

down and helped banish their negative energy long enough for you to do the work. Really, it's sometimes little things that make a difference." She looked me over and gave me a hug. "You should probably be going soon if you're to reach Lisbon before dark. Not that I'm eager to get rid of you . . ."

Ben and Brian chimed in on that note but Mara was right—I needed to go, though I wasn't comfortable with it. I looked over toward the couch, but Sam and the kids were still huddled together and the last thing I wanted to do was disturb them.

I said some quiet good-byes to the Danzigers, picked up my things, and headed for the door.

On the sofa, Soraia raised her head, whispered into her mother's ear, and slipped out of her grasp to run to me. She stopped a step in front of me, looking up at my face, anxious.

I crouched down to make it easier.

"I saw you," she said.

I smiled a little. "Thought so. Are you going to be all right if I go?"

"Why are you going?"

"Because I have to help your uncle and Senhor Carlos stop the people who hurt you from hurting other people."

She nodded. "All right. Are you going to hurt them back?"

"It's tempting. Really tempting, but my job is to make things better, not worse. Not even if they deserve it."

She nodded, looking grave, and hugged me, saying nothing more.

SEVENTEEN

Traffic had not improved on the way back and since I hadn't driven the route the first time, I got lost and came toward the city on a different highway. At the outskirts of Lisbon, I had to wait in slow traffic near the air base in Montijo. A modest group of protesters with signs I couldn't read blocked the road and an equally modest contingent of police was trying to move them out of it. Both groups seemed peaceful enough, but as the demonstrators were pushed away from the road, some of them began shoving back, shouting and hitting at the police with their signs for no reason I could make out. Singly, the cops lost their tempers and their collective, steady push became curt, rough, and finally angry. A dark shape, barely visible in the westering sun, circled over the seething lines of demonstrators and cops, and even though it was difficult to see, everyone ducked as it moved. Someone yelled and, as the dark thing swept away into the sky, the peaceful protest turned into knots of pointless violence scattered along the roadside. I stared at it, rolling down the window and cocking my head to look into the Grey. Another shape moved around the edges of the infant riot, seeming to nip at the cops and protesters like a dog herding sheep. It was made of red energy and silver mist, and where it walked, the violence escalated. This had to be the work of Purlis's Ghost Division and there was nothing I could do. I closed the window in haste and found a path through the traffic.

The conflict seemed to spread outward like crystal growth and I had to detour several times to get onto the bridge that would deliver me into Lisbon proper. Paranoid that something might have seen me, I took a circuitous route, checking frequently for any kind of paranormal tail. I never saw one, but I took the precaution anyhow and arrived at the house in Alfama after sunset.

Nothing had changed inside since I'd left and that bothered me more than it might under other circumstances. Trying not to imagine the worst, I raced up the stairs to our suite and burst through the door to the sitting room.

No Quinton at the desk. I ran through to the bedroom.

He was sitting cross-legged on the bed with his laptop open in front of him and a pair of long cables running off across the floor. I breathed heavily with relief. He looked up, craning his neck to see me better.

"Hi. Everything OK? Sam and the kids made it all right?"

"Yeah. We made it to the Danzigers' all right, but it's going to be a rough road for Sam and the kids. They'll be OK, though. What about you?"

"I'm fine. I slept like the dead."

I let that go. "No signs of anything unpleasant in the streets?"

"Uh . . . not up here. There've been a few incidents around town today, though. Some disturbance happened at the Banco do Portugal headquarters that the news is vague about and some kind of protest down at Montijo Air Base went wonky."

"I know—I was there. And so was your father's band of invisible agitators."

He frowned a little. "Are you sure?"

"Yes. There was something—a ghost of some kind I think—working the edge of the crowd, making them angry and volatile, and something I could barely see had descended on the protesters and police from the sky, and they all acted like they'd been strafed. After that, it went to hell."

"Damn it. That sounds like the same sort of thing I saw in Paris. Damn it! I keep missing him," Quinton snapped, and started to get up.

"Nothing you can do right now," I said, waving him down. "Tell me what else you found—that may be more important to us than getting a closer look at the wreckage your father's group is responsible for."

He frowned. "All right . . . I've been working on your bones-in-the-news question."

"I had an idea on that—or rather, Ben did. Anything about ossuaries? Or bone chapels?"

"Yeah. They weren't connected by the press or police yet, but there have been a series of vandalizations of small ossuaries here in Portugal—did you know that Portugal has the largest number of extant ossuaries of any country in Europe?"

"No. What does that mean?"

"It means that while there may be bigger, better-known piles of bones in places like Italy and France, there are more of them total and per square mile in Portugal. And with a comparatively small population, that's a lot of dead bones for every live one running around. It seems to me that would make this country very attractive to bone mages—which could be why Dad is concentrating here at the moment."

"I agree," I replied in haste. I still felt wound up from my trip to the house while Quinton seemed to vacillate between anger and a strangely distant curiosity. "What happened with these small ossuaries?"

"Well, over the past few months, there are four ossuaries along the coast in the Algarve that have been vandalized. Algarve is a coastal vacation area that's very popular with European travelers. Anyhow, bones have been removed, causing the ossuaries to shift or fall in some cases. In another, it was basically a shrine in a wall and someone took the arm off the crucifix, which was pretty obvious. But no one's been saying the crimes are connected. So far, all the reports read like it's just a local annoyance and the press is blaming the tourists, but locals are disturbed by it. The ossuaries are old and small, but sacred, and with the other problems in Portugal, it seems like a bad sign."

"Any idea how many bones have been taken altogether?"

He shook his head. "No. Something's always missing, but no one is really sure what, except in the case of the crucifix."

He put the laptop aside and unfolded himself from the bed. He stretched, his spine protesting with a series of pops and snaps and his joints joining in the complaint. He shook himself out and closed the distance between us to put his arms around my waist and kiss me. When I didn't respond in kind, he gave me a curious look. "Are you all right?"

"I could ask you the same."

"Why?"

"You just . . . don't seem like yourself."

He shook his head as if dismissing my concern. "Probably lingering effects of whatever that was last night. You're a little prickly yourself."

I stepped back from him. "I'm sorry. I'm obsessing a bit about these bones and this business with the Ghost Division suddenly popping up. . . . Carlos said he thought he could learn something about what the mages are up to tonight, but I want to give him all of this information before he goes out and does whatever he had in mind."

"Oh. Well, I think it's too late. He's not here."

"It's not that late yet. The sun just went down."

"About forty minutes ago. I almost didn't hear him leave, but the door up to the tower stairs makes a noise when it passes over the floor. It sounds like someone trying to sweep the tiles with a very stiff broom. I looked out and saw him going down the stairs right after the sun went down."

I scowled. "He'd have had to sleep in the tower all night. Not very safe."

"Safe enough, apparently."

"I wish I knew what he's up to."

Quinton pulled me a little closer in a jostling manner and said, "Hey, a guy could get jealous when all you want to talk about is bones and some other man."

"Carlos isn't a man. He's a vampire."

"That is not my point, Harper."

I stopped glaring into the wall and turned my attention back to Quinton. His aura was still streaked with green, but at least it was more of an apple color than olive. He frowned at me.

"You're not joking," I said. "You're jealous of Carlos."

"I wouldn't call it jealousy. . . . It's more like . . . preoccupation."

"There is no point in it. I love you. I spent most of this past year without you because you had other things you needed to pursue. But there's no one else I want to be with. Not for the moment, or in the situation, or if I can't do better. No one at all. Ever. And you know it. You know it right here," I added, touching the bright pink line of energy that always pointed me to him, no matter where he was, no matter how far away.

He winced as I touched it and his energy corona flushed with a flurry of little sparks in green, black, white, and, finally, pink, like a Roman candle. "Ouch."

I frowned. "That shouldn't hurt."

He blinked and shivered. "It doesn't, exactly. It's more like the sensation after you pull out a sliver."

I thought of Amélia's ghost floating over him as he slept and I felt furious. "Oh, I'm going to kill that interfering little specter twice over."

"Who?"

"Amélia—Carlos's dead wife." I raised my head and looked toward the ceiling, then around the room, just in case I could spot her, but she wasn't in evidence. "I hope you're eavesdropping, Amélia, because I don't want this to be an unfair fight. I'm going to turn you into a pile of sparks and ghost dust and send you back to the ethereal nothingness if I catch you playing with his mind again. So keep your incorporate hands off!"

"Is there something going on that I should know about?" Quinton asked.

"Yet another meddling ghost getting up to nothing good, I'm sure, though why, I don't know."

"That's going around."

"Oh?"

"Well, aside from this interesting half a conversation, the vandalized ossuaries, and sudden surges of violence that seem to be my dad's work, this morning someone broke into the tomb of King Sebastian."

"Who is that and how is it relevant to our problem with the bone mages?"

"You remember I said something about there being people in Portugal who believe in the 'Sleeping King'—O Desejado—who will return to save the country in its darkest hour? A sort of Arthur figure with a cult built around him?"

"Yeah, a little."

"That king was Dom Sebastião. He was a bit of a mess. His mother took off soon after he was born so she could be regent of Spain for the remaining twenty years of her life, so he was raised by his grandmother, Catherine of Austria—who was a bit of a hard-ass. He became king at the age of three in 1557. He was Jesuit educated and did a lot of important stuff, like establishing standard measures, reforming civilian and military law, creating medical and science scholarships, abolishing slavery of Brazilian natives, and mandating a school for navigators that taught them math and cosmology. Just that alone increased the number of ships that made it home from their voyages—and that's a big deal for a seafaring nation. Portugal was an economic powerhouse in the Renaissance largely because of Sebastian. But he was kind of a misogynistic jerk—he never got married, and he was more interested in flouncing off to fight crusades against the Moors in north Africa than having kids or watching out for things back home.

"Anyhow, he was killed at the battle of Alcácer Quibir in 1578, but his body was never found, and he left no direct heir. It was kind of a boondoggle, and an expensive one as well, because Sebastian had borrowed money to do it. Phillip the Second of Spain became king of Portugal, and in 1582 some human remains that he claimed were Sebastian's were entombed here in Lisbon at the Jerónimos Monastery. But most people were sure the body wasn't actually his and that led to the idea that Sebastian was still out there somewhere, waiting for the chance to come back and save Portugal. Which he never did. That's the 'Sleeping King' legend. But the tomb is still an important icon of its own and someone—or several someones—broke into it very early this morning."

"What did they take?" I asked.

"No one knows if anything was taken at all. The body and contents weren't very well documented and it's all dust now, anyhow. But I'd be willing to bet—given the way these things work—that the dust of a legend's bones might be as useful to some people as the bones themselves."

"So we put a kink in their plans, but not as much as we thought." But something was nagging me even as I dismissed the case as trivial.

"Assuming that the break-in was perpetrated by our unfriendly neighborhood bone-twiddlers."

"Not too likely to be the work of an unaffiliated group—what are the odds?" I asked.

"Slim, I agree. So . . . is that the sort of thing Carlos was after? Because there were a few other stories, but they were older and farther afield. Oh, except for one thing that's not in Carlos's search, but it kind of gave me the creeps, so I bookmarked it for you."

He turned the screen in my direction, showing a very short news piece about a man found dead in the quake-damaged area where we'd seen what might have been a drache the day before. "It sounds like the pickpocket you chased down. . . . I'm sorry."

I stared at the story with its scanty details and bad sketch, asking for information about the deceased—a petty criminal who'd died of a heroin overdose.

"Damn it. I feel like I'm responsible. If I hadn't given him the money . . ." I said.

"He'd have found it another place. You're not responsible for his choices."

"No, but . . . I shouldn't have. How is it connected . . . ?"

"Maybe it's not. Not every crime, no matter how appalling, is my father's fault."

"No, but there's something . . ." I muttered, thinking and going over it again. . . . There'd been two priests. . . . No. There'd been three. "Hang on," I said as my mental pieces fell into place. "The priest this guy robbed was walking with a man in a black suit and clerical collar. They met another man in the same sort of outfit— black suit and clerical collar. An older man. I would swear that it was the same man who was in the middle of the circle last night— Griffin's master. I didn't see him well, but the general description and the aura were the same. Even if it *wasn't* the same man, it was one of the bone mages—they have a fairly distinctive aura. We were that close to them!"

"How does that make a positive connection to the robbery at Jerónimos?"

"I'm not sure, except that it has to have been them—who else would want to break in to a tomb and disturb the dust of a fake king? But . . . it's a monastery, isn't it?"

Quinton was puzzled. "It's mostly a museum now—but there is a secularized church and members of the old royal family were buried there."

"Carlos said a lot of the bone mages come from the religious community. They wouldn't be much noticed coming and going from a church of any kind and in this case, there would have been people in and out all day."

Quinton took back the laptop and looked at the report again.

"Witnesses around the area said they saw a priest near the building about the time the vandalism must have happened, but . . . there are a lot of those in Lisbon."

"Black suit, clerical collar, old man . . ." I listed.

"Sounds right."

"No way to prove it, but it has to be the same guy—or another bone mage."

"I didn't think they were that common. It's hard to maintain a low profile when you've got a large group."

"But it's not a large group. It's the same thing your dad is doing: He breaks his men up into smaller units and plants them in strategic places. The fact that they have—or had—a bone church here in Lisbon must be significant, but it doesn't mean they're high profile."

"Small, discreet units, spread over Europe?"

"I'm thinking they're modeled on religious organizations instead of military ones. It's more likely there's a handful of chapter houses near significant ossuaries and a moderate number of mages who move around." I was speculating, but it fit and I spoke as the ideas formed. "Your father has some kind of deal with them—that's how he got the shrine he brought to Seattle and how he's been able to continue advancing the Ghost Division after you destroyed his lab. They know how to make those ghost boxes and how to pack a spell into something that allows a mage to use a dissimilar magic—that would be how Griffin produced a Night Dragon when that's not within her normal powers as a bone mage, according to Carlos. But it's likely that the Kostní Mágové's *physical* resources are thin. Their wealth is in knowledge that your dad wants. But they want something, too. Last year, Carlos implied that they didn't care about your dad's goals, but had plans of their own and would use the Ghost

Division and your father's obsession to their own ends. What if this . . . thing they're making is part of their price for helping your dad?"

"That would imply it's at least part of their own long-term goal."

"And therefore worth any price."

"That doesn't explain why Dad would give them Soraia."

"What if they have persuaded him that this thing is useful for his goals as well? Necessary, even? Carlos said . . . What was it . . . ? Something about scorched earth . . ."

Quinton looked grim. "I remember what he said. 'They will starve and burn Europe to scorched earth.' They lost Limos, so the starving part's out, but there's more than one way to start a fire."

"All these little actions . . . little horrors—riots, bombings, disease, uprisings—they're the fire."

"But if what these guys are building can make it burn faster or hotter, they're only a spark."

"That's got to be what Carlos was after. Can you summarize all these incidents for him? Even the ones you think aren't as likely to be connected?"

"Yes. I'll have to start on it right now—it's a lot of material if I go back over the past eight months."

"I think you can just stick with what's happened since you traced your father to Portugal."

"I hope this helps Carlos figure out what Dad and his cronies are up to."

"And I hope he shows up soon so we can discuss this business. This just gets worse."

"It does look pretty bad. But you've had dire cases before."

"They were mostly boring until I got killed."

"The first time."

"Actually, it was the second time. Didn't I mention drowning when I was a teenager?"

Quinton was appalled. "I think I'd remember that conversation and I don't."

I blushed with shame. "I'm sorry. I should have said something before now. I think I'm up to death three or four, depending on how you count them."

Quinton swore. "How many times can you expect to bounce back?"

"I'm not sure, but I think it's not many—if at all."

He pulled me into a too-tight embrace. "No more dying, OK?"

"I can't promise that if you keep squeezing me like a boa."

He winced and loosened his grip only enough to keep from suffocating me. "I'm sorry. I know you can't make that promise, but . . . just don't die for a long time. I want to be an old, grizzled curmudgeon with you."

"So, you've been practicing?" I asked with a grin I didn't feel, trying to lift the moment out of the deadly track it was heading into.

"I am not a curmudgeon. I'm socially maladroit."

"You are not maladroit at anything," I said.

"Oh, you flatterer, you."

"I'm only trying to get you into bed."

"Then why are we still standing up?" Quinton made a bad imitation of an evil laugh and dragged me backward onto the bed he'd only just left. Somehow, neither of us landed on the laptop.

"You know, this is going to be really embarrassing if Carlos comes in," Quinton observed.

"That won't happen," I said.

"How can you be sure?"

"If you were more than three hundred years old, would you really want to watch *us* tumbling around like two squirrels in a knapsack? Besides, I'd kill him."

"You would never kill a friend."

"OK, no. But I might threaten him with sunlamps."

Quinton laughed, which was the most perfect sound I'd heard in eight months. We did our best squirrel impression and unmade the bed in spectacular fashion until I fell asleep, snuggled into the crook of his arm.

I was so tired that I didn't notice him get up and leave the room a little before ten o'clock. I was startled to wake in an empty bed to the sound of a woman sobbing, the room lit only by the dim glow of the laptop screensaver.

Socorro, ajude-me! Help me! Help me!

It is a concept so universal that the words needed no translation, carried as they were on the throbbing strains of panic. I sat up, looking for the speaker, but the words were in my mind, not in the air, and it took a moment to recognize that the damsel in distress was Amélia.

"What? What do you want now?" I could barely see her, so faint was her manifestation. Even sinking toward the Grey, she remained as transparent as mist. She was in full panic, rushing from side to side in the room, whipping up an uncanny wind by her passage.

Resgata-lo! Carlos precisa de sua ajuda. Ajuda-lo, eu lhe imploro! She spoke so fast, I couldn't follow the exact words, only that Carlos needed help—a notion that seemed completely ridiculous at first.

But he had needed my help in the past, more than once. As powerful as he was, Carlos was not invincible and with enemies from his past—not to mention the night before—still around and angry, it was possible that even he could be in danger.

I scrambled out of bed and yanked on clothes, clumsy with the dress and flat shoes so unfamiliar compared to my trusty jeans and boots. "Where is he? What's wrong?" I demanded, wishing I could grab her and make her stop her paranormal pacing. I tried to catch her, but she passed through my hands, even in the Grey, as if she weren't there.

But she wasn't. I was in the presence of the impossible: the crisis apparition of a ghost—a woman long dead.

"Amélia!" I shouted at her, exerting my will to force her to pay attention to me, even at a great distance. It made my body ache as if I'd been crushed in a vise. "Amélia, listen to me. Where is he? Where is Carlos?"

Carmo.

"What is that?"

But she was too upset to answer in a way that helped me. I grabbed Quinton's laptop off the floor and opened a search window, typing in the word as fast as I could and hoping I'd spelled it right.

The Carmo Convent was one of the structures that had remained in ruins after the quake—the broken vaults of the soaring medieval church I'd seen from Rossio. Directions on the map showed the fastest route was to head for Rossio and then go past it, westbound, to the Santa Justa Lift—whatever that was. It was now ten o'clock and the lift closed at eleven. I'd have to run.

EIGHTEEN

I ran into Quinton walking up the stairs with a tray of food as I went leaping down. The tray toppled, spilling food everywhere.

"I'm sorry!" I called as I ran past. "Carlos is in trouble. I have to find him."

Quinton turned and followed me. "I'll come with you."

"No. Stay here in case I miss him or something else goes wrong. I'll call the house phone if I need help. Don't leave until I do!"

I rocketed down the stairs, sounding like a troop of cavalry on the move. Although I'd spent a large part of the day in a car, it was better than the coffin. My legs didn't protest my movement as they had before, though my lungs, working overtime from anxiety, were less easygoing. Since I'd done most of the route in the daylight only the morning before, I had no trouble most of the way and turned left onto the Rua de Santa Justa one long block before Praça da Figueira. The blocks were narrower east to west, but there were still seven to go and ahead was the improbable sight of a slender, illuminated, Neo-Gothic tower rising into the air out of the middle of the road.

The city was still warm, though cooler in the night breeze off the river, and there were people strolling the streets of the Baixa after dinner, or just going out for a late evening's entertainment. A few heated arguments colored the air as I passed bars and late-night cafés. I heard the words *"dragão,"* "Sebastião," "Montijo," and "O Desejado," but the words, while familiar, didn't stop me. Even the debaters paused and stared as I ran past, panting, and skittered up to the doors of the tower only fifteen minutes after leaving the house below the castle.

It was the lift, Elevador de Santa Justa, not just some mad tower out of an Edwardian science fiction story. White-painted ironwork and cement pretending to be Gothic traceries rose seven stories from the steps of black-and-white tile, connecting to an elevated walkway that stretched toward the hill where the dark bulk of the Carmo Convent loomed, casting a Grey pall cold enough to make me shiver. I had no idea what had prompted the people of Lisbon to erect an elevator in the middle of a street, but the steep rise behind it made the hills of Alfama insignificant and I thanked the lunatic impulse that had put it here.

The operator at one of the two doors raised his eyebrows at me and asked for a ticket. Out of breath, I tried to explain why I didn't have one and how badly I needed to get up to the top. He sighed and pointed at a ticket-vending machine, much like the ones we'd used in the metro.

I bought a ticket and was just able to squeeze into the next lift. I barely had a chance to notice the well-rubbed woodwork and brass fittings of the car's interior as it rose to the top of the tower. I was thankful to be so close to the doors when they opened that I could bolt from the crowd that had ridden up with me and run down the metal walkway decorated with the lacy shadows of delicate ironwork railings and chain-link safety mesh.

The walkway led directly toward the ruins of the Gothic church. I ran forward, over a steel bridge and under an age-stained flying buttress, into an alley lined on one side in the standing stones of the ruins, and on the other with a plastered wall of lipstick red. In my hurry, I could see no breaks, no doors, so I kept on down the narrow, tiled alley, just ahead of the rest of the passengers from the lift as I slowed in the nauseating chill of the church's endless memory of wrack and ruin.

I stepped out from an iron gateway into the lighted square ahead. Surrounded with fern-leafed jacaranda trees and filled with the memory of soldiers carrying rifles with red carnations protruding from the barrels, the square lay before me, heavy in icy Grey mist. In my eyes, the shadow of the convent ruins ran across the tiled square like a spreading black pool of blood. The restored parts of the building beside what was now a museum had shed much of their grim memory in constant use, but the wreck remained, more virulent now for some fresh horror that leaked out from behind the bright red doors and empty windows.

The doors were locked. The museum had closed at six, well before sunset, yet I knew Carlos was somewhere on the other side. The charming square on my side of the building was far too busy for me to call out for him without drawing unwanted attention to myself. But Amélia was here, more visible and present than she had been at the house. She stood at the corner of the building beside the alley I'd passed through and beckoned me closer.

I walked back to her, my legs feeling rubbery from exertion and alarm.

"How do I reach him?"

She pointed down the alley and I, shivering with a sudden sweat, walked back into the shadow of the ruins. At the point where the metal walkway diverged to swing out around the building as the ground dropped away on the steep side of the hill facing the Santa Justa Lift, a smaller red door huddled under a pointed Gothic arch. It was almost twelve feet below the walkway and I saw no way to get to it but to jump, which I didn't feel very good about. But if the door was there, there must once have been a way to get to it. If I could find the right temporacline, I should be able to walk through the door in the past to emerge inside the ruined church in the present. I slipped into the Grey and started searching for the right slice of frozen time.

In the silver-film mist of the Grey, the earthquake's shuddering, rumbling discord dominated everything and though I ran my hands over the razor edge of temporaclines, the only one I could lay hold of was the worst—All Saints' Day of 1755. Shivering with dread, I slipped into the glassy memory of the past.

I plummeted down and hit the ground in front of the door with a jarring impact. I'd always wondered what would happen if I moved from one time to another at a different physical level, and I now knew that the ground and buildings remained as solid in the memory of time as they were in normal life. I crumpled and rolled as the earthquake shook the ground, heaving chunks of the paving up as other sections sank. Colored glass from the windows and white stone from the walls and flying buttresses showered from the height of the buckling building as men in brown monastic robes and white mantles ran from it, carrying whatever holy objects they could rescue. Most of them didn't acknowledge me, but passed around or through me—here, I was the ghost. One paused to stare at my sudden appearance. I stood up and began to fight the tide of monks and occasional nuns who rushed out from the church like water down a sluice. The one man seemed on the point of stopping me, but he had no free hand, busy as he was, clutching a huge, jeweled book to his chest.

I shook my head as I passed him, bouncing off the other monks like a ball as I struggled into the failing building. The doorway led into a staircase that ran steeply up to the main floor and into a small room that finally led into the side aisle of the great, falling church building.

The roof along the central beam of the main aisle began crumbling, plaster and stone tumbling into the nave ahead of me. A carved grotesque plunged from high on the wall to the ground, striking a monk down and shattering the floor tiles where it hit, throwing up a spray of blood and a cloud of sharp stone shards. I felt their sting as several nicked me. I dodged to the side, cowering against the sturdy curtain walls that had withstood the earth's rage, and waited for the shaking to stop.

It seemed forever before the earth subsided, but not knowing how long I had until the aftershocks would hit, I ran from cover and toward the highest ground I could find, willing to risk another tumble rather than be embedded in the floor when I emerged. I nearly tripped over the dead monk crushed by the carving, his blood sinking into the ground where the tiles had been cracked open like the thinnest sheets of ice. Layers of Grey fog lay across the point where the monk had fallen, turning the ground into a carpet of broken silver, and I stumbled to my knees, falling hard against the small chapel doorway from which the monk had come, the niche above it now hollow. I picked myself up and staggered over the broken floor, rushing from column to column for safety as the ceiling continued crumbling down.

I struggled up to the altar, to the highest point I could think of, and threw myself out of the temporacline, hoping I was high enough for safety.

I fell again, but not quite so far, and hit the ground with a little less force, rolling into a long, narrow patch of grass that now grew between the main columns, dividing the ruins into the nave and side aisle with strips of tended green. The nave and aisles were paved in the ubiquitous white stone tiles. The roof gone, there was only the night sky above, with a crescent moon and stars shining down through the skeletal fingers of the side arches. The devastated church appeared empty but for me and the dark shapes of archeological displays along the side aisles.

I shook from the fading adrenaline spike as I picked myself up and dusted off my limbs. My hands came away sticky with blood from scrapes and nicks. I stumbled onto the firmer paving stones and began searching for Carlos among the memorials and relics arrayed around the edges of the vaultless church. I blundered into tombs and statues and tripped over the iron uprights of displays, biting back my curses with every new injury and disappointment in discovering another shape that wasn't Carlos.

I found him in a niche that must once have been a small chapel. At first he was only a dark shape in the shadow of the wall, the light picking out only a small gleam of white within the blackness. I shuffled toward it, picking my way through a collection of heavy stone objects until I could see that the white telltale was a reflection of moonlight off the surface of his open, staring eyes.

Utter stillness and silence are no great feat for a vampire, but the feeling of the space as I drew near was colder than all the surrounding silver mist and stone of the Grey. A familiar tangled web of energy lay over the place like a shroud as white as bone. Carlos did not move or make a sound. A glimmer of bright metal shone at the side of his throat. He appeared to have been crushed and thrown down as easily as a rag doll, as Griffin had nearly done to Quinton.

The spell was better constructed this time, and I couldn't draw closer to Carlos with the mesh of energy around him, so I began tearing at it and shoving it aside, interposing my limbs and shoulders where I had made a hole. Then I forced my way in until I could use my whole body to heave the mass, which sizzled against me with a stinging pain, making my body quake and my sight fade toward blackness shot with points of glittering, colored light.

When I had pushed aside enough of the veiling magic to kneel down in the clear beside Carlos, he didn't respond to my presence, but seemed to collapse a bit as if the energetic web that had covered him had also held him in shape and he was now decaying before my eyes. A black, insubstantial haze rose off him through the glimmering fog of the Grey, faltering and thinning into smoke that spiraled up toward the sharp sickle of the moon.

"Blaine. . . ." It wasn't his voice, exactly, but more like the echo of it in my head.

The vaporous black pall drew together for a moment, taking a vague resemblance to Carlos, before it drifted apart and began, again, to flow away in streamers of darkness. I felt the sharp pang in my chest that told me he was dying—if you can say that about the undead.

It did not occur to me that without him, any chance of stopping Purlis was remote at best, nor did I think for an instant of Amélia's bizarre behavior or of all the incidents when Carlos had brought death, madness, or pain. I didn't pause to consider all the times he'd caused me grief. I could have stood back and let him pass away into the restless mist of the Grey world, but I threw myself at the dissolving shreds of night-black soul and tried to capture them, force them back into the strangely broken shell they were escaping. But they slid away, eluding my grasp.

I touched the metallic gleam at his neck and found a dagger hilt, the blade driven through this throat from side to side. Whoever had taken him down had known what they were up against and stopped him from speaking any sort of spell. The dagger radiated a dread, black aura—a dark artifact—and the touch of it against my skin felt like ice that was cold enough to burn. I yanked it from his neck and threw it down on the ground. It clattered on the marble and slid away into the grass, but still Carlos didn't move.

I grabbed his arm and felt no shock of nausea, pain, and horror as I usually did, only a low, disturbing static that made the hairs on my arms stand on end. I shook him, as if he were only asleep and my desperation alone could wake him. "Hang on," I begged.

Carlos frightened me—he always had, even as we'd become reluctant allies and, eventually friends of a sort—but I didn't recoil or think for more than an instant about what I was about to do. I shoved back my sleeves and dragged him to a more upright position against the wall, which was pockmarked with tombstones. Then I sat beside him, right arm holding him up, and I pressed the thin-skinned underside of my left wrist to his mouth. I might have cut my arm instead, had I thought of it, but I just hoped there was enough survival impulse left to make him bite.

For a second, nothing happened and I thought I'd left it too late. Then I felt the sharp tearing of my flesh as he bit.

The pain wrenched through me, making me buckle and cry out. My cry turned into stifled screams and gasps for air as he gnawed and sucked at my arm. My stomach lurched with nausea from the agony and the sudden, flooding odor of vampire. In stories, the bite of a vampire is a sensual thing, soporific and addicting to mortals who succumb, but to me it was anguish. He had once told me there was more than bloodlust in the vampire's need to feed from humans; there was some intangible life force within us as necessary as blood itself. My senses reeled in torment, and I thought I could feel the blood and life flowing out of me, torn away as if every corpuscle fought and clung with barbs of steel to my tortured flesh.

I started to yank my arm away, but his hands flew up and gripped my forearm, pulling me closer to his cutting teeth. I thrashed, feeling weakened and faint as I tried to escape.

"Stop," I gasped, twisting feebly. "Carlos, you're killing me. Please . . ." My free hand groped for anything I could use to make him stop, to strike him or cut him, as I prayed I wouldn't have to use it. I felt myself draining away so quickly. . . .

As I tugged and begged, the pain stopped. For an instant, I thought I had reached the threshold of death, where sensation ends as the body gives up, but I was still writhing, still alive, however frail. I felt him hesitate, his mouth touching my torn wrist, but still now.

I felt the word against my skin as much as heard it. "Blaine."

"Yes." I sighed, slumping a little in relief from the ache and terror that had held me. I tried again to draw my arm away, but he held it firm.

"Not yet."

"No," I protested, trying to rear back from him. If he drew another drop from me, I was sure I would die, and my mind went numb at the thought of what might happen to me in the state between Greywalker and vampire. What new horror would I become?

But the sensation on my ripped flesh now was not the tearing and torment of his bite, but a silk-soft brushing and a touch of cold breath. Finally, he let me go and I drew my wrist back to cradle it against my chest as I moved away from him, scraping against the stones of the earthquake-shattered church.

I pulled free of his weight and squirmed into a corner, feeling too weak and shocked to support myself any longer, and bent over my savaged arm that tingled with a strange flushing sensation of cold followed by heat and then the harsh prickling of flesh knitting together in a fire of magic.

Carlos had slumped to the side as I sidled away. Now he pulled himself up again to lean against the wall beside me, his movements rough jerks. He closed his eyes as if exhausted by the effort and seemed to be panting.

"Thank you," he murmured. "I'm in your debt. Yet again."

"I thought you were going to kill me," I whispered, still pressing my throbbing wrist between my breasts, harder than I may have needed to.

"I might have, had I not realized it was you."

"That would be some thanks for coming to save you."

He made a coughing sound and sighed. "It is our nature to take what we need. I apologize for frightening you. How did you come to find me?"

"Amélia. How did she know you were in trouble?"

He gave a weak, lopsided shrug. "She was my wife and it appears she cares for me still, though I was the worst sort of human monster to her." He twitched and frowned. He took a breath. Then he raised a shaking hand to his own chest. "How . . . strange that feels."

"What?" I asked, finally daring a glance down at my wrist. The moonlight revealed only a set of faint lines on the inside as if I'd worn tight sleeves that pressed their seams and wrinkles into my skin. I stared at the soft, whole flesh, too surprised to speak, almost too surprised to listen, except that his words cut through my daze.

"My heart . . . is beating."

"Doesn't it always?" I asked, recalling the way I'd seen it once, a torpid red gleam in his chest that pulsed less than once a minute.

"Very slowly, yes. Not like this. Not like yours."

Carlos reached for me and had to crawl to close the distance between us. He stopped and remained on his knees, leaning against the wall as he put out his hand. "Please. Your hand. Only for a moment."

I held out my right, since it was closer to him and seemed less vulnerable. He took my hand in his, rubbing his thumb across my palm as if he'd never touched skin before. Then he pressed it against his chest, above the scar I knew lay there, scribed into his skin almost two hundred sixty years earlier.

I could feel throbbing, like a distant, uneven drumroll beneath his cold flesh. His heart beat like the reflection of my own. I looked at him in confusion.

"It's been almost three centuries. . . . I didn't think that I had missed it." He frowned, thinking. His face went blank and dark and he peered at me from the corner of his eye. For just a moment, the edge of a cruel smile danced along his lips, his grip tightening on my hand until the bones ground together, keeping me close. Then he let me go and slid away, sitting back against the wall again at a short distance and no longer looking at me. Through the Grey, I could see shades of darkness and pinpricks of light gathering around him like a constellation slowly burning into being.

NINETEEN

I watched his power reassemble around him, changed and yet the same: dark as night, but no longer blood streaked.

He seemed surprised. "I cannot fathom what has happened. I feel. This blood moving within my veins, pumped by a heart that has not beaten thus in centuries, demands breath like a babe howling newborn from the womb. I feel all this, and memory of how precious it is brings me shame that for even a second I thought of killing you. Thought of consuming you and drawing this from you for my own selfishness."

"For the sake of a heartbeat, for breath?" I asked. I was afraid, but it wouldn't do me any good to give in to it. "For a mortal thing that can stop like an unwound watch?"

He turned his head toward me. "You do not appreciate what it is to feel this after so long."

"No," I agreed. "But to feel my heart stop, to die, I know that. And the surge of my heart beating again, my lungs hungering for air, my body wanting to live, however broken it is, I know that, too. I die and I wake changed, and hope it won't happen again, over and over. How many times have you died, Carlos?"

"In my own body, but once, and very nearly a dozen times more. But every life I take, I feel as if it were my own death and rebirth. Like you. But you live—truly alive—from heartbeat to heartbeat, and I exist in the bitterness of death," he said. "But I had forgotten life's tang, how sweet and sharp, like the taste of your blood on my tongue."

His gaze on me burned with conflicting desires that sent chill and sorrow through me. I turned my head away and let it fall forward, tired and weak and unable to fight if it came to it. "If you're going to . . . at least make sure I'm really dead this time. I don't want to know what happens after this. After we fail."

The small sound that came from him was not a laugh. "Oh, Blaine, you mistake me. I forfeited my soul for power, my life for knowledge and existence beyond my due years. Tonight I reached again into the abyss of that power, but I miscalculated and should have died. Because of you, I have survived. No, I live! Every fiber of my being cries to cleave to this sensation and I know it is nothing more than a fleeting semblance that will fall away, but that does not cheapen the gift, nor change my gratitude to you. For now, I feel the phantom of your heat in my body, my heart beating, my lungs striving for breath, and I know to whom I owe this. If what you see in my eyes is an unholy desire, it is only because I am an unholy creature."

"That does still leave desire," I said, still feeling weak and small and uncertain.

"I've never made a secret of my interest in you."

"Yes, but your interest never looked like lust before."

"I am too hungry to disguise all my appetites, at the moment, but where you are concerned, I promise, they are not of the flesh. Mostly."

I laughed, but it was strained, and I looked at him again. "Oh, you wouldn't. . . ."

"Wouldn't I?

"Not with me, you wouldn't."

He sighed and leaned his head against the white marble wall. "Alas, true. Though not, perhaps, for the reasons you imagine."

"I *imagine* that you forgo forcing yourself on me because our friendship precludes any action that . . . transgressive. And you are the one who has several times pointed out I'm married, even if not in the eyes of the law, and bound to others as well as the Guardian Beast."

He grunted. "And now how shall we go on?"

"You mean as friends, or 'how do we get out of here'?"

"The latter. I don't think I've laid waste to our rapport by acknowledging that I have no interest in raping you."

"Goody. Because I have no idea how to get out of here. I had to walk through the earthquake to get to you. I'd prefer not to return by the same route. Also, I don't know if I can stand up on my own yet."

"Perhaps we should wait a while longer."

"Fine with me." I paused a moment, dizzy and weak just from talking. After a minute or more I asked, "Are you still breathing?"

Carlos seemed to have to test it before he replied, "Remarkably, yes. And my heartbeat seems to grow stronger, rather than fading away."

"Maybe you've discovered a cure for vampirism."

"No. I do not believe that aspect of my nature has changed, only the state in which it continues."

"So . . . are you going to stay up and watch the sunrise?"

"I'm not persuaded that such a course would be wise." Even in the dim light of the stars, I could see him scowl and raise his hand to his throat. "The knife . . . Where is it?"

"I threw it into the grass. I could barely stand to touch it long enough to pull it out."

"Ah." He crawled forward and ran his hands over the grass until he found the blade. He cursed as it nicked his fingers. Still, he picked it up and put it into his shirt, then sat in the grass and leaned back against the nearest column, facing me across the distance of what had been the south aisle, long ago. He looked wan and weary, but not dead, at least. I hoped I looked that good, because I felt awful.

"We can't rest for too long, but I owe you a tale, since I can't show you the window from here," he said. "In the days of this church's glory, I was a student at the University of Coimbra, in the north. Several years earlier, my father had decided, after much vacillating, to acknowledge me and provide an education and establishment befitting a younger son of an influential family. As I had begun late on my formal education, I was several years older than many of the students I studied with, but already arrogant in my power, which had come at a young age. I had discovered a tutor in the necromantic arts quickly and, with my mother's help, I had thrived and learned to hide what I was.

"At university, I offended a certain gentleman of a wealthy family—not noble, merely rich—but he was a very distant cousin of mine and we were often thrown together. We were like sparks and gunpowder—always one setting the other off. Of me he knew two things: I was a bastard and I was a practitioner of dark arts, but of the latter he had no proof. The other was a well-known fact, but since Nuno Pereira himself—the great general who saved Portugal from Castile and built this convent—was born on the wrong side of the blanket and still became Condestável do Reino and a greatly honored man, it didn't seem much of a bar. And one didn't argue about the rights of an acknowledged son with my father. That my mother was Moorish and I dark in looks and dark in soul seemed to offend my cousin to a far greater degree.

"He was brilliant, an intellectual, but also a prig, a bigot, a hypocrite, and ambitious, with a hidden fear of the ancient nobility of which he was not a member. I hated him, as boys do, with a great misplaced passion, and he felt the same for me. We played at cat and mouse for years, he hoping to lure me into an act or admission that could send me to the Inquisition, and I hoping to shame and discredit him. And so it went. . . ." He closed his eyes and the light from the dim moon seemed to tremble on his skin as the black strands of magic wove around him. His voice drew me into the scenes of his tale, wrapping me in the moving shadows and fog of his recollection, his language and cadence becoming subtly more formal and archaic, as if he passed backward in time.

"When I removed to Lisbon with Amélia," he continued, "my family name allowed me access to the thousands of books then kept here and I far preferred their company to hers. I was not merely callow, but thoughtlessly cruel in my self-absorption. I was still striving toward a goal of power that was ill-defined—and foolish for that—and I was obsessed with it. The city was also rife with the pitiful deaths few pay heed to, which suited all my plans.

"My antagonist had gone into politics and had family in the church as well, so it was no surprise that he, also, was in Lisbon frequently. When I came to read, I often saw him here. I baited the gentleman at every opportunity and in a fit of rage one afternoon, he attempted to stab me with the knife you drew from my throat. When he was unsuccessful, he threw me from a window in the library of the chapter house. That building is now obliterated but for the rear wall, in which my window still stands as part of the new building that rises like an ungainly phoenix from the ruins." He paused, opening his eyes for a moment to stare at the wall above my head as if he were studying the tombstone mounted there. Then he shook his head and continued.

"I fell and should have died, stabbed to the gut and nearly all my bones broken, but death and I had already a fond acquaintance and though I had to be carried home, I lived. There was debate whether this confirmed my demonic associations or just the opposite. My adversary's brother was a favored son of the church and through him, I was nearly brought down, but I escaped that fate as well. The excesses of the Inquisition were long over, but what remained were still terrible enough, however useless in the actual discovery of those like me. I learned caution. I began keeping to myself, showing myself less frequently and avoiding the men I'd known in college in particular. I also avoided Amélia, and when she would not let me to my own devices, I was brutal to her—in every way you can imagine and some I pray that you can't. She left me for a year or so, but came back—for what reason I never knew—and found me more changed than she could have anticipated.

"During her absence, I discovered what I had been searching for—another master who could unveil a greater mystery of death, a higher state. I worked—lived—for that 'Becoming' with all my energy and passion. I searched for artifacts of power—one of which you know, the Lâmina que Consome as Almas—and destroyed what stood between me and them. I did murder in the dark and took the tribute of death for my own ends, spending all the hours of my mortal life in that pursuit. I had no time or desire for anything else, spared no thought for those that I harmed, and only a little more on those I killed. I did not even know Amélia was ill until she died and the whimpering release of her exhausted spirit passed through me. And I cared nothing but for the modicum of power it gave me. She died of fever I could have cured, wasting to nothing below my tower and I neither knew nor cared, such was my obsession.

"I attended the funeral and Mass, as I had to, and there I saw again my adversary, who was awaiting an influential political post. His brother had risen to bishop, and I had remained as I was—the wastrel younger son of a powerful man by his half-Arab mistress. It should have been a moment of rejoicing for him to see me no further advanced in the usual ambitions of society. But there was only silence when I appeared. My first thought was that they knew what I was and believed that I had killed Amélia, but it was far simpler than that. I was nearly fifty years old, yet I had barely aged past twenty-five. While they were men in their thirties, men of consequence with estates and children, I was as I am now. This was not only a prick to their vanity, but a proof that I was, if not actually in league with the Devil, at least uncanny.

"I knew they would come for me, confirmed in their own minds, even if they had not convinced anyone else, that I was in league with demons. I went then to my master, Lenoir, as I came again tonight, to ask for knowledge that would aid me against my enemies. Then, as now, a double-edged sword that cut deeper than I had expected."

"That's why you were here? To ask for help?"

"To discover what the Kostní Mágové are making from their bones. I may know now, but I'll need more information about which bones they possess to be certain. Did you uncover that information?"

"Quinton did and I have some other information. We don't know which bones, though—the news articles mostly recorded vandalism without specifics. And a robbery, a death, and a possible connection between one of these vandalisms and the bone mages . . ."

Carlos murmured to himself. "I shall have to ask him for the details."

We fell into silence for a minute or more as we each tried to rally whatever reserves of energy we had. After a few more minutes, I asked, "So, this old master of yours—Lenoir—helped you tonight but he also tried to kill you?"

"No. He no longer has the power of life and death. He is a shade, but his knowledge of his old brothers in the art has not faded. Nor has his treachery. A young friend of his discovered our meeting and crashed the party. I suspect he would not cavil at telling the place if he were asked, and would have cared not at all whether I lived or died as a result. Our association was a study in betrayal and power. As I spoke to him, he eked his knowledge out by small degrees, teasing me with it, and I told him what had become of his creations, of the one I destroyed for you in particular. It infuriated him, but there was nothing he could do to harm me here. I had not counted on the reappearance of Maggie Griffin."

I wasn't surprised. The web of bone-white magic that held him down had been too much like the spell that I'd torn off Quinton the night before to be coincidence. "Griffin. How?"

"She is of the Kostní Mágové and she asked the right question of the right ghost. She was not unprepared or overtaxed this time, but she did come alone—which was my only piece of luck. Lenoir chose not to warn me when she moved to strike." Carlos shrugged as if it hadn't nearly killed him. "As I said, I miscalculated."

"But she didn't stay to finish you off. That wasn't wise."

"She had no choice. Rui may still be incapacitated, but he is her master and would demand her attendance, even if he were the one to send her. And her powers are limited here, for there are few bones left in this place. The tombs contain only dust now and even the bones of dead monks are scattered like straws in the wind. But there is the shadow of death in plenty here—my element and strength. Her only chance was to silence me and cast what spells she had already prepared. She did her work well, though she had little time to craft it and could not stay to see the end. Her art would have destroyed me without your intervention."

"Your old master is a hard case to stand by and let his star pupil die for pissing him off."

"What makes you think I was ever a star pupil?"

"You said you pursued the knowledge he offered with all your passion."

"Ah. I did. And when I had what I wanted from him, I slaughtered him. A peculiar kind of stardom. The irony was that he killed me first and should have known I would repay him in kind. He did not warn me that the ascension I desired would be a journey through hell from which I would emerge a vampire and the only way to reach that state—the Becoming—was to be murdered, torn open while alive and bled like a butchered animal. Not merely to die, or to sink into the Bliss and change painlessly in the addiction of blood. For that alone, I enjoyed destroying his creation when you brought me to it."

"His creation . . . ?"

"The organ. The object of your first client's desire. Sergeyev's prison. Just like the small boxes assembled in the temple last night."

He'd mentioned it before and it had been on my mind, too. A ghost had come to me in my first days as a Greywalker and asked me to find "an heirloom," which proved to be quite a bit more than that. I hadn't known what I was into, that my client was dead for centuries and that the solution of the case would require me to leap into the occupation I hadn't wanted. "Oh gods . . . You wanted it. Mara and

I believed it was because it was a dark artifact—a thing of power you could use for your own ends."

"That was true. But even greater was the satisfaction in undoing what he had done."

"I nearly got you killed then, too."

He looked amused. "It was a close thing." He pressed his back against the column and pushed slowly to his feet. "Which of us can stand well enough to carry the other this time?"

"I think that's you."

"This may also be a close thing. . . ."

I found it harder to get to my feet than he had, but though I flinch from the touch of vampires in most cases, this time his hand on my arm didn't send a bolt of nausea or pain through my body or shake my mind with unimagined horrors. It was a cool touch— unnaturally cool—but not grave-cold, and though it raised the hairs on my arm and the back of my neck, it didn't make me ill. "I think I'm getting used to you," I panted through weakness and the persistent cold of the Grey.

"I may find that inconvenient."

"I said 'used to,' not 'fond of.'"

He laughed and leaned back to counterbalance my awkward struggle to regain the upright. When I'd attained it, he put his arm around my shoulder and I put mine around his waist. It felt very strange to be half hugging someone who spoke casually of slaughtering others and ripping souls into shreds as if we were boon companions—though in our horrifying way, we were. Between us, we reeled like a pair of drunks.

"Where's the exit?" I asked.

"Griffin went through the doors to the north chapel. There should be stairs to the crypt from the ambulatory or the transept."

"I was never a good churchgoer. I have a rough idea of what the nave, aisles, and altar are and beyond that, I'm a heretic."

"I never imagined I'd be pleased to have been a Catholic in life."

We made our unsteady way out of the ruins through a door that deposited us on a bare roof.

"The apse . . . is gone," Carlos said, and stopped, looking out at the city.

"You didn't notice that when you arrived?"

"No. I came another way." He stared into the distance over the Baixa and toward the castle of São Jorge. "The streets were never so straight when I lived here."

"Quinton told me it was all rebuilt after the earthquake by some nobleman called the Marquis of Pombal."

Carlos jerked as if I'd electrocuted him and turned to stare at me, nearly letting me fall.

"Pombal . . . didn't rebuild anything. He was no nobleman. He was secretary of state—what would be the prime minister now. He *ordered* it done, the same way he ordered an end to the Inquisition and to the purity of blood laws—which was well-done—but in the same autocratic way he decided who would die after the Tavora affair. He was only Carvalho e Melo then, but by his hand he would have wiped out every member of the Tavora, Lencastre, and Ataíde families if he could have. He hated and distrusted them and it was a fair excuse. He was made Count of Oeiras for his duplicity and Marquis of Pombal ten years later. It was the end of the old families—all but Bragança and Periero de Melo. He took the rest down like hares in the field."

"Your name is Ataíde."

"Only a bastard son."

"How do you know what became of them after you left? You said you never came back."

"I was neither blind nor deaf. News always comes. I did not know at the time that this would be the result of what I went to do on All Hallows' Eve. When I survived another betrayal, when I found out what had happened, I knew it would be the seal on my doom. He was the secretary of state—the voice of the king—and he hated me. His brother was the patriarch of Lisbon by then. Had I, a man who would not die, nor age, reappeared in the ashes, alive and whole when all the city was still in flames and ruins, that would surely have been taken as sorcery—he threw me from the window of this holy place and I lived, but it fell! Even without the Inquisition, little would have stopped them from having me burned at the stake."

"Wait, wait . . ." I begged him, not sure I'd caught the implication that was circling the back of my brain like a shark. "The Marquis of Pombal . . . was your cousin? The one who threw you—"

"Out that window," he confirmed, pointing with his free hand to the back wall of the old chapter house that still stood on the sheer side of the building next to the church. "Yes. So, you see why I did not return. After a time, I closed my eyes and ears to Lisbon. I forgot what I did not wish to know. This was my city and these are my ruins."

"It rose again, like your clumsy phoenix."

"Under the hand of the *Marquês de Pombal*." He spat the name. "Is it any wonder that my plans are frustrated in this place as if his very ghost opposed me?"

I found his almost superstitious reaction strange and disquieting. "We can leave Lisbon as soon as we know what the bone mages are up to."

"We'll have to leave soon, regardless."

I frowned at him, but he said no more and led me across the bare roof to a set of unattractive iron railings that secured a short flight of steps to the edge of the curtain wall. More steps led us down by stages until we stumbled past a gate, into the Rua do Carmo and into the path of a policeman strolling along the road.

The cop called out to us, sounding suspicious but not yet alarmed. Carlos drew in a breath to reply, but I cut him off.

"Oh thank God!" I said, playing the dizzy tourist. "We got lost by the church and we don't know how to get back to our hotel." I even giggled like the inebriate I appeared to be. I felt a bit light-headed from blood loss, so it wasn't a stretch.

The policeman peered at us, his English not quite up to my chattering speed.

"*Nós estamos perdidos,*" Carlos said, in Portuguese that made mine sound fluid and dulcet. "*Nosso hotel . . . Rossio.*"

I wouldn't have believed he could sound so befuddled and foreign. The cop seemed to buy it, however, and pointed north, down the road toward a bright smudge of light one long block away. "Ah! You have luck. Rossio is there."

We thanked him as if we really were drunken tourists and we staggered onward. A few feet from the intersection, Carlos winced and swayed and I nearly fell into him. He caught me without grace or sign of affection and we leaned against the edge of a doorway. I felt unsteady and ill from the heaving and rolling of the Grey's constant replay of tragic history—a history the creature beside me had helped cause.

"You don't do well," Carlos observed, sounding rough himself.

"No," I replied. "History is too persistent here and I'm too weak to push it back. A cab might be a good idea," I said, swallowing bile and breathing too hard.

"That is why I chose the Rossio. If there are taxis to be found, they will be here."

"Is that because some things never change?"

"Yes. And no."

The driver who pulled over at our hail gave us a sideways glare that measured up the likely origins of our bloodied and rumpled appearance and found us questionable, but not bad enough to blow off. He was English and became much happier to brave the narrow twisty streets of Alfama once we started speaking English also.

"Right," he said, "top of the hill. Hang on."

A better piece of advice he could not have given, for he took off into the late-night traffic with a jerk and a jink that slipped us between a bus and a limousine in a cacophony of horns.

TWENTY

This time, the house was illuminated—it even looked welcoming as the taxi driver let us out at the gate. He'd barely squeezed the small car through the medieval streets of Alfama with close calls at every turn and passing. I'd been too exhausted to react and Carlos had spent the short ride brooding out the window at the city he no longer recognized.

The taxi fare was surprisingly low and even with my meager collection of coins, I was able to tip the guy to a degree that earned me a huge grin. "You'll want to be more careful with your money around here, love. Neighborhood's gone to the dogs since the smart set moved to Chiado and Bairro Alto. Still, it's lovely, ain't it? Can't complain about the view, eh?"

"No. And thanks for bringing us up."

"Pleasure's all mine."

We watched him drive away, threading the twisty streets once again with inches to spare and no apparent care for his paintwork. Carlos and I limped through the gate and courtyard to the house.

Quinton and Rafa awaited us in the dimly lit doorway.

"Look what I caught," Quinton said, waving his arm to indicate the phantom housekeeper.

"How?" I asked.

"With the key. We're in her version of the house right now. That's why I left the gate and door unlocked for you. Holy crap!" he added as we stepped from the shadow into light. "What happened?"

He lunged to grab me as if he thought I'd fall at any moment, leaving Rafa to attempt an escape while he was distracted. Carlos made a gesture and spat out a word, and she froze in place as if time had stopped.

He turned back to us and, in the light, I saw a smear of dried blood on his forehead and long streamers of it stiffening the black fabric of his shirt from collar to waist. In the dark it had been invisible, but here it was plain. "You look like death," I said.

Carlos bowed his head with an ironic smile, just out of Quinton's sight as my lover said, "You look worse."

"Do I?" I glanced at my arms, but the left was fine. The right was covered in small nicks and filthy scrapes that had bled and dried closed again already. My shins below my skirt were covered in worse scrapes and gouges where the stones of the broken church had cut me while they fell and my outfit was filthy and ripped in several places. I'd never taken that kind of damage in a temporacline before. I already felt weak and uncertain, and the sight didn't improve my sense of being barely in the normal world at all.

But Quinton was looking at my face, not my body. He smoothed a warm hand over my cheek and forehead and into my hair. "You look like you've been in a wreck."

I gave a rough laugh. "A ruin. But we survived."

Quinton finally turned back to look at Carlos. His eyes widened, but he said nothing.

Carlos raised an eyebrow, but I noticed he was leaning back against the wall with more of his weight than usual. His skin was waxy, not merely pale, and he seemed smaller, thinner, or diminished. In his own lifetime, he must have seemed a giant. Now he just looked tall, broad shouldered, and worn down.

I watched his chest for a moment, just to be sure he was still breathing. He was, so the odd change in his state of existence was still operating.

"We should adjourn this discussion to a more comfortable location," he said.

"I don't think I can make it up the stairs yet," I said.

"There used to be a salon in this house," Carlos said, and led the way out of the entry and through one of the other doors at the back. The door opened into a room that ran from the front to the back of the house and had long windows on both sides to let the air through. The room was clean, if sparsely furnished, and we settled into a pair of couches that sat at right angles near the back, overlooking the small garden through tall, Moorish arches. The heat of the day reflected off the stone wall that held back the hillside and the house above to flood the room with the scent of orange trees, jasmine, and bougainvillea. It might have seemed romantic and pleasant if I hadn't been exhausted, bloodied, and woozy. I snuggled against Quinton, feeling unseasonably cold. He put his arm around my shoulders and pulled me close, unknowingly repeating the gesture Carlos had made earlier. It gave me a chill.

"Now . . . will one of you tell me what happened? Harper bolted out of here as if you were dying."

"I was and would have been gone from this world if she hadn't arrived when she did. She would have sacrificed herself to save me and I was almost thoughtless enough to accept that offer."

I felt Quinton bridle and start to lunge for him at Carlos's implication, but he fell back as the necromancer held up his hands.

"I said almost. Your spouse-in-soul is remarkable and only a very great fool would allow her to leave the world for so little good purpose. I am no fool and I don't value friends so cheaply. More immediately, I have an idea of what the Kostní Mágové are building, but not the specific details. Tell me what you have discovered about bones. . . ."

Quinton still felt tense and the color of his aura shifted as he spoke from a red-tinged anxiety to a softer blue color shot with occasional sparks of red, orange, and olive. He repeated the information he'd discussed with me earlier and Carlos was able to tease more specifics from him by precise questions based on knowledge neither Quinton nor I had had. When they were done, Carlos was pale and a sheen of sweat had appeared on his forehead. He looked ill and I felt equally terrible, huddling against Quinton's side.

Rafa stepped into the room and stood still in a shadow, barely visible to me from the corner of my eye, but in Carlos's line of sight.

Quinton scowled at Carlos. "What's wrong with you?"

Carlos swayed in his seat. His voice was low and barely audible when he replied. "Mortality. By a quirk of blood, I seem to be temporarily . . . human again." All remaining color drained from his face and his eyes rolled back a moment before he collapsed across the sofa, unconscious.

I felt the edge of the same blurry nothingness pulling over me, too, and fought against it, unwilling to leave Quinton alone.

Quinton stared, appalled, between Carlos and me, his mouth

open in protest. "No . . ." He fixed on me with a beseeching expression. "You didn't. . . . Say you didn't."

I tried to speak, but my voice failed and I had to nod, falling over the edge of irresistible unconsciousness as I felt him clutch my shoulders and let out a cry of despair.

The day and night faded to bad dreams and I woke up in the bright, warm morning, disoriented to find myself in bed instead of still on the sofa in the salon. Quinton was sitting on a chair near the bed, watching me. I felt more groggy than seemed reasonable until I remembered that I was operating about a quart low on blood—which will make anyone a bit slower than normal.

I hauled myself up in bed to sit leaning against the wall and take a look at my watch. "Ugh, why am I still in bed at ten a.m.?"

"Staying up until three a.m. can have that effect," Quinton said. "How are you?"

"Confused."

"About . . . ?"

"Why you're sitting over there like I have a highly contagious disease."

"I admit to being a little nervous."

"Why?"

"I don't know what happens next."

"Next? I think the plan was to figure out what the bad guys are up to and then blow town before they take another shot at any of us."

"OK. Now I'm the one who's confused."

"About what?"

Quinton hesitated. "Last night . . . I had the strong impression . . . that you . . . had let Carlos bite you. Maybe more . . ."

I stared at him with my mouth hanging open, blinking like a stunned owl. "Oh. . . . Uh . . . That's not quite how it went."

"But—"

I put up one hand to stop him from saying more. "No, no. Just listen. This is difficult. Amélia told me—not as such, but let's just go with that in lieu of a longer explanation—anyhow, she told me that Carlos needed help and passed on the impression that the situation was desperate. So I raced out of here—as I'm sure you remember—and up to the Carmo Convent. Those are the ruins—"

"The church ruins you can see from Rossio, or from the castle if you face west," Quinton said.

"Yes," I agreed, nodding. "Those ruins. It wasn't an easy or pleasant job, but I found him there. He was dying."

"He's the undead. How could he be dying?"

I gave him a stern look. "Don't split semantic hairs with me right now. The upshot is that whatever it is that passes for life in him was almost gone. And I didn't stop to think about the ramifications or complications of the situation—I didn't even consider that we need him if we're going to figure out what your father and the Kostní Mágové are up to and stop them. It didn't occur to me. I just did what I could to keep a friend from dying."

"You let him bite you."

"No. I pretty much had to force him. But that was all—just . . . blood. And something happened that I have no explanation for—and I'm sure Carlos doesn't, either—but whatever it was, it changed his state of existence, at least temporarily. This thing seems to have been a one-way expression only. I'm not affected, except to be a bit anemic. From something Carlos told me while we were trying to get out of the ruins, he's not a vampire in the same mode as, say, Cameron is. He may not even function quite the same way, but for whatever reason, I'm not blood-bound or turning into a vampire or anything dramatic or treacherous like that. I'm still just me, running about a quart low, but otherwise fine."

"Quite fine, from what I see."

We both turned our startled attention to the bedroom doorway where Carlos stood, backlit by the morning sun through the sitting room windows. I couldn't see his face in the glare, but the light cutting his silhouette made him appear reed-thin.

Quinton jumped up from his chair and stood between us, and it occurred to me that I was still sitting up in bed with only a sheet lying loose across my legs. I considered pulling it up over my exposed breasts and then thought it was not only too late, but a ridiculous gesture, given the company.

Carlos turned his gaze aside. "I beg your pardon. I knocked, but no one replied." He took a step into the room and turned deliberately to look only at Quinton, giving me a clear view of his profile, but putting his back to the rest of the room. He looked less filthy, tattered, and exhausted than the last time I'd seen him, but still tired and less kempt than I was used to. His voice and presence still left an impression on the Grey, but with less intensity, as if his paranormal volume had been turned down. "I believe we left a conversation unfinished last night," he said.

Quinton scowled at him. "You're up."

"Indeed."

"In daylight."

"It comes as a surprise to me, as well. Do you wish to discuss the phenomenon right now?"

Quinton thought about it. "No."

"Good. We have many other things to talk about." He turned and left the bedroom.

I slipped out of the bed and snatched up Quinton's nearest shirt on the way to the bathroom. An uncomfortable tension buzzed in my chest and I felt a little light-headed. I hoped nothing unpleasant was about to erupt between Quinton and Carlos.

Throughout my shower, the vibrating discomfort in my chest continued, easing a little, but not entirely going away. I got dressed, annoyed that my jeans were still unwashed and too filthy to put on, so I was stuck once again in a dress that had only the saving grace of pockets. I saw no sign of Quinton in the room, but the sitting room door was now closed, and even through the thick plastered walls I could hear a murmur of male voices.

I'm a snoop by nature and I couldn't resist putting my ear to the old-fashioned keyhole to discover what they were saying.

". . . My girlfriend!"

"Your wife, more properly. But the relationship does not make her your property and I did nothing to influence her. If you imagine that I would, you do her considerable insult and no less to me."

"I know what the effects of surviving a vampire's bite are."

Carlos laughed and this time it shook the floor. "You know nothing. Most of those who give us blood go their way with no more effect upon them than a slight euphoria. Those who succumb to the Bliss bear a mark—that is how we know them. I assume you've searched every inch of her body looking for it. . . ."

Quinton said nothing.

"You found nothing because there is nothing to find. She is not my thrall. I have no call upon her beyond our mutual respect."

It was very quiet, and I thought they'd left, but in a moment, Quinton spoke again.

"You said it was risky—what she did for you. But if you respect her, why did you let her do it? Why didn't you stop?"

"I did stop, though I admit it was difficult. In extremity and offered rescue, it was hard to temper the drive to survive with the knowledge that her life lay in my hands. And I did not 'let her' save me. Blaine made that decision for herself. You made that decision once for me, also. Did you think I would forget that you didn't leave me to die in a fire?"

"That was Cameron's doing."

"Not alone. You don't credit the breadth of your own compassion."

Quinton scoffed. "For vampires? Your lot nearly killed me a dozen times."

"Not 'my lot,' but all the others, and for her. It's what makes you a terrible spy—you feel and cannot resist acting on that empathy—and it makes you her perfect mate. But it allows you to know—or to imagine—*too* much, which is why you want to kill me for touching her," Carlos added with a chuckle.

"That's not true. . . ." The rattling discomfort in my chest fell apart.

"It is. But, as I am useful, you have no choice but to tolerate my presence a little longer. I know what your father wants."

"An invisible company of invincible, undead spies—a whole department's worth of Sergeyevs to bring Europe down. I know."

"For how long?"

"I only really put it together last night. Harper saw my dad's project in action yesterday and we all saw the boxes at the bone church. Harper recognized the master bone mage from last night—we saw him just before that . . . drachen thing fell apart down the hill yesterday. It was just like the one at the bone church. The ossuaries that have been vandalized, the places my father has been, and what we all saw two nights ago . . . I knew there was some piece of information I had that made it all fit, made my suspicions true, but I hadn't been able to tease it up to the surface. Now I know. That organ . . . the bones . . . You said at the time that you knew the man who made it. You said that you knew this bone mage when he was an apprentice and how would you if you didn't study under the same master? It all comes together. The Kostní Mágové promised my father the secret of packing ghosts and monsters into boxes so they can be moved around like furniture and that's what he wants, but there's something else that has to come first— something they want and have convinced my father he wants, too— something that will burn Europe to the ground. You know what that is."

"They must have their apocalypse—their dead in legions unburied, an endless sea of bones. O Inferno Dragáo will give them that. And then, we all die."

TWENTY-ONE

I gave them a chance to leave before I emerged from the bedroom and went downstairs, assuming they'd be in the salon, which proved to be empty. Quinton was in the kitchen with Rafa, asking her questions.

"Where?" he said.

"In the Alentejo. The olive trees were all that was left. I'm sorry. . . ." She stopped speaking when she saw me. *"Bom dia, Senhora Blaine."*

"Good morning, Rafa. How are you?"

"I am very well, thank you. It is good to see Dom Carlos as he should be."

"Where is he?" I asked.

"In the garden."

Carlos in a garden in the daylight. This I needed to see. I started to go, then turned back. "Rafa, where did Dom Carlos sleep last night?"

She frowned. "In his bed. Where else should he sleep?"

"I mean where in the house. The cellar?"

She shook her head. "No. In the master's chamber on the second floor. I had to take him there myself."

"How did you lift him? He must weigh more than two hundred pounds."

She blushed. "Avó helped me. He is light as a child with her hand on him."

"And where is she now?"

"Oh, I think she won't come for some time. It was very hard for her to bear him up after all that happened."

There seemed to be more questions opened than answered, but I let them go and nodded to her, thanking her and starting for the door to the back garden.

"Oh, the key!" she cried. "Take the key."

That was interesting: The garden apparently didn't lie in her time frame of the house. I took the key off a hook by the door and went out.

In the modern daylight, the garden was shabbier than it had seemed the night before. Jasmine climbed up broken trellises against the house walls, growing from pots that had seen much better days. Three dwarf orange trees set in a shallow V were dusty and seemed in need of attention while the bougainvillea had overgrown the wall and was encroaching on the tiles around a fountain mounted to the surface. The pool and fountain were dry, the tiles and plaster cracked and chipping here and there. Carlos sat on the rim of the empty pool and squinted upward at the sun through the dusty leaves of an orange tree. A shaft of light struck blue highlights off his hair and warmed his skin with a ruddy glow across one cheekbone. It was like seeing some young relative of the Carlos I knew, one who hadn't yet gained bitter knowledge and a taste for blood and power.

"You're not supposed to look directly at the sun," I said.

"I am also not supposed to be alive and sitting in my own garden. It's run-down—I shall chastise the management company for that—but as I am somewhat run-down myself, I shan't be too harsh on them."

"I'm afraid I overheard part of your conversation with Quinton."

"I know it. As, I suspect, does he. But we each pretend the other does not and thus we save our foolish male pride."

"Why aren't I attached to you, blood-bound, because of what I did?"

"Always direct, Blaine."

"Why should I be otherwise?"

He replied with nothing but an ironically raised eyebrow.

"Come on, man of mystery. Tell me."

"I've already told you. I am not blood-bound to another because I did not die of the Bliss—of the blood addiction. I Became, my blood poured onto the ground to feed something else. While I can—or could before this change—create blood kindred, it must be carefully and deliberately done. You gave me your blood. I gave nothing back—or at least nothing that I intended."

"There's still something more to this. . . ."

"Yes, but I cannot tell you what it is. I don't know. I think I know what I've received from you, but what may have passed *to* you, is unknown. But it isn't the blood tie, nor any form of control. You are not in thrall to me. Although it might be interesting if you were. . . ."

I rolled my eyes. "Please."

He smiled a perfectly ordinary smile, the sun showing every bone-white scar where the glass of the church window had cut him, and finding tiny wrinkles around the corners of his eyes and mouth that darkness had never revealed. The smile faded quickly; then he shook himself and stood. "Let us not bait your beloved any longer. We should go inside and speak of dragons."

He put his right hand out in a courtly, old-world gesture and I, laughing at it, put my left hand onto his, aligning our fingers.

For a second, our hands were one oddly shaped construction of four overly long fingers and two opposed thumbs that sprouted from both our wrists like the overlap of conjoined twins. I gasped and flinched, yanking my hand up and back without thinking.

The bizarre double hand divided at the knuckles of our middle fingers as if hinged there. All the rest of our hands were free and normal, the fingers sliding past one another, but our middle fingers remained connected at the medial joint. It was creepy to look at and impossible, like some kind of optical illusion where it appeared that my finger passed through the knuckle of his, without displacing either of our bones more than a micron or two. But it wasn't an illusion. Our middle fingers were somehow locked together at that now-aching joint, mine pointing slightly downward from the plane of his hand.

Carlos winced but didn't move otherwise. I felt a stab of hysteria as well as pain through the joined finger and up my arm.

"Don't twist," he warned. "The joint isn't meant for that."

Quinton stepped out of the kitchen door, looking puzzled as he walked toward us. "What's up? You guys look spooked."

"I misspoke about there being nothing between us," Carlos said.

Quinton glanced at our oddly joined hands and blinked, then stared. "What the hell is that?"

"The ghost bone. It appears this is my gift to Blaine in exchange for my life. I haven't seen the phenomenon in a considerable time. I had thought it died out."

"Apparently, not so much. And it hurts," I said, holding still at the expense of growing discomfort in my forearm and hand from extraordinary pressure on the conjoined digit. The rest of my finger was below Carlos's hand and I couldn't see it, though I was sure it was still there from the tingling ache. "Is the rest of my finger still attached? I can feel it, but . . ."

Quinton ducked his head to see. "Well . . . it's there. What it's attached to is in question, since it looks like it's just growing out of the middle of Carlos's knuckle on each side."

I curled the finger, causing Carlos to take a sharp breath and close his eyes.

"Sorry," I said.

"It's wiggling, so if you're doing the bending, it's still your finger, babe."

"I'm not sure how much of a relief that is."

"It is better than the alternative," Carlos said. "Perhaps we can reverse this action."

"Worth a try," I said, lowering and rotating my hand back to the position where my fingers had aligned with his. I could feel each finger brushing past his and back into position. The conjoined knuckle hesitated and balked like a tumbler in a rusted lock. I let out a little whimper and squeezed my eyes shut for a couple of seconds. The agony in my hand and arm was less, but the intensity of the ache in the finger was profound and after losing blood the night before, I felt a bit more weak in the knees than I wanted to admit.

Carlos scowled at our still-joined hands. "Hmm . . ."

I peered through the Grey at the knuckle. The bones looked like glass pipes filled with steam and outlined in white light. Thin red filaments of energy stretched along the bones and tangled at the joint, creating a mess I couldn't make sense of. I leaned closer to the knot and slid a bit more into the Grey. The joint became less solid as I became less corporeal and the tight wires of red energy loosened, uncoiling slightly. I could see how the two bones of his hand and mine had—impossibly—slipped past each other and rotated just a little, locking the rounded ends together in the complexity of the joint. I twitched my hand a touch counterclockwise and arched the finger. . . . With a pop and a spark of discomfort, the bones slid free and our hands separated.

"Ow!" I yelped, jerking all the way back into the normal world.

I clasped the aching fingers in my other hand and looked up to see Carlos doing the same, cradling his right hand in his left. His eyes were still closed and he wore a thoughtful expression. "I see . . ." he muttered.

"What?"

He didn't seem to hear me. He just said, "This could prove useful." Then he opened his eyes and turned to the house. "We had best go back into Rafa's memory of the house before anyone we would prefer not to talk to takes an interest."

Inside, we walked up to the tower, having agreed that privacy was necessary for what we were going to discuss even in Rafa's version of the house. Carlos opened the heavy curtains over the windows and pushed the casements wide, reveling in the touch of sunlight. A hushed flurry of minute rustlings and shuffling sounds rose at the intrusion of the light, and died away again, leaving an odor of newly turned earth and cut grass behind.

The chamber was cleaner than the last time I'd seen it, which surprised me at first, since I had expected the remains of whatever conjuring had drawn Carlos to Carmo to still linger in place. When had there been any time to straighten up? But the nevoacria—the shadow creatures that Carlos had drawn forth—had consumed and hidden away all traces of dust and disorder. Even the cobwebs and dry-rotted wood beside the fireplace were gone. Of the creatures themselves, there was only the smallest trace—persistent shadows in corners and under objects that cringed from sunlight and smoked when it touched them.

Carlos leaned against the edge of a table near the front window, so Quinton and I took the seats we'd occupied the last time, on the bench in front of a nearby table. The breeze through the window was pleasant, but the perfume of the garden had been muted by the odor of hot dust and old buildings.

"What about this ghost-bone thing?" I asked.

His expression was grave and remote. "We have little time for details. You will have to accept what I tell you without much explanation."

"All right. Give me the short version."

"It is a rare phenomenon—an affinity, not spell work. It's related to but not the same as the bone magic you saw two nights ago. You noted then, I'm sure, that bones have resonance. If the practitioner can match the resonance and an appropriate bone is available, the bones can be exchanged or grafted to a degree. They do not have to touch or lie atop each other as ours did, but in this case, it appears the position completed the requirements. One of the bones of your hand and one of mine share the same resonance—as unlikely as it seems."

"It doesn't seem very useful to me," I said.

"It is limited. True bone magic is more complex and broader in scope, but it requires tuning or reshaping the bones—utilizing them as the material and instruments of the spell work—as well as the ability to match resonance and draw a bone, living, from the body. This phenomenon is more use in healing bones—that was my mother's skill."

"I'm not sure I'm getting it," I said.

"She would heal people of broken or diseased bones by grafting a small portion of her own bones to theirs through this ghost bone. Like you, she healed very quickly and barely noticed the loss of her bone matter most of the time. If the injury was severe enough, she would replace the bone with her own and bear the injury herself for a while. It was not pleasant to observe and I learned a great deal about pain, damage, and death by her side." He saw me frown. "Not all of her experiments were successful and some of those she would have helped were too greatly injured to live. Some didn't deserve her attention—I took them."

I shuddered and felt the same reaction in Quinton, beside me. "How did this happen? Today, I mean—I think I know all I really want to about your relationship with your mother."

Carlos chuckled. "In our case, it was simply luck. The hands of men and women are usually so unequally sized that one bone or another would have to be carved or reshaped—usually in the body. Grafted bones must be of the same status—living or dead. A dead bone doesn't quicken in the body. But in our hands, there is something similar enough that the bones slipped past each other for a moment."

"Because I'm tall and have large hands for a woman."

"Paws," Quinton added.

"Thank you, Captain Obvious."

Now Carlos didn't smile. "Regardless, tuning and assembling the correct bones—living and dead—weaving the appropriate spell through them, and binding them by power and sound are the processes of the Kostní Mágové. Theirs is a learned craft and the discipline doesn't require that the practitioner have the ghost-bone affinity. It was not one I seemed to possess, but it appears that I've passed my mother's latent ability on to you, temporarily, in exchange for what you've given me."

"I'm not sure that there's any . . . use for this ability, if I do have it. I mean, how would you even know you had the right bone to swap?"

"Practice and tuning. You should be able to hear the bones, if you have the skill."

"Ugh. That's a sound I'd like never to hear again, thank you."

"Then you did hear it, even without this strange gift."

"In the bone temple? Yes. The whole room was full of these tuned bones you're talking about. It whispered everywhere. Every time Griffin cast or adjusted a spell, the whole room . . . wailed."

Carlos turned an inquiring look on Quinton. "Did you hear this?"

"I heard something, but it only got loud once. Otherwise it was like a constant low whistling or whining that made my skin crawl."

"I heard more, but not what Blaine describes." Carlos returned his focus to me. "As a Greywalker, you hear the voices of Grey things more clearly, even without this strange, new gift."

"All the damned time," I said. "Lisbon sounds like it's crying. Seattle hums. Mexico City rattles and whines like a steel guitar. I used to hear voices in the Grid itself, but I don't anymore—which is fine by me. They almost drove me insane. Noisy is manageable, chatty . . . not so much."

"It is something to bear in mind as we deal with the Kostní Mágové and their drachen."

"Drachen?" Quinton asked. He looked at Carlos. "You mentioned something this morning. . . ."

"O Dragão do Inferno—the Hell Dragon. It is not the fragile thing that Griffin conjured two nights ago—she didn't cast that herself, but released it from the small, carved bone she carried with her from the altar. That bone was another form of Lenoir's spirit box.

The Night Dragon and Hell Dragon require drachen bones and the work of a dreamspinner. Griffin is not one of those. But the Kostní Mágové here clearly have drachen bones and a dreamspinner in their company. They still need other bones and the chance to carve them with the appropriate spells and tunings, since they have yet to replace your niece. If they complete the skeleton and give life to the song of the bones, it will be a living nightmare."

"And how are we going to stop them?" Quinton asked. "We took back Soraia, but there are other bones out there. We can't protect every little girl. . . . Whatever they're up to, they're moving faster than we are. This morning, there were near riots outside the Jerónimos Monastery about the possibility that the tomb of Dom Sebastião might not have been vandalized, but that 'the desired one' is coming back. Which is, frankly, an 'End of Days' scenario in my mind. You don't want the Sleeping King to show up for anything less than—" He cut himself off and turned his head sharply away from both of us, staring out the front window.

"Less than what? An apocalypse?" I asked. "Why wouldn't your father want that as well? It would do everything he wants and much faster than his current work with ghosts and undead agitators." Then I turned to Carlos. "It's what you said they—these bone mages—are after, too. We saw the master mage from the temple meet with another priest just before we saw the Night Dragon here in Alfama. And he matches the description of a priest seen at the monastery when it was robbed."

"Rui," Carlos said. "Are you certain they were the same man?"

"Not entirely—no one described his aura in the news report— but the one we saw just down the hill here? Yes. It was him—Rui. It's not likely there are two priests of the same description involved in *unrelated* crimes concerning bones," I said, "aura or not."

Quinton and I told him about Purlis's disruptions in other places—riots in Paris, bombings in Turkey, epidemics in Spain and the United States, the riots at the bank and the air base, the Night Dragons and monsters, and then about the dead pickpocket, the priests who must have been bone mages, and the other ossuaries that had been vandalized, coming at last back to the robbery at Jéronimos and the angry mutterings I'd heard the night before as I ran through the Baixa to Santa Justa.

"There is no Sleeping King," Carlos said, but he was thinking as he did. "Sebastião was not entombed in that crypt. But the dust of those bones would still be of use. . . . A great deceit—a pauper buried as a king. And they are aware that they can benefit from fear and unrest without having to cast a single spell to achieve it."

"So that's what my father has been doing in the past months, here in Europe—sowing discord and unrest to benefit the Mágové—as well as working for their ends more directly by acquiring materials and destroying resistance to economic and political decline. Europe is facing a crisis that's not just about money or national boundaries— it's the loss of hope for an entire generation. The system is failing them and they're becoming desperate enough to do something rash. Or that's what I think, from what I've seen in places like Ukraine and Syria. He still needs to create the same degree of division and despair here, but I'm not sure that rousing the hope of a few nuts in Portugal is going to do what the Mágové want."

Carlos wore a speculative frown. "The numbers of those who truly believe in the Sleeping King may be small, but it will take very little to convince those whose despair and desperation can be romanticized into supporting a foolish cause. Poverty, unrest, disillusion, dispossession . . . This modern Europe is full of it and the number of those who feel hopeless and angry is growing. And from what I see, my countrymen are not what they once were. The world, the passage of time, has crushed them, reduced them from a people who once ruled an empire girdling the globe to those who barely rule their own country. With the Inferno Dragão, the Kostní Mágové could burn Portugal to ash and that alone would not be enough. But a legendary monster rising in a time of fear? It fits the myth of a coming apocalypse that they have sown, and it amplifies the irrational. It is something so far beyond what normal men and women believe in normal circumstances that many—most, eventually—will reject any more logical attempt at explanation. It will turn their logic against them. They will be hopeless, unable to imagine what to do, in the face of the impossible made flesh. Not all of the relics the bone mages have taken are intended to build the creature—only to sow discord and create other, smaller engines of terror. We will have to deprive them of the remaining pieces of their puzzle."

"How?" I started.

Quinton interrupted. "None of this conversation is going to matter if we get captured," he said, taking a step away from the bench and the window near it. "Look out the window, discreetly, and tell me what—or more to the point—who you see across the street."

Carlos leaned his head to one side and peered down. I turned my gaze sideways through the Grey, looking for energy signs that were familiar or dangerous. There were three distinct and unpleasant forms outside in the Grey and a fourth, weaker one, farther down the road. The first was a violent tangle of colors tightly contained in bands of white that rose from the cold lines of the Grid in the street below—I knew the shape of it, but the colors weren't as I remembered them. Beside it were two shorter shapes: One was a brittle black and bone-white with towering spikes of blood-red erupting from it; the other was a less-complex black-and-white I recognized from two nights earlier as Maggie Griffin. I couldn't tell much about the fourth one—the colors were strange shades of aqua, violet, and marine blue, their curling, calligraphic shape unfamiliar. I stepped away from the window also and pushed myself back into the normal plane, casting only a glance out the physical window to confirm what I thought.

Well down the road, a skinny teenager crouched at the edge of the sidewalk, looking around with strange, dreamy eyes as he chalked something on the stones. I wasn't sure if he was part of the party closer to the house or not. Across the street, at its widest point, where the road turned and flowed around a huge old tree that was now in the center of the lane, Maggie Griffin stood with her back to us, dressed as before in her narrow black dress and heels. She stood just in front of two men as if arguing with or being chastised by them. One I recognized instantly: Quinton's father, James McHenry Purlis. He leaned heavily on a cane and his stance was awkward, his left trouser leg falling unevenly over the clumsy shape of a badly fitted artificial leg. Beside him stood the old man I'd seen with the priest and again at the bone temple with Griffin. He was short and slim, but age hadn't bent him and where his wavy hair hadn't gone gray, it was the lusterless black color of soot.

"Rui Araújo e Botelho de Carreira," Carlos said. "When we both labored under Lenoir—the mage who imprisoned Sergeyev—he was called O Anjo do Dor."

Quinton scowled. "The Angel of Pain? That seems kind of anti-climactic. Why not the Angel of Death? It has more gravitas."

"That is what he called me when his education passed into my hands."

"I should have guessed."

Carlos only lifted an eyebrow.

"And of the others, one I don't know, one's Griffin, and the other's your father," I added. "And like Sam said—his left leg is missing from the knee down and his energy color is . . . way off. That can't be good."

Now Carlos scowled. "This presents a complication, but possibly an advantage to us. Rui cannot leave Portugal and plainly he is the master at work here. Whatever else they need to complete the Dragão do Inferno, it must be in Portugal and they will set it aflame here."

"That's nice. In the meantime, we need to get the hell out of Dodge," said Quinton.

"There are tunnels—" I started.

"Those will only take us into the castle," Carlos said. "With Rui and Griffin this close, that would be an insufficient distance. We can buy time, but with no safe harbor to flee to, time is not enough."

"Let's start by getting out of this room where they can see us," I suggested. "Apparently, Rafa's temporacline doesn't operate here, since we see the contemporary world through the windows, and not the world of her time—as we did in the salon last night."

Quinton looked to Carlos. "My dad's a hell of a tracker. What about this Rui?"

"Only fair, without recourse to the bones, but he has the scent of us from our visit to their circle. He knows we are here as well or better than your father does."

"Would he be able to detect our presence when we're in Rafa's time frame?"

"Yes, but it would be confusing, even with Griffin's assistance. If they were in the house and we were outside it, however, the difficulty would be greater, since the house traps magic and contains many temporaclines that scatter and dissipate spells attempted by those unfamiliar with the building's peculiarities. I could also ensure that they have difficulty leaving. . . ."

"Then we should get into the kitchen, where Rafa's effect is strongest. That will buy us a little time right now to figure out where to run and how to get them stuck in here when we do."

"I have no doubt that they will enter on their own if we leave any opening. You trust our mysterious Rafa's effect more than I," Carlos said, but he started for the door with us right behind him.

"It's not that I trust it—or her," said Quinton as we began down the tower stairs, "but that I've been stuck here more hours than either of you and had the chance to study her more. There's something very strange about Rafa."

"What, aside from being dead?" I asked.

"Yes. She's aware of the passage of time since her death, and yet she really isn't. It's as if events happen in a vacuum and they all occur simultaneously."

"Ghosts lose their sense of time and chronology," I said. "They have no reference for events outside their own lifetimes. Or at least most don't."

"I've been trying to figure out how she's connected to this house, aside from having been the housekeeper. She seems to know Amélia, and yet, their lifetimes have no overlap. Ghosts aren't usually aware of other ghosts, are they?"

Carlos and I exchanged glances over Quinton's head, but it was I who answered. "If they were aware of an older ghost before they died, they might know about them afterward. But it's rare for them to know a ghost from a different time frame the same way you and I know living people. It's not like there's some ghostly party going on where they discuss their afterlives with one another."

"But that's the relationship they seem to have. Rafa calls Amélia 'Avó,' which means—"

"Grandmother," Carlos supplied.

Quinton stopped at the second floor hallway and offered an expectant look.

Carlos shook his head. "I had no children and most of my near family was executed. There were a few surviving women and children, but their descendants would be remote nieces or cousins at best."

"But it's possible she is a relative."

"In a distant fashion."

Quinton looked thoughtful. "Did your family have any . . . estates or land elsewhere in Portugal?"

"Yes, many."

"Any that grew olives?"

"Probably, but they were no concern of mine since I was a bastard and would not inherit any of them."

"What about your wife?"

"Her family had no title, but they were wealthy and I believe they gave her a small property as a wedding gift. It produced income, but it was in the east. I never saw it."

"You mean, like . . . the Middle East?"

"No. Eastern Portugal near the Spanish border. It was an area frequently in dispute between the two countries."

"They grow olives in the east, but are more famous for cork, wheat, livestock. . . . No wonder she apologized. . . ."

"For what?"

"She said there was nothing left but olives as if that were a disappointment. If, when you were alive, the estate made its money off the cork oaks or other products but those are all gone now, she might have felt she'd let you down . . . Dom Carlos. She talks about you like you're some kind of family legend. You're certain Amélia didn't . . . have an affair or anything like that . . . ?"

"No. It would be surprising if she hadn't. But there was no pregnancy, no child." Carlos frowned. "But if Rafa is a granddaughter of Amélia's through adultery, she should have no tie to this house. It is mine alone."

"Well, she's somebody's kid. Maybe we should have a chat with Amélia before we blow town," Quinton suggested, and turned to continue down the stairs to the kitchen.

Outside, I heard a distant boom and a crack like that of giant wings, while a shiver of heat passed through the Grey.

TWENTY-TWO

The kitchen proved a difficult place to summon Amélia. It had probably been a room she rarely frequented when alive—the realm of domestic servants, not the lady of the house. Carlos was becoming frustrated, when Rafa come into the room behind us. He caught her, pinning her in place near the stove with the same word and gesture he'd used the night before. She looked alarmed but didn't fight.

He leaned close to Rafa. "Who is the lady of this house?" Carlos asked her.

Rafa was confused. *"Sua espousa, meu senhor."*

"My wife?"

"Sim. Ela é minha bisavó." Rafa seemed to find the whole conversation odd and she frowned at him. *"Por que você está tão cruel com ela? Por que você trouxe essas pessoas—"*

Carlos moved his hand in front of her as if he were brushing her speech aside and Rafa fell instantly silent. He looked at Quinton and me, standing on the other side of the old wooden kitchen table. "In Rafa's temporacline, Amélia is the mistress of the house. She resists coming when I call her, using the power Rafa has given her as leverage. She has no such strength in other versions of the house."

"But we aren't as safe," I said.

"True. But if we move swiftly, we can capture Amélia and escape before Griffin, Rui, and Purlis can get past the gate."

"That's assuming they haven't been busily working their way in while we've been hanging out with Rafa," Quinton said.

"They have, but I have a little control over how fast they come. It will be sufficient, so long as we are swift," Carlos said.

"Do you have something to catch her in?" I asked. "I've done this before, but I had to have a reflective container."

"I need no such object."

Carlos started to gesture as if he would dismiss the temporacline and Rafa with it, but Quinton threw up one hand. "Wait! What about the estate? If it still exists, it might be the perfect place to hide, since only Rafa ties any of us to it and she's a ghost."

"Rui is not above torturing the dead for information. Though without her bones in hand, it will be more difficult for him."

"Then we'll take her with us, too."

Carlos gave him a narrow, assessing look. "For a man who distrusts and despises me, you seem to have high expectations of my abilities."

"I trust you. I just don't like you much. And I know better than to underestimate your skills. Snatching two ghosts out of the ether instead of just one isn't going to be any sort of difficulty for you."

Carlos looked at me and raised an eyebrow. "Birds of a feather."

"Hey!" I objected.

Carlos offered a thin, unfriendly smile. "It is not quite as simple as you believe, but, indeed, it's no hardship. However, her temporacline may collapse as soon as I take her and we'll have less time in which to move."

We both nodded. He turned back to Rafa and removed whatever magical gag he'd placed on her.

She let out a stream of indignant words while Carlos waited for her to stop. It didn't take long for her to wind down.

"Where is Amélia's estate?" he asked.

Rafa blinked as if surprised and replied in rapid Portuguese, gesturing as though giving directions I couldn't begin to follow. Carlos scowled, but Quinton nodded the whole time. When she was done, she smiled at Carlos as if he'd just paid her a dazzling compliment.

He bowed to her. *"Perdoe-me,"* he muttered. Then he swept his hand through her as if grabbing a coat off a rack.

She was solid in the temporacline we occupied. For a moment her form resisted, and she gasped in surprise and pain as his hand ripped into her. Then she collapsed into a shape of silver mist and pale blue sparks that Carlos gathered into his fist, rolling the ghostly steam into a small wisp he thrust into the chest pocket of his shirt.

The house shuddered around us as Carlos collected the remnant of Rafa. The kitchen seemed to waver and grow icy, then flush into searing heat and a flash of harsh yellow light as the house settled back into the normal time frame. Cold white mist rolled across the floor. Shrieking, scrabbling, and pounding shook the front of the house, resonating through the structure and reflecting off the garden wall in waves of sound and magical force. The Grey shivered silver and green with every blow.

Quinton was a little shaken, but he looked around, assessing the situation. "That's not another earthquake."

"No," Carlos said. "Our guests have grown impatient. Are you both ready to leave as soon as this is done?"

"Not quite," Quinton said. "I can't risk leaving the laptop where Dad can recover it. Can you do without me while I go get it?"

"We can, but bring everything you'll need and be sure the tower door is closed and the lock engaged. Meet us in the cellar."

"Will do." Quinton bolted out of the room and I could hear him running at full pelt across the foyer and up the stairs.

Carlos looked at me. I shrugged. "I travel light. What I need is in my pockets. Remember—I came with nothing." I blessed the habit by which I'd stowed my ID and cash in the pockets of unfamiliar clothes as I dressed.

"Good. Catch Amélia when she arrives. She won't be as easy to take as Rafa. She knows me better."

He glanced at my hand and seemed about to ask me to extend it, but then he chuckled in his throat and looked down at his own hand. He picked up one of the kitchen knives and pricked his left index finger. Very fast, he wrote something on the kitchen table in his blood and drew something from his shirt that was black and shining darkly through the Grey. It was the Lâmina que Consome as Almas—a black blade he had killed for and nearly been destroyed by, later. He let fall a single red drop of his blood onto the knife and the blade rang as he slammed his palm down on the table over the words he had scrawled there.

"Come, Amélia Maria Desidéria Leitão e Sousa de Neves Ataíde. You have no choice."

She appeared with a screech of fury and flew at him before I could lay a hand into her energetic substance. *"Monstro!"*

He batted her aside and I caught a few fingers into her chilly tangle of ghost-stuff. She strained against my hold, toward Carlos as if she meant to strike him, and her words made hollow echoes in my mind, heard and only partially understood in the confusing fog of her fury.

"Monster?" Carlos said. "First you save me, then you revile me. Dear wife, you're more interesting than I realized."

"Deixa a minha filha em paz. Deixa!" Let my daughter go. . . .

"Your daughter? Rafa? Impossible. Many-times-great-granddaughter, perhaps . . ."

She fell back a short distance, her shade quivering in the shaking house as the tension between her energetic form and my crooked fingers eased. *"Minha neta . . ."* My grandchild . . .

"By whom? By whom did you have a child that begat still more children, little wife?"

"Você! Por causa de você, Carlos, a minha grande maldição, e o meu grande amor . . ." By you, Carlos, my curse, my beloved . . . Her voice trailed away and she tried to withdraw as if ashamed or appalled at what she'd said. I held her where she was, though I longed to let her go.

"You never told me," Carlos said, the air around him waxing hot and red with his anger.

"Eu temia que você faria. . . ." I feared what you would do. . . .

"As well you should have. I took you against your will, forced you—" He seemed almost pleased to remind her of the things he'd done to hurt her and drive her away.

Amélia shrugged. *"Forcei você a fazê-lo."* I made you do it.

He roared at her.

The house rattled and Quinton skidded through the door with his bag over his shoulder. "No more time, folks—the storm troopers have arrived!"

Carlos cursed, but his fury dissipated as suddenly as it had come and he drew his hand over Amélia's phantom face. "Sleep." Then he slipped the point of the Lâmina into the swirl of her ghostly fabric. I yanked my hands away, feeling the tool's hunger as it cut. Carlos twisted the ghost's substance onto the blade like thread on a spindle. The knife drank Amélia in until no sign of her remained.

I backed toward the door as he pulled a match from the box near the stove and lit the smear of blood across the table's surface on fire.

Then he turned to us, the black blade still in his hand. "Why are you standing still? Run!"

We bolted out the door, but Carlos didn't follow immediately. I turned to see why.

Griffin had skittered into the hall, her black heels clattering on the tiles. She stopped as she saw Carlos and gaped for a split second before making a flinging gesture at him.

A rattling swirl of ivory and black whirled toward him. Carlos flicked the Lâmina through it and the spell fell apart, littering the floor with white grit.

Griffin jolted backward, spitting, "Why can't I kill you, you bastard? You should be dead!"

Silent, Carlos sprang toward her, the gleaming blackness of the blade thrust forward in a blur that sliced into Griffin's chest almost faster than I could follow. Her mouth fell open in shock as his hand pushed wrist-deep under the arch of her ribs. I gagged.

Carlos leaned close, as if he would kiss her, and murmured words that seemed to settle on Griffin like dust. She writhed, smoke rising around her. He yanked his arm back, tearing something pulsing and dripping blood from her chest.

I doubled over in an agony of reflected death as Griffin collapsed to the floor, blood and dark vapor pouring from the hole in her torso. She blinked twice, her mouth working like that of a fish out of water. Then she was still and I could barely breathe from the shock of her death as it moved through me.

Rui ran through the archway with a fleetness that belied his age and stopped, taking in the body and the blood on the floor with a strange gleam in his eye. He raised his head to look at us, his gaze narrowed, as if he was trying to decide which was more important: catching us or dismembering his dead student.

Before he could move farther, Carlos flung Griffin's heart at the bone mage's head and whirled back to drag me to my feet and across the hall to the cellar door.

He slammed it closed behind us, muttering swift, barbed words that sparked and sealed themselves across the door.

We fled down the cellar stairs, snuffing candles as we went, tumbling and staggering down to the cool, dry darkness of the rooms below where Quinton waited in a foment of impatience and worry. Carlos led us through the last door and bolted it behind himself once again before showing us the concealed door on the other side. Beyond the odd little portal, a narrow tunnel sloped upward toward the castle that lay on the summit, dreaming in the sun. We stepped inside, Carlos pausing again to work some more complicated spell at the threshold of the secret door, and then we began up the steep stone passage.

The house echoed behind us with the sound of Rui's rage.

By the time we emerged on the far side of the hill near the castle wall, we could no longer feel or hear the shuddering of the house, but there was a new sound in the air. The chatter of morning tourists on the castle ramparts above us was louder than it should have been, breaking into shouts and sudden squeals as a shadow passed over with a sound of leathery wings. Housewives on the terraced streets below looked up and screamed. Seabirds cruised through the blue sky above, letting distant cries into the air perfumed with the river and the scent of Lisbon's streets and moved aside in the sudden rush of air as a churning, dark mass of wings, eyes, and streaming cloud-stuff that looked like tentacles dove from above. It spread in my vision, obscuring most of the sky in inky green horror.

Quinton had stopped just within the concealment of shrubs and trees that covered the mouth of our escape tunnel. "What in three kinds of hell is that?"

Carlos tilted his head. In the slanting light through the shrubs there was no sign of the gore that had splattered him as Griffin died. "Someone's nightmare. Rui brought his dreamspinner along."

"So he or she can do more than raise weak drachen," I said. "Is it dangerous or just an illusion?"

"Even an illusion can be dangerous, but this one is weak. A dreamspinner's work is always stronger in shadow and night than in daylight," Carlos replied.

"We've seen some of his work in the daylight before on this trip," I reminded him.

"True, but this one is decaying already. It won't last more than a few minutes longer."

"Why bother with it, then?" I asked.

"I suspect he's as pleased with the diversion and fright it's creating as with any practical aspect."

"But can we afford to wait for it to dissipate?" Quinton asked. "How much time do you think we've bought ourselves?"

"Perhaps three hours," Carlos said.

"Well, I guess we've got a few minutes to wait, whether we like it or not," Quinton said. "I'm thinking that if we split up and get far from here before they get free from the house, we might improve that lead. How long do you think it will take Rui and Griffin to catch up?"

"Griffin will not be catching up, which may remove Rui from the equation for a day while he deals with her remains. If our trail goes cold here, it could be two or three more days before he and your father find other ways to track us. If the estate proves to be remote enough, we may confound their efforts completely—when we reach it."

"And you don't know what they still need to make their Hell Dragon?"

"We know they still need the bones of a child. They may require the bones of a repentant thief, among others. If the bones are touched by power, the strength of their spell is greater, and the same is true if the bones serve more than one purpose. Rui will take some of those from Griffin, but he will find them unsatisfactory. Your niece would have sufficed, but they have lost her. They will look elsewhere for their woman's bones, once they realize Griffin's are tainted. Without knowing precisely what's already been taken from the ossuaries and whom they've killed, I can't know what's still wanting. The recent damage has all been in Lisbon or in the south along the Algarve. There are ossuaries in the Alentejo—the most important is the Capela dos Ossos in the church of Saint Francis, in Évora where the skeleton of a child hangs in chains, but there are two more in the area. One at Campo Maior and another at Monforte, both to the northeast. They are more likely to find their woman's bones and their thief at one of those."

The boiling cloud of wings and tentacles turned in the sky, growing smaller and thinner. "I think it's fading out," I said.

"Good," Quinton replied. "The sooner it's gone, the sooner we go. If we split up here, they'll have to decide who's more important to chase after and that will tell us what they're most worried about—you or us." Carlos looked dubious while Quinton continued. "I know where the estate is from what she said and since you have Rafa . . ."

It was hard to credit, but Carlos appeared uncertain. Since we'd arrived, I'd seen him use magic as casually as if it cost nothing; he'd called the nevoacria without any apparent effort. He was on his home turf, one of the most powerful mages I'd ever met, and yet he hesitated. But nothing was as he remembered and he currently existed in a more fragile state than he'd experienced in nearly three hundred years. Now he faced traveling alone in daylight, which had become as foreign to him as living on the moon. For five years I'd thought of him as invincible, infallible, but now he wasn't. His aura had changed so profoundly in the past twenty-four hours that I could no longer read it, but I could see it shift and contract around him. Was it possible Carlos was overwhelmed and didn't want to part company with us for reasons that had nothing to do with practicality or safety?

"What of Blaine?" Carlos asked.

"I always know where Quinton is—or at least which direction—if I concentrate hard enough," I said, laying my hand on my chest for a moment to touch the point of our paranormal connection. "I'll just head northeast until I find him."

Both men frowned at me, but they didn't have any more choice than I did. "It's nearly gone," I noted, watching the nightmare spark and thin in the air before it swirled and dove for the ground. "Are we agreed on a plan?"

Their replies were drowned in the shrieks of the people on the castle rampart as the dreamspinner's work plunged toward them, in its last act.

"It would be unwise for us to travel farther together," Carlos conceded. "I will go through Évora and then find my way to the estate. I will meet you both there."

He stepped out into the sun and walked toward the castle, just another slightly dusty tourist—not a sign of bloody murder left on his skin or clothes. I watched him until Quinton pulled me the other way—there was only one other direction to go on the road below us and no way up or down without wings. We'd have to walk together for a few minutes.

"He'll be all right. He's the baddest badass in Portugal."

"I'm not sure about that," I said as we walked down the north slope of the hill and away from Carlos and the Castelo São Jorge. "He's vulnerable—mortal, at least temporarily—and this isn't the same Lisbon he's used to anymore."

"He's still more dangerous than six of anyone else put together. He stopped Griffin, didn't he? She wasn't a pushover."

"He ripped her heart out."

"Good for him. No one better deserved the loss of a major organ. You don't see Carlos as others do, Harper. No one who doesn't have a death wish is going to mess with him."

"Those aren't the people I'm worried about. What if Rui and your father catch him?"

"They won't—if he doesn't have to watch out for us, he has more options about how to stymie Rui than we do. We're a detriment to him at this stage. Besides, who would you bet on in that fight? The apprentice or the master? Seriously."

Even in my uncertainty and the lingering ache in my chest from Griffin's death, I had to give him that point. "How do you think they found us?" I asked.

"Taxi driver."

"What taxi driver?"

"You didn't notice? Down at the end of the block where the street turns, there was a taxi parked. The same cab you and Carlos came home in."

"I can't believe I missed it."

"You were both in pretty bad shape last night, so it's not that surprising. And don't kick yourself about not having identified the driver as a villain. Dad and Rui just did what the cops would do—they checked for anyone who fit your or Carlos's description. My dad's seen you both before, but we got lucky, because the old man wasn't quite prepared to see Carlos at all, much less running around in daylight. They knew he survived, but Griffin obviously didn't stay to see the finale. I guess Carlos was right about her vanity being her downfall."

"I'm just afraid we're throwing him to the wolves. And after what I did to keep him alive." I had to trot to keep up with Quinton's agitated pace.

"Rui and my dad won't want any of us alive to stop them. They both know how dangerous Carlos is to their plans and Dad can't risk having me on the loose for similar reasons. And while my father may not be sure what you are even if Rui's told him—and he strikes me as the sort who likes to keep a few cards hidden at all times—he knows you're not normal. With or without me, you're a wild card far too dangerous to leave in someone else's hands. We're all running from the wolves, now. I'm frankly worried about whoever may be with Dad aside from Carlos's dearest enemy. I can't plan for what I don't know. On the upside, Dad's not going to be moving very fast with that leg."

"On the downside, when we're talking about bone mages, I'm more concerned about where his original leg is now. It happened before he took Soraia, so it's not a substitute for her. . . ."

"I'm trying not to think about that."

"Maybe you should."

We both shut up and jogged on down the hill. At the first corner we came to, Quinton stopped, gave me a quick kiss, and turned aside, taking the other road and leaving me to my own devices.

I had no doubt about my ability to find my own way—strange city or not, figuring things out was my forte—but I was still worried and other bits of my mind continued pursuing the calculus of destruction and the unacknowledged weight of fear.

TWENTY-THREE

I started walking the other way, feeling the slightest pull of Quinton behind me, but knowing better than to turn around. At each intersection, I turned away from that tugging sensation, looking for some way out of town. I finally came down from the castle hill on Rua Cavaleiros at the north end of the Baixa, where the next of Lisbon's seven hills began to swoop back upward. Ahead of me lay Praça Martim Moniz—another open plaza with trees and fountains set in a huge oval park of ubiquitous white tile. The area was scruffier than the nearby Praça da Figueira with only a few of the Pombaline Baroque buildings looking slightly down-at-the-heels here amid flat-fronted modern construction. Low-set half walls of bland concrete shoehorned an antique church between what appeared to be a commercial building coated in peeling paint on one end and a hideous 1970s apartment block on the other.

On the near side, I spotted a bus stop that was nearly a block long across the street from a sign for an underground metro station. I ran across the road, dodging traffic, to the station stairs. I figured I could find my way out of town if I could get to a train or bus station.

Whatever I did, I knew the train station at Cais do Sodré lay south-west and I wanted to go northeast, so as long as I moved in the opposite direction of the trains Quinton and I had used to go to Carcavelos, I should get closer to my goal. I was less worried about catching up to Quinton once I got out of Lisbon. Though it was illogical, I knew I wouldn't have any trouble finding him once I started trying—we always seemed to fall back together. The curious, pulling sensation in my chest that connected us through the Grey thrummed and vibrated with the nervous quivering of my heart.

Negotiating an unfamiliar transit system can be nerve-racking, but I got to do it in a foreign language while trying to stay off the radar of anyone—or anything—associated with my almost father-in-law. The paranormals were much easier to avoid than the spies—I could see them coming. The Martim Moniz metro station wasn't very busy. With Purlis and his uncanny companion in mind, I moved with care, first finding a restroom so I could clean up a little, and then slipping into the Grey to peek at the station from that vantage point before I strolled out into it.

I saw two of the uncomfortable, rolling auras I'd spotted at Cais do Sodré and something that looked like a transparent human skeleton. My guess on the last one was some kind of ghost working for Purlis—whether it wanted to or not. I wasn't sure if the men and the skeletal thing were looking for me at all. I have a distinctive glow in the Grey and I thought it might be better if I didn't find out the hard way that they could see it. Chances were good the two dark auras belonged to humans who couldn't see through walls, so if I knew where they were, I could avoid them. The skeleton was more of a problem, especially since, being a bone construct, it had to be the work of the Kostní Mágové. I had no idea how it functioned. It wasn't close, however, so I slipped back to the normal and out of the restroom. Looking down the concourse, I guessed that the Men with Ugly Auras—I dubbed them the MUAs for convenience—were inside the gates, but it appeared that the skeleton was outside them.

I slunk down the concourse toward the ticket-vending machines, keeping my vision partially turned to the Grey until I spotted the edge of the skeleton. I looked toward it and saw one of the many art installations that seemed to be common in Lisbon's metro stations. I shivered, realizing that the gruesome thing was embedded in an otherwise nondescript bit of construction board that covered a wall repair in progress. It faced the turnstiles I'd have to pass through to get to the platform. I guessed that there would be some similar thing at any other set of turnstiles for this station, so there wasn't much to be gained in checking and a lot of time to be lost. I'd have to find a way through this chokepoint.

I stopped well back from the turnstiles as if I couldn't find my ticket and pushed myself back against the tiled wall, studying the construction through the Grey. It reminded me of something I'd dealt with before—a sort of paranormal security system that had been set up by a blood mage using a dead dog. I'd been able to get around that with a combination of my skill and Quinton's theory, but this didn't seem to be quite as complicated. It was more like a silent alarm that looked for something specific and sent a signal to whoever was at the receiving end, by paranormal means, without alerting the subject. The skeleton probably sent some kind of alarm to the MUAs so they could converge on the turnstiles once I—or whatever they were looking for—was committed and couldn't back out easily, since the gates were the automated stainless steel variety that took the ticket at one end and gave it back on the other side of their automated wing doors. It wasn't a complicated system and to someone without my ability, it was undetectable and inescapable.

But it had a couple of weaknesses—the skeleton used as the detector was embedded in something movable and the chances were good it saw in only one direction—forward from its hollow eye sockets.

I studied the board and how it was supported, wondering if I could just . . . tip it over and walk past. The thing might alert when it fell, however, and that wasn't any better than just setting it off to begin with. I almost laughed at myself as I realized I could slip behind it through the Grey and step out on the other side of the turnstiles without ever passing in front of the skeleton. It was a good thing Quinton hadn't come with me, since he had no such ability.

I waited for a rush in the late-morning commuter crowd and slid past the skeleton alarm. Now I just had to deal with the MUAs on the other side. I was pretty sure they knew what I looked like by now—Rui and Papa Purlis both knew, and it was unlikely that anyone working for this group had no discreet communications. I'd have to spot them before they spotted me.

I walked to the system map on a wall and studied it, planning my route. I also checked for the locations of the two creeps I'd spotted as I did so. It appeared that the route was faster if I went south, but there were more chances to lose a tail if I went north, and the zoo's metro station connected to the northernmost train station in Lisbon. I was sure I'd be able to find a bus or a train going northeast from there. . . .

The platform announcement system made a noise and someone spoke in Portuguese, followed by English, French, and Spanish repetitions of the information that a northbound train was approaching the platform and everyone should remain behind the safety lines. All subways seem to have the same message. I made my way down to the platform, barely staying in the rush of people hoping to make this train while I kept an eye out for the MUAs. One was pacing at the end of the platform nearest me and the other was at the opposite end, covering both exits. I wondered if they'd spot me without an alert from their bony alarm system. . . .

I didn't dare slow the traffic flow by stopping since that would only call attention to me before I was near the train. I wished I had my hat, but without it, I'd just have to rely on another technique. I eased closer to the stair edge on the open side of the platform so I'd be as close to the train as possible when I reached the next level. By slowing just a little near the wall, I forced other passengers to flow around me, blocking me from the sight of the man at the bottom of the stairs.

The train rushed in and sighed to a stop, the doors opening on a trickle of passengers—not enough to make a good screen, but not enough to clog the cars, either. I stepped down onto the platform and walked without a glance past the man who was looking for me. He apparently wasn't able to see my aura, so at first he didn't notice, but I heard him shout, followed by the sound of feet and cursing as he pushed someone aside to reach me. I dodged into the nearest car and ducked into a seat by the door.

The MUA lunged into the car and paused to look for me. I dropped to the floor and he ran up the aisle as I popped back up and sat down as if nothing had happened. He stepped out of the car through the next door, looking around as if not sure how he could have missed me. He was about to turn back into the car, when his partner ran up to him and distracted him long enough for the doors to shut them out. Both men stood there, staring into the car, annoyed. I turned my back and hunched down in the corner of the seat, making myself smaller, just another brown-haired woman on the metro. . . .

I don't know if they saw me or if they just called ahead on general principle, but I had to make several transfers and jump through a complicated change to the Red Line at Alameda station, then another change to the Blue Line at São Sebastião before I lost them. At first, I was surprised at the resources Purlis had put into bottling up the transportation hubs, but this unspeakable project was the object of his years-long ambition. He'd already tried to sacrifice thousands of innocent people in Seattle to move it forward. It appeared he'd engineered other acts of equal horror throughout Europe to keep his plans on track, so placing a few spies in transit stations wasn't such an outrageous idea, though I knew his resources had to be limited. He seemed to have everything he needed except the right bones, though, so maybe it was a matter of putting the nonspecialists to the grunt work, even if they weren't that well suited to it, while Rui and his cronies did the magical dirty work alone. There had to be a limit to the number of men Purlis could place in metro stations, however, and it looked as if I'd finally exceeded it.

Although I was braced for more of the MUAs at the Jardim Zoológico metro station, I didn't see any. Maybe it was too far outside the downtown core for Purlis to cover, or bother with, since he'd located us in Alfama, which lay a good distance in the opposite direction. I hoped the lack of Men with Ugly Auras and creepy bone-based cantrips and alarms didn't mean they were busy elsewhere, lying in wait for Quinton or Carlos.

But I'd underestimated Purlis.

I came up from the metro station on the side next to the zoo and started to the crosswalk to go under the elevated highway to the bus and train station on the other side of the road. A dark blue sedan with tinted windows pulled in awkwardly at the curb, partially blocking my path. I started around it, looking for other trouble, and had to scramble back a step as the rear door opened and Purlis un-folded himself from the backseat.

He wasn't quick and I could have just run back down the metro stairs to elude him, but it was obvious he had agents with him—and probably a lot of others around that I hadn't pegged because they weren't magical or unusual in any way. He must have figured out that I could detect paranormal elements and pulled the MUAs and mages back out of the area. Ordinary spycraft was all he needed here unless I wanted to make a scene. I couldn't be sure he didn't have Rui, another bone mage, or even the dreamspinner in the car, since the steel and glass of an automobile make a pretty good filter for Grey effects. On the other hand, if he was wasting time with me, he wasn't chasing Quinton or Carlos.

Purlis closed the car door and leaned on his cane, looking at me with a benign expression that sent a chill over me. "Hello, Harper. I thought we might have a little chat."

Even with his aura going green and red as an Italian flag, he was still keeping it under tight control. He looked so much like Quinton, it was startling, though he was older and not in the best of health. His skin was an unpleasant color even in the sunshine, and the ten-sion in his shoulders could have held up a bridge. Tiny lines of pain etched the corners of his mouth and eyes, and a faint odor of putre-faction clung to him.

"I think the last chat we had didn't go very well. Why should we have another?" I asked, trying to devise an escape without giving him any sign of what I was thinking. The area was completely un-known to me in both the Grey and the normal and I had no idea what resources he had on hand. I needed a break. . . .

"Well, this time no one's trying to kill anyone." His voice was almost identical to Quinton's, but it was flat and devoid of emotion. It made the skin at the back of my neck crawl.

"Strike one."

"Pardon me?" he asked.

"It's like baseball," I said. "You get three strikes and then one of us is out of here. Every blatant lie you tell me is a strike, and you just whiffed one in a major way."

"Will you simply walk me if I tell you some uncomfortable truths?"

"Maybe."

"Then perhaps you'd stroll with me to the zoo." It was like talking to Quinton's evil doppelganger and the experience disturbed me. But turning would give me a chance to look the situation over and I could stand his disquieting presence a little longer for that.

"I'd rather not, but if you insist, I'll go as far as the gate—if your leg is up to it." He could have anything waiting in the emotional chaos of the zoological gardens. Here on the street, I was in public view, but the pedestrian crossing was a little more public than I thought our conversation could handle—especially if I had to make an escape through the Grey.

"It's a small price to pay." He waved to the car and it pulled off to park not too far away, but certainly not close enough to overhear us without equipment. I backed up a few steps and Purlis closed the distance in lurching strides. He covered a grimace with a strained smile that didn't light his eyes.

"So, what happened?" I asked before he could own the discussion. "Your knee was healing fine the last I heard."

"I don't find your question germane to the discussion at hand, so let's say that my work has taken a toll on my health and leave it at that. But I have been asking a lot of questions about you. . . ."

"Me? I'd say I was flattered, but that would be a strike for my team," I said, crossing the dark paving stones of the parking area and onto the white stones of the walkway.

"You almost had me fooled. If you hadn't shown up with the vampire, I might still have thought you were just a bit odd."

"I've always been a little odd. Vampires are just the icing on the weird cake that is my life."

He forced a well-practiced laugh that in some other circumstance might have been charming. "You interest me, which is why I wanted to have this little talk." His words came out in small puffs as he walked, each movement jarring them into the air as he lurched on his unstable prosthesis and put too much of his weight on the cane, watching the grooved and patterned ground as much as he watched me. "You see, I don't understand you. Everything I hear about you— even from your enemies—indicates you have a strong sense of what is morally right, that you're driven by a desire for justice, without worrying too much over the letter of the law. I understand that position—I've been there, am there, myself. What we do may look unfathomable—even wrong—to outsiders, but we know it's the right thing to keep the world in balance."

"Are you implying we're of the same moral type?" I wasn't sure if it was his presence, the situation, or just the conversation, but I felt nervy and overwound as if the air were filled with static.

"From different approaches, but yes."

"Hmm . . . And yet I've never felt there was any excuse to kidnap and kill a child. You not only thought so; you took your own granddaughter. I think that's pretty far out of the ballpark of moral rectitude."

Jagged red sparks flew in Purlis's aura. He didn't like what I was saying, but he continued to keep his cool and replied in the same low, featureless voice, "Any true sacrifice is painful."

"It's not a sacrifice when you force someone to do it against their will—that's just murder. Why would you even consider such an action reasonable? What 'sacrifice' did you need a six-year-old child to make for you?" The electric feeling on my skin was intensifying with my anger.

"Necessity—"

"Strike two. There is nothing reasonable and necessary about kidnapping and murdering a six-year-old girl for spare parts. Your own granddaughter!"

He stopped walking just where the walkway divided to head for the zoo and turned to face me directly. "It was a hard choice, but Soraia is special and Sam has another child."

His face was calm, but the colors in his aura were now heaving and flickering in a polychromatic display I'd seen only once before. In the past year, Purlis had progressed from a fanatic who believed in his cause without wavering, to a full-blown psycho. For the first time in my life, I was certain that the world would be better off if I shot a man in the head and bore the consequences. And I didn't have a gun.

"She is special, but she's not a box of Tinkertoys for whatever unholy purpose your friend Rui and his ilk have in mind. And without her, you . . . what . . . would have settled for Martim if you could find him?" My disgust was heightened by the irritation of his energetic presence.

"No. He wouldn't have suited the work." As if anyone should have understood that without having to be told.

"He wouldn't . . . Oh yeah, because Soraia is a special little *girl* as well as your granddaughter, so she becomes a piece of the construction, along with your left leg and all the other bones you've looted from ossuaries all over Europe."

"There's always a price for the acts that redefine a nation—or the world."

"So your leg was the buy-in for world domination? Surely you don't think the Kostní Mágové are going to give you any real control over whatever it is they're making?"

He didn't give any sign in his expression that I'd hit home, but his energy corona sparked and he shifted his weight off his bad leg by the tiniest bit. "I've been at this game long enough to know how to control my assets."

"Assets? This bunch of religious fanatics? You told me you were a patriot."

"I am."

"I'm not sure how you square that ideal with plans to bring down some kind of apocalypse. It just seems to fly in the face of individual liberty."

"Individuals rarely stand high enough to achieve the scope of vision that will allow them to see what's truly the greater good."

"But you do, standing on your pile of bones with the likes of Rui Araújo."

"We can't always choose our allies."

"I'd bet Trotsky said the same thing about Stalin." Purlis gave me a sideways glance but held his tongue as his aura gave off a shower of annoyed orange sparks. "And since you've lost her, I suppose now you're looking for something to replace Soraia. . . . What kind of diabolical engine are you building, Purlis, that you need the bones of children and family? Are you planning on killing your wife or your son for this, too? Bear in mind I feel pretty strongly about his continued existence." There was no need to tell him how much I knew. If I didn't find a way to get out of the area, I might have to go with him for a while, and every piece of information Purlis and Rui didn't have was to my advantage.

"I don't need them. We have more than sufficient supplies of betrayers and spies."

"And you're both. So what else are you after? The innocent? The pure? The unbaptized babies of women born in a full moon? Or maybe those with a gift your skeleton-sucking friends don't have?"

The mad strobing of his aura shut down suddenly, becoming a tightly controlled spiral of blood-red and gold energy bound in white bands of force. "Some of those, yes, but the talented *and* pure prove much harder to find. Sadly, you don't have the vision I thought you did. You could have been useful to me, but associating with monsters seems to have derailed your sense." I could see him shift his weight and reset his grip on his cane.

I made a more subtle shift—reaching for the Grey. "The only monster I know is you."

TWENTY-FOUR

I had no more time and saw no other way out. I dropped toward the world between as fast as I could, not worrying about the location of temporaclines or what paranormal things might be nearby. Purlis was about to do something and I had to get away from that—before I strangled him with my bare hands. If he had traps for me in the Grey, so be it, and I hated that my precipitous vanishing act would probably give him more information about my own abilities than he already had.

But as I fell, something jerked me hard back toward the normal world and down to the ground. Purlis's cane slashed, gleaming oddly, through the air where I'd been standing, and he stumbled as he recovered from my sudden flicker. The force of the strike alone would have broken my legs, but the trail of oil-slick glisten it left in the Grey told me there'd been more to his attack. That cane wasn't just a bit of steel and wood, and I didn't know if it was connected to the cold or the breathlessness that now held me against the white paving stones.

Something pulled me down like a net drawn tight. I cursed myself as much as him, and I could feel the spell digging into me the same way the floor of the bone church had tried to do. I snatched at the ivory lines of the trap that I could now see inched in bones between the cracks of the white paving stones. This was plainly some work of Rui's and I hadn't seen it. Purlis had done an expert job of maneuvering me and keeping my attention on him, not on a potential pitfall. I ripped a piece of the spell out, but that left me with no better escape route.

I struggled toward the deepest layers of the Grey, down near the Grid where energy rules and the world devolves to wire frames of light and color in the void of physical matter. I could see it, but I was unable to drop any farther than the most superficial layer, my physical form refusing to sink or soften into the realms of mist and shadow that lie just outside of normal. It felt as if my own body were holding me back and my every move toward the Grid made me ache in every bone and joint. Usually I travel through the realm of ghosts and shadows securely housed in the armor of my physical body. However tiring it is, my ability to bestride all three planes—the normal, the paranormal, and the Grey—intact and whole is my one unique attribute. Everything else I can do or see or experience is within the power of someone or something else, as well. That ability is what defines me as a Greywalker—and now I couldn't do it.

I knew, much as it galled me, that I could lie struggling on the sidewalk, growing colder in the grip of Rui's bones and exhausting myself, or I could give up, save my energy, and hope to find another way to extract myself from the situation later. Not a great choice, but there was no better alternative and prisoner is still a better position than corpse. I didn't think Purlis or Rui—wherever he was—cared which they got.

I let go and was yanked back into the normal world. I slumped on the sidewalk as if my own bones were water.

"Welcome back," Purlis said, looking insufferable. "You'll forgive me if I don't help you to your feet."

"No," I muttered, unable to raise my voice any louder. "You're unforgivable."

"You've an interesting set of talents. It's a pity we have to be enemies."

"Who says we have to?" I asked.

"You don't like me and I can't trust you. . . ."

"Oh, but we won't be enemies forever. Eventually one of us is going to be dead." I found I was looking forward to it, since I had a much better chance of giving death the slip than Purlis had.

Purlis chuckled in spite of his physical discomfort as people who were obviously working for him converged on our position. "True. And sooner rather than later, I suspect."

He limped away as his team encircled me, hiding my strange, crushed posture from public sight. In a moment, Rui Araújo parted the circle and stood looking down at me. He seemed pleased, the red spikes in his aura jumping. He made a small gesture, murmured a word in Portuguese, and the force pulling me to the ground vanished.

I unfolded and stood slowly, wincing more than was strictly necessary, brushing the dirt off my dress and a few drops of blood off my abraded knees. He watched me with eyes brighter than one would expect of someone who had to be more than two hundred fifty years old. The penetrating quality of his gaze was disconcerting. I stood still and looked back at him, saying nothing, doing nothing.

Rui studied me a few moments longer. "You are not injured," he said. His voice was at odds with his appearance, low and soft, moving slowly, but not old at all, rather the opposite. He also had clear English, but a strong Portuguese accent and though there was nothing unpleasant in his tone, I felt like I was listening to a scorpion discussing the pros and cons of stinging me to death.

"You can't possibly know," I replied.

"No broken bones, no cracks, or bruises. Old injuries only. And a few scrapes on the skin," he added with a shrug and a dismissive snort. "I see everything." He pointed as he continued. "Feet, leg, knees, hip, spine, ribs, wrist, shoulder, neck, nose. What interesting scars your bones have."

"I used to fall down a lot."

"I see two . . . three that could have killed you."

"I also bounce."

"So I see. Come."

He beckoned and I discovered I had no choice. The men and women encircling us stepped aside and flowed out into the crowd again, but I followed jerkily after Rui like a reluctant pet on a leash, whether I liked it or not. I could resist and strain, which slowed my movement down, but didn't stop me; it only made me tired and sore. This could be a problem. I tilted my head and peered at the space between us through the Grey. A fine net of white lines ran from Rui's hands to various positions on my body and he towed me along like a badly strung puppet. There were a lot of them, but, individually, the lines wouldn't be much to break when I had the luxury. I just didn't at the moment. I guessed that he had literal control of my skeleton—probably created while I was in his trap where the bits of his ivory spell had burrowed toward my bones. I could oppose him, but the force of magic overcame the force of my currently weak muscles. I was still a bit on the anemic side after what had happened with

Carlos and I didn't have the stamina to bother resisting more than necessary, especially if I meant to break away when a better chance arrived.

"Where are we going?" I asked, walking along of my own accord now.

He relaxed a little and let me catch up to him. "Ah, you're being reasonable. Purlis said you would not. I disagreed. At my temple, you did nothing that was excessive or impulsive—unlike your companions. You understand when you are beaten."

I said nothing and Rui seemed to think that meant I agreed with him. He pointed ahead to a silver car with dark-tinted windows. "We shall take a ride. I have many questions for you."

"Will you be upset if I don't answer them?"

"Perhaps not answering them will be the answer."

There was a man behind the wheel of the car. Rui waited while I got into the backseat. He got into the front and the locks clicked down, leaving no manual lock buttons or levers for me to toy with. There was still the opening above the front seats that I could have reached over to wreak some havoc, but the arithmetic of whom to take out first and if I would survive it was trickier than I liked. And there was the option of digging through the seat's back into the trunk, but it wasn't viable in this situation—I'd be shot or enchanted before I could get past the center armrest. I sat still and waited for Rui to ask his questions.

"What are you?" he asked, looking at me in the vanity mirror. I could see his eyes and the back of his head, but not much else from where I sat behind him.

Funny: I now expect every magic-user and paranormal I meet to know what I do in the Grey, because Carlos and a few others nailed it even before I knew, myself. But, in fact, most have no idea such a thing as me exists and they don't need to. If they want help that I can give, they seem to find me on their own. I frowned and blinked at Rui. "I'm a licensed private investigator."

Rui glared and I saw his shoulders tense. My ribs seemed to collapse inward as if a giant fist were crushing my chest. Breath gushed out of my lungs and I clapped both hands over my mouth to stifle my scream. It felt as if my guts were being squeezed up through my throat. I was dizzy and thought I was going to vomit. Then the pressure vanished, though it took several seconds for me to refill my lungs, fighting the gripping pain as my ribs and intercostal muscles moved back into their accustomed positions.

"Don't toy with me," he said, his eyes looking back from the mirror crinkled at the edges as if he were smiling. "I can break every bone in your body, individually or all at once, as I choose. I do not need your bones for my work."

"No?" I gasped, still having difficulty breathing without a hitch or ache. "Griffin, I suppose, is good enough. . . ."

Rui's eyes narrowed and his silence was telling. I'd hit a sore spot. "Carlos must think me a particular fool not to check the body for curses," he said, and made a spitting sound. "Her skeleton is quite useless, thanks to him."

I nodded as if this were all news to me. "He is a bit of a bastard."

Rui chuckled. "You can't imagine. He won't come for you. Not even if he had more time."

"Didn't think so. . . . We're not that sort of friends."

"What sort are you, then?"

I finally got a full breath and had to hold it a moment while my chest got used to the feeling again. "I work for his boss. Had a personal problem, needed some help—"

"Your problem—the younger Purlis."

I nodded. "Called in a favor. Carlos is a mage and I'm not—I know better than to bring a knife to a gunfight. Also, he wanted to come. I guess that's partially because of you. He hates Purlis, but he despises you."

"Good, good . . . What he underestimates will kill him. Finally."

"Bit of a disappointment to see him walking around in the daylight, I imagine."

"I'd have punished Griffin soon enough for that mistake. He's conquered death a dozen times, so why not once more? Within his own house, it would be easy enough to overcome the paltry difficulty of sunlight. Outside of it, he will be nothing but a burden to your lover. They cannot move until nightfall and we will find them. As we found you." I was pleased to hear that the cloud of terror that had circled the castle had not given Rui any advantage after all. "They cannot return to Carlos's house, since it's now a murder scene. My dead student is useful after all."

I concentrated on my physical discomfort to hold back the spark of satisfaction that Rui didn't know as much about either Carlos or vampires as he should have. I hoped it would be enough of an edge when the time came—if I was able to pass the information on to Carlos and Quinton.

"How *did* you find me? You didn't just cover every bus station in Lisbon."

"Hah! No. You are unmistakable. Inside my shield, although I couldn't see you, once my little burrowers had touched you, left their hooks in you, I could hear the song of your bones. They sing— off-key, out of tune, but those are matters easily corrected—and at the house, I simply listened. I was surprised that Purlis's son had purged himself of them, while you hadn't. We followed your bone song and the agents in the metro confirmed the direction. We knew where you must be heading and came to wait. Your plan might have been clever if not for that, and what could you do about it? Nothing! It's, literally, in your bones. Short of breaking them or tuning them again by blade and fire and blood, you cannot evade me long, now that I know." He closed his eyes and I felt the ripple of his anticipation through the Grey. "As close as this, I can hear them now. We have only four days, but you will be magnificent once I'm done with you."

I didn't care for that idea. I preferred my bones as they were, scarred and remodeled and in my own skin. I restrained the urge to ask what he intended to do, in spite of his obvious wish that I would. Rui seemed to enjoy the discomfort of others. I wondered if it went with the territory or if it was just Rui.

He reopened his eyes, watched me, and tried to wait me out as the car wound through strange streets. Away from the Pombaline downtown, Lisbon and environs seemed designed to confuse with few straight roads up the hills and lots of traffic circles and streets that sloped or angled into intersections with far too many outlets. It would be a challenge to retrace the way, and the fact that no one was trying to conceal it from me didn't bode well. I thought we were taking a longer, more circuitous route than necessary, but the details mattered less than what would happen once we got wherever we were headed.

"I shall ask again," he said. "What are you? Not a mage, not a witch . . . a conundrum: powerful and powerless at the same time. What are you?"

I hesitated. I thought he wouldn't be familiar with the term "Greywalker," and since he didn't know in the first place, why help him . . . ? "I'm . . . sort of a . . . security guard. . . ."

He glared and I saw the tension gather in his shoulders and neck again. I cringed into the backseat, putting up my hands as if I could shove his spell away. "No! No, please! Not again. I'm not teasing you. I just . . . It's hard to explain." I did lay it on a little thick, but he didn't know me and without Purlis in the car to break my cover, there was no one to tell him I was exaggerating my fears. Pain is not the most effective way to motivate me—I had spent enough time in toe shoes and physically abusive relationships to be inured to that.

"I work at the edge of the magical world. I keep the normal stuff on one side of the line and the paranormal stuff on the other. That's pretty much what I do. Not my choice, just what I got stuck with."

Rui appeared less than completely convinced, his eyes slit in doubt. "I suspect there's more to it than that," he said.

"Well, of course, but the details are not what you asked for—and frankly they're more complicated and long-winded than you probably care about. I'm not sure that the ability I have would remain if you . . . adjusted me. . . ."

"Possibly not, but it would not be important then. There would be you as I had made you, which would exceed anything else you have ever been."

"Am I . . . going to survive this . . . ?"

He gave me a sly look but didn't reply. The car passed through industrial gates and dove into a tunnel cutting down under the ground at a mild slope that seemed to go on for a long time in darkness. Then the sound around the car changed and we seemed to be in something like an underground parking structure that was so poorly lit, the car navigated by its headlights through a field of cement pillars up to a double-wide loading door. A guy in street clothes sat at the edge of the loading dock platform with a compact automatic rifle resting on his knees. He hopped off the dock as we pulled in and held the gun at the ready position. Purlis was taking no chances this time. Though I supposed he might be nervous about the monster he'd tied himself to, it seemed more likely that he wanted a bit more insurance on my account.

Our driver got out and opened the door for Rui, and then for me. Rui waited without speaking for me to sidle out of the car, acting a little cowed and nervous.

I darted toward the rear of the car at my first opportunity and crashed to the ground in breathless agony, unable even to scream this time as Rui pulled his little crushing trick on me again, as I'd thought he would. If I hadn't tried, Purlis's agents would have felt things were going too easily. I couldn't let them think that I was just as happy to be here, wasting their time and making them keep their eyes on me, rather than letting them chase down Quinton and Carlos. In spite of the demonstration he'd made at the zoo, I knew Purlis's resources were limited and Rui had no easy way to track my companions, in spite of his bragging, so the more of these guys I kept bottled up here the better.

"Come, Senhorina Blaine, I have a great deal to show you. Don't make me force you."

I had the impression Rui would be delighted if I did. I didn't have to fake breathless dizziness and discomfort as he let me back up. He and Purlis were well suited. I added another name to the very short list of people who'd benefit the world by taking a fatal bullet.

Another armed man awaited us just inside. With one guard ahead and one behind us, Rui conducted me into the facility. Past the roll-up doors, it changed from generic work space to horror-film set.

Ahead lay a long concrete hallway with intermittent steel doors and flickering overhead fixtures, but the walls were covered in bloody runes and murals of bones that seemed to move in the intermittent light. I pulled my shoulders in to avoid touching the walls and tried to watch where I put my feet on the red-splashed floors. Ghosts wandered through the halls in a haze of Grey, as if they couldn't find the way out and weren't sure where they were. This base hadn't been in place as long as Rui's bone temple, but it wasn't brand-new, either, which made me queasy. A few of the doors opened onto ordinary rooms filled with office or surveillance equipment, supplies, guns—or men carrying them. But the rest opened onto visions of hell. We walked through more ghastly corridors and by rooms that held the memories of screaming and the song of bones like reeds in the wind and fingernails on chalkboards. A few robed figures passed us or could be glimpsed through doorways crusted in bone and blood. Even the floors writhed with marks that raised every fine hair on my body. I winced and gagged, feeling battered by the continual assault of re-membered death. I was raw and had lost my sense of direction for a while, but a peep into the Grey reoriented me, and the cold steam playing in my vision seemed, for once, welcoming and soothing, wash-ing the present horrors of the Kostní Mágové's lair out of my senses and leaving the distant chime of the Guardian Beast in my ears.

The psychic abrasion made me feel that escape was not as certain as I'd hoped. I looked for any relief I could find, grasping at the smallest detail. My occasional snatched sight of the deeper Grey was my touchstone. Since the Grid tends to run north-south and east-west, with certain energy colors dominant in their direction of flow, I was able to reacquire my bearings whenever I thought I would fi-nally collapse from the disorientation of the haunted corridors that ran ruler-straight yet seemed to twist and writhe like snakes. My glimpses of the Grid weren't much help, but at least I knew which way I'd have to head to catch up to Quinton if I did manage to get out of here alive.

"Do you know the story of the girl and the ghost bone?" Rui asked as we walked. Our guards ignored his question.

For a moment I thought he knew about what had happened in Carlos's garden and the discussion we'd had, but as I stared at him, there was no shift in his aura to indicate that he was baiting me. "No," I replied, letting my fatigue and fear color my voice.

"Ah, it's a folktale my grandmother told," he said, "but an interesting one. . . . You'll understand your purpose much better once you know the story.

"Long ago, in the hills, an old and terrifying witch with four arms and three legs captured a clever but lazy young girl who had run away from her family. The witch made the girl her slave. As she had three legs, the witch wasn't very spry, but she was very powerful and she forced the girl to perform a great deal of manual labor that the witch was incapable of because of her mismatched legs. The witch also had no fingers on two of her four hands and this meant she did a great deal of her work by raising bone golems and skeletons, but a living servant was much stronger and smarter, and so she kept the girl in her house and forced her to work." He told the tale with unholy glee, sending frissons up my spine and twisting my stomach into knots. I walked along with him, not bothering to hide my horror and disgust.

Rui grinned, showing crooked teeth, and went on, pleased with my revulsion. "The girl knew that the witch planned to devour her eventually but not all at once, for the witch was a frugal old monster. Every month the witch cut off one of the girl's fingers and ate it, then threw the bones onto the fire. And each morning after the witch had consumed the finger, the girl saw that the witch had grown a new finger of her own, and so it went for several months.

"The girl was no fool and she knew her fate, so she watched the witch for an opportunity to escape. She noticed that the witch always sang a song to the bones as she burned them to ash and then took the ashes away to make soap. The witch saved the soap to wash her face at the end of the month before she decided which of the girl's fingers she would dine upon the next day.

"The girl, in spite of having no education and being very poor, was very astute. She made a hole in the hearth and hid it with a bit of pitch so that when the witch went to scrape the ash from the fireplace, the pitch had melted away and some of the ash had fallen, unnoticed, into the hole. Once the witch had gone to weave her other spells and work her wiles, the girl scraped up the ash and made her own tiny bit of soap with which she washed her own face. When next she looked at the witch, she could see that the witch's skeleton was made of bones from all the children she'd eaten over the years. The girl knew then that once the witch had eaten all her fingers and made her useless for work, her own leg bones would become the witch's new leg and all the rest of her bones the instruments of the witch's magic.

"So the next time the witch cut off one of her fingers, the girl watched everything and discovered how the witch made the bone her own. Then the girl laid her plans and waited for the day the witch would come to cut off her leg. On that day, the girl washed her face with the rest of the magic soap and recited the magic words that she'd learned from observing the witch. When the witch arrived with her knife, the girl pretended to be asleep until the witch had cut off her leg. Then the girl snatched the witch's own leg away, ate it herself, and pushed the witch into the fire. Once the witch had burned to ashes, the girl then picked all her own bones from the fire, put them back where they belonged, and burned the witch's hut to the ground. Then the girl returned to her own village and lived happily ever after. . . ."

"Somehow I don't think 'happily ever after' is how that really ended," I said.

Rui stopped by a door and opened it into darkness as our guards flanked us with their weapons trained on me. "That would depend upon whether you were the girl or the villagers. I preferred to be the girl. Please step inside the room."

I shifted my gaze to the shadowed space beyond the open door and shuddered in dread as a cold white cloud choked with bones and black coils of death poured out. "Do I have a choice?"

"Of course you don't." He clutched my arm suddenly with his free hand and flung me through the open doorway with a surge of red energy.

I tumbled over the sill and rolled into the darkness, hoping I could gain an advantage and jump him as he came through the door, but Rui was prepared for me. The lights snapped on, making me blink as he stepped into the room. Although I lunged for him anyhow, he fended me off with a rough thrust of clattering bones that flew from the floor like a fence and shoved me back. The door closed with a sound like doom.

TWENTY-FIVE

The room was something more akin to a torture chamber than a hospital operating room, though there were aspects of both present. The bones arranged around the walls and scattered on the floor definitely tipped it over into horror-movie territory. A large book bound in bone and skin lay on a small lectern as if in a pulpit, the atmosphere around it black as murderous thoughts. I saw tables and instruments in the normal world; piles of bones, pools of blood, and seething, unformed ghost-stuff in the Grey, but nothing that looked like a way out short of a body bag. Cold panic swelled over me as wailing ghosts rushed to surround me, patting and snatching at me with incorporeal hands that left ice in their wake.

Rui smiled, more crooked teeth and a gleam of blood-tinged delight in his eye. "When I was a child," he said, "I knew that the story was supposed to frighten me into behaving and never straying from doing as my parents and my grandmother told me to do. But to me, the girl was a hero. She learned even from those who did not wish to teach her and she turned their strength against them when she seemed powerless. I also learned more than my masters wished me to and used their tricks to gain power over *them*. One in particular left me to dwindle and stagnate, cursing me, hoping to weaken my power by refusing to teach me further. He alone eluded my revenge, and you, my beautiful creature, will help me have it. Please remove your clothes."

"What?" I said, gaping at him as I backed toward the farthest reaches of the room and openly looked for any way, however Grey or obscure, to get out of there and away from Rui.

"Unless you wish to walk about in a tattered and bloodstained dress when I'm done, you'd be wise to remove it now."

"You're not going to kill me?"

"Not your body. I have a great deal more for you to do, once you're perfected and your soul stored away for Purlis's collection. I think he'll be particularly pleased to add you to it—since you and your friends destroyed most of my work when you burned down my temple." His voice rose and sharpened in anger and the red spikes in his aura reached upward like fountains of blood. "It amuses me that his ridiculous scheme will bring our Great Plan to fruition and has finally brought my last enemy within reach."

"Carlos? All this is about . . . getting even with Carlos?"

"There is so much more than that, but that one small thing adds such savor. He was my master and he abandoned me. I had to teach myself, just like the girl in the story. But he never would have expected me to be stronger for it. He cursed me, tied me to the land of my birth so I could never travel to the great bone churches to sit at the feet of another master, never pursue him, and yet . . . he returned." Rui chuckled. "Oh, how I will relish using you against him. It's even worth losing my student and the little girl to do it."

His laughter escalated into a cackle of sadistic glee. He yanked the lines of energy that spun from his hands to my bones, dragging me toward a table that reminded me more of the equipment in the mortuary than anything from a doctor's office. "It's time for you to do as you're told, *senhorina*."

I made enough of a fuss that he had to work to haul me in, but not so much that I exhausted myself. My hope of escape was ragged, but it wasn't gone yet. As long as he had his bone hooks or an energetic tie to me, I couldn't go anywhere without him pulling me back, or hunting me down. I had to break the strands that connected us or get him to do it.

Rui seemed to be enjoying himself, grinning as he forced me onto the table. The whole setup reminded me of *The Pit and the Pendulum* and made me regret all those Roger Corman films I'd watched with reprehensible boyfriends in college. Rui, having gotten me on the table, strapped me down at the wrists and ankles.

"What are you doing?" I demanded, letting panic color my voice. "Why are you doing that? You don't have to do that—you already have control over me."

"Ah, but the sounding is easier if I don't have to maintain your restraints as well. The little burrowers change the tones and I want to know everything about your bones. A few straps won't interfere once I've removed the hooks." He stoked my shoulder and upper arm, smiling. "Lovely, lovely bones . . ."

I felt sickened. I kicked and struggled and thrashed, but it didn't gain me one centimeter of slack. It did, however, grant me a view into a few obscure corners of the Grey and across the edges of the temporaclines that lay in the room. He dropped the white threads that connected us and seemed to draw fine white spirals from my body, like ivory worms. I gasped and writhed, but there was as much show as actual pain and disgust—I needed to distract him while I studied my options. If I could get into the Grey long enough while unencumbered with Rui's hooks and threads, I might be able to escape through the correct temporacline and, though he might find me again, he wouldn't be able to hold me. . . .

He didn't bother with my clothes and I guessed that his request that I remove them had been more of a psychological tactic than a necessity. He did take off my shoes, though, and in a moment I knew why.

Whispering sharp, black words, he smoothed his hand very lightly over the top surface of my left foot. As his hand passed, it felt as if my bones strained toward his palm like iron filings rising toward a magnet. I yelped, as much in surprise as pain. I wasn't sure, at first, that I heard a whistling, singing sound, but it grew louder as he moved his hand up toward the larger bones of my leg.

My left shin lurched upward, and I shouted in startled pain as the bone yanked toward his hand violently, sending out a loud, low tone like a clarinet.

"Ah, that is interesting. Nearly the same as the one Purlis gave," he said, allowing my bones to fall back into their normal position. "Remarkable that this bone should sound the same as that of a man with legs so much shorter than yours."

I was panting and tears blurred the edges of my vision. "I broke it . . . when I was a kid," I said. I'd also screwed up the knee a few years earlier and done any number of other injuries to the joint over the years, but I didn't think I had to tell him.

"So I see," Rui replied, touching my leg again right over the place the bone had snapped when I took a dive off a stage. He moved his fingers up and down the line of the bone at that spot, wringing from me a wailing chord of the bone's song mixed with my own shrieking.

Rui smiled at the sound as if it were heavenly music. "Ah, I must find the right one. . . ."

He put his free hand on my other leg and that bone also jerked toward him, wrenching the joints at knee and ankle and sending another jolt of pain through me as my bones sang a discordant chord, out of tune with my howls of agony. He "played" up and down my tibias for a few moments, replaying every bit of damage I'd taken in the joints and connecting bones over the years, but he was unable to find a more pleasing resonance. He slid his hands around, first displacing my fibulas, then moving upward over my distressed knees— which he rejected and moved past immediately. I almost sighed in relief, except that there was none: His hands slid up my thighs and elicited more reedy tones from my femurs as I screamed.

It was hard to concentrate on finding a sign of a useful temporacline when every movement of Rui's hands on my body racked me with new colors of anguish. He passed his hands over my hips and up the sides of my ribs, then ran his fingers over them in an excruciating glissando. He toyed with the loud bones of my chest until my voice was cracking. Then he slid one palm flat between my breasts, stroking the length of my sternum. Unable to scream now, I whimpered, and tears ran from the outer corners of my eyes in hot streams.

"Smaller, smaller . . ." he murmured. "A pity about the scar . . ." I thought I could feel the memory of a ghostly knife that had once scored my breastbone. Then he pulled his hands away and stared down at me, his eyes darting from point to point, seeking something.

"What?" I whispered.

"The key. The one bone that aligns to one of mine. How else will I tune you? How else will I bind these songs together? I must have that one for Coca."

I knew I'd heard the word. . . . What was it . . . ? Not the soft drink . . . "Coca," I repeated.

"The dragon," he answered, offhandedly. "Inferno Dragão. The legends align. But there will be no Sleeping King to save them. Only the fiery Coca, before which all others will fail. You see what a clever plan it is? Take their own myth and turn it against them? The dragon has already eaten the knight! He cannot save them!"

"Eaten the knight . . . Oh. The tomb at the monastery," I whispered, thinking out loud. "But . . . the bones weren't really King Sebastian. . . ."

"Of course not. A common soldier, but buried as a king. The dust of a great deception will make it seem to burn like flesh."

He turned away from me in frustration and snatched a bone off another table. As he raised it, I could see it was carved into a flute with rows of strange, blood-red characters running down the length.

He held it up, his eyes shining. "Do you see? This is my own song. I drew this bone from my own body, carved it to my own song. And its twin will lie in our dragon."

I gaped at him, but I couldn't see that he was in any way crippled or missing a significant bone—even though the flute was small, it wasn't as small as a finger bone or one from the ear, and I couldn't spot where it had come from.

His expression bloomed into delight as he saw me looking, as if my understanding was a thing of joy for him. "You're clever. I found others to take their places. I have sacrificed for the work, but I couldn't finish if I left my own body broken. Purlis believes he can control the drache by giving one bone, but I have given three—keys to the song. I hear the melodic complement in you—small, like a grace note—and I will take that for our dragon, too. Not a key, but it will be beautiful. No, no . . . It will be exultant. I will exult you. You will be perfected."

He was enthralled with his idea and didn't hear my muttered, "I'd rather remain flawed."

He brought the macabre instrument to his mouth and blew, working his way through the tones, each seeming to flay me and touch my skeleton like live wires.

Dark shapes and ivory vapor oozed out of the pipe as he played a disturbing tune that made my spine ache. As the coil of magic wafted closer, the pang intensified and spread. It felt as if my skeleton were vibrating, every bone separately at high speed. The tormenting song rattled and hummed into my body, making me arch and writhe in pain as my joints seemed to be tearing themselves apart. One clear, piercing tone seemed to cut into the ring finger of my left hand like a physical blade, the bone shivering and ringing with the same note until the very fingertip was as cold as ice, singing back to the flute. It felt as if the farthest bone of that finger no longer belonged to me, although it was still attached.

The spell of Rui's music wove through and wrapped me, crawling through my bones until it reached my stinging left hand, which shook and jerked without any impetus from me. Constrained so close to my side, the twitching hand fought to rise, falling back to pound the table and then fly upward again as the rest of my body drew tighter and tighter in a bow of anguish.

Rui pounced on my thrashing hand, dropping the flute to the floor. He yanked the restraints away and dragged me off the table, toward another part of his chamber. Released from the torment of the song, I went limp on the floor, falling into a heap. Without a glance at me, Rui dragged me forward by the wrist, far stronger than I'd anticipated of such a small man.

The bone flute rolled ahead of us toward a butcher block and Rui pulled me in its path. He heaved me up, yanking my hand onto the surface. I fell back down, too enervated to manage any resistance and too stubborn to contribute to whatever he had in mind.

"Stand up!" he snapped at me.

I shook my head and lay on the floor. "Too tired . . ."

He let out a growl of frustration and threw my hand down as he turned aside again, saying, "Selfish, useless creature." He grabbed for something and I didn't bother to look to see what it was. I snatched up the bone flute in my right hand, shoving it into the pocket of my dress, and dropped toward the Grey now that I was free—or nearly—of his hooks and strands of control.

"No!" he shouted, and I felt the bone-web prison try to close on me again as it had at the zoo, but he could not force me to the ground. I could feel the peculiar cold in the tip of my left ring finger, and before he could crush me or catch me by that resonance, I pushed back up to the normal, rising to my feet. I mustered all the strength I had left to stand and pick up the knife that lay on the block. Rui was too far away for me to use it on him, so I slammed the blade down on the farthest joint of my left ring finger. The tip of my finger fell off the edge of the butcher block in a spurt of blood and the drawing, tingling cold of Rui's last connection vanished.

I threw myself into the Grey and rolled into the temporacline I'd been watching, dropping away from Rui's chamber of horrors, free for the cost of my fingertip.

TWENTY-SIX

I had exchanged one type of paranormal cold for another and spent more of my own blood. I was free of Rui—at least until he wanted to try to track me by the song of my bones again—though I wasn't sure how well that would work now that he no longer had his flute or a resonant connection to me. I had the impression he'd have to be pretty close to listen for me in the song of Portugal's Grid, so the farther I got from him, the better my chances. I could have put an end to his tracking option by breaking a few of my bones, I supposed, but I was damaged enough as it was and now I was also bleeding from an amateur amputation. While I do heal preternaturally fast, I didn't think that was going to save me today.

But without Rui's traps and connections, I could drop deeper into the Grey and look for energetic signs that might get me closer to Quinton and Carlos faster. I couldn't travel far or for long in the Grey even at the best of times—it was chilling, exhausting, and dangerous—and right now I was vulnerable. I needed to get back to the comparatively safe world of the normal—safe, that is, once I was far enough away from Rui.

Tired, shaking, and worried about what might come after me next, I crawled through the temporacline, swarmed by ghosts, until I seemed to be outside the current building. Then I slipped out of the frozen blade of time and dropped deeper into the Grey, awash in a silver fog of nascent souls and shrieking phantoms following the trail of my blood. I'd never bled in the Grey before and I hadn't been sure that every hungry thing within it would come drooling after me like a pack of hunting dogs. I probably should have guessed, though. I needed to get out again, quickly, before anything nastier than a few ghosts caught up to me.

I could see the wild tangles of energy that were humans and mages rushing around on my right and the sweep of distant darkness that was probably the river. It was too far for me to reach. I looked in another direction—northeast, I thought. And there, like a ridiculous beacon, was a blazing pink line that led to a frantic coil of brilliant blue shot with arcs of orange and red. I couldn't think of anyone else in all of Portugal to whom I would have a pink familial connection aside from Quinton. I fixed the shape in my sights and moved toward it as fast as I could, rising from the Grey and dragging a train of bleeding, biting specters as I went.

I tumbled out in a cold rush of blood-gorged ghosts, into the falling dusk at the edge of a thick planting of trees. Quinton had been crouching in the undergrowth and turned to look for the source of the whimpering sound I made as I hit the ground and felt the normal world jar my aching, abused bones and joints. It wasn't a loud sound, but it was enough. His expression was grim as he prepared to do any violence necessary to get to me . . . and there I was without his having to manage any at all.

Quinton threw himself forward, scooping me to his chest as we both sprawled on the ground. "Harper. Harper," he kept saying, kissing my face as if he hadn't seen me in years. "I thought they were killing you. I felt—horrible things. Dear God, are you all right?"

"No," I whispered. My voice was still a wreck. I held up my bleeding hand. "Lost a finger, screamed myself hoarse."

Quinton grabbed my hand and wrapped something around the end of my chopped-short finger—some cloth that he tightened into a makeshift tourniquet with a pen and a piece of duct tape from his pockets.

"I felt that. The finger. Who did it? Rui? My father?"

"I did."

He stared at me, confused and a little freaked-out. "Why?"

"Long story. Get me out of here. Please."

I barely managed to keep on my own bare feet and not need to be carried away. Quinton led me down a hillside and out to the edge of a road where a tiny car was parked. It barely had room inside for two adults and a box of chocolate, but since we had no chocolate, we fit.

I felt dizzy. I patted the door pillar of the passenger seat as Quinton drove. "This . . . ? How?"

"Stole it."

"Hidden depths . . ."

"Not so hidden. You always knew I was shady."

I nodded and my head felt wobbly on my neck.

After a half hour or so, he pulled the car over and loosened the tourniquet for a few minutes before tying it back down and driving on. "You're in bad shape, but I don't want you to lose the hand to gangrene. There's no medical kit in this car or I'd do more."

"Superglue?" I suggested.

"Not on a bleeder like that—the glue won't hold in that volume of liquid with no flesh to pull over it—the whole tip's gone. The vein needs a couple of stitches first. Then glue. Jesus . . . You did that to yourself?"

"Had to. Later." I faded out and fell asleep, uncomfortably close to not waking up.

I did come to again in lamp-lit night, curled in a white bed that smelled like bleach. My hand throbbed and felt swollen, but I couldn't see much because someone had bandaged it up. Quinton was snoozing in a chair nearby and woke with a start when I moved in the bed. We weren't in a hospital, but the room had a feel of medical competence and I wondered where we were. Then I wondered why I was feeling a lot less muzzy than I'd been when I fell asleep. Just getting some rest and a clean bed wouldn't have had that strong an effect in the face of the damage I'd taken.

"Hey," Quinton murmured, pulling his chair up to the side of the bed so he could lean closer to me. His eyes were bloodshot, his face puffy, and his hair was a disarrayed mess that stuck out in dirty spikes.

I tried to reply, but all that came out was a breathy echo. "Hey."

He put his head near mine and picked up my uninjured right hand, holding it loosely in his as if he thought he would hurt me with any greater pressure. I tried to squeeze his hand in reassurance, but mine ached and felt bloated, resisting closing much farther.

"Don't try," he said. "Everything's a little swollen and you'll feel like you've got arthritis all over for a while. So, right now, here's the situation: We're in a little city called Borba about halfway between Évora and the Spanish border. Me, I'd call it a town, but they say it's a city and the locals are a pretty fierce bunch. It's a wine-making area and this week they're swearing in a bunch of newly elected municipal officials before the crush starts. It's pretty busy here this time of year with the wine business and the marble quarries, so we don't really stand out much. Even your injury doesn't look too weird to a doctor who patches up vineyard workers and quarrymen all the time. He was a little annoyed we didn't have the fingertip, but he didn't have to remove any more of the finger, so once it heals up, you'll be pretty normal. Though it's going to be a bitch to relearn how to type."

I tried to laugh and it came out sounding more like a steam radiator with a bad pressure valve.

"Medically, the doctor says the rest of the injuries almost look like a case of the bends or an industrial accident. He's kind of curious how you got them and not completely satisfied with my bullshit explanations about falling into a quarry, but it's not like you've got a bullet hole in you, so he's not pushing. I think he kind of wants us gone before whatever trouble we're obviously in comes knocking on his door. And he gave you a couple of pints of blood—lucky for you I'm a good donor. Also a whole lot of other fun stuff like antibiotics, anti-inflammatories, and pain meds—not to be taken with wine, he was careful to tell me. Apparently that can be a problem around here."

I nodded some more.

"The estate is about an hour's drive from here, but it would take most of a day to walk it. I had to ditch the car, so we're going to have to find alternate transportation to meet Carlos. So . . . how are you feeling?"

"Tired," I whispered.

"Too tired to move?"

"Not if it puts more distance between us and your dad's monstrous friends." The length of my speech dried my throat to a rough soreness. I coughed a little and Quinton played nursemaid with a glass of water.

When I finally pushed the water away, Quinton closed his eyes and shook his head. "I wish you hadn't stopped me. I wish I'd shot him dead last year."

"No, you don't."

"None of this would have happened if he were dead."

I tried to shrug and ended up wincing instead. "Maybe."

"I don't see any way to end this without killing him. And if I have the opportunity, I'll take it this time."

"OK."

He gave me a sardonic look. "Oh, now you're all right with it."

"It's not the same."

"How?"

I shook my head since my throat was too sore for me to want to make long explanations. "Later." I shifted in the bed, trying to find a way out of it. I didn't have any great desire to leave the comfortable nest of blankets, except that something Rui had said nagged at me. "We have four days. Three."

"What?" Quinton asked, frowning as he helped me out of the bed.

"Rui . . . said four days." I had to pause and drink again. "Don't know when that clock started running."

"We'd better assume today was Day One."

"Still . . . ?"

He glanced at his wristwatch. "Barely, but yes." He put his hand up as I sat on the edge of the bed. "Hang on. . . . Let me get you some clothes."

I made a face, imagining the condition my dress must have been in by now and wondering if I'd bled on it. Quinton fetched his pack and pulled out a slightly wrinkled button-down shirt and a pair of cotton trousers. He offered them to me, saying, "Your stuff was pretty trashed. I saved everything from your pockets, but I'm a little short on lingerie."

I sighed—which hurt but still felt better than not breathing—and took the clothes. "I can go commando."

Quinton is shorter than I, but he's broader in the shoulders and men's shirts are always longer in the arms and torso than a woman's shirt of the same chest size, so the top wasn't a problem—especially since I'm small-breasted, so there was no chance of inappropriate "barn door" syndrome with the buttons. The pants were a bit of a strange fit, but the biggest problem was their length. I rolled them up to midcalf and figured the heat would account for my lack of fashionable style. I looked at my bare feet and dreaded having to go very far without shoes. Mine were probably still on the floor of Rui's charnel house and I wasn't going back for them.

"Just a minute," Quinton said, and slipped out of the room while I restored the contents of my pockets. He came back quickly with a pair of sandals with insoles that looked like an aerial view of clear-cutting.

"One of the nurses gave them to me," Quinton said, seeing the look on my face. "They're cheap, but they'll get us out of here. We can't afford to sit and wait for the shops to open."

We didn't have the luxury of being picky, so I put them on and we slipped out of the clinic.

The clinic was housed in a long, low two-story building that was faced in white marble. Most of the buildings I could see along the narrow street were white or pale pink. Even those that weren't faced in marble were painted similar colors so the whole town glowed in the moonlight reflected off the pale buildings. Sounds of revelry came from several of the taverns and restaurants open farther down the road.

It was Friday—Saturday now—and I'd lost track of the days completely since I'd arrived. There'd been no chance to rest or be bored. I'd hit the ground running, and the sound of people having a good time reminded me of all the dinners I hadn't had with Quinton in the past eight months or more before we'd gone to rescue Soraia. It seemed like a week had already passed since I'd arrived in Portugal, but it was only three days and I was as hungry as if I hadn't eaten the whole time. There really was no time to stop to see whether any of the bars had food available. We needed to get to Amélia's estate as quickly as possible.

Quinton steered us away from the main highway and down a road that became increasingly industrial and dusty. The road came to a traffic circle and the buildings thinned, leaving miles of dusty white road winding between fenced yards filled with slabs of white and rose marble gleaming in the moonlight.

Just beyond the circle was a driveway leading into one of the stone yards. A dust-covered truck stood idling in the driveway as the driver walked around it, using a flashlight to search the underside of the large, empty flatbed. He muttered to himself and reached to grab something, shaking it with a muffled rattle.

The man lay down on the ground and tried to move something while still holding his flashlight. Something slipped and the light broke with a crash. The driver rolled out from under the flatbed, shaking off debris and swearing. *"Filho da puta!"* he added, kicking the nearest tire and drumming his fists on the flatbed.

Quinton and I exchanged a glance and walked toward him while Quinton pulled a small flashlight from his pocket. "Hey, do you need a hand?" Quinton called out as we drew near and turned on his flashlight, aiming the beam at the ground.

The man whirled, wide-eyed, not expecting anyone to be walking along this road after midnight. He stared at us and at the flashlight for a second. *"Sim!* Yes! I could use an extra hand." His English was good enough, but his accent was thick. "You have a light."

"Yup," said Quinton, stopping next to the driver. "What's the problem?"

"This pile of shit—the lift is jamming. I had the bolt out and then one of the scissor arms fell off. . . ."

The conversation became an exchange of technical terms that meant nothing to me, but Quinton understood. And that led to a few minutes of talking, then lying on the ground under the flatbed with flashlights and tools and cursing. Finally both men were satisfied with something and got back to their feet, dusting themselves off and smiling at each other as if they'd slain a troll with butter knives.

"Thank you!" the driver said, offering his dusty hand to Quinton. "I would have been here all night without you."

Quinton shrugged. "It wasn't much trouble, once you could see it."

"It was a lot of trouble for me. *Obrigado*. What can I do to thank you?"

"Don't know. Where are you headed?"

"Vila Viçosa. It's not very far down this road, but I'm glad I don't have to walk it."

"Well, we do. Can you give us a lift?"

The driver looked me over and made a "not bad" face as if I were a bit of livestock he was considering. *"Sua namorada?"*

Quinton shook his head. "No. She's my wife."

The driver stiffened and stood up straighter. "Oh. *Desculpe*. Sorry. Uh, yes . . . I can take you to Vila Viçosa. Where you need to go?"

"As far as you feel comfortable taking us."

The driver nodded and walked up to the cab to open the doors. "Get in."

We scrambled aboard. I sat on Quinton's lap in the narrow cab while the guys made small talk. I fell asleep as we passed through an endless plain of holes where the marble quarries had been carved into the earth. We parted company from the driver a few miles down the road in Vila Viçosa, outside the Palace of the Dukes of Braganza and walked through the early-morning silence toward the industrial edge of town, once again. As the sun was rising, we negotiated another lift with a man who was delivering sausages to Ciladas—the next town closer to our destination.

The route twisted along a narrow highway through dry, tree-covered hills with the rising sun in our eyes and the dusty smell of olive and cork trees mingled with the odor of cured meat as the breeze twisted through the open windows of the delivery van's front seats. I was considering a raid on the man's cargo almost the whole time—my empty stomach now becoming insistently loud. I wasn't sorry to see the last of the too-redolent truck when we reached the tiny outpost that turned out to be Ciladas.

I felt we'd been transported back to some wide bit of the road in Southern California's eastern desert near San Bernardino or Riverside. Even in the early morning with the sun barely up, the place was hot, dusty, and smelled of agriculture. But it was still a Portuguese town of low, plastered buildings with red tile roofs, stone-paved sidewalks, the sound of the Grey atonally melancholy, and all the rest of the world as remote as the moon. And yet, once again, I was reminded of places I'd grown up, the scent of ocher dust, the color of the light, and the weight of sun like a veil lying on my shoulders and winding up my neck and face, as tangible as a touch. The town rolled along the edge of the road, which wasn't even a highway anymore, with some of the houses hiding behind stubbled brown humps of land or perching on the ridge in rows like red-crowned birds. The only notable landmarks were the police station at one end of the main street and the soccer field on the other. The road stretched away, east, out of town, into more rolling, sunburned hills dotted with dust-laden trees. It seemed like we'd come to the end of the world and the road was only an illusion that would vanish under our feet and return us endlessly to the same intersection.

I looked at Quinton. "Where to?"

He frowned and pulled a pad of paper from one of his pockets. "East. The directions say it's a little more than three kilometers— about two miles. Can you walk that far?"

"I don't walk on my hands."

He gave me a tired smile and we started on our way.

Usually, I stride along at a good clip and could have completed the trip in less than an hour, but it was warm and I wasn't at my best. Two hours later we turned onto a dirt road that went up a long rise landmarked by crippled cork oaks. The driveway curved to a rambling white house perched on the height so it looked down into a valley of wheat stubble and olive groves that tumbled to the edge of a small river. The energetic colors around the house were soft, as if they were as worn by time as the rolling hills. The sign at the edge of the road indicated that the house took in guests and I hoped we were in the right place. I could hear kids behind a courtyard wall and the splashing of water. A painted tile sign beside the gate in the wall identified the building with a number and the name A CASA RIBEIRA NO VALE DAS OLIVEIRAS, and a hand-painted addition just below the tiles read TURISMO RURAL.

"The name's right—if I understood Rafa correctly," Quinton said, "But the *turismo rural* is a tourist bureau, which would make this a sort of . . . very nice B and B, for lack of a better term. Most people call them *turihabs*."

"Is this bad?" I asked, my voice still no louder than a whisper.

"Not necessarily, but I wasn't expecting this. It's not quite a hotel, but it's not really a private house, either, so, while it's all right to just walk into the courtyard and see what's what, we have no guarantee about who else may be here."

I opened the gate and walked through into a white-walled corridor between the building and the courtyard wall. The ground was covered in slate slabs, and I followed the walkway along the side of the house until the wall turned and I came out into the courtyard itself. The wall ended a few dozen feet ahead, leaving an open, falling-away view of the shallow valley below. A wide blue swimming pool stretched across half of the revealed terrace and a small band of children played in and around it, screeching with delight. Carlos sat in a deck chair at the far end of the terrace from the pool, brooding out into the view. He raised his head and turned toward us as a petite woman stepped out from the house through a door on my left. She was almost a dead ringer for Rafa.

She peered at us with a knowing smile. "Mr. and Mrs. Smith? Cousin Carlos told us to expect you in a day or two, but we're pleased to see you sooner. I'm Nelia. Welcome to A Casa Ribeira."

Carlos had left his chair and was a few steps away from Nelia. As he closed the distance and stopped beside her, he also reached forward and took my injured hand. For a moment he said nothing, glancing at me, then frowning at Quinton, and then down to my bandaged hand before he looked into my face.

"What have you done to yourself?"

TWENTY-SEVEN

Nelia settled us indoors away from the noisy children in the pool and brought food, then left us to our discussion in a quiet room that would have looked onto the terrace when the curtains were pulled aside. We were the only guests in the house—the children all being either the family's or the other local kids who were too young to be much help with the tail end of the harvest season. Even though it was Saturday, the grapes and the olives were both disinclined to wait on human convenience, so nearly everyone who could work in the fields was, leaving us with only the company of Nelia and a few family ghosts who were mostly disinterested in us—gliding through their remembered business in endless, silvery loops or simply passing by without paying us much attention. A plethora of temporaclines littered the view in the Grey and gave a streaked and smoky appearance to the mist of the world between worlds, making the auras of the people in the room harder to see through the fog of the building's memories.

Carlos was not pleased about my being captured and examined

by Rui, but he was willing to wait for a report until Quinton and I had eaten.

"I had to remove the fingertip once Rui said it matched one of his," I explained, still feeling—and sounding—like I'd gargled broken glass. "Once he'd done whatever he was up to, I'd have been a danger to you two if I escaped, and completely in his power if I didn't."

"But you had to leave the bone behind, which gave him part of what he desired."

"It was a trade-off. Rui has no direct connection to me now, but he did get the bone. On the other hand, he said it was a mere 'grace note,' and I got information and I got out. With Quinton's help."

"Now they know what you are capable of," Carlos said, scowling, "and will follow."

"They only know that I can drop through the Grey. They may find me eventually," I croaked, "but I think they'll have to be closer than Lisbon, or even Borba. Rui only caught up to me this time by listening to the resonance of my bones through the bone hooks that got into me at the temple—and which neither of us thought were significant at the time—once he was outside the house. He had to be that close. Without the hooks, he could only hear what he called my 'bone song' when he was a few feet from me."

Carlos's expression blackened. "I underestimated his skills. I expected your own healing ability to deal with it, but I . . . was wrong." I could tell it was difficult for him to say so. He rarely made errors, much less the sort that came back with consequences later, and he'd made several here. I wondered if the memory of his power when he lived here had made him incautious and thoughtless of the changes time had wrought, but I wasn't going to suggest it. We'd survived and had to look forward, not back.

"I haven't been in top form. My body just hasn't been able to keep up," I said.

Carlos shook off my attempt at mitigation. "Nonetheless, I left you in danger that could have been avoided."

"Could Rui find you the same way he found me? I mean, he must *know* what your bones—"

Carlos waved the comment off. "He's had little success thus far—my bones have changed since the days of our association. And it's hardly impressive to bribe and threaten a taxi driver to find my house."

"Which is a crime scene now," I said.

Carlos shrugged. "We could not have returned in any event. Tell the rest."

"We may have some breathing room. Even with that bone, he's not got much. It's the only one of mine he seemed to have an affinity for. I don't think Rui was paying much attention to what he told me—he was too focused on his plans."

Quinton looked ready to throw up, but Carlos was intrigued. "What did you discover that was nearly worth the cost of your life?" Carlos asked.

"Rui doesn't know about—or understand—your change of state. He thinks the house protected you from the daylight and that you're a sitting duck outside of it. He doesn't seem to have much knowledge about vampires in general, either, and he's . . . excited by the thought of exacting revenge from you. He hates you to a point of blindness, but he figured out what you did to Griffin pretty much on sight, so that was a wasted effort."

"Not entirely. It deprived him of his best assistant, stopped him from salvaging anything from that loss, and he will still have to find appropriate bones."

"He does have one of mine," I said, "and he talked about 'adjust-ing' my bones to make me . . . something else—he didn't say what."

"He did not and will not have that chance. The bone is a pity, but there are still others to collect. I have been to Évora. The skeleton of the child is missing, but they had no opportunity to take more—perhaps because Rui was too busy with you to oversee his minions' efforts." He looked at Quinton. "They have recovered from the loss of your niece, but they are no further ahead."

"And there are only three days left, according to Rui," I added.

"Only three days?" Carlos scowled. "What is significant about that date . . . ?"

"He didn't say."

Carlos made a dissatisfied growl. "Go on. What more did you discover?"

"Rui confirmed that Purlis gave up his left tibia for some control of the drache—and he was amused enough to tell me that my own left shin is a near match in resonance, but again, he'd have to be close enough to touch me for that to be useful. I guess it tickles some Kostní Mágové sense of irony. Anyhow, he said it wouldn't matter that Purlis had sacrificed a major bone for some control of the project since Rui had placed three of his own bones in the construct, which he seemed to think would mitigate the effect of Purlis's."

Quinton shook his head, muttering, "Jesus . . ."

"Yeah . . . your dad's completely past the sanity line. I—we had a really disturbing discussion before he let Rui catch me."

"I'm sorry—" he started, leaning forward as if to pull me into his arms.

I put up my hand. "It's not your fault," I said in my strained, half whisper. "Both of you stop apologizing or I'll never get done before I lose my voice."

It took him some effort to sit back and let me go on.

"So," I said, regathering my thoughts and swallowing a few times before I continued. "Rui told me a nasty story about a girl and a witch and I think I may have figured out how the ghost bone swap thing works, but I didn't have time to try it out and I have no idea how it's useful." I pulled the bone flute from my pocket. "This is Rui's bone song—he said it's made from the twin of one of the bones in the construct. He used it to locate the finger bone I . . . left behind."

Carlos smiled one of his wolf grins and took the flute from me as I held it out. "Ah, now this may be useful, once he can't hear it." He looked it over, listened, and pulled a long, kinked strand of white energy from the small bone. I watched him through the Grey as he stretched the white thread across the table, then picked up a sharp, serrated knife from the food tray and stabbed it into the wiry filament. He held it tight, muttering, as the energy strand whipped and writhed like a snake. Every word he murmured to it seemed to slide down the blade of the knife and stain the thread darker and darker, damping its vitality, until it lay limp and black. He pulled the knife away, picked up the strand, and wove its inky length around the bone again. Then he handed the modified flute back to me. "He cannot hear it now, but it may be best if you keep this, else I may be tempted to do something rash."

"I don't see you as the impulsive type," Quinton said. "More the brooding, plotting type."

Carlos gave him a sideways look that bordered on amusement. "At the moment, the balance of my impulses appears to be positive. Don't tempt me to upset the scales."

Quinton made a dismissive snort, as if he had no fear of what Carlos could do to him. It was an interesting reaction, but I was too worn down by sleeplessness and pain to give it much thought.

Carlos turned his attention back to me, saying, "If you must use it to call to Rui's bones, remove the binding I've put around it, first, or the sound will die in the air. It should do you no further harm now that you no longer own the bone it sang to."

"All right," I said, my voice barely audible even in the quiet room as I accepted the flute. "There is one other thing," I added. "Rui mentioned Coca and the Inferno Dragão as if they were the same thing. He said . . . the dust from the tomb of King Sebastian . . . Let me think. . . . 'The dust of a great deception will make it seem to burn like flesh.' I'm not sure what he meant, but I thought . . ."

Carlos picked up where my flagging voice gave out. "It will lend the drache the illusion of solid flesh that burns without being consumed."

"But if it's only an illusion—" Quinton started.

"The illusion of flesh. 'A great deception,'" Carlos repeated. "But the flames will not be a mirage and there is no Saint George or Sleeping King to save the people that this burning death will descend upon, although Purlis's agents have done a great deal to give the distressed hope of such a miraculous rescue."

Quinton added, "After creating or contributing to their distress to begin with."

Carlos nodded. "And when there is no rescue, their resistance to fear, despair, and the rhetoric of hate will be shattered." He closed his eyes as if he were worn out and covered his face with his hands before running his fingers back through his hair in a gesture I'd never seen him use before. "Ah . . . now I know what he needs and where he'll have to go to find it."

Quinton and I both stared at him in expectation while he fell silent, thinking, the colors of energy around him whirling like the view through a kaleidoscope full of volcanic glass.

"What?" Quinton demanded after a while.

Carlos replied slowly, as if dredging his thoughts from long-faded memory. "The day Rui and the Kostní Mágové have chosen to raise the Dragão do Inferno is the memorial day of Saint Jerome. That sharp-tongued aesthete is the patron saint of librarians, translators, and encyclopedists, and in that regard, the Kostní Mágové consider themselves Hieronymites—followers of Jerome. I had almost forgotten. They are gatherers, translators, and protectors of the knowledge of the bones. Jerome himself was fascinated with the bones of the dead and the righteous. He walked through the tombs and catacombs of Rome regularly as penance for his sins when he was a young man—he considered it a vision of hell. His biographies say that he cited a passage from Virgil's *Aeneid*: '*Horror ubique animos, simul ipsa silentia terrent*' to describe the horror and repentance that he felt in the silent judgment of the dead. It is ironic that the bones of a common soldier were entombed and venerated as those of a king—the dust of a great deception—in the monastery of Saint Jerome. And now that profane dust lies in the hands of fanatics who consider themselves the hidden acolytes of that same saint.

"On Saint Jerome's Day, they will bring forth their monster, clothed in fiery deception, blessed by the saint's own, and constructed of bones from both the innocent and the depraved, carved with the song of an unholy resurrection. The perversity of their plan is magnificent. It binds the sacred indivisibly to the obscene. The drache cannot be killed, because it is not alive. It cannot be cursed away by darkness, nor banished by light, since it is made of both. Rui has advanced better than I'd expected. It's too bad I'll have to kill him."

"You make him sound . . . commendable," I murmured.

"I would be lying if I said I did not admire tenacity and ingenuity. Especially since I hadn't expected him to survive ten years after I left.

But how he's chosen to use his talents and with whom he's chosen to ally himself do not please me in the least. I will consider the return of his powers to me as a worthy apology for the small matter of his sending his student to kill me. . . ."

Quinton shuddered beside me and I felt no happier about the idea myself. "He gave me the impression that Griffin either did that on her own, or didn't follow his instructions," I said, compelled to be fair.

"A detail of no consequence. Rui seems to have forgotten that I am also tied to Saint Jerome—I was born and died on the saint's memorial day. That will give us some additional strength, but we would be better served if we could stop him and the rest of the Kostní Mágové before they can assemble the final form of the drache. Given what we know he has and what he intends to create, how he means to weave the holy with the blasphemous, I know what else he must have that can only be found in the ossuaries of Alentejo. He has already taken the bones of a sacred, virgin child from Évora. Now he will need the bones of someone infected with a plague that killed thousands, and he will need the skull of a repentant thief who died in a fire. I know where both of those might be found. If they yet lie undisturbed, we may be able to upset Rui's plans. But if we cannot, we must be prepared to fight a monster that may be nigh on unstoppable."

"How come this doesn't surprise me?" Quinton asked the air of the room. "Leave it to my father to hook up with a bunch of bone-waving spell-slingers who can raise an undead and unslayable dragon that breathes fire."

"Not merely breathes fire. Is made and born of eldritch flame that burns everything it touches except the beast itself."

"So . . . fire extinguishers aren't going to help?"

I snorted a laugh and winced as my whole aching body seemed to nag at me for moving.

Carlos turned to look me over again, his face creased with unaccustomed worry, and held out his hand for mine. "May I see it?"

"Not pretty," I warned him—more for Quinton's benefit since Carlos wouldn't care one bit how my mutilated finger looked. I put my hand into his and he unwrapped the bandages with great care.

Beneath the gauze, my whole hand was swollen, discolored, and misshapen. I winced with an unexpected pang as Carlos removed the last of the packing around my dismembered joint. I hadn't looked at it since I'd cut off the tip of my finger and was taken aback by how terrible it looked. The skin remaining on the palmar side had been stretched over the cut end and stitched down, leaving a hideous line of bloody sutures and bruising across the top of what had been the upper joint of my ring finger. The wound had wept blood and serum and the doctor hadn't been overly nice about his work. It looked as if there were no remains of the bone I'd hacked off, but I didn't know if I'd managed to remove the fingertip so cleanly myself or if the surgeon had done that, cleaning up some chopped-off bit I'd left behind inadvertently. I hoped the latter hadn't been the case, since even a sliver of the bone might draw Rui to the doctor who would have no reason to lie for us even if the bone mage didn't do anything to persuade him.

Carlos glowered and shook his head. "It could have been better done."

"The chopping or the sewing?" I asked, my voice nearly faded to nothing by now.

"Both. And you waited too long in repairing it." He held on lightly and laid his free hand over mine. His hands were cool and dry, his touch more soothing than I could have imagined. I closed my eyes and let the sensation flow over me, not caring where it came from. "I can't make it whole again—the tip is unrecoverable—but the remaining bone and tissue are dying," he said, his voice very low. "For that I have some recourse."

The relief of pain I hadn't even acknowledged was so great that I cried and was dizzy. Tension that had held my shoulders rigid for hours faded away. I could feel Quinton supporting me, his arms around me, pulling me to his chest. I went limp against him, his breath stirring my hair. The constant, red ache in my body eased and flowed away, replaced by a cool, creeping tide that seemed to loosen all my joints and draw me toward a sensual floating sensation. I felt adrift, aware of the room as if from a distance. Then the coolness began to warm to an uncomfortable degree. I moved a little, trying to pull away, trying to make an objection with my sleepy, ruined voice, but it came out as a weak whimper. I forced my eyes open as Carlos let go of my hand, surrendering it to Quinton with a thin smile.

Carlos rose to his feet from the chair he'd occupied and turned toward the door. "I shall ask Nelia for more bandages."

He left us alone in the quiet room and I looked up at Quinton, fighting to keep my heavy eyelids open.

"Are you all right?" Quinton asked, watching me with clear anxiety.

"Hand's better," I whispered.

"It still looks bad but not like something from a train wreck anymore," he said. "I can't say I'm pleased with Carlos about it, though. Something felt . . . weird about that."

I tried to laugh but didn't make it past a snort.

Quinton started to smile. "All right, how 'bout one snort for 'you're imagining things' and two for 'you may have to challenge him to a duel'?"

This time I did manage to laugh.

"I'm sorry. That sounded like 'You're imagining that I want you to challenge him to a duel and die tragically.'"

"Never," I said, my vocal cords having received a small benefit from whatever Carlos had done, as well. "Showing off."

"Me or Carlos?"

"Him."

"What sort of showing off are we talking about here? Because I'm grateful for the healing thing, but if he's been messing around in your head . . ."

"No. My head's fine. Funny that you're still jealous."

"Of a dead guy? I am not."

"Liar."

"All right. I am jealous of someone who has a connection to you that I can't have. And I'm jealous of the time I haven't been able to spend with you while I was chasing after my father, giving in to my own obsessions instead of being with you. I'm envious of my sister. She has a family and a home, and she can hold her loved ones close and be with them all the time, wherever and whenever she wants. And I wish I had that. I hate what I've done in leaving you alone and I wish I'd quietly broken Dad's neck when you weren't looking last year."

"I'm glad you didn't."

"Why? If he'd died, none of this would have happened."

"You've said that before, but we can't know that, and you would have become a man who had murdered his own father in a fit of rage."

"But I still think the world would be better off if he were dead."

"I agree, but a year ago, you weren't thinking of the world. You were caught in your own fury and fear. If you had killed him, your remorse and your horror at what you'd done would have torn you to pieces. What's happened is terrible and I feel for your sister and her kids, but you can't preempt every atrocity in the world by perpetrating more—that's the route your father has taken. It would be unwise for you to be the instrument, no matter how necessary his death may become. You don't need the guilt and you would carry it forever. I know you. It would weigh you down even more than knowing the end results of what you did for the government does now. I want you to be free of that, but I can't take it away and you would never let yourself off that hook, so don't put yourself there. Let someone else carry the guilt."

"You?"

"No. I think he ought to be dead, but I won't be the one to do it. He is very ill. Rui and his plans may be all it takes. Let him go."

"I will. I'll have to work on it, but I will. I would rather hold on to you." He looked at me as if asking permission, and the colors around his body were fluttering, unsure.

"Right now?" I asked, feeling there was something that pressed on his mind that he was afraid to say, and was trying to get around to, or escape from somehow.

"Yes."

"All right," I said.

He pulled me closer into his lap, swinging my legs over so I was snuggled sideways to his body. I nestled my cheek into his shoulder and, in spite of the topic, I wished I could purr with the contentment of being quiet in his arms. Quinton wrapped those arms around me and we sat like that for a while, me listening to the reassuring constancy of his heartbeat at rest.

After a time, he pressed his cheek against the top of my head. "I love you so much," he said, "and ever since I saw you again in the doll hospital, I can only view the world in the context of you. Every step I take without you beside me or in front of me seems like wasted motion. I feel you in my heart like a separate but indivisible part of me. Not just the magic thing; the everything. If you died, I wouldn't know how to live. I would be like an old-fashioned watch that had lost its spring. I never want to be far from you again."

An electric wariness tingled over my nerves. "What if I didn't die, but I couldn't be with you? What if we had to be apart for a while through no desire of our own?"

"Like this past year? Are you hinting at something I should know . . . ?"

"No," I replied too quickly. "Just hypothesizing. But what if . . . ? Would you wind down and die?"

"No. Because I would know you were still in the world, still spinning the little gears of my existence, if from afar. I wouldn't like it much, though."

"I wouldn't, either. I didn't like this past year much at all."

"Maybe we should do something about it."

I made a small interrogative sound, confused and apprehensive about where he seemed to be leading the conversation. . . .

"This isn't how I pictured this moment. . . ."

"What moment? What's wrong with it?" I asked, startled, and twisting out of his lap to get a better look into his face.

He let me back away, but kept his gaze on me, his expression so soft and full of longing that tears pricked in my eyes. "Will you marry me? Harper? I want . . . us to be . . . together."

"But we are."

"Legally."

I blinked at him. "You think you're going to die."

He stared and then broke out in startled, uncomfortable laughter. "No! If I thought *that*, I wouldn't be asking. I know I'm supposed to do this differently—I'm supposed to get on one knee and have a ring and all that, but I suck at that kind of thing."

"But . . . you'd be stuck with me. You'd be out in the open. Everyone would know how to find you and you'd never be able to hide again."

"I don't want to hide anymore. I think I'm too old for hide-and-seek."

"What about your father?"

"What about him? When this is over—one way or another—he's not going to matter anymore. It's not about him—except what dealing with him has taught me about myself. About what I want and what I don't want. Back at the agency—the other one—the field guys were all single because they were wild cards, mobile, replaceable . . . expendable. When a guy moved up, he got a desk job, got a house, got married, because now he was a real person with a real place in the world—not what we used to call a 'wild dog' with no permanence, born to roam, born to die. I want to be permanent. With you. Out in the open."

I was panting and sweating, couldn't answer him while I wrestled with a fear I hadn't faced in years. I thought I wasn't afraid of anything so paltry, but the impulse to flee that captivity and everything that I associated with it hadn't quite let go of me, as regressive and stupid as it was.

Quinton frowned and leaned forward, reaching to brush my cheek and then pulling back, his eyes widening a little. "You're panicking. Which I sort of understand. But you don't have to. What I'm offering is not a prison and a wedding ring is not a shackle. You wouldn't be my property. The only thing that would change between us would be the light."

"Light?" I repeated, confused and disoriented.

"It's that condition that isn't shadows, secrets, and darkness. And we could live there." He looked down at my injured hand, biting his lip.

"It's OK to touch me. I won't shatter into pieces," I said.

He took my hand into his and studied it, then turned it upward to press a kiss into my palm. A warm tear fell onto my upturned wrist.

I felt as if something cold and hard were breaking inside me and I started crying. Quinton pulled me gently toward him and I threw myself back into his arms, flooding tears and sobbing. I wished I could blame my display on exhaustion, injury, and low blood sugar, but none of those was the cause. I was still sorting out if what I felt was relief, joy, or terror. Or all three.

So, of course, the door opened and Nelia bustled in with an armload of boxes.

TWENTY-EIGHT

N elia was more flustered than either of us. She put the pile of boxes on the nearest table and started back out.

"No, no," Quinton called out. "It's OK." He swiped at his eyes and cast me a questioning glance as I sniffled and wiped my face with the back of my right hand. "It is all right, isn't it?"

"Yes. We'll finish this later. I can't think—"

He shook his head and gave me a small smile. "It's OK. I'm not going very far away."

I nodded and moved aside so he could stand up. He paused to give me another kiss—a soft, slow brush of his lips over mine—and helped me to my feet as he got up. "I love you more than Roger loved Jessica," he whispered.

I snorted a laugh as he left the room. Nelia watched me with a sideways glance of curiosity. "Are you all right, Mrs. Smith?"

I laughed again, thinking that I wasn't even sure which last name I'd have if I were to accept Quinton's proposal. I had no desire to adopt "Purlis" or any of his various working aliases. "Smith" might work just as well. Maybe I should get used to it. "Yes. Well, mostly." I moved to lean against the sofa on which I'd been sitting with Quinton, and my injured hand brushed over the upholstery, sending a sharp pang up my arm. "Ow," I gasped.

"Oh, your injury. Cousin Carlos said you needed a bandage. Let me see." I held out my hand and she peered at it. "Nasty. What happened to your finger?"

"Accident."

She gave me a sideways look but didn't ask again. "It needs washing."

She led me out of the room and down a corridor to a small powder room near the back door. It was obviously more of a family space than one for guests, situated as it was near the kitchen and work areas, but it had a large cabinet filled with useful supplies such as bandage tape, gauze, and medicines. "There's always an injury this time of year," Nelia said. "Someone is always cutting their hand instead of a vine, falling off a ladder, or out of a tree. . . . It makes me glad I only work here."

"I thought you were one of the family."

"I am," she said, pulling me up to the sink where she started water running to warm and fussed with various packages of gauze, tape, and disinfectant. "But . . . I have a gypsy heart. I married an Englishman once and thought I could settle down if I were just rich enough. But I couldn't. I prefer the caravan to a house. I come to visit and help out when the harvest is on because this is my blood family. But I always think my real family is the wind and the sun and the campfire at night. It's hard to be indoors so much when the weather is so fine, but even a gypsy has a duty to family. Up to a point."

I scrubbed my hands carefully—the hot water stung the skin of my injured hand and I had to go around the finger with care, not sure if I was supposed to keep the stitches dry or not. I did my best not to wet the sutures, but they looked a little damp anyhow when I was done. Nelia handed me a towel and waited while I dried my hands; then she made me hold out the cut hand again and began bandaging my finger very neatly.

"Is Carlos actually a cousin of yours?" I asked.

"Probably not. He knew all the family history up to Carlos and Amélia, but he doesn't fit. I know everyone living who's part of our family and there are very few Ataídes left in our direct line. The first of Amélia's children was a girl, but the second was a boy and so the only direct descendants of Carlos and Amélia who bear the family name are the male children and grandchildren of Damiao-Maria Ataíde." Nelia looked up at my face. "Why are you frowning?"

"Two children? I . . . thought there was only one."

"Carlos said the same. The rumor was always that Amélia's daughter, Beatriz, was the child of her lover, but I was never sure."

"Why not?"

Nelia shrugged. "I can't say—I just think so. When did she have time to become pregnant by anyone but her husband? She was too young to conceive when he left for college and too proud to present him with a bastard before she'd given birth to a legitimate heir. She may have had lovers, but she wasn't fool enough to let one of them compromise her position. Damiao's birth killed her—her maid said it was 'childbed fever.' They thought the child was dead, too, at first, and didn't tell Carlos about it—he had a famous temper. He went into mourning and somehow no one ever told him about the boy, who had already been brought here to be raised by one of Beatriz's nurses. That was how they did it then—children raised in the countryside far from their parents. Carlos became a recluse for years—

they said he was a sorcerer and he was even interrogated by the Inquisition once, but he was released. The stories say that the lights from his room cast doleful shadows on the night and let demons out to roam the streets of Lisbon. And some of them say he consorted with the Devil and that his enemies dropped dead in the street when he passed—which I never believed. Then he disappeared in the earthquake and no one ever knew what had become of him. His body was never discovered, as many weren't, and he never knew he had a son. Or that's the family legend."

"That is a lot of legend."

Nelia shrugged. "You know how stories go. I think he just didn't care that he had children."

"What about the sorcerer part?"

She cocked her head in thought. "Hmm . . . That I might believe"—she held up her thumb and index fingers less than an inch apart—"a little. All of the diaries say he was a very strange man."

"Whose diaries are these?"

"Oh, Amélia and her maid left some. They aren't very complete. The maid hated Carlos, so I don't take anything she wrote about him seriously. When she wasn't complaining about Carlos, Amélia was mostly whining about household things, social gatherings she couldn't attend without her husband, and being bored, or being ill. She was a dissatisfied woman who became obsessed with providing an heir. I think she may have been a little crazy. She was of two minds about her daughter, too—some days she loved her with all her heart and others she was angry that Beatriz wasn't a boy."

"How much older was Beatriz than Damiao?"

"Twelve years. She was more like a mother than a sister to him, I suspect."

"And which child are you descended from?"

"Beatriz." She finished off the bandage and patted my hand with a smile. "Good enough, don't you think?"

I nodded, still trying to work it out. . . .

"How do you know Carlos?" she asked as I started to turn away.

"We work together."

"He seems very . . . fond of you." She said it as if unsure she'd used the right word.

I laughed. "In an odd sort of way, I suppose he is."

"Why would he say he was my cousin when it just isn't possible?"

"I don't know. Are you sure he's not related?"

Her eyes narrowed. "He can't be, but he *is* an Ataíde—he looks just like the first Carlos."

That drew me up short. "How does anyone know what he looked like?"

"There's a portrait, of course," she said, tilting her head toward the front of the house.

"May I see it?" I asked.

"If you like, but it will be there later, if you would prefer to see your room now, instead."

"No. I can rest in a few minutes. I'd really like to see that painting."

Nelia shrugged. "I'll show you where it is. I have to take the wine crate out of the salon anyhow."

"I didn't see one. . . ."

"The wooden box I brought in with the mail. It shouldn't sit like that for long—the room gets too warm to preserve the wine. So inconvenient—the last thing this house needs is more presentation wine in fancy crates. You can't drink the stuff or someone will have a fit, so it just takes up room and goes bad. A waste."

She led me back toward the room we'd left earlier and stopped at the door, pointing to a heavy frame that hung on the wall a few feet away. I couldn't see the painting within from my angle—the frame's thick carving obscured even an oblique view. "That's it. Amélia painted it herself. It needs restoring, but she was so haphazard, that it's hard to tell which bits are dirt and which are just Amélia's poor work. She was much better at needlework and music."

I walked toward the painting while Nelia went into the salon to retrieve the packages she'd left. I wasn't holding out much hope about the portrait's quality or likeness, no matter how much Nelia seemed to think it looked like Carlos.

I was surprised. Even in the subdued light of the west-facing room, the windows of which weren't yet lit with direct sun, it was startling. The work was terrible, the colors muddy where they weren't slashes of primary tones like a modern abstract. There was a lot of black, too, and not all of it was the color of paint. The uncanny darkness hung in streamers of Grey and gleamed in the thick body of the paint as if mixed into the oil and pigment. It could have been age that made the painting as a whole seem dark, but I thought it might have been the subject, because the man glowering out of the canvas was unmistakably Carlos.

The portrait showed him in a library or study, standing beside a table covered with books. He wore a loose white shirt under a long, pale blue garment that was something like a dressing gown. He was younger than I knew him and his hair was cut close to his head, almost shaved. His beard and mustache were much smaller and softer, just framing his mouth and not extending onto his cheeks at all, leaving his jaw and neck exposed without any sign of the scars that he now had there. His left hand rested on a human skull, the long fingers curled slightly as if caught tapping the bones in impatience. In his right hand he held something that could have been a scruffy quill pen or a badly rendered knife. The hand's position was awkward, as if Amélia couldn't recall exactly what a hand looked like when she got to that point. She'd worked very hard on the details of the man's face and clothes, but the arrangement of the painting was odd, the room exquisitely detailed on one corner and barely blocked in at another. Carlos's figure was pushed off to the left, leaving the skull his hand rested on at the center of the picture, while the man simply ended at midthigh, though there was still empty canvas below into which he could have been painted full-length. In the upper-right corner, a bird descended into the picture as if it had flown in through an unseen window and been captured by accident.

I stared at the painting and shook my head.

Nelia came back out of the salon with the wooden box and two smaller cardboard parcels in her arms. "It's an awful painting," she said. "I think she may have been insane by the time she finished it. But you see why I say he must be a relative. How could this Carlos look so much like that Carlos and be anything but a descendant?"

I felt something ruffle across the surface of the Grey, scattering a few ghosts, and I started to turn as a footstep sounded behind us.

"It is a disturbing likeness," Carlos said behind me.

Nelia yelped in surprise and spun around, fumbling to keep hold of her packages. She pulled them tight to her chest and stared at him.

Carlos offered a restrained nod and didn't smile. "My apologies. I didn't mean to startle you. I came to see how you were—both of you. Mr. Smith has gone to bed. I think he was hoping one of you would be coming to join him soon." He raised an eyebrow at Nelia.

She blushed and excused herself, turning and walking away at just less than a scurry, clutching her boxes in a swirl of gold and silver energy while streamers of Carlos's black pall followed in her wake. I frowned after her for a moment, feeling dull-witted and thinking I'd just missed something other than Carlos's not quite flirting with her.

"I think it's a very bad painting," I said, just to say something as my exhaustion caught up to me.

"It is yet another thing I did not know about my wife."

"That she was a terrible painter?"

"That she had an imagination. That room was the library in her home, where she lived when I was at Coimbra. I was rarely in it and I don't recall ever wandering the shelves *en déshabillé*. I don't remember a skull or stuffed ravens. However, I may have owned some garment like that once, though not while I was at college. It appears she created this portrait from her own mind, weaving pieces of memory together with some ideas of her own—and I had thought her rather brainless. I didn't realize her depths. Plainly, I underestimated her." It didn't sound like a compliment.

"Plainly," I said, shaking off a surge of heavy-lidded sleepiness.

"I may need to speak with her again."

"This seems like the place for it."

"Yes. I should unbind her and Rafa here—it would be appropriate."

"You're getting sentimental in your old age."

"Hardly. Practical. I can't carry them forever and they may be useful."

I grunted, unable to put my thoughts together fast enough to make a better reply.

Carlos looked me over. "You need rest and your spouse-in-soul expects you." He put his hand out. "I only want to know how you do."

I put my injured paw in his palm and shivered at the touch, feeling a little ill. "I do all right, I think. Very tired, though."

He peered at my bandaged hand. "Hmm . . . It should be well enough with time. Sleep, and I will talk with you more later."

"Are you sending me to bed?"

"I am."

"May I borrow your bathrobe? Mine was lost in transit."

He growled at me and I was too tired to care.

"Where is my room, anyway?" I asked, feeling drunk from lack of rest.

"I'll show you. Otherwise you may wander off and lose some other bit of yourself," Carlos said, taking my arm and walking me through the room toward a staircase.

"Is that a shot?"

"It is a threat."

I kept my mouth shut for the rest of the walk upstairs to a bedroom, where Carlos handed me off to Quinton as if I were a found pet. "Take her to bed and keep her there until she stops babbling."

Quinton raised his eyebrows. "Well, I was planning on doing that anyway. . . ."

"Good." Carlos turned and stalked off in disgust.

"I think he's mad at me," I said as Quinton closed the door.

"Nah. If he were mad, things would start dying . . . or exploding, I think. Definitely impatient, though."

"Why?"

"Well, it must be frustrating to finally be awake in the daytime and not be able to get anything done because your companions are too exhausted to be any help. I don't think he's comfortable waiting around."

"He is capable of managing on his own."

"In this case, I suspect he needs our assistance—or at least our presence—to get the work done. I'm not sure why I think that, but I do."

"Hmm . . . Intuitive thinking."

"Right now, the only thing you should intuit is the bed. As in 'get into it.'"

"Oh, ha-ha."

"I'm not kidding. You're swaying on your feet."

"I need a bath. . . ."

"Not as much as you need to sleep," he said. This time he did not ask permission but picked me up and carried me to the bed.

"Too much to do . . ." I objected. "Carlos—"

"Obviously thinks it's more important for you to rest. So in you go," he added, rolling me onto the quilt laid over the bed.

Every part of my body seemed to become heavier the moment I was horizontal and the thin blanket Quinton pulled up over us both was like a magical veil of sleep colluding with the pillows to draw my eyes closed and drown me in slumber. I barely acknowledged the comfort of his body curled around mine with a drowsy mumble before I sank away.

TWENTY-NINE

The sun was still up when the stifling discomfort of sleeping in clothes and blankets forced me awake. I wasn't entirely rested, but the feeling that we were already pressing too close to a deadline goaded me. My attempts to get out of bed without waking Quinton were unsuccessful and he caught my good hand.

"No. Please," he begged. "A few minutes . . ."

"There's too much we have to—"

"I know. I know," he said, sitting up and shaking his head in resignation.

Quinton followed me into the bath and we managed to get clean without soaking my stitches or having uncomfortable, hurried sex—my hand still ached and the timing was just too wrong, though the desire lay plain between us. We were both anxious and wound up, but he didn't press me about his proposal and I didn't talk about impending doom or the ghosts that seemed to peer from the walls and flow through the rooms like smoke.

The shirt and trousers I'd borrowed from Quinton were dusty

and sweat-stained, and I thought it unlikely I'd be much help in the nude—though Quinton probably thought otherwise. As much as I appreciated that, I couldn't push aside the nettling feeling that there was too much to do and not enough time.

There were noises outdoors and something thumped in the hall-way outside. Quinton stuck his head out and talked to Nelia for a moment, then backed into the room with a large, heavy suitcase. He shut the door with his foot and turned around, lugging the case to the bed.

"Nelia—with some prompting from Carlos, I suspect—has un-earthed a collection of things left by guests and family. If we're un-lucky, something will fit you."

"Unlucky?" I repeated.

"Well, unlucky for me, because then you'll stop pacing around the room in nothing but a towel."

"I think it would be luckier, since that way you won't have to watch the pacing part of the equation."

"It is a little annoying."

"Let's see what's in there."

The case was stuffed with mismatched clothes and, once again, I had to make do with a blouse and skirt that were both a bit loose-fitting but long enough to cover my midriff and knees as well as all the essential bits. The outfit was comfortable enough and didn't look too bad once we'd found a belt. The skirt even had pockets, which seemed more common with European than American clothes, the assumption of American designers being that you'd rather look slim than have a convenient place for your keys.

"I'm becoming tired of borrowed clothes," I grumbled. "I never thought I'd miss my closet more than my truck. At least the sandals are more comfortable than they look."

"I, for one, am not complaining. You have fantastic legs. Especially when—"

I put my hand over his mouth. "Oh no. Don't go there."

He pushed my hand away and kissed me, pulling me in tight to his body. I could feel the tension and desire he was trying to suppress for my sake. "I'm sorry that this is such a bad time, but no matter what clothes you're wearing—or not wearing—you're always going to make me feel this way," he said. "Did I ever tell you that the first time we met, I wanted to take you to bed?"

"Yes."

"Damn. I thought I was revealing something."

"Oh, you're revealing something, all right," I said. "And if there weren't bad guys to stop and dragons to slay, I'd be flattered flat onto my back."

He laughed and let me go. "Then we'd better go slay them."

I moved and my thigh brushed against him. He bit his lip. "Maybe you'd better go first," he added.

Downstairs, the house had become busy near the kitchen and a group of long tables had been set under the cork oaks at the end of the driveway. Nelia and the children were coming and going along with several other women and a man who limped, carrying food, wine, and utensils out to the tables.

Trying to stay out of the way, I stepped out onto the terrace around the pool, which was now deserted except for Carlos. He stood at the edge of the drop and watched the bustle from a distance.

"What's all that?" I asked.

"Dinner for the fieldworkers. The house provides for those who've labored during the day. Most of them are local people—about a third are family, the rest neighbors and seasonal workers."

"Your family . . . ?"

"Yes," he replied, sounding a little irritated. "I can see the ties, some faint, some stronger. . . . "

"I don't understand how you couldn't have known, couldn't have felt them. . . ."

"Do you feel every connection in your web of family? Even once you saw it?"

"Only Quinton."

Carlos nodded with a slight scowl. "I had no such connection to any of them."

"Are you sure Beatriz and Damiao-Maria were your kids?"

"Yes. While you slept, I spoke with Amélia."

"So she's loose."

He inclined his head a few degrees. "For now."

We were both quiet for a minute, watching the bustling around the dining tables as other people began arriving, walking across the fields, or driving in to park nearby on the stubble of crops already harvested near the house. Even the ghosts streamed out from the house and wove among the living, remembering the harvest meals they'd eaten under the same trees. I spotted Rafa, but I didn't recognize any others as more than swirls of white, silver, black, and blue, and the vague mist-shapes of bodies and faces. The man with the limp paused to stare back at us until Nelia grabbed him by the arm and laughingly pulled him along with her to the kitchen. He followed her with a hungry gaze and stumbling feet.

"This is a burden I never wanted," Carlos said, his low voice making the air near us quiver. "I had thought, as I first saw them, 'In a very different world, might this have been mine? Might I have been other than what I am?' But there is no different world in which any of that could be true. There is only this one, where I have descendants only because I raped my wife and I see them only because of you."

"Me?"

"Yes. I would not stand here, now, if I had not met you. I would not be as I am now if you hadn't come asking foolish questions and if I had not taken Cameron under my wing because of you. Because you are who you are—not *what* you are. I have met other Greywalkers—I knew Peter Marsden when I lived in London under the heel of my hate. He is a weak creature, compared to you, and driven mad by what he is."

"Marsden is twice the Greywalker I am."

"And half the man. Less than half the woman."

I laughed a little at that, but it didn't distract Carlos from his strange humor that seemed to balance on the razor's edge between anger and awe.

"I saw it when you first looked at me and wanted to run away, but you didn't because you were more worried for the safety of a fool-hardy, loyal boy than you were for yourself. Your compassion, your sense of justice and righteousness, your ridiculous bravery—I've laughed at you over them, goaded, and pricked you about them, but they are what fascinated me from the first. They are what keep you from falling into madness and make you superior to all the others of your kind. Until that night, I would have killed a creeping, questioning fool like you out of hand. A lamb walking into a lion's den gets eaten and I am a vicious, ever-hungry lion. But you shone like a star and I wanted to see what you would do, strange creature, if I told you the truth."

"And I went outside and threw up."

"That may be, but from that moment, my life—my *unlife*—

began to change. Before I met you, I had only one emotion: hate. And only one desire: vengeance. You destroyed them. And rather than having nothing, I had everything—including a student I didn't want, whose only ability is his charm. You challenged me and I discovered I was still curious, still passionate about something other than my desire to see Edward destroyed. Then you made a proposal that no one had ever made before."

"I did?"

"Yes. You suggested that even a vampire who had no ability with magic might still exert pressure upon it, because we exist as magical creatures. That through one such as me or Mara Danziger it might be directed, rather than passive. And you were correct. It is that which makes Cameron the better leader—because of your suggestion I trained him to enhance what is natural in him. My fascination with you grew and other things became less important. I ceased to see myself only as the creature that Lenoir and Edward had made me. The rift between Edward and me seemed smaller, less . . . worthy of my energies. Every question you brought to me challenged me and whetted my desire for knowledge and greater consequence as nothing had in centuries. Cameron was hopeless as a mage, but as a leader, he is passionate, mindful, and fair, and determined to make us all better than we were—which he learned from you."

I had fought—usually in blind ignorance, fear, and fury—to wrest my fate from the control of others and do something better with what I had become. Cameron had been led to it. "You don't give yourself enough credit," I murmured.

"I promise you, I am neither decent nor humane and my passions are far too dark to be reflected in what Cameron has become. Except for one. In both of us, there is a high regard for you."

"Oh no . . . not that . . ."

"No, not that. Not what you feel for your husband-in-soul—whose true name is almost too painful to utter—not even lust."

"Are you making fun of my beloved He-Who-Must-Not-Be-Called-After-His-Father?"

Carlos curled his lip in disdain at my attempt to derail the uncomfortable conversation. "Perhaps. Your empathy, your foolish, irresponsible compassion, even for walking horrors like Ian Markine, drew me to watch you, to help you, even when I wanted to take your light from you. That is why I did not kill him and it is why I broke his mind. You believed he should be stopped because you believe—you *know* by your own action—that there is such a thing as justice even if it isn't what the laws of man would prescribe. You imagined he could be saved, made whole, because of your burning, beautiful compassion, but he would not have stopped in his plans to murder you and all the rest. He intended it—I saw it in him the way you see the fire in the warp and weft of the world. I recognize evil too well. I cared nothing for the fates of the others, but I could not let him live to kill you and I could not let him die and damn you. For its own sake, because it fed my own power, I destroyed him, but because it preserved you, it was a pleasure to drive him mad."

The emotion that colored his voice then ran over my skin like a caress, a hedonistic thrill more erotic than simple flesh. Shivering, I had to look away and watch the people at the tables as the sun began to slide down in the west, turning the sky to gold.

I watched the limping man catch up to Nelia and turn her around for a kiss, which she returned, laughing. He ran his hand into her hair, which she had let down to tumble in dark curls onto her shoulders. He bent to kiss her again and then pulled back, leaning away, staring at her, his expression changing from ardor to anger. He spoke sharply to her and I couldn't hear what he said, but the way he leaned toward her and the color of his aura, suddenly flushed red, was enough. Nelia glared back at him. I turned my gaze aside.

I felt Carlos step up close behind me and I winced as the almost-forgotten cold of his aura enclosed me in nauseating discomfort. "I have told you these things because I am falling away," he whispered. "This gift of yours is flickering out. By Monday night I will be what I was. I will not forget what you gave me and I will not profane it by doing you harm. But if you don't say yes to your lover's proposal, I may—"

Quinton walked out of the house and toward us, calling out, "Harper?"

It didn't take Carlos's unfinished threat to decide me and I turned toward Quinton, smiling, happy. "Yes!" I called back.

Something shrieked and a whirlwind of mist and malice descended on us. "No! No, no, no!"

Amélia swept between us, throwing Quinton into the pool and pushing him down. "She is not for you!" the ghost screamed into my head.

I winced at the eldritch sound and dove toward the pool.

Carlos spun and plucked me out of the air. "No!"

"She'll drown him!" I shouted back.

"And you also, if you go in now."

He reached forward, the jet-black shroud of his aura expanding like wings and folding over us, and yanked Amélia backward by the clawed extension of his power.

She screamed and thrashed in his grip as I dove into the pool and grabbed hold of Quinton. I pulled him up under one arm and kicked for the surface, giving no thought to my injured hand, even as it throbbed and stung. Through the water I could see Carlos holding Amélia down while she continued to fight him.

I broke the surface and gasped for air, squeezing my arm tight around Quinton's chest as I made for the shallows. He coughed and sputtered, gasped, then kicked and fought me for a moment before he realized I wasn't the one trying to kill him. I could hear Amélia screaming, her words in Portuguese and echoing in English in my mind, making a clamor that made my head ache.

Quinton got his feet under him and pulled free of my arm. "I got it. I'm all right," he panted, slogging for the nearest rail.

"Are you sure?" I asked.

"Yeah, yeah. What the hell was that?"

"Amélia."

"Still here?"

"Yes, and wants to kill us both."

"Jesus, everyone wants us dead except us. Go. I'll get myself out of the pool. You go deal with the ghost."

I pulled myself out of the water, clumsy with only one good hand, and dripped to where Carlos was struggling with Amélia. She fought and screamed at him, tearing at him with taloned hands, her face distended into a horrifying visage full of fangs—the expression of her rage.

"She is for you! For you! Not for that weak creature! I did this all for you, Carlos—my love, my curse. . . ."

"It is not for you to determine my life, Amélia. You are dead! Your power on Earth is passed," Carlos said, his voice sharp. He shook her and she diminished, becoming more human-looking, but no less disturbed.

She giggled a shrill, mad sound. "I brought her to you! I gambled your life, my beloved, so she could save you. So you could take her. You should have taken her then! Why did you not make her yours at Carmo?"

"At Carmo?" he asked, and now his voice trembled at the edge of rage. "What had you to do with that, Wife?"

Amélia laughed hysterically, sliding to her knees in front of Carlos as if begging him for something. "I found Lenoir and I spoke with the woman who wanted you dead. I tricked them! They thought they controlled me, but I was the one who turned them to my purpose! They lured you out and tried to kill you, but I knew you could not die. Not my love, my Carlos. And *she* would save you and you would love her and be happy! I tried to make you happy. I tried to give you a son. I failed and failed and failed. . . ."

Carlos shook his head. "Foolish woman . . . You failed at nothing. Look out there, in the field. Who are those people?"

Amélia turned her head toward the tables under the trees and the diners all stared back. I don't know what they saw, but it must have been strange, judging by the expressions they turned our way. Carlos sank to one knee beside his wife's shade and pointed at the family and neighbors. "Who are they?" he repeated.

"Fieldworkers," Amélia said.

"Look harder." He placed his hand on her phantom back and beckoned me closer. "Rafa . . ."

Amélia smiled as she saw Rafa. "My granddaughter."

"And the rest. All your children."

"My children. Our children." She broke into sobs. "I loved you and I gave you children, but you never loved me!"

"I am not capable of love."

"You love her. . . ."

"I do not—I am a monster." His voice thrummed on the strings of the Grey, resonant, and unbearable. "I raped you and beat you. You died to give me a son and I did not care. I hated you and wished you dead long before that. I would have killed you eventually if you hadn't the luck to die before I could do it. You deserved better than me. You deserve to be free of me." He shifted his focus to me for a second. "Hold her."

I reached for Amélia's tangled threads as he continued. "And I deserve to be free of you, treacherous bitch."

I was stunned by his words and barely had my fingers in the knotted gyre of her energy, which sent a sharp, electric pain stabbing into my cut finger and running up my hand like fire, when he pushed his free hand against his own chest and tore away the tiny energetic filament that held them to each other. Amélia shrieked and writhed in my grip. Carlos spat a word at her that coruscated with spikes of obsidian black and bleeding red thorns. Then he plunged his hands into her spectral form, ripping her into shreds with two violent swipes. The hot, bright core of her energy snuffed out and she unraveled in a swift tumble of gleaming threads and a waning cry that dropped to a whisper as she fell apart and then vanished into silence.

She was gone. Still dripping wet, I stared at Carlos, aghast, shivering not from the water, but from shock and the electric feeling that had coursed through me until he tore her apart. I had seen him dissipate ghosts before, but never with such brutality, and I had never felt so much as if a small part of me had been shredded with her.

Carlos closed his eyes, his chest heaving as if his actions had cost him dearly.

"I don't understand," I said, rubbing my arms and trying to silence the buzzing sensation touching her had brought on.

He caught his breath, looked up at me, and got back to his feet. He glared out at the family, neighbors, and workers, arrested in their dinner, until they turned their heads and returned to their food. He swung back to me and Quinton, his expression bleak as a wasteland.

"She had to be released, but she tried to kill us all and—unlike you, Greywalker—my compassion is limited."

"Amélia . . . knew Lenoir? The one who made Sergeyev's box?" Quinton asked, coming to put an arm around my shoulder and hold me close—though for his own sake or mine, I couldn't guess.

"Yes. My old master. The man who murdered me."

Carlos walked past us and disappeared into the house. I glanced out at the people in the field, but they conspicuously didn't look back.

"I think I missed something. What has Lenoir to do with this?"

"I thought—but I never did tell you, did I?"

Quinton gave an exasperated sigh. "Tell me what?"

"The night I went out after him, Carlos had gone to talk to Lenoir's shade at Carmo and Griffin tried to kill him—that setup appears to have been Amélia's doing—but how would Amélia know Lenoir? Carlos wouldn't have introduced them during her lifetime and ghosts don't usually—"

"Get chummy after death? Yeah, I remember your saying that before. But I don't think it would be smart of us to ask Carlos about that right now, do you?"

I shook my head.

He looked at me, still rubbing my arms. "Are you all right?"

"Feels like static all over my skin. And I never thought I'd say I feel cold here, but I do."

"We'd better go in and dry off," Quinton said.

"Yes," I replied, turning with him as he led me back toward the house.

Nelia was in the doorway when we reached it. Her eyes were too bright and she smiled at us with a strange feverishness. "I knew it," she said.

"Knew what?" I asked.

"He *is* Carlos."

"You know that's not possible," I said.

She smiled and held out some towels, but she didn't say anything beyond, "Put your clothes in the hall and I'll dry them for you." Then she walked away, leaving Quinton and me alone in the salon.

We exchanged a puzzled look and returned to our room, dampened in more than our clothes.

THIRTY

arlos met us at the head of the stairs. "Change clothes. We still have work to do tonight."

"Wait," I said.

He gave me a cold look.

"Why?"

The thin edge of a razor smile pulled one corner of his mouth, but he didn't give me the answer I wanted. "Rui will not ask that question if we fail," he said, and turned away.

"Still as warm and friendly as a crocodile with a toothache," Quinton observed as the necromancer walked away down the hall.

I found myself scowling and reserved any comment.

"What was that business with Nelia?" Quinton asked as we entered our bedroom. "She's a little obsessed with our scary companion, I think."

"She also seems to have a male admirer who isn't happy about that. If we hadn't made a scene, I think he would have."

"Ah, the joys of family dynamics."

"As if either of us can talk."

He pressed his lips together and didn't say anything.

I had to sort through the suitcase of mystery again and find dry clothes, but at least I knew I'd be running around in the dark, so it didn't matter how presentable they were. I found a dark shirt and a pair of men's pants that fit a little better than Quinton's had and were long enough to cover my ankles. It was an inelegant ensemble, but I didn't care.

A knock came on the door and this time I opened it while Quinton stuffed the unwanted clothes back into the suitcase.

Nelia stood in the hall with a tray. "I thought you would want food before you go out—Carlos has arranged for the car, but he isn't hungry. And I can take your wet clothes and towels now if you like."

"Yes, thank you," I said, accepting the tray and turning to put it down inside the room. Then I picked up our wet things.

I stepped out into the hallway and closed the door, looking around to make sure we were alone before I spoke to her. I dropped the wet clothes to the floor and caught her arm. "Nelia," I started, "I would avoid Carlos if I were you. Your boyfriend doesn't seem to like him."

She made a dismissive shudder and pulled her arm from my loose grip. "Eladio. He can go to the Devil."

"You seemed fond enough of him an hour ago."

"He's a possessive prig. I don't need another of those in my life. If I must have a man, I'd prefer one who appreciates my wildness as much as my body." She smirked a little and bent down to pick up the wet clothes, pushing her loose hair back behind her ears. There was a tiny flicker of color along her collarbone that gave off an unnatural gleam when no light from the lamps could strike it. I peered at her through the Grey, unnerved, and saw it: a small red mark like a tiny dagger nestling in the hollow of her collarbone, right where blood would pool as it flowed from a wound high on her neck.

There was no such wound—no sign of one, but there was an odd purple thread in her aura, a subtle thing I had not noticed before and might have missed—like the tiny mark—but doubted I had. Carlos had mentioned a mark by which vampires could recognize those who fed them and to whom they belonged. . . .

I reached out and touched the mark on Nelia's clavicle. She gasped and stood up, staring at me, eyes bright and startled. Then she shook herself and took half a step away. "What are you doing?"

"I thought I saw something on your neck," I said.

"You, too? It's nothing."

But it wasn't nothing, not the way it had sparked at my touch and she'd jumped to turn toward me, only to see I wasn't whom she'd expected. But there was no one in the hall besides me.

"I still think Carlos is not a safe choice for you," I suggested.

"It's none of your business, Mrs. Smith."

"No, but I know him better than you do and he's not a nice man. I think you saw what happened earlier. Is that someone you want to be close to?"

She gave me a cool look. "It is none of your business," she repeated, then picked up the laundry and walked away with it.

Of course it wasn't, and Carlos, for all he was mortal and warm for the moment, was still a vampire and a necromancer—a monster, as he had said, who would return to his undead state by Monday night if we all survived whatever we were going to do between now and Saint Jerome's Day. Nelia was an adult, old enough to have adult children if she had started young, and old enough to make her own decisions about whom she was going to lend her body to in whatever capacity. But it still gave me a queasy feeling, since she was his granddaughter, however many generations removed. I didn't want to think about the implications of that kind of consanguinity.

But I was still thinking about it as we drove toward Campo Maior. Night had fallen and the roads were empty. My hand prevented me from driving and I had been a bit surprised that Carlos had chosen to take the wheel.

"You're a font of the unexpected. I didn't think you drove," I had said as we approached the small car that sat in the driveway, dusty from the trip to the house for our use.

"That I do not choose to does not mean that I cannot." His voice had been chilly and I'd wondered if Nelia had mentioned our conversation to him. "I find the effect of the steel and glass . . . disconcerting."

It sounded like the flip side of the comfort I took in my truck's ability to filter out the random energy of the Grey. "You never seem uncomfortable in the Land Rover," I'd said.

He had given me a sideways glance as he got into the car and closed the door without another word.

Campo Maior lay in a small bulge of the border between Portugal and Spain, surrounded by the sometime enemy on three sides. It was a small city, placed as it was on a hill with a river on one side, and fields that rolled down to Spain on the other. Even from the highway, I could see the rigid shadow of a castle at the top of the hill, its fortified walls like arms reaching for the city beneath a quarter moon. On the outskirts, the area smelled of mown fields, dusty olives, and pigs, which I could hear grunting even in the dark as they moved restlessly in their yards. I imagined that even with the pigs, it was a striking place in the daylight. We passed a large, rambling building bearing a sign for the Delta company, and the odor of coffee reached in through our open windows. We wound up through the town to the second-highest point—the Igreja Matriz de Campo Maior.

The Mother Church of Campo Maior stood in a road that was

wide by Portuguese standards, but still narrow by mine, completely surrounded by red-roofed buildings sprouting old-fashioned television antennas like a harvest of metal wheat, gleaming silver in the moonlight. It was another Baroque building with little ornamentation other than the contrast of dressed stone edges against white plastered walls. The edifice was six stories tall and as wide as a city block with a central arch between two square towers that made the massive doors to the sanctuary seem small. I had to crane my neck to look up at the huge structure.

We left the car a block away and walked back, not looking too unusual even after dark, since the town hadn't gone to bed yet, it being Saturday and only an hour past sunset. Like Borba and Vila Viçosa, the town was white with marble and plaster except for the church itself. A small staircase led up between the massive stone-edged church and a smaller building on the east that was so perfectly white it looked like a house made of sugar and decorated with restrained piping of white frosting around the top, windows, and doorway. Facing the staircase, a delicate black iron grille protected an arched window below a white plaster frieze of leaves and curlicues with the words CAPELA DOS OSSOS painted in neat black lettering between the plasterwork and the top of the window arch. Behind the window, barely lit by a candle from within and streetlight without, rows of white skulls lined the ledge like pies in a macabre bakery. A priest in a long cassock was walking up the stairs ahead of us, one hand clutching a fold of his robe to keep from stepping on his hem, a ring of keys held in the other.

Carlos caught up to him in two long strides and said, *"Padre, um momento."*

The priest turned, an expression of mild surprise on his long, bland face. *"Sim?"*

They spoke for a minute, the priest shaking his head and gesturing to the chapel.

Carlos turned back to us, his eyes gleaming. "The priest says that the chapel is closed—it was broken into and vandalized this morning."

"What was taken?" I asked.

"I hope we may discover that ourselves."

He turned back to the priest, who was frowning at us. "I speak a little of English," the priest said, his voice very soft but carrying down the marble stairs clearly. "What interests you in the bones here?"

Carlos provided an edited version of the truth. "Other ossuaries have been desecrated recently. We wish to discover if there is a pattern to the vandalism." I could feel the weight of his persuasion bearing on the priest through the Grey. "May we see what happened here?"

The quiet priest narrowed his eyes, resisting Carlos's magical nudging. "You are from the government?"

"The church. These two have brought reports of such damage in other parts of Europe. We fear the current economic and political stress may be causing anger misdirected at us—at God. It may be nothing," he said, then added, "But . . ." He spread his hands, as if he were shrugging, but I could see a thin strand of magic pulling between them, growing ugly spikes of compulsion.

I stepped close, tilting Carlos a questioning look. He lifted his eyebrows, giving way to me in silence. I knew from experience that any such spell of Carlos's tended to do damage and I didn't see the point in harming the priest just to get a look in his chapel. If the Kostní Mágové had already been here, our only interest was in figuring out what they'd taken so we could guess what they'd go after next.

"Father," I started, leaning lightly on the Grey—just enough to incline him to like me, "it is an imposition, I know, but while my colleague may have doubts, I don't. You've heard about the ossuaries in the Algarve, I'm sure, and the desecration of the tomb of King Sebastian in Lisbon. But there have been so many others, in Poland, in France, even in Rome itself. We must stop this. We must not let people lose faith when they need it most."

The priest was taken aback and blinked at me. "Oh. No. I had not heard. You wish to see the damage here?"

"Yes. If you can allow it."

"Yes. Yes," he repeated, walking to the chapel door with the keys ready in his hand.

I walked past Carlos, giving him a smug smile.

"Well played," he muttered.

"Persuasion is my gift," I whispered back.

Quinton ran up the steps and joined the tail end of our parade, pulling a pad of paper and a pen from his bag as if his job were to record what we discovered. Few people notice or question a secretary.

The priest unlocked the door and we filed through a small vestibule with a drinking fountain, a small counter, and a chair. Then we followed the priest down a short set of steps, into low light and the odor of crumbling mortar, must, and beeswax as he went to the altar to pay his respects to the cross above it. I found my chest tight with an unaccustomed pressure as I stepped into the room. It boiled with ghosts that thronged against me, whispering and sighing, crying, screaming in pain, or moaning in despair. I had to stop and close my eyes, my breathing short and sharp until the feeling eased and the shadows of the jumbled dead made room for me.

I opened my eyes and saw the priest looking up at me, concerned. "Daughter? You are unwell?"

"No. It's just the chapel. It's . . . overwhelming. There are so many. . . ." I stood still and looked around. Streetlight and faint moonlight shone through the large round window that took up most of the back wall and through the arched one on the side where we'd entered. The light limned the bones embedded in the mortared walls with silver, while a single fat candle glowed below the crucifix. The priest lit the four wax tapers on the altar, and four more in tall stands beside it, turning the illumination golden.

"Yes," the priest replied. "You are sensible of them. There are many bones, many bodies. There was an explosion in 1732, then the Spanish siege, the wars, Napoleon. . . . So many in the graveyards . . . Then the cholera in 1765. We built the chapel for them—there were so many taken by the illness—but there are others here. All the bones here wait, as a reminder. We are all bones and all bones are dust. Only the glory of heaven is eternal."

The room was much smaller within than it had looked from the outside, the walls a foot or more thick from the long bones that had been piled up, ends facing out, and mortared into place. The walls' bottom third was all covered in skulls, like bizarre wainscoting, and the skulls were protected by thick sheets of clear Plexiglas. Every joint of the walls and the arched ceiling was delineated with lines of skulls. The floor was a smooth mosaic of small colored stones below the wing-like patterns of the bones and skulls that covered the wall surfaces and pillars that supported the roof. Even the ceiling was covered in the bones of arms and ribs, mortared in place like thatching above the shadowed niches and pointed arches made of the smallest bones.

Playing our parts, Carlos, Quinton, and I approached to genuflect and cross ourselves at the altar in the golden light. Only I hesitated, uncomfortable with my deception, wondering if the God of the Old Testament would take exception to the way I did my job. But there was no lightning or thunder, and I turned away to look over the room again.

The priest knelt on one side of the altar and switched on a small electric floodlight that aimed its beam from the floor to the wall above. For a moment, the plain crucifix in front of a Plexiglas-covered bone altar piece was brightly lit, as were the vases of wilting flowers below. Then the priest turned the small light toward a section of the wall that lay farther back, near the rear windows, our shadows huge across it.

I caught my breath, seeing the crumbled section of wall, thick with bones and skulls, but now torn and raked as if by giant claws. I turned in a small circle to see the whole room. There were three niches in total, two on the wall facing the door and one on the door-side wall. It was the niche beside the door that was now empty, hidden from first view in the darkest part of the room by the way the stairs deposited visitors next to the altar, with their backs to the niche. The other two niches were untouched.

The long-faced priest took a taper from the altar and lit a silver oil lamp that hung from the ceiling by silver chains, adding to the golden light that touched the desecrated wall. He returned the candle and stopped near the lamp to look at the damage. "It is profane. The whole skeleton that stood in that niche is gone."

"A whole skeleton? Of a single individual?" I asked.

The priest shook his head. "I cannot say for certain. This other one has mummified flesh which binds the bones," he added, pointing to the niche across from the ruined one, "but the one that was taken did not. It is not recorded who the bones were in life."

"This is terrible," I said, walking up to the ruined wall and putting out my hands as if I could recall the missing skeleton by touching the place it had stood. The priest laid his hand on the back of mine, stopping my movement as he said, "They are very old and fragile."

"Of course," I replied, lowering my hands. How could I talk to the ghost if I couldn't touch the bones to make a connection to it . . . ? I looked at the priest again. "Could you allow us a moment to confer?" I asked, giving a little more psychic weight to the trust and persuasion I'd already established with him.

He looked uncomfortable, but he nodded as I leaned harder on the compulsion, feeling it like cold quills piercing my skin. "I shall wait in the vestibule," he offered.

He walked through to the tiny antechamber and sat on the wooden chair at the head of the steps, but he didn't close the door, keeping a benign eye on us from a respectful distance—or as much distance as the small space allowed. It would have to do. I stood staring at the wall for a moment, awash in ghosts. If only they would cleave to their own bones, this would be easier. I turned toward Carlos and moved close to him, which in such a small room required only a few steps. Quinton followed.

Carlos waited for me to speak, offering nothing. "I have an idea, but it depends on you," I murmured.

"Go on," he replied, matching my low tone.

"Can you, without touching the bones, force the ghosts to retreat to, say, their skulls? All of them. At the same time."

He frowned. "All of them?"

"Yes. The ghost who has no skull to retreat to will remain isolated in the room and then I can hold him while you talk to him and find out what he or she can tell us."

His frown darkened into a scowl as he thought about it. He turned to look around the room, raising his eyes toward the ceiling. It almost looked like he was praying. He turned his gaze back to me and I shivered. "I can, but not without touching something of the chapel's bone walls. To control them all will be difficult enough, but to do so with no contact is impossible. Your chance to catch the spirit in question will be short even then."

"We'll have to find a way. I know it will take a lot of energy and won't be easy, but I can manage my end if you can manage yours."

"I know how it can be done without the priest becoming upset. If you are ready . . . ?"

"Hang on," said Quinton. "Maybe I can help."

"You would have to die. That would not do."

"No. I'm just thinking there might be another way. . . . Is there any reason to keep all these ghosts captive here? Aren't they . . . kind of miserable? If you can isolate the ones that have bones still here, why can't you just . . . absorb them? They *are* dead after all. . . . Then you'd only need to expend enough energy to isolate the first one and the rest will simply replace the energy used for the start cycle. The tricky bit is making sure you don't suck up the one ghost we need."

"That I will leave to your beloved."

Quinton was pleased with himself for the idea and I was certain it wasn't just because it was clever—Carlos in need of energy could become dangerous and unpredictable, and none of the humans in the area wanted to die to make him feel better.

"But I will need your help," Carlos added.

Quinton paled. "Mine? What do you want me to do?"

"Pray."

THIRTY-ONE

"Wat?"

"Kneel, fold your hands, and let them rest on the edge of the altar while you bow your head. The balance of life and death is maintained so long as we each touch the edge of the altar—which is made of their bones. The ghosts will flow through you to me. It will be unpleasant, but it won't kill you," Carlos said, then added with a sharp, white grin, "It doesn't matter if you pray or not, but I suspect you will."

Quinton made a face and turned to look at the altar, muttering, "This is not what I had in mind."

Carlos chuckled at him and sank to his knees, crossed himself, and clasped his hands, letting them rest at the edge of the Plexiglas barrier, tilting forward until his long fingers pressed against the altar built of skulls. He gazed up for a moment at the cross. Although I couldn't see his face where I stood, his posture changed and he seemed to be truly praying to God. Then he dropped his head over his hands. I had to remind myself that he had been raised in the faith and had fallen from it. It was doubtful his mind was on anything other than the task at hand, but he appeared to be one of the devout.

Quinton copied him, though his performance was less inspirational.

The air of the small chapel chilled and the room seemed to compress, the ghosts all stirring at once and looking toward the altar. One by one, they slid toward it, suddenly fluid. Quinton gasped and shuddered as the first glittering stream of spirit energy touched him. I wanted to run to him, to pull him away, but I stepped back, looking for the one phantom that was not mesmerized and turning toward the altar. In the writhing, silvery sea of them, a single oddity was hard to find and several more slipped away, making Quinton twitch and utter muffled cries of distress with their passage. It tore at me and I started moving around the room as if my pacing could break apart the impenetrable cloud of specters.

One eyeless face turned to watch me and I hurried to it, sinking slightly into the Grey to clutch the remnant of a soul more securely, the stinging burn of the thing's energy piercing through my damaged fingertip, and slicing up the long bone of my arm. "I have it," I said, ascending to the normal with the ghost in my grip, panting and shivering with tingling discomfort.

For a moment, nothing changed and I wanted to scream. "I have it!" I repeated, louder.

Carlos and Quinton stood up, and the priest in the vestibule did as well. I pulled the phantom closer to me so my hands didn't seem to be clutching empty air a foot in front of my body. The tension among the remaining ghosts ebbed away, the room returning to its normal temperature as all three of the men came toward me and the ghosts drifted back into their muddled, endless flocking.

Quinton was shaking and had turned a terrible shade of pale.

He'd bitten into his lip and a small trail of blood had started from the corner of his mouth. Carlos glanced away from him and kept his eyes on me as the priest stepped down from the vestibule into the chapel.

"What have you found?" the priest asked as he walked toward me.

"I believe I know what the vandals took and why."

He looked at me, expecting something. I made a gesture at Carlos, which was more by way of passing the ghost off to him. He took the motion as intended and caught the fine tangle of silver and white that I had held, drawing it into his own grip as he had done with Rafa.

"The bones of the infected," I said, for Carlos's sake and not the priest's. I could see Carlos nodding behind him, but the priest only looked confused. I was guessing, based on what Carlos had said Rui would need. This chapel's bones were unlikely to include those of a thief who'd died in a fire, but according to the priest, many had died of something that would qualify as "a plague that killed thousands."

"Infected? The cholera?" the priest asked.

Carlos took over the conversation, forcing the priest to turn to him while I went to Quinton's side. I put my arms around him until he stopped shaking. Then I wiped the blood from his lip, out of sight of both the priest and Carlos.

"Yes," Carlos continued. "The missing skeleton was that of the man we would now call Patient Zero—the first person to have the disease and spread it." That had the ring of truth and I supposed Carlos had gotten the information from the ghost in the scant time he'd had so far.

"Cholera comes with dirty water," the priest said.

"Yes. But it can be passed by contact with the patient. These thieves may believe—in error—that they can culture the disease from the bones. This is like some of the other cases," Carlos lied.

Quinton gave me a questioning look as the color began returning to his face. I just nodded. He closed his eyes in relief.

"How did they know . . . ?" the priest asked. "One hundred and twenty of our parish died in a single month of the disease. All of them are laid to rest here."

"I cannot know how they knew. But . . . I know what God told me." I wondered if Carlos felt any qualms using the priest's faith to misdirect him, but necessity is a bitch and the story sounded good. "I don't know if we'll be able to recover your skeleton, Father. It may be dust by now."

The priest sighed. "A pity. And no help in catching the vandals."

Quinton nodded at me and stepped a little to the side. "I'm OK," he whispered.

I gave him a worried look but turned back to finish our job. "It's helped more than you can guess," I said, using the priest's shifting attention as cover to withdraw the compulsion I'd created between us. "Thank you for letting us see your chapel."

"It was my pleasure to help the church," he said, looking relieved as the thin needles of persuasion dissipated. With luck the feeling would linger and he wouldn't feel any need to question who had really been in his chapel tonight or why.

We avoided any protracted conversation and hurried off with our ghost in Carlos's pocket. The necromancer led us to the heights of the castle walls to examine the ghost in the moonlight, but, unable to tell us where its bones had been taken or why, it wasn't a helpful specter. It only confirmed the details of its death and complained of the pain Rui inflicted on it.

"Carving runes in the bone," Carlos noted.

"That's not good," I said.

"What kind of 'not good'?" Quinton asked, looking much better now that we'd walked and been in the fresh air for a while.

"The bones must be in tune with the correct spell," Carlos said. "If the bones were not already in tune, then they must be carved or grafted to match the song of the spell. The only reason for taking on the extra work such bones require is to add an aspect to the drache that is not a normal part of the spell. Whatever survives the fire of the Dragão do Inferno will not live long, but sicken and die, and spread more disease."

"Oh God . . ." Quinton said.

"Now you pray?"

"No, I've been praying since we got here, but the situation just gets worse."

"And we still do not know where they are or where they will call their drache," Carlos said.

"Can we do any more tonight?" I asked.

Carlos shook his head. "We had luck here, but there will be no accommodating priests roaming the stairs in Monforte or Évora."

"I thought you said you'd already been there."

"I have, but without Rui to guide them the first time, they may have to return."

"The Capela dos Ossos in Évora has very limited hours—according to their Web site," Quinton said. "Unless you feel like trying some breaking and entering in a major church in a fairly large city at midnight, we'd probably be better off going there first thing in the morning."

Carlos's mouth almost turned up enough to call the expression approval. "I agree. And your suggestion in the chapel was . . ." He paused as if having changed his mind about what he was about to say, then finished. "It was genius. But we have all expended too much energy today to face any of Rui and Purlis's company with a hope of emerging unscathed. The morning will be soon enough."

We returned to the Casa Ribeira. Seeing no one and finding the door unlocked, we headed upstairs to our rooms and retired to our respective beds without further discussion. We'd talked enough in the car and could sort out any details in the morning. The constant aching and itching of my injured hand was the least of our troupe's discomforts. Quinton had continued to wince with sudden pains and had grown paler and more sleepy throughout the drive back. Even Carlos looked tired—mortality seemed to wear on him badly.

In the morning, I woke up restive and stiff, too aware that I'd been abusing myself in the Grey, but neglecting any more reasonable physical routine. I knew it wasn't what most people would do, but I figured it was better to risk pushing myself too fast than to stagnate, stiffen, and chase my own thoughts into useless corners. I left Quinton in bed while I went downstairs for a swim—I'd had little proper exercise and while the stitches in my hand were a problem, I needed to move and let my mind drift without the distractions of desire, worry, regret, or still more conversation about the current problem.

I passed Carlos's door, seeing it standing an inch ajar, and heard the low rumble of his voice without being able to understand the words or hear them clearly. Portuguese, I assumed. A soft gasp that faded to a small moan followed from someone who was definitely not Carlos. I turned and continued down the stairs, not even wanting to pull the door closed and call attention to the fact they'd been overheard—the whole idea made me shudder.

I went to the kitchen to find some plastic to put over my injured hand and emerged into the courtyard in my borrowed bathing suit to find Eladio skimming invisible leaves from the pool's surface while glaring up at the bedroom windows. The wine crate that had so annoyed Nelia was propped on one of the chairs near him, its lid hanging a little askew.

"What is that doing out here?" I asked.

Eladio seemed startled at my presence, as if he hadn't seen me walk past him. His concentration on the windows of Carlos's room was so intense that perhaps he hadn't. He shook himself at my words and blinked as he looked at me.

"*She* gave it to me to take to the storage shed," he said.

His emphasis on "she" sent a green spark of jealousy arcing from his energy corona, which was a tangled mess of green, red, and orange that sparked pink one moment and sickening olive the next. He had it bad.

"You love her, don't you?" I asked.

He swallowed a sound of longing and pain, shaking his head. "It is nothing."

"We won't be here much longer," I said.

He just grunted and pulled the skimmer from the pool. He put it away and returned to tuck the box under his arm. *"Bom dia, Senhora Smith."*

He limped away, his right leg and spine slightly twisted, and disappeared around the edge of the house. I hoped I was right about leaving soon—the atmosphere at Casa Ribeira was becoming unhealthy.

I swam for about twenty minutes before I was too winded and aching from the uneven stroke of my arms to do more. As I got out of the pool, Quinton sat waiting on the chair that had lately housed the wine crate. Several ghosts were hanging around the edges of the courtyard as well, but I ignored them in favor of my boyfriend.

"Hey," he said, smiling at me.

"Hey, yourself," I said, reaching for my towel.

"You look wonderful when you're wet."

"I bet you say that to all the sea life."

"No, only tall, gorgeous brunettes. And eels."

"Eels?" I asked, pausing in removing the plastic from my hand.

"Yeah. I figure if I distract them, they may not bite me."

"Just how many eels do you know?" I asked, getting frustrated with trying to pick the plastic and bandage tape off my hand.

"None, but I like to be prepared."

I held my hand out to Quinton. "Can you remove this mess?"

"Certainly," he replied, turning his attention from my body to my mutilated hand.

Carlos walked out onto the terrace. I saw no sign of Nelia.

"And speaking of slithery things that bite . . ." Quinton added under his breath as he freed my hand.

I gave him a hard look—he'd seemed less antagonistic toward Carlos until this moment. Quinton returned a warning shake of his head.

"Coming for a swim?" I asked as Carlos stopped at the pool's edge.

"No. I may bask in my mortality for a time, but I'm not fool enough to risk it by drowning."

"You can't swim?"

"I could when I was younger, but water is rarely kind to such as me. I prefer the wrath of fiery stars—if I miscalculate, at least I shall die warm."

He'd almost died in a fire once before and I couldn't see the advantage of one death over the other; but I did notice he'd made a vampire joke, so he was in a good mood—"warm" being the uncomplimentary term some vampires used for normal humans and their state of life.

I finished drying myself off and sat at the edge of Quinton's chair. He kissed my cheek, but he didn't pull me into his body and I missed the reassuring affection of his touch.

"So," I started, "what's the schedule today?"

Carlos narrowed his eyes at us, as if surprised we were leaving him in charge. He raised an eyebrow, but neither of us made any move to enlighten him—he was decidedly more knowledgeable in this instance than we were.

"I suggest we go to Évora, and then Monforte," he said. "The city is a much greater risk for us. We'd do best to manage our business there quickly and move on to the less-likely ossuary afterward."

"I guess we'll know everything we need to by then," Quinton said. "There aren't any untouched ossuaries left in Portugal and if Dad and Company are going to do this on Saint Jerome's Day, they won't have time to move their show."

"No. And your father's efforts at destabilization have concentrated here in the past week, aimed specifically at the unconscious, cultural beliefs of the Portuguese, their economic desperation, and their unfortunate relations with the European Union. Even with the Spanish border so close, Rui cannot leave Portugal. The plan can only be set in motion here."

"OK. Then I'll get dressed and we can leave," I said, standing to go.

"Hey, one thing," Quinton said. "I drive."

Carlos scowled at him and I was equally curious.

"No offense, Carlos, but you're . . . out of practice at the driving thing."

Carlos had no reaction at all. "Very well."

And that settled it.

I ate and dressed hastily and joined the men at the car.

They were standing outside it, having a discussion that came to an abrupt halt as I drew near.

". . . Some idea of what it's like," Quinton was saying.

"A very pale one," Carlos replied.

Quinton looked dismayed, but he smiled at me and didn't allude to the conversation again. We drove to Évora in near silence.

If I'd been a scholar of things medieval, Évora might have been a delight, but for me as a Greywalker, the place was a nightmare. The old city sat on a hill, fortified by walls that still enclosed the town, and surrounded by the ubiquitous olive trees and mown fields going to golden stubble in the late-summer sunshine—pastoral and lovely, but the narrow, cobbled streets within were filled with the memory of the misery of generations of slaves, wars, sieges, and plagues. I was gaining an appreciation for living on the West Coast of the United States where the history of humankind's inhumanity was shorter and more scattered. It was no wonder that other Greywalkers, like Marsden, went insane if they lived in such constant, inescapable knowledge of horror. I thought Carlos was wrong: It was more luck than any quality of my own that kept me from joining them.

But our trip was for nothing—the Kostní Mágové had beaten us to the chapel once again. A docent in the church of Saint Francis informed us that the chapel was still closed due to vandalism and that the child's skeleton was still missing, but had been joined in its disappearance by the bones of one of the founding monks, which had been stolen from a marble casket beside the chapel altar very early that morning. While we'd been at Casa Ribeira making plans, they'd been here, harvesting the bones of the devout.

Carlos waited until we were outside to mutter something under his breath about the spawn of demons and swine. He'd been restrained while inside the church, as if trying to avoid the eye of God. I'd wondered if it was a lingering effect of being born and raised a Catholic, or the caution of a man who'd withstood the Inquisition. I was surprised to hear him swear at all and more so since we were still in the porch of the church when he did.

"They seem to know what we'll do. I hadn't thought Rui knew me so well . . ." he said.

"Maybe we have a spy in our midst?" Quinton suggested.

"Where? How?" Carlos demanded, his annoyance making the words snap and spark in the Grey like firecrackers and leave a sharpness in the air of the normal world that stank of burning sulfur. "We are the only guests at the house, and the family and workers have no time to spare for us."

"And Nelia won't betray you," I added.

Carlos turned a narrow glare on me that was intense enough to force me back a step.

Quinton grabbed Carlos by the arm. "Don't be an ass," he said, turning the necromancer away from me. The force of Carlos's anger doubled him over as if he'd been punched. "Anyone can see," he said with a gasp, backing up to sit on the church steps and catch his breath. "Anyone. The way she looks at you . . ."

Carlos turned his head sharply away, closing his eyes a moment. "Is like the way you look at Blaine."

"No. When I look at Harper, I don't *want* to die for her. I'm only willing to."

Carlos turned and looked out at the street for a moment before he turned back to both of us. "I pray that my indiscretion hasn't destroyed all chance of stopping Rui and Purlis."

"It's not like there's much to be done now, except get to Monforte and hope we're not too late this time."

THIRTY-TWO

Quinton found a route that took us north and east, avoiding Estremoz and a reported traffic accident that had brought the main route along IP2 to a standstill. It was longer, but I doubted we were losing any time if Purlis and Rui had gone the other way. The countryside was rugged and dry, dotted with standing stones, strange mounds, ruins, and tiny towns with a single street of low plastered buildings scattered along the edges of fields and groves of olive and orange trees. We passed by a cork plantation and the musty odor of the thick, spongy bark drying in barns off the roadside clung to the car for miles.

I could see dark flights of birds rising into the sky far ahead, flocking in momentary illusions of monsters and gods, then falling back toward the ground again. Ghost armies marched over the harvested fields and clashed in the roadside barrens, safely at a distance behind the glass and steel of the tiny car.

We were still a few miles away from Monforte when a dark shape exploded into the sky ahead.

"What was that?" I asked.

Quinton and Carlos both craned their necks and peered at the sky.

"I don't know—another flock of birds?" Quinton asked. "It's hard to see."

"Drive faster," Carlos said. "It came from the ground ahead."

"Do you know what it is?"

"We all do."

"What?" I asked.

He shook his head but kept his eyes on the sky, leaning forward from the backseat to stare over my shoulder.

The road dipped toward a bridge over a lazy curl of river and we sped along, flying for a moment as the slope dropped below the wheels. In the distance I saw the dark shape, like a mirage shimmering in the sun, turn in the sky and swoop back toward us, diving toward the land.

It vanished into the landscape just a mile or so ahead, shaking the earth for a moment. Then the air was still and unnaturally quiet except for the whine of our engine. A disturbance of dust hung in the air where the thing had crashed just off the road amid a ragged stand of cork oaks in a narrow band of ground between the highway and the river. The land was below the embanked road and partially hidden from view by scruffy shrubs and trees planted at the highway's edge, but the late-summer heat had left them drooping and even with the river water, the screen of leaves was thin enough to see into the sunken field.

"It's down," I said, excitement and anxiety clutching my heart and lungs and leaving a silvery taste in my mouth.

As we approached, a second smaller shape leapt up from the ground and rocketed into the sky while a man-sized thing darted away into the emptiness of the Alentejano plains with the nasal scream of a two-stroke engine being hard pressed.

Quinton jerked the car to a stop off the side of the highway a few yards from where the plantings gaped and showed a group of stones that stood side by side over a circle of gravel amid the wildflowers and grass. We all scrambled out of the car and ran toward the stones and the lingering smell of gasoline exhaust and motor oil.

"Dirt bike," Quinton said. Then he pointed across the river. "Must have been waiting on the other side of the water and took off across the next field."

Carlos and I weren't looking at the fields. I was staring at the stones—three taller than he was and one cut halfway down—while he looked into the sky.

"Night Dragon," he said, and shoved us both to the ground as a shadow spread over us and then stooped like a bird of prey.

It made no sound and the shade of its passing was insubstantial like that made by a thin cloud passing the sun. But the effect of its claws scraping the gravel was not—two sets of three straight lines scored the small rocks on either side of us with a stinking chemical odor and trails of smoke.

We all scrambled to our feet the moment it was past and ran for the rocks, crouching to remain below them so the flying monstrosity would have to come down where the odds were in our favor. With the sun shining, it was hard to see the construct of bones and magic as it wheeled in the sky.

"Someone has been practicing," said Carlos.

The Night Dragon swooped for us again, silent and leaving only the trail of its shadow in the sky.

"Avoid the claws," Carlos said as he ducked out from the shelter of the stones.

"I remember," I said, recalling the Night Dragon that Carlos and I had destroyed the previous year. The claw Carlos had picked up from the wreckage of the thing had smoked and dripped corrosive acid.

The shadowy construct tilted its wings to pursue Carlos and clipped one against the ground, pinwheeling as it lost control and crashed toward the rocks. It was much more solid than any of the previous versions and the ground quivered as it hit. Quinton and I ran in opposite directions as the nightmare beast plowed into the standing stones, dissolving into a scatter of bones, smoking claws, and the stink of rot.

"That felt a little too easy," Quinton said.

"It wasn't meant to harm us. The dreamspinner simply ran away before he could be caught here and left the creature to self-destruct," Carlos said. "The drache would have fallen apart like the others."

"Does that mean we got lucky?"

"Very. Chances are good the rest of the party is at Monforte. We may have a chance to stop them if we go before the boy can warn them. It's a pity we won't have time to collect the bones and deny them that resource if we hope to catch them."

He started back to the car at a run and we followed, but I was the slowest.

"What is this place?" I asked, looking at the rocks over my shoulder.

"It's a dolmen—ceremonial standing stones."

"I know that, but look at the rocks themselves."

They turned and saw what I'd seen.

The rocks, three just taller than a man making a jagged row and the fourth cut short later, huddled together at one side of an oval of gravel that stood at their feet. They seemed like unremarkable stones colored gray and tan with green lichen eating slowly on the tops until a cloud moved aside and the sun struck, leaving a deep red stain the color of blood splashed on the rocks. Another errant cloud passed by and the stain disappeared, leaving the rocks a simple gray again.

"That's eerie," Quinton said.

"Do you have a camera?" I asked.

"I have the laptop—it has a camera and the battery is good."

"Take a picture of the rocks. I want to find out if there's anything more to know about these."

Carlos was impatient with my request as Quinton grabbed his laptop and used the screen camera to take the photo. "Most likely the stones are merely convenient to where Rui is now—in Monforte."

"What if they're not?" I asked. "If we miss something at this stage, we may never catch up to them in time to stop their plan. Once the Hell Dragon is loose, our odds go down."

He glared at me. "If we continue to linger, we shall have no chance of catching them at all."

"Our chances aren't great on that score no matter how you look at it. If we don't have a backup, we're screwed," I snapped back.

He growled but didn't reply.

By the time we were done arguing, Quinton had packed the laptop back into the bag and was ready to drive on. Carlos didn't insist on further delay to pick up the bones, though I could tell it irritated him.

We pushed hard to reach Monforte and hoped the boy who'd been playing with dragons hadn't paused to watch what happened.

Monforte was a village just off the IP2, but it had the unusual distinction of having seven churches to serve a listed population of three thousand people, a shrine, and the expansive Roman ruins on which the current town was built, as well as the remains of an encircling castle wall. It was quaint, well maintained, and haunted as hell. The churches weren't the problem so much as the location. Armies had clashed in the fields nearby for millennia. Seen in the Grey, the soil of tiny, pastoral Monforte was red with blood.

We drove past a group of three small churches that climbed up the hill from the highway, a stone wall enclosing them and a steep path winding from the lowest to the highest, each drastically different from the others. The lowest one, sitting beside the highway like a mushroom, was a cross-shaped building with a central, cylindrical tower and small square projections on each side, all plastered smooth as a wedding cake and painted white with wide bands of deep yellow trim. The shape of it reminded me of Eastern Orthodox churches without the onion domes. Farther up the hill was a tall, narrow church with pointed square towers and peeling white paint that revealed hints of the stone underneath. At the top was a wide, low building with a crenellated roofline, plastered a newly painted white with the same deep yellow trim as the lowest church. The middle church looked drab compared to its neighbors that were so clean and bright that the white plaster glowed in the sunlight. On the road opposite the middle church tilted a tiny white and gold building with a cross on the roof over the date 1883, and a sign nearby that read RUA DO SENHOR DA BOA MORTE—Lord of Good Death Road.

We continued past the churches and the shrine to dying well and into the red-roofed village arrayed around the hill like the skirt of a ball gown. The steep, narrow road was interrupted by crossings that led to staircases instead of sidewalks as it wound up the hill to the heart of the village. We passed a grove of the ever-present olive trees and an apartment building with children's playground equipment inside a white-painted wall. Then we turned and crossed suddenly into the old village itself, crumbling stone walls holding back the hillside behind squat buildings with red roofs and peeling paint. A modern steel staircase led from the side of the road up into the remains of an old castle through the embracing fortress walls. We drove past and around, into a small town square called Praça da República, where we parked the car and continued on foot, diagonally through the square toward the farthest of the church towers that faced the open plaza.

The streets were paved entirely in gray stone, and the sidewalks and central square in marble cobbles. Young lemon trees had been planted at regular intervals along the perimeter of the square, and the leaves gave a citrus fragrance to the air around the central fountain and its tiny potted palms. The buildings here were also white trimmed with wide bands of golden yellow. As we passed into the narrow street at the corner that led to our goal, we saw the Igreja Matriz do Monforte was painted the same way. It was a small, square two-story building with a single window above the door and a narrow three-story bell tower on one side. Just next to the bell tower was an even smaller, narrower building that bore a skull and crossbones over the narrow, arched doorway.

The church door was closed and we could hear the sound of the priest and parishioners within, praying aloud. We walked toward the tiny chapel of bones next door, past a rambling house in some state of reconstruction or renovation that had peeled back parts of its stucco to reveal old wood and stones beneath and release the musty smell of ancient plaster and rot into the sunlit air.

A slim monk in a long black robe stepped out of the chapel. He had something cradled in his arms and as he turned to close the door, the cowl of his robe fell back.

I felt as if I'd been stabbed in the gut.

"Rui," Carlos said.

As if he'd heard him, Rui turned and looked at us. He made a gesture and my hand ached for a moment before I screamed in agony, falling to the cobbles as if I'd been sucked down by the earth itself.

Quinton threw himself down beside me, trying to scoop me into his arms while Carlos seemed to reach out for his old student as he had for Amélia when she held Quinton underwater.

But the bone mage had another trick ready. A wall of bones and rocks flew up between them, knocking Carlos back and disrupting his spell as he vanished from my sight.

Nearby, a two-stroke motorcycle revved its engine and though I could hear running feet, I couldn't turn my head to see anyone but Quinton.

As suddenly as the pain and pulling had come on, they ended, and I sat up so fast, I clocked Quinton on the jaw with my forehead. I couldn't see Carlos anywhere, but a handful of people had emerged from the church to see what was happening.

Quinton scooped me up and put me on my feet, saying, "Are you all right now?"

"Yes," I said, leaning back against the partially deconstructed building to catch my breath. "We have to find Carlos."

He held my good hand and we started forward, passing the curious churchgoers and climbing over the mess of uprooted cobbles and bones that now littered the road in front of the church in a straight line from side to side. The parishioners watched us go and turned as a body to return to the church, wearing puzzled expressions as we paid them no heed and offered no explanation. The priest had come to the door to usher them back inside and he, too, stared at us as we went past.

The street beside the church was as narrow as an alley and opened into a much wider road and a sudden blossoming of bigger streets and intersections at acute angles. A row of elderly men, sitting in plastic chairs beside a café that wasn't open, stared down the road toward the green triangle of a park ahead. They muttered and gossiped to one another and looked us over with curious glances.

Quinton ran to the nearest one and asked, "Which way did the motorcycle go?" He clenched his hands in frustration and made a face, thinking until he could formulate the question in bad Portuguese. "Uh . . . *Para onde foi a motocicleta?*"

The old men exchanged glances, canvassed their opinions, and then pointed downhill toward the park.

"*Obrigado!*" Quinton called back as we ran toward the park and the swiftly diminishing sound of the unseen motorcycle.

The park was empty for no reason I could see and we found Carlos sitting on one of the benches, angry and a little dazed. He had pressed his left hand to the back of his head and there was blood dribbling slowly between his fingers.

"What happened?" I asked, sitting down next to him.

"I . . . am not sure. Rui seems to have been prepared for me. His young friend with the motorcycle—the dreamspinner—raised a construct . . . something I haven't seen before, as was the illusion over Castelo São Jorge." He was puzzled, distracted, annoyed more at himself than Rui and the dreamspinner. His speech continued to wander a bit as if he were thinking aloud as he continued. "It might have been something prepared and simply thrown, as Griffin did with the Night Dragon at the temple. But, be that as it may, it blocked my path and threw me here. I had no time to dismantle it. It fell apart in a moment—his constructs are powerful, but they don't last—but by then the motorcycle had outrun me."

"They do that," Quinton said.

"Not to me."

"Yeah, well, you aren't your usual indestructible Angel of Death self at the moment, are you?"

Carlos winced. "No."

Quinton stood up. "I'll get the car and we can backtrack to the church to find out what Rui took."

"I'm not incapable of walking the distance."

"Maybe not, but if you try it and don't make it, I'm not going to be the one to pick you up and carry you," Quinton replied.

"You are the soul of generosity," Carlos said.

"You must be feeling better—your snide is showing."

I stayed with Carlos, who grew increasingly snarky as his head stopped bleeding and his frustration increased, while Quinton brought the car and we all went back to the chapel together.

Monforte's Capela dos Ossos was a surprise—especially in contrast to the dark, dour atmosphere of the famous chapel at Évora, which had been, frankly, horrible. Monforte's chapel of bones was tiny—the smallest of the three we'd seen—and oddly charming. The sun streamed in through the open door, bouncing off the white walls of the narrow street outside and augmented by discreet lamps and candles. The room was only four or five feet wide by six or seven feet deep. The altar, not much more than a deep shelf, was covered in candles and flowers obscuring nearly all of the plain white cloth covering it. The cross was hung above it in a small white plaster niche flanked by two square white columns topped with gilded leaves. The scent of flowers and candle wax wiped out any stink of mortar or rot in the walls that were almost entirely faced with skulls and the rounded ends of long bones. A garden stood behind the chapel, and the smell of fruit trees and flowering plants seeped in as well.

A section of the bony wall near the altar had been knocked in and a skull was conspicuously absent.

"I don't think we have to guess what was taken," I said.

"Skull of a repentant thief," Carlos confirmed, looking at the hole.

"And we'd better get out of here before Mass ends, or someone may think we took it," Quinton added, hearing the bells above us beginning to toll the end of service.

We hurried out, closing the door behind us, and made it to the car as the first attendees exited the church.

As was fitting for a Sunday in a churchgoing community, we drove sedately out of town. We backtracked past the dolmen, but the drachen bones were gone and Carlos's glower was so black that Quinton and I both had to retreat to the car until he'd caught his temper. Then we investigated the dolmen for any clues we could gather. The stones sat above an energy nexus, which wasn't unusual for a dolmen, but it wasn't quite like any nexus I had seen before—the fringe realm of the Grey seemed more present and yet thinner over the pool of gravel. The worlds seemed slippery and unstable there, and I felt slightly drunk walking across the bed of small stones as if the frozen temporaclines scattered over the ground were actual sheets of ice, enveloped in an intoxicating fog.

"This is the strangest nexus I've ever been near," I said, moving with care back to the scruffy grass at the far edge of the dolmen.

"The barriers between the worlds are always particularly thin at a dolmen," Carlos said, irritated and frowning at the ground.

"I know that, but this is not like any other I've seen. It doesn't feel more powerful—it doesn't feel particularly powerful at all, really—but it feels . . . different."

Carlos growled, staring at the stones and their oval of mussed gravel. "As if something waits . . . but there is nothing to be seen. The young dreamspinner has talent, but little training. This nexus may be especially easy for him to access, particularly amenable to his talent. He needs to make a good show. I don't imagine Rui is pleased with the boy at the moment for risking the bones in the open."

"On the other hand, the kid did save his ass, and he *is* just a kid," I said. "I saw him from the window of the house in Lisbon. He's probably hoping to impress Rui and doesn't really know what he's gotten into. But I don't see how the Kostní Mágové are going to raise their Hell Dragon with such a weak dreamspinner no matter how easy the nexus is to use—you told me only ley weavers and dreamspinners can raise drachen."

"That is not what I said," he snapped. "A Night Dragon can *only* be raised by such mages. Some drachen require them, but the dire beasts—the Inferno Dragão, being one—are compound constructs. They require more than one discipline, and considerable power. The dreamspinner's work is a mere spark to start the spell. Rui will not care how young or ill-trained the boy is so long as he gets his spark." He turned his back on the dolmen and started for the car. "There is no further profit in this discussion."

The drive back to Casa Ribeira was tensely silent and far too long. Each of us kept our thoughts to ourselves, constrained by a feeling of failure. Purlis and the Kostní Mágové had all they needed to raise the Hell Dragon and we had nothing to stop them.

THIRTY-THREE

I sat in the courtyard and stared out at the fields, watching the distant figures of people working in the olive grove and among the grapevines on the opposite hill above the river. Quinton was next to me, poking at his computer, trying to get more information about the standing stones. Carlos lurked in the shadow of the courtyard wall, sunk in a glowering introversion no one wanted to disturb.

"They still have to cast the actual spell," I said. The only person in the house besides us was Nelia, and I figured that since she already knew Carlos was a vampire—if an unusual one for the moment— she wasn't likely to be too freaked-out by discussions about death and magic if she overheard them. "If we disrupt the casting, the whole thing collapses."

"Yes, but the timing must be perfect and the spell scattered im- mediately," Carlos said behind me, "or they will simply dispose of you and begin again."

"I thought you weren't listening."

"I had nothing to say. It is not the same."

I stood to turn my chair around and include him in the discussion, even if it meant losing the view. A heavy object, which had been leaning under the chair legs, fell onto my foot. I glanced down and saw the wine crate Eladio had been carrying around earlier in the day. I bent to pick it up and saw that the box had fallen with the hinges up. The top gaped toward the stones of the terrace, spilling something onto the ground in a coil of black and white energy strands. The spell whispered and cried, and I backed away from it.

"Oh crap," said Quinton, scooting away as well. "That looks like one of those boxes from the bone temple where we found Soraia."

"Just like," I said.

Carlos stepped closer as we backed away. "A Lenoir box." His mouth quirked into a bitter smile. "I believe we have found our spy."

"But it's not a dark artifact. It's barely even holding together," I objected, mostly out of embarrassment for not recognizing it sooner.

"It was not made by Lenoir."

"It's not one of Griffin's. Rui told me they'd all been destroyed at the temple," I said. "He was displeased about it."

"Yes. This is rushed and shoddy work. More of Rui's poor mastery passed down to unready students. Now . . . where is the ghost it contains . . . ?" he said, looking around.

There were a few of them wandering about, but even after Carlos picked up the box and muttered over it, the ghost didn't appear.

"It's not at home," Quinton said.

"It is somewhere nearby. But it resists coming to me or cannot come directly. If we wait, it will make its way here."

"We could just destroy it and send the spirit on its way," I suggested.

"But then we would not know what it has told our enemies."

"I think we can guess most of it," I said.

Nelia came out from the kitchen with glasses of chilled wine on a tray and set them on the table nearby. "You are all looking very upset. I thought you might like a cool drink." She paused and looked over Quinton's shoulder at the photo of the dolmen. "Have you been to Anta Serrinha?" she asked.

"What?" Quinton asked.

Nelia pointed at the photo on the laptop screen. "The rocks— Anta Serrinha. It means 'the Little Sawtooth Dolmen,' but some people call it 'the Devil's Pool.'"

"You've been up there?"

"Yes. I've ridden or walked over every mile of Alentejo. There are dozens of those stones and other places like them, full of magic. Old places that they say open to fairyland or to hell itself. That one, they say, is where Lucifer first fell to Earth and wept in his fury at God, his tears turning to sand and stones as hard as his heart. When the pool was wide enough to drown in, he threw himself in and swam to hell where he became king of all that is evil and damned. The stones turn red when the sun is just right, as if they were bathed in blood. They say that if the stones ever *are* covered in blood, the mouth of hell will open there and belch out demons and minions of the Devil to set the earth on fire." She shrugged. "I say why should they come to Alentejo—it's already hot as hell and no one cares what becomes of us."

The rest of us exchanged glances but said nothing, wary of the possibility that the spy was near enough to hear the tale also.

Nelia looked at us and gave a sly smile. "Dinner will be served in an hour. You should drink your wine. Wine calms the soul," she added, giving Carlos a look that would have melted glass.

"Not this soul," Quinton said, glancing at the box.

"Blast Eladio!" Nelia said, instantly angry and coming to glare at the box. "I told him to put that in the storage shed, but he opened it up, and then he didn't even put it away! Oh, I'll beat him with a stick for this!"

Carlos caught her by the wrist, turning her to him and tilting her head up with one finger so she would be forced to meet his gaze. His eyes blazed with banked fury, but his voice was soft. "Eladio opened the box. Are you certain?"

"Of course, Carlos," she replied, her voice melting and soft, her body swaying toward his. I could see the dark, sparkling twists of his glamour wrapping around her and she responded as if to a caress. She looked like a doll beside him, almost a foot shorter, black hair falling around her shoulders like a storm cloud, and brown eyes wide and liquid enough to drown in.

"What was inside the box?"

"Nothing but a bundle of twigs and a cloud of dust."

"When did he do this?"

"This morning. While you were out."

I noticed that her answers were precise, with nothing volunteered that wasn't asked. She was enthralled. I'd never appreciated what the word really meant until that moment.

"Where is Eladio now?"

"In the vineyard on the hill."

"Will he return to the house with the others for dinner?"

"No."

"Why not?"

"I told him to leave me alone, not to come back if he couldn't."

"Thank you, Nelia. Go back to your work," Carlos added, letting go of her arm and dropping his glamour as he dropped his hand from her chin.

She seemed to become smaller as she stepped back, letting out a held breath and blinking very fast. She turned without saying any more and went back into the kitchen.

"At least I have not diminished completely," Carlos said as if to himself. "We have discovered our spy and know where it is."

"We have?"

He turned to look at Quinton sharply. "Yes. The spirit from this box is attached to Eladio—or has moved to one of the other vineyard workers for the moment. It cannot observe us, for now."

"Shouldn't we banish it as soon as possible?" I asked, remembering the long, difficult process of releasing Sergeyev years ago.

"Soon, but not yet. Now we should lay plans while we know it cannot hear or observe us. This," he added, kicking the box, "explains how Rui kept ahead of us. But he'll learn nothing more. So long as the ghost has not been banished, he will believe his spy is still here, gathering information."

"But the last time was not quick or easy. . . ."

"This shall be. You could do it yourself just by tearing the box and its contents apart and banishing the spirit as you already know how to do. You are no longer a stranger to the Grey and this isn't the work of Lenoir or even Griffin. It's the construction of a raw apprentice with insufficient time to lay the spell."

I hesitated to agree. "Are you sure . . . ?"

"Yes. It would fall to you in any event. My own powers beyond death are weak—that is why I lost Rui and his apprentice today. This state between mortality and undeath is ending, and I am neither one nor the other, no stronger than I was before Becoming, mortal and weak until the sun goes down again on Saint Jerome's Day, taking the last of your gift with it."

"And after that . . . you return to being a vampire?"

"Yes."

"What are you now?" Quinton asked, truly puzzled and frowning.

Carlos surprised me by answering without rancor. "Something between. Part of each, most of neither. The only power I now can be sure I command is that which I was born with and trained to while I was still alive. But necromancy is a complex magic, ill-suited to quick work. I am, or will be from the moment the sun goes down, unable to touch the power without death on my hands."

"And that would kind of ruin the dinner party," Quinton said.

Carlos chuckled. "It would. But we can plan now, before the time comes, and I will simply . . . withdraw until tomorrow night. As you saw, the drachen are weaker in sunlight, so Rui and his mages will summon their Inferno Dragão after dark. They'll use the Devil's Pool—what better place than one reputed to have a doorway straight to hell? That is why the young dreamspinner was practicing there. He wishes to prove his mettle tomorrow night. Casting a smaller spell in the same location would give him a feel for the ley lines and flow of power there."

I nodded. "It sounds likely to me. So . . . we need to be at the Devil's Pool tomorrow before they can get started. But how are we going to disrupt the spell? You said the timing had to be perfect and the spell dissipated quickly. Could we use Rui's bone flute?"

"Perhaps, but the risk is high," Carlos replied. "The flute sings only to his bones and that would also require excellent timing. If you cannot remove the bones before the spell is begun, the song of the flute will reinforce the song of the spell, making it stronger until the bones are out of place. If you call the bones, you must assume them, or they will pull you into the construct instead."

"Assume? You mean . . . take them as my own?" I felt sick at the idea. I'd embraced a ghost once and held its struggling energy captive within my own flesh for a little while. It was an agonizing ordeal and one I could sustain for only a short time. I was better at this business now, but I doubted I could stand what he was implying. "What happens to *my* bones?"

"Usually they would take the place of the bones you had assumed from the spell, but they could also return to the matching bones' original owner. It's a difficult action to predict. Using the ghost bone, you could control it, but with both elements to manage, it would be extremely difficult." He looked thoughtful. "But you wouldn't need the flute to call a bone you have an affinity to—such as the finger bone you sacrificed—so long as the ghost bone is functioning."

"I'm not sure that bit of me would break their spell—Rui said it was a 'grace note,' not a 'key.'"

"A pity. If you were able to send the bone back to Rui, the effect could be . . . interesting."

"Is that one of those 'Oh God, oh God, we're all going to die' kinds of interesting?" Quinton asked.

"Yes. And no. The spell-transfer effect would occur only if the bone were moved after the spell was fully active—which has never been done, if, in fact, it can be done."

"Never?"

Carlos gave Quinton a curious look. "How often do you imagine anyone has tried to raise O Dragão do Inferno?"

"I'm sure someone's tried it once or twice," Quinton replied.

"Fewer than a dozen times in human history—and most attempts have not been effective."

I frowned. "What's the spell-transfer effect?" I asked.

"As it sounds. With the bones out of place once the spell is in action, the full animation of the drache fails, but the other effects would continue for a time."

"So . . . with this drache . . ." I started, unable to finish describing the grotesque image that my mind was conjuring.

"He would burn with the fire of the spell until the bone was consumed," Carlos replied. "But as fitting as such an end might be, the danger in it is too great. A small miscalculation of location or timing would kill you in the same manner. It would be better to stop the spell before it's cast. The timing would still be delicate—if the bones are moved or the spell disrupted too soon, Rui will simply destroy us and begin again—but I know the moment where the casting is irretrievable. The song of the spell rises to a sustained chord that ignites the flesh of the drache, and the breath of the fire then sings the song of the bones and sustains it. For our sake, the spell must break as it weaves the bones together—making them unsalvageable—but before the chord resolves."

"It's a good thing that's going to be your job," Quinton said, "because Harper can't sing."

Carlos scowled. "A dancer who can't sing?"

"It's not that unusual," I said. "Have you ever heard Fred Astaire sing? Flat, off-key, imprecise, but right on the beat. I'm tone-deaf. I can dance. I can count time. I can tell you a touch from a shuffle and a heel tap from a toe by sound. I can syncopate with the best of them, but I can't carry a tune in a bucket. I might *feel* where the chord is resolving, but I couldn't anticipate it without knowing the song well enough to dance to it first."

"Then it is as well that you won't have to."

"It's too bad there isn't more dancing magic around—I'd probably be brilliant at that."

"You are brilliant now."

I felt myself blush, taken off guard by Carlos's flattery, but he could also just have been alluding to my aura.

Quinton smiled at me, his eyes alight with love, but sparkling with amusement as well. I smiled back. I was lucky to be in love with a man who had a sense of humor.

"Hey," Quinton said, "couldn't we just arrive early and steal their bones or something? Dad and his corps of creeps are going to have to do some setup first, aren't they?"

"Yes, but there are many of them and only two of you. I will be nearly useless to you except as manual labor until the sun is fully set."

"Damn. And here I was thinking I was having another genius idea to keep up with my brilliant girlfriend."

I smiled a little in spite of the situation ahead. Then I picked up a glass of wine, enjoying the feel of the condensation as it touched the skin of my hand. "So, it's tricky, but we have a plan?"

"We do."

"How do we manage the clan of bone-waggers and spies?" Quinton asked.

"I will kill Rui as soon as the casting breaks. The disarray and destruction caused by the unresolved spell and his death will affect the other mages involved. They may or may not survive, but they will be too damaged to be any danger to us. Bystanders who are not mages may die, but they will certainly be confused and frightened even if they are otherwise unscathed. Given the state of health Blaine reports for your father, he may not survive any effects reflected by the bone he gave up."

Carlos paused to watch Quinton's reaction, but Quinton only tightened his mouth into a grim line around whatever he might have said. "It will be his own hubris and folly that bring him down, not one of us," Carlos said, "but he is still your father, in spite of what he's done and would have done. This won't be easy."

"I didn't expect it to be." Quinton stood up and folded the laptop closed to tuck it under his arm. "I need to go upstairs for a few minutes. I'll come back down for dinner."

I put my glass down, stood, and started to go with him.

He put his free hand out to stop me. "Please don't. I need to . . . put my thoughts in order. I've been thinking about this for a while, but it didn't feel quite real until now."

I glanced at Carlos, but he was blank. "I'm sure something could—"

"No," Quinton said. "His survival is not an option. You know all the reasons why. But I need to resolve it in my mind, myself. By myself." His breath was growing ragged and his face was paler than it had been the night before in Campo Maior. His expression implored me to understand and say nothing.

I took half a step back from him, offering a nod, without speaking.

He kissed my cheek and I turned my head to brush my lips against his. As he broke away, he gave me a thin, stumbling smile, then turned and left the courtyard.

Carlos was still watching me, his arms crossed over his chest and his head cocked down so he looked up from under his brows. "He is a remarkable man. You two are well matched."

I sighed as the moment broke. "I know. And I know I haven't answered his question yet. I tried yesterday, but it doesn't seem right to talk about the Happily Ever After when we're in the midst of plotting the deaths of others."

"Death is incidental. Putting an end to madness that would kill millions is what we are after. If it could be done without bloodshed, then it should be, but I see no way to accomplish that."

I didn't, either, but I let the words I might have said dissolve into the air. Instead, I turned back to look out at the river valley again, the light across the stubbled fields and dusty trees turning golden as the sun moved to the west. I thought how appropriate it was that Sunday evening, as the demands of the harvest waned and the field-workers began to trudge back up the hill to dine and rest, was the moment for contemplation that Quinton had chosen to take for himself. A day of rest in which there had been no rest for us, a day of peace in which we plotted destruction. I hoped he would resolve his emotions as easily as Amen, but I doubted it.

I saw the long communal tables under the trees being laid once again for dinner, the food brought out as the workers drew near. Nelia ran up and down, smiling and laughing as if this were any other Sunday dinner. Days turned like a wheel, each seeming like the last, yet each different and as inevitable as time itself.

The gate from the driveway creaked, the sound startling me from my melancholy thoughts. I turned a little and raised my head to look toward the gate that lay beyond Carlos's back as he stood near me.

I recognized the sound of the dragging limp before the light fell on Eladio's face. He emerged into the waning sun on the terrace with his hands fisted at his sides, his face set in lines of cold resolve and his aura bloody red. He walked toward Carlos as if there were no one else.

We both turned toward Eladio. I took a step and Carlos stopped me with a barely raised hand.

"It's the ghost. It rides him. Banish it while he's distracted with me. The rest will resolve itself."

The box was still on the ground where Carlos had kicked it. I was a foot or two away, but it was only a step to return to it. I bent down and grabbed the wine crate, carefully turning it so as to scoop up the contents with it.

I glanced over my shoulder.

Eladio had drawn closer, and the golden sunlight glinted on a knife in his hand. Carlos shifted slightly as if looking for a way around the pool that didn't force him to shorten the distance between himself and the advancing man. The only other route was past me and while I was working on the box, it wouldn't be wise for Carlos to be too close to it or me.

I hurried and put the box on the table Quinton had been using, shoving the sweating wineglasses aside so they tumbled and smashed on the ground. I couldn't give Carlos more room, but I could try to give him more time. I tore the lid away in my haste and grabbed the bundle of bones within, tied with sinew and bound in the ivory and black strands of bone magic.

"Come to me," I said, feeling the spirit resist my demand and the barbed bone magic cut into my hands like blades.

I snapped one of the bones in two, clumsy with my bandaged finger, and a burst of shimmering light blinded me for a moment, but even dazzled, I could see Eladio still advancing. Carlos had barely moved, his head cocked to the side as if he saw something odd. While I appreciated that Carlos didn't want to harm the man if the ghost was the real problem, I wished he'd at least . . . do something. "This is not right . . ." I heard Carlos say. He moved away from me, but I was focusing on the box of bones again and didn't spare a moment to look up.

As I concentrated on the ghost, I broke the rest of the bones into pieces as fast as I could, panting with effort and the pain from the spell and my hand. "Go," I ordered. "Go. You're free. Get out of here."

The silvery shape of a young man—the same thin, quivering, addicted man from whom I'd retrieved the priest's wallet in a Lisbon alley—coalesced before me. He looked terrified. I ripped away the last lingering bits of the binding spell, kicking the box apart and letting it all fall, glittering, to the ground to dim and die away. Then I plunged my throbbing hands into the ghost's shape, groping for the burning-hot sliver that held him in the memory of himself.

From the kitchen door behind me, Nelia screamed, *"Não, Eladio! Não!"*

I grabbed the core of the ghost and pulled it free, letting his tangled strands unwind and fall away.

The shivering phantom vanished with a sigh and I turned, breathing easier, too.

But Eladio didn't stop coming forward and Carlos started walking toward him with his hands out. "You have no need to harm me," he said. "Her heart is not mine."

But Eladio wasn't listening. Now the fury and jealousy in Eladio's face burned hot instead of cold, and the color of his aura was no longer simple red, but dripping around him like visions of running gore and flashing with bolts of green and crimson.

"Oh no," I whispered, starting to move toward Carlos.

His head came up sharply and then he looked back over his shoulder at me. He held up one hand as if to stop me running toward him. "Blaine, I've thought of a better way."

Nelia had run halfway around the pool, but she was still too far away to stop Eladio any more than I could, on Carlos's other side. We both shouted at once, "No!"

Carlos took one more step, turning his head back to face Eladio as the other man lunged forward, closing the gap between them. Clutching Carlos's arm with his free hand, Eladio stabbed the knife upward into the necromancer's chest, just below the arch of the sternum—upward, just like another blade had cut into Carlos's heart ages ago.

I felt it in my own chest and gagged on the sensation as I reached for Carlos and he staggered back.

Eladio spoke the same words Amélia had shrieked at Quinton: "She is not for you." He jabbed the knife into his rival's chest again and Carlos doubled over, collapsing.

Nelia gave a wordless shriek and threw herself at Eladio, clawing and kicking at him while other members of the family began to run into the courtyard from the kitchen.

Carlos fell on his back, curled around the gushing wound in his chest, his hands clutched over it as if he could stanch the bleeding with the pressure of his fingers, an expression of shocked surprise on his face.

He convulsed and rolled to his side, his lips moving and his fingers scrabbling across the stones soaked in the blood that ran from his wounds. I fell to my knees beside him, feeling the gash in his chest as if it were in my own, and feeling a breathless choking sensation of blood rising in my throat.

Red foam bubbled from Carlos's mouth and he choked, gasping for breath he couldn't catch. His body shuddered with every beat of his heart as it pumped blood to spurt onto the courtyard slates in a widening swath of red. Black needles of magic sparked a moment at his fingertips and then fell away, failing, fading. . . .

The family converged on Eladio and Nelia, pulling them apart, surrounding Eladio—who gave no resistance now—and holding Nelia back as she howled her grief.

Carlos fought for air and I leaned over him, racked with his agony. His eyes turned to me and I knew he could see me there, but no sound escaped him other than the choking rattle of his borrowed life flowing out on his breath.

The pang of his death shook me, and I convulsed over him, gasping and choking for a moment before being taken by a quick-fading dizziness that left me shivering with sweat as his life passed swiftly. It was over so fast, I thought he must have been closer to death all along than I'd ever imagined. Shaking, I struggled to my feet and backed away from his still body where it lay on the edge of the drop into the valley. His blood ran into the pool, making red swirls in the water Eladio had skimmed clear that morning. I stared, panting, at Carlos's face, his eyes and mouth open, blood and foam at the corner of his lips.

THIRTY-FOUR

Quinton had been at my side in moments, pulling me to him and away from the terrible scene in front of me. My clothes were soaked in blood, my legs red with it and my arms smeared in gore to the elbow. I looked more like a murderer than Eladio, who turned white and sank to his knees, huddling in silence and shivering as we waited for the police.

We were up until midnight. Everyone who had come to dinner and some who had joined the scene later to fetch their families or employees were forced to stay until the territorial police allowed them to go. The crime was so obvious and pathetic that the police barely questioned anyone after Eladio confessed, his voice calm with quiet mortification. Nelia raged at him at first and then sank into weeping grief so profound she couldn't stand. One of the family—a burly man with cowlicked hair—carried her away. The family seemed to have agreed she shouldn't stay at the house.

As for Quinton and me, we followed the police back to Estremoz when they removed Carlos's body to the mortuary. As the night grew deeper, I kept expecting him to sit up, but he never did.

The police officer who'd accompanied us back to town knew where we could find a guest room even at such a late hour, and it wasn't until I was standing in the bathroom, seeing the dried red-brown stains of blood on my body, that I started to fall apart. I had noticed and cataloged everything as it had happened, but it was a blur now, a nightmare of gore-soaked fragments that played over and over as I blinked in the light of the washroom: Carlos standing calmly, turning to me; the knife; Eladio's furious face seen over Carlos's shoulder; the shock of the blade stabbing into flesh; the touch of death, and the heart that beat only because of what I'd done at Carmo pumping blood onto the stones around the pool; Carlos's lips moving without sound; his hands twitching in the rushing tide of blood from his body; Nelia screaming; and then the stillness; Carlos's eyes turning to mine a moment before life ceased.

I sank to the floor, shaking and gasping, my throat closing around my horror and grief. Quinton had to help me up and into the shower, wash me off, and put me to bed—there was even blood in my hair and covering my feet. Only the still-healing demands of my body and copious amounts of a bittersweet/sour cherry liquor called ginja let me sleep at last.

I woke up feeling drained and sick—I preferred to blame the ginja for the latter, but the malaise was more emotional than it was a hangover.

When Quinton and I quit the hotel, there were hours yet to kill until darkness would fall. Once again I was in his spare clothes since mine were unsalvageable. I didn't want to look in any mirrors to see whether I appeared as wretched as I felt, but Quinton pointed out that I needed clothes. Even if we left Portugal that day, I still would have to dress in something other than his shirt and trousers, eventually.

I despise shopping at the best of times, but this chore at least took my mind off half the problem. I still winced and choked in horror every time I saw myself in the mirror, reviewing grisly flashes of the night before with every piece of clothing I donned, seeing it for a moment clinging to my body, soaked in blood.

After that, I found it almost a relief to discuss the rest of the problem with Quinton, sitting in the sunshine on a café's patio while picking at necessary food and wanting only coffee.

"Can we?" I asked.

"We can't not try."

"I don't know if we can pull it off without Carlos. . . ."

"We have a plan and we'll do our best with it. If that won't work . . . we'll improvise."

"I can't hear the notes. You know that."

"Yeah, but I can. We'll work together. My role was basically to protect the two of you and that's less complicated if I only have the one of you to guard. I can do more than one job, but it's simpler if it's all centered on one person. It won't be easier, but it will be simpler."

"What if we fail?"

"Not an option."

Panicked, I grabbed his hand and looked at him, imploring. "Seriously. What if?"

He put his hands over mine and returned a steady gaze. "I don't know. Whatever happens, we'll find another way. I'm not kidding when I say 'improvise.' You're good at it. So am I. It's our strength. Dad and Rui have to have a plan. They don't have the option of winging it. If we can't make the plan we have work, we'll force them into their weakest play and make the best of it."

"I'm not sure. . . ."

He slipped his hands under mine and closed his fingers gently, pulling my hands to him across the small table. He kissed each hand and looked back to my face. "I would never lie to you. I believe we can do this. What's breaking you up so badly? Are you worried we can't make it work without Carlos or is it that he's dead?"

I had to close my eyes, shutting my lids over the wet heat of tears before they could escape down my cheeks. I swallowed with difficulty and tried to reply without my voice wavering and cracking, "Is it crazy to feel . . . bereft over a vampire?"

"There's nothing crazy about mourning the passing of a friend. Monster, mage, murderer—those things are *what*, not *who* he was."

"How do you know?"

Quinton glanced away, nervous. "We talked a few times lately."

"About me."

"Every time. Some of the things he revealed weren't pleasant; some of them were hard—" He returned his gaze to mine. "He told me off plenty and didn't let me off any hooks in that regard. But what he said about you . . . I was not his biggest fan, I admit, but he never hurt you. And he could have at any time. You said you respected him, that it was mutual, but he went you one better—he admired you. I think, in some weird, twisted, Carlos way, he almost loved you, and that made it harder for me. I wanted to keep on despising him, but I couldn't. Well . . . except for the Nelia thing, which still creeps me out. But he supported you when you needed help and made you work things out for yourself when you didn't. He cared what happened to you, even though he didn't have to, and he told you things you didn't want to hear when you needed to hear them. Sounds like a friend to me. And you were a friend to him, which I think was very rare."

"But for friendship . . . He wouldn't have died like that if I hadn't given him blood at Carmo. It changed him and that change killed him."

"No. An angry, jealous man killed him. You saved him—at least twice. You're not guilty of what another person did in destroying your gift. And . . ." He closed his eyes and shook his head as if throwing something aside. He looked back to me, his gaze clear and certain. "And I am not guilty of what my father does just because I didn't ruin our lives by taking his. I know that what he's doing is wrong and since no one else believes me, the task of doing the right thing in stopping him and his magical thugs falls upon me. And upon you if you choose to come with me."

"Why wouldn't I?"

"It's not your fight. You didn't let this happen and the Guardian Beast hasn't been around pushing you to fix this, so . . . I guess it's not the apocalypse I fear it is and it's not your responsibility in that particular sphere."

I found myself shaking my head, convinced he was wrong. My uncertainty and tears dried up like water in the Alentejo sun. "No. That's not why the Guardian hasn't been around. I've seen it nearby—it's concerned in this. But, I think . . . I think it's decided I'm not a child anymore who needs to be taught her responsibilities. It expects me to make my own evaluations. It didn't push me into the possession case last year, though I heard it at a distance and it helped me when I really needed it, but it didn't interfere. It was watching, but it wasn't directing. It's up to me, now. It's my road to walk and screw up or not, just like Marsden and every other Greywalker. Hands of the Guardian, not a pawn."

Quinton smiled and glanced down at my big hands. "Maybe Paws of the Guardian in your case."

I laughed, surprising myself. "Well, it is a guardian *beast*, after all. And even if this weren't my job, on that account, it's still my job on your account."

Quinton's eyebrows rose. "Mine?"

"Because I love you. And I won't leave your side. Ever."

He closed his eyes and breathed a sigh, all the energy around him going a soft blue, like clean water. I knew he was still thinking about the question he'd asked and I should have given him my answer again—the last time seemed to have gotten lost in the chaos of Amélia—but part of me didn't want to promise something death might negate if we didn't meet our goals tonight.

THIRTY-FIVE

Lying in wait. That was the only phrase I could think of for what we were doing. Quinton called it "camping." The fields around the dolmen rolled slowly up from the river, into gentle hills covered in cork oaks and grazing cattle and down shallow valleys until it climbed all the way to the castle walls of Monforte, which I could spy even at this distance. There was very little cover down near the standing stones, so we'd crossed the river and climbed the nearest hill until we came to a stand of trees on a bit of high ground with a mostly clear view back down. We lay in the last of the summer grass with Quinton's small automatic pistol between us to watch what Rui and Quinton's father would get up to. We'd have to work our way down with care once they arrived, since the low slope and the trees made it difficult to watch the dolmen from any greater distance than about a quarter mile.

For hours there'd been no activity at all. Then a handful of trucks arrived and set up around the bridge as if they were road mainte- nance. There was a farmhouse about a mile to the west up the rising road, but the sloping, rolling terrain hid the little hollow by the river and only a car approaching from the east would see anything going on at the standing stones.

The trucks were useful cover. They parked one at the far end of the bridge and another farther up the road to the west, just before the road dipped down. With lookouts in each, there would be plenty of time to warn the group working at the dolmen of any visitors coming from the road. They plainly weren't worried about anyone crossing the road in between the trucks since that stretch was visible between the two vehicles. The only blind spots would be on our side of the river, but it appeared they were counting on the water itself to hold off intruders. The mages were conspicuous in their black robes as they headed to the dolmen. Papa Purlis's guys spread out to create a perimeter near the trucks and patrol the field near the standing stones. I counted fourteen of them, all armed with compact weapons of some kind—shotguns or rifles, I wasn't sure—and there would be a few more in the trucks.

"It looks like they've heard about Carlos and are writing us off," Quinton said. "They aren't putting out many sentries I can see. Anything magical?"

I peered into the Grey, but aside from a growing network of lines over the dolmen, there was nothing new. "No. They're probably shorthanded without Griffin, but if, as you said, they've written us off, they won't be too worried about redundancy."

"Or spares." Quinton returned to staring at the standing stones through the binoculars. "It's frustrating that the graveled part is on the opposite side of the stones. It appears Rui's decided the Devil's Pool is the place to do the job, but I can't see what's going on there with the stones blocking a big part of the view."

"It's more important to know where they are than what they're doing until nightfall. Carlos thought they'd have to wait until after dark to raise the dragon—which looks likely—so I think we can make our way closer once the sun goes down without a lot of risk, so long as we know where all of your father's guards are."

"We've got a few more hours. Do you want to sleep for a while and I'll keep watch? We can swap in an hour or two—you'll be a better observer than I once the sun starts heading down."

We agreed to the schedule and I curled up to nap, sleeping poorly with more dreams of blood and death. Quinton woke me as the sky turned orange and I took over, peering through the Grey to keep track of the living bodies down below. I was grateful that none of the bone mages were undead, since their smaller, darker auras would have been harder to spot in the growing darkness.

I could see a spinning circle of silvery fog around the dolmen and thought Rui had probably created an alarm system, in effect, by posting the ghosts from any remaining Lenoir boxes to watch. They would be a problem only in bringing our presence to Purlis and Rui's attention, but by then we'd be so close, the element of surprise wouldn't be much anyway. I looked at the other sentries and look-outs, trying to map a path down to the stones without alerting any-one. Without Carlos, I'd have to be right at the edge of the casting circle to have any effect on the spell. I studied the landscape of my preferred route, looking for potential problems like tree stumps or sudden hollows in the ground.

As it grew darker and the sky was turning purple, the stars begin-ning to shine while they waited for the moon, I switched my atten-tion to the dolmen, watching the slow building of the casting circle and the assembly of the bones within it. Since they were parts of the spell that would become the Hell Dragon's skeleton, the bones gleamed through the Grey, leaving soft threads of ivory with streaks of blood red and ink black hanging in the silvery mist world. They were beautiful in spite of their dire purpose as was the strange chanting of the Kostní Mágové. I recalled Rui's bone flute that I was carrying in my pocket, the bone, smooth and pale, carved with red runes that molded the tones that would come from it. I wondered whether I was going to have to use it since we didn't have Carlos with us and whether it would be better to take that risk and use it soon, rather than gambling on getting close without Carlos to back us up. Just how close would I have to get to make it work . . . ?

I sank a little deeper into the Grey, holding the bone flute in my hand. The world seemed to leap and tremble in shades of silver and gunmetal as if the planes of the normal and the paranormal fluttered here like sheets of cellophane in unearthly breezes, with almost no Grey fringe in between. The longer I stared, the more obvious it became: The Grey really was only the thinnest curtain here. And on the other side of it lay the true, deep paranormal—the realm of things that should never escape into the world of mortals, things I had only glimpsed and with which I wanted no closer association. Whatever Rui's mages were doing with their lines and their chanting, it was thinning the Grey. If they could tear the barriers between the worlds open, I didn't know what manner of horror would pour into the normal plane.

"Oh shit," I whispered, rolling over to wake Quinton. "It's not a nexus—it's a portal."

Quinton woke instantly. "What?"

"We missed it, Carlos and I. That's not just a nexus. It's a door. The Grey is thin here—there's barely space between this world and the next. Whatever they're doing right now, it's pushing the Grey aside and tearing a hole in the barriers. If that nexus actually lies in the paranormal, it's not as weak as we thought and once they've made their hole, it's not just power that will come through. Carlos thought something was waiting there—he almost told me something just before he . . ." I had to shut my eyes for a moment to banish the choking memory. "Just before he died. He started to turn back, said he had a better plan. . . . I can't possibly exert enough control from here if that opens up. We need to risk using this," I said, holding up the flute, "before they're done preparing, or we'll have to move a lot closer—and I mean breathing close."

He blinked at me for a second or two. "Well . . . I guess we needed to get closer anyway. When's the best time to go get captured?"

"Captured?"

"Yeah, whatever I can do to create maximum disruption, at this point, is what I need to do. You need to get as close as you can if you're going to use that thing, so I need to pull them away and buy you the chance. How many of the people down there are bone mages? Or mages of any kind?"

"Six—one is Rui and one's the dreamspinner. We know the kid is weak, so there're only four to worry about aside from the Big Bad."

Quinton nodded. "All right. Can you pinpoint my father? Assuming he's here at all."

"Yes. I know his aura. He's down by the Devil's Pool. I'd guess he plans to test his control of the drache as soon as possible."

"Probably wants a good look at what he's paid for, first. It's so convenient of them to gather close together. This is one time I wish I had a rifle."

"Are you any good with one?" I'd seen him handle rifles before, but I'd only seen him fire my automatic and a shotgun and that had been in close quarters. This was more like four hundred yards.

"Passable, but I'd settle right now for any mess I could cause from a distance. This small-caliber pistol won't do much from here but make noise," he added, patting the gun that lay on the ground nearby.

"Sort of the same problem with the flute."

At the center of the Devil's Pool, someone lit a fire. The flames jumped up initially and cast shadows into the falling night, then died back down to something more like a moderate campfire.

"Looks like gasoline," Quinton said. "Flares up quick, but burns fast, too. I wonder how much of it they've got. . . ."

"Does it matter?"

"It could. I'd feel bad for the farmer, but I could do a lot of damage and wreak a lot of havoc with a couple of cans of gas, especially around these dry grasses and trees. Even more if I also had some rags and some matches. Gasoline makes a pretty impressive explosion if you know how to make it go 'boom' in the first place, and then there're little fires all over the place afterward."

"They've lit a fire of their own, so my guess is that they're going to start this show soon," I said. "The sun's already down. They're probably just waiting for the last of twilight to burn away. It has to be a pretty complex spell with so many parts, so it's not going to advance quickly. At my guess, we've got maybe an hour. If they already know we're here or if we draw too much attention too soon, they'll try to grab us."

"A pair of megalomaniacs like them? Yeah, they'll want to make us watch the whole show. I'd better get to causing trouble so you can get into position. Where are you thinking of stopping?"

"Near the short end of the standing stones—I need to see what's happening on the gravel, but I can always retreat to the river if I have to."

"I don't want them to hurt you. . . ."

"This is not going to be a damage-free fight. So long as we're alive and they're dead at the end, I'm willing to risk some hurt."

Quinton looked grim at my reply, but he didn't argue. He nodded. "All right. You start down to the stones by an indirect route. I'll start moving toward the truck on the bridge to play pyromaniac."

Once again, Quinton and I were moving in opposite directions; I digging the bone flute from my pocket and he slinking through the long shadows of the freshly fallen night like a snake in the grass.

Getting down the hill wasn't simple. I wanted to keep one eye on the Grey and one on the ground, looking for a location that would be close enough to try the flute, but far enough out to give me room to run when Purlis's guys started after me. I also didn't want to step in anything that might slow me down—like a hole or a cow patty. Pastoral hillsides look benign and lovely in photos, but they're full of potential pitfalls. I made my way to the top of one of the paths I'd been mapping earlier, crouching and moving with care while keeping to the shadows as much as possible.

At the top of my path to the stones, I stopped and, remaining crouched, slid a little farther into the Grey to look around. I could see Quinton's energetic form moving down the hill closer to the bridge and no one seemed to be paying him any mind. I could see the fluttering of the planes and the growing white shape of the casting circle with its enclosed bones, sending ripples through the Grey like something rising from deep water. I thought that once I was within the radius of the ripples, I should be able to disrupt the spell with the flute. I had no idea what noise I was supposed to make with it, but I'd have to hope I could fake it—it only had four holes, so the tone combinations were limited and when Rui had used it, he hadn't been playing a song so much as progressions of notes and listening for a matching resonance. If I could get it to make a noise at all, I'd try to do the same thing, except I'd be watching the glow of the bones to see if one stirred.

I checked for anyone moving nearby and estimated my distance to the first ripple. Then I backed toward the normal and started down the hill. I was going to be closer than I liked, but I didn't think I stood any kind of chance at a greater distance.

Going downhill in a crouch was more difficult than crossing the face of the hill. I started to lose my balance once and bit back a yelp as I put my injured hand out to catch myself. I may have been healing faster than normal, but the flash of pain was sharp and left my hand throbbing for a minute. I would need both hands to play the flute and couldn't risk doing myself more damage at this stage. Maybe later . . .

I could feel the ripple in the Grey when I snuck into it. The world seemed to roll like the deck of a storm-beset ship. With the contradictory evidence of my eyes saying nothing was moving and the remaining discomfort in my hand, I felt a bit queasy. It was nothing compared to my initial nausea in the Grey years ago, but it wasn't easy to ignore—it reminded me too much of vampires and of one in particular. . . .

I squatted in the churning cold and unwound from the flute the black thread that Carlos had made. I shuddered at the thought of putting my mouth on the nasty little instrument, but I forced myself to do it and started to play, the random notes warbling out into the night like disturbed birds, screaming in distress. I played as terribly as I sing, being tone-deaf. The initial notes from the bone flute caused a flurry of sparks to rise from the bones assembled in the center of the casting circle and, for a moment, the spell burned phosphor-white. I didn't see any of the bones move, but I did observe the black and white energy around Rui eclipse in a storm of red as he heard me. The chanting of the Kostní Mágové faltered and the spell dimmed, wavering as Rui moved, shouting first at the mages and then at Purlis. The chanting resumed and the spell gleamed not quite as brightly as it had and the red spires of Rui's anger fell back only part of the way. Apparently I was irritating him and that was adversely affecting the spell. It was not the effect I wanted, but it was still a good one.

I could see the tangles of energy that were more-normal people scrambling around near the dolmen as three of the guards broke away to find me. Others spread out into the edges of the river-bound area, the non-magical working their way farther out, crossing the water to search for anyone else who might be with me. I could no longer see Quinton's aura clearly in the mess of movement and the rolling of the Grey. While Purlis's men were quiet and careful, I had confidence in Quinton's ability to avoid them long enough to make some trouble at the very least. Me, I made noise and tried to keep an eye on the bones in the circle as well as tracking the three men coming across the river to catch me.

Every note I played made the spell waver, but I needed to move or be a sitting duck. It didn't take long for the three men tracking me to converge and try to grab me. I slipped sideways through the Grey and forced them to chase me, playing different notes on the flute whenever I got away and waiting as long as I could for any bones to respond.

On the third try, I saw something flicker, dim, and quiver in the illuminated skeleton within the circle. That was the note I needed. I only had to remember which holes to cover and how hard to blow. Down near the bridge, I spotted Quinton's energy signature slipping toward the truck. I figured we both needed a few more minutes and I wasn't sure I could get them.

I dove back into the Grey as the men stalking me drew close to my position. I struggled through the thin, heaving Grey as if I were trying to swim in a storm-wracked sea. It was becoming difficult to keep both my positions in mind—where I was and where I needed to be—and watch everything that needed watching, but I saw the men turn, realizing I'd moved, and start searching for my new location. They were pros and knew I wouldn't be far away, but I still wouldn't be where they expected.

I dodged around behind them and dropped for the normal. . . . Then one of them stepped left when I'd expected him to go right, and I fell into him, knocking him down as I slipped out of the Grey. I tumbled a few feet down the slope toward the river and the dolmen. I felt the flute break in my hand as I rolled and my injured finger took a beating even as I tried to pull my fist in against my body.

The man I'd knocked down shouted for his comrades and they bounded down the slope after me, my movement making me easy to track under the quarter moon and the light of millions of stars. The quickest of the three caught up to me and stopped my downward somersaulting by throwing himself across my path and onto my body. The second guy jogged up and started to haul me to my feet as the first stood up and then slipped and fell in the unmistakable stench of cow flop.

"Shit!"

The second one laughed. "Yes, it is! That was fucking hilarious, Bara."

"Fuck you, MacPherson."

Apparently the guys in Purlis's team were Americans and they had the usual sense of humor that young men in combat acquire. I put my feet down more carefully, avoiding the dung, as the last of the trio trudged in, feeling no need to hurry now that someone had captured me.

"Remove your heads from your fourth point of contact, gentlemen, and tell me what we've got here," he said. I immediately thought of him as "Leader."

"It's a woman, sir," said the laughing one—MacPherson, I reminded myself.

"Must be Blaine." Leader looked at the one who'd fallen. "Jesus, Bara, you stink. Go back to the truck, clean up, and see if you can find something less . . . shitty to wear. If not, stay at the truck. This isn't going to be much of a job now. The only remaining threat is Junior."

"He's a sneaky bastard," MacPherson said as the fallen one trudged away, muttering. "I'd be more worried about what he's going to do than what this skinny bitch is up to." He shook my arm slightly to make his point.

I back-kicked him in the knee and ducked, yanking him over my back and into the same pile of manure his buddy had found. Then I lunged at Leader.

There was a reason he was in charge of this group, and he demonstrated by stepping aside and smacking me on the back with the stock of his compact shotgun. I thumped to the ground, winded and facedown, in the opposite direction from MacPherson.

This time Leader pulled me up, twisting my arm behind my back and snatching my free wrist into the same hold while I was still off balance. I gave up a sharp bark of pain as he grabbed my injured hand to manage the maneuver. He ignored me and secured my wrists behind my back with a riot cuff. "Yup, not going to be much of a party now," he said. "Gotta watch out for skinny broads, MacPherson—they'll kick your ass." He yanked the broken flute from my good hand and turned back to me, holding it up. "What's this?"

"Not mine," I said.

He peered at it in the moonlight. "Looks like one of the creep's toys. You take this with you the last time you escaped?"

I didn't reply. He took that for an answer and started me walking downhill with a slight push. "All right. Find out soon enough."

We trudged on down the hill with MacPherson in the back and slogged across the river at a shallow ford, getting wet up to the knees. At the edge of the gleaming circle of ghosts, Leader stopped and sent MacPherson on the same errand his partner had gone on.

It was fully dark now, but the area around the stones was illuminated by the fire in the center of the Devil's Pool. Without the flute, I'd have to buy Quinton time and hope one of us got an opportunity to disrupt the spell up close; otherwise I had only one shot left and it was such a long one, I wasn't sure it would work.

Leader gave me another encouraging shove and I walked forward, into the firelight and toward Rui and Purlis standing at the edge of the graveled circle. Rui looked thrilled to see me, clasping his hands together as if he had to force himself not to unwrap me like a Christmas gift. Purlis appeared ill, leaning more heavily than ever on his cane, but smug at my return.

Rui started to reach for me as we drew near and Purlis waved him back. It annoyed Rui, but he stepped aside to let Purlis address me as Leader caught my arm again. He wasn't taking a chance that I might bolt.

Papa Purlis smiled and his eyes gleamed as he said, "Hello, Harper. I knew you'd be back. Rui was displeased with your departure."

Leader leaned forward, keeping his grip on me, and handed Purlis the broken flute. "She had this."

"Thank you, Mancino." He took the flute and Rui snatched it from him. Purlis offered no objection.

Rui examined the bone flute and turned a stormy face to me. "What happened to it? Where's the rest?"

I nodded toward the hill behind me. "Broke when I fell. Sorry."

Rui growled and threw the broken flute to the ground, crushing it underfoot.

Purlis smiled at me, a sick, tired smile. His aura was a terrible dark green, threaded with black. If he wasn't dying, he would be soon. "Where is J.J.?" he asked.

"I don't know. We split."

"I doubt that."

"It doesn't matter," Rui interrupted. "We must call the dragon. Now."

Purlis ground his teeth, frustrated at having to delay the pleasure of grilling me, but he was as anxious as Rui to see what the spell would produce. "Yes. Yes, we should. Go on." He turned his head to Mancino and nodded him away.

I started to jump forward as soon as Mancino's grip left my bicep, but he snatched me back and gave me a hard shake. "No, you don't. Sit tight or one of us is going to shoot you."

Rui glanced at Mancino and then at me. Then he took my arm in a proprietary manner, waiting for Mancino to let go and step away before he said, "I look forward to perfecting you later. This will be exquisite. You'll understand why the flesh is a poor vehicle for enlightenment after this. All that matters is the bones."

It reminded me of what the priest at Campo Maior had said: "All of us are bones and all bones are dust."

Rui turned to gaze at the circle of gravel on which the skeleton of his beast had been laid. Hundreds of bones, carved and illuminated with runes and sigils painted red with blood, some grafted together to form a different shape than nature had provided, others whittled down while still in the living body they'd come from. It all formed a single creature with a long snout full of teeth, massive wings, and taloned feet, and it now rose slowly into shape, held aloft by a complex web of light that the Kostní Mágové chanted and wove into existence.

"Begin," Rui said.

Four men in long, black monk's habits had been walking slowly around the bones as they chanted. Now they circled around the edge of the gravel and stopped, one at each point of an invisible compass. The young dreamspinner edged past the rest, coming close to where Rui and I were and stepped in front of the standing stones. He stooped beside the bones and began whispering to them in a voice so low, I couldn't hear him, but every word sparkled and burned on the glowing bones, coloring them and drawing fine silver ligaments between them. Muscles of ghost-stuff and glimmering flesh began to knit over the bones before my eyes. The mages at the compass points continued to murmur, but quieter and lower, slowly withdrawing the support of their initial spell as the shining skeleton began to stand on its own.

I had to stop it and I wrenched myself from Rui's grasp, diving forward, hoping to break the circle or disrupt the boy's voice. But I had made no more than a few inches' progress before Rui snatched me back, clutching my injured hand. But even my shout of pain didn't distract the dreamspinner, his expression enraptured as he slowly rose to his feet, opening his arms as if he were conducting the misty monster upward, raising it with his own strength.

"Levanta-te, meu sonho!" the boy shouted, rising up onto his toes.

The monster of bones and magic stood in the gleaming circle, fully fleshed in silvery skin, taller than the stones, and barely contained in the circle of the spell, the bones held within its shape of ghostlight and magic burned like white-hot steel. Then it opened shimmering wings that arched over us in a starfall of pearly light. I was too stunned to move or breathe as the monstrous, beautiful thing stretched its neck, raising its face to the starry sky. The moonlight touched the unreal flesh with a lambent glow that rippled across its surface as if the thing drew breath, waiting only for a command to take wing.

The dreamspinner spun to face the stones, his face glowing with joy. He threw his arms up and flung his head back, shouting at the stars, *"Vive! Voa!"*

Rui pivoted on his off-side foot, coming up behind the dreamspinner, and cut his throat. Blood gushed from the boy's neck, splashing onto the stones and turning their gray faces red.

The swift death doubled me over and I fell to my knees. My only solace in the moment of agony was knowing that the boy had barely understood what was happening before all the world went dark for him. The tiny, shining thing that had been his life energy flashed away, soaring toward the stars, and disappeared as I gasped, still coiled in the shock of his death.

The ground trembled as the dreamspinner's body struck it. Rui shoved the remains slightly with his foot so that they fell outside the "pool" of gravel and crumpled against the bottom of the standing stones that were wet with the young man's blood. Rui looked me over with a wide smile and a gleam in his eye and yanked me back to my feet, my aching hands still caught behind me, unable to drop into the Grey while the pang of death still dazed my mind and crippled my body.

Rui resumed his place beside me, staring into the circle that began to burn around the straining shape of the luminous dragon within. A line flowed swiftly from one monk to the next and the shaking of the ground increased.

I heard three quick shots, and the truck by the bridge exploded as I folded once again over the stabbing torment of death, barely keeping my feet.

Everyone turned their heads. All the men who weren't in the circle ran outward, searching for Quinton, turning into black silhouettes against the brightness of spell and flame. In the momentary distraction, the white fire that connected the mages in the circle around the bones began to dim and the shape of the dragon trembled like the surface of a pond. I pushed myself toward the circle, hoping I could break the edge, but Purlis swept his cane across my legs, so I twisted and fell onto my injured hand, screeching in pain.

"Go on!" Rui screamed at the mages as he stepped into the dreamspinner's place and reached for the incantation, closing his eyes. The white lines of the circle folded him in, and he seemed to burn, adding greater light to the fire of the spell.

Purlis hooked his cane through the loop of my arms and hauled me backward until I was lying facedown in the dirt in front of him. He rested the tip of the cane against my spine and leaned on it, letting me know he could break my back in a heartbeat.

The bone mages had turned their attention back to the circle, singing and spreading their arms wide so the white lines of magic seemed to pass through them. Light shot upward, then rushed back to them, spreading into the circle and crawling along the bones. Burning light shot from each rune to shine on the eldritch dragon's skin from the inside, mixing with the gleam of moonlight and lending the eerie appearance of living, rippling flesh that glowed from within as if lit by a growing bank of candles. As they illuminated, each bone sang. More notes joined the bone mage's song, building into a complex melody that coiled in minor keys around my spine.

This was the moment Carlos had spoken of and there was only one thing I could do. I tried to concentrate on the odd feeling of the ghost bone, hoping to have the same strange, aching sensation that had linked my finger with Carlos's. . . .

Above me, Purlis turned his head from side to side, shouting, "J.J.! J.J.!"

Another, smaller explosion disrupted my concentration and sent the black shapes of Purlis's men scurrying and shouting. More gunshots punctuated the singing of the bones like drumbeats and I convulsed in a knot on the ground as someone died.

Purlis yanked me up with the crook of his cane. "Where is he?" he demanded.

"I don't know!" I spat back, shaking with fury as much as pain and barely making myself heard over the growing noise in the circle. "Try looking at the next thing that's on fire!"

He slapped me so hard, I crashed back to the ground and he staggered, barely catching himself with his cane. He leaned against the edge of the nearest stone and slashed his cane at me. "Don't toy with me!" Each word brought the cane down in a crashing impact on my body.

I squirmed away and ran into Rui's foot. He moved within the edge of the spell and flipped me over onto my back like a beetle. "Let me deal with her," he said. "I know what will bring your son running. . . ."

The light from the circle was intense, searing white around a core of yellow fire, the incantation's song a mighty roar of sound, shivering on the verge of something. . . .

Rui thrust one shining hand down at me, and I felt my ribs arch toward him, the bruises Purlis had just inflicted burning like na-palm. I screamed in agony, and I could see the sound flow out of me and into the spell through Rui's outstretched hand.

The sound clashed with the song of the conjuration, and Rui made a sour face. He moved his hand over my body, his dissatisfied expression turning to smiles as the timbre of my screaming shifted along the scale, shivering against the music of the bones.

Quinton bolted from the darkness, straight for me and Rui.

His father, still leaning on the stones beside us, drew a gun from under his jacket and aimed it at Quinton's face.

Chest heaving, Quinton skidded to a halt, the small pistol waver-ing toward his father, but useless—the slide was locked back and it was empty.

"You may not have had the balls to do it, Son, but I do," Purlis said, just loud enough to be heard over the sound of the spell yearn-ing toward resolution. "You move, and I'll shoot you in the head. And then her."

Rui drew his hands over me again. The tone of my screams blended to the voice of the incantation and the world shouted fire into the sky. All other sounds fell away and I sagged to the earth, aching.

From the column of flame a shape emerged, flapping massive, blazing wings of nightmare sinew and ghost-stuff stretched over fire-limned bones. It flew upward, and all of us, even Rui and his mages, stared after it, struck with awe or terror. Everyone stopped to watch it, and the stars vanished in the glare of the monster as it raced to swallow the moon.

Then the Hell Dragon arched down, turning as it fell away from the apex of its flight, graceful as a falling leaf. Someone shouted and the rattle of automatic gunfire broke the awestruck stillness beside the river.

The beast opened its mouth and roared a gout of flame, for a moment illuminating the silhouettes of men with rifles trained on it before they vanished in the conflagration. The bellow of the dragon was a bass chord that shook the ground and blew trees aside, a sound like mountains shouting. The thing, like living flame, swept across the dry grass, setting fire to the hillside where I'd lain beside Quinton in the sun. I jerked into a ball around the agony of several fiery deaths.

More shouts and screams came from the still-burning truck near the bridge as the dragon bore down on it. It slapped the truck aside and snapped at the men who had been moving behind it, snatching one up in its mouth. The victim screamed, the sound trailing as the Hell Dragon leapt back into the sky with a clap of wings and a sweep of its tail that set the river steaming and flung burning trees and the charred bodies of men into the air to rain down again in the farther fields. It circled into the air and turned, sweeping for a moment over Monforte and setting the hillside village aflame.

I couldn't hear them, but I felt the panic and death of the people in the town and those on the ground nearby as the drache burned a turning path back toward us. I couldn't think or concentrate enough to do anything through the haze of anguish and death. I felt our failure crushing my chest and twisting through my guts as I tried to hear anything of the bones, do anything . . . but it was beyond me.

I lay immobile on the ground, barely breathing, sick from pain, remorse, and the continual shocks of death. Then cold flowed over me, drawing the anguish from me as darkness that did not give way before the fires of the Hell Dragon emerged from the shadow of the standing stones.

"I'm late. I apologize."

I almost sobbed in relief at the rumbling, impossible sound of

Carlos's voice beside me. His presence seemed to draw death away from me, like a lightning rod attracts the fury of the sky. It did nothing for my other pains, but at least I was able to move and breathe again.

Rui laughed and turned to make a mocking bow. "Hah! The very last Count of Atouguia. I thought you were dead."

Carlos reached for him, hands like claws and black wings of power spreading wide. Rui swept his hands upward. The stones seemed to buck and thrash, throwing Carlos back, but this time he wasn't knocked to the ground. He turned and swept behind the blood-splashed rocks, Rui pursuing him as the Hell Dragon swirled in the sky and roared back at the ground.

The farmhouse on the hill above the dolmen burst into flames and distant screams erupted with the fire and smoke. The light of the conflagration cast the scene in hellish, flickering light.

The monstrous thing swept onward, raising a bank of flame that caught the second truck and flipped it, tumbling like a toy along the road in the sudden superheated wind. Men crawled from the twisted vehicle, burning like the morbid candles of Rui's temple and threw themselves down to roll or simply to fall and lie burning on the ground. But their agony was a glancing blow to me now. Carlos had done something to me—or at least for me—and I was grateful.

Quinton started forward under the distraction of the newest assault, but his father twitched the gun a little to get his attention. "Let the mages kill each other. I have other plans for you and your girl-friend."

"My wife."

Purlis raised his eyebrows. "Oh, so you did it, did you? I hoped you wouldn't."

Brightness fell on the ground and we all looked up, seeing the brilliant flare of the Hell Dragon swooping downward again. It sped, blazing from the heights of the sky toward the highway. Its fiery breath would set the width of the road and a dozen yards on each side aflame. Already the river steamed from the heat of the fires on the hillside, spreading across the dry fields with a crackling roar and the stench of destruction.

I squeezed my eyes closed, rolling onto my shoulders to free my hands and slip them, still bound together, under my hips. The riot cuff cut into my wrists and made my injured hand feel like it was going to explode under the pressure. I screamed into the dirt and rolled into a ball to pass my hands below my feet. Flat on my back, sweating in the heat and pain from every part of my body I concentrated on the skeleton of the Hell Dragon, reaching for the one bone I knew—my own.

It resisted and rang like steel, refusing to come at first. Then it sprang free to fall hot on my hand, blazing and trying to fuse to the finger I'd cut it from. The song of the Hell Dragon altered only slightly and it rippled, the fire within it turning slightly golden, but otherwise the burning construct was unaffected by the removal of the bone.

It wasn't a key—it wasn't important enough to bring the beast down. If I kept it, it would burn through my flesh and set the rest of my bones on fire. I yelled and let go my mental hold. The bone leapt back to the Hell Dragon and the light of the dire beast flared white and red again. I could hear it roar and turn in the sky with a sound like wind tearing through the sails of a foundering ship.

I had no other choice: I'd have to swap bones if I could. It would probably kill me—a fiery death from which I wouldn't stand a chance of waking. But it would be worth it to stop Rui and Purlis. I hoped Quinton would forgive me.

I kept my eyes closed as I tried to remember all the bones, tried to reach for one that I had an affinity for, mentally scrabbling. . . . It seemed far away, but I could hear Purlis talking to Quinton nearby. "She's too much like your mother. She'll never really give up her life to be with you. She'll leave you in the end, like Liz did me."

"Mom left you because you're a monster. And you had her locked up in a mental institution because you can't live with the truth, while your actions only confirmed it. You are a piece of work, Dad."

I remembered and reached with my hands and my mind for the bone Rui had found such an amusing match—James Purlis's left tibia. It was the bone of a man who was shorter than I, older, smaller in every way. The bone now inhabited the Hell Dragon Purlis had hoped to control to bring Europe to its knees, but he hadn't even tried yet because he was too obsessed with his anger at his son to realize he couldn't. I'd have to take it—it was the only shot I had left.

Heat and light rushed toward me and I felt a tearing, splintering pain in my left leg, my knee and ankle seeming to twist themselves apart as my own tibia started to pull toward the dragon's skeleton to displace Purlis's. I resisted the scream that rose from my gut, wrenching my will against it as if the sound would ruin my intent. I could feel blood running from my knee and along my leg like a line of fire, pooling around my ankle and heel. Then a steely cold wrapped around a burning shaft of light seemed to sear me, blinding me through my closed eyelids with hot illumination that rose from inside my own body. But it wasn't like the burning of my finger bone against my severed knuckle. It felt as if the bone had ripped itself loose and left a hollow filled with some living light that tore through my flesh like a knife, burning with cold instead of heat.

I should have been dying, burning from the diseased and fiery magic that animated the Hell Dragon, but something wasn't happening as Carlos had said it would. I had no strength to try again, even if I could figure out what to do. I wanted to shout, to scream, to weep, but I couldn't. I was done and I was broken and it was for nothing. . . .

The strange singing sound in the night broke and soured, the ground beneath the standing stones seeming to shudder in revulsion at what it had vomited forth.

I opened my eyes, mere slits against the anguish gnawing on my body and the despair clouding my mind, and looked into the brightness of the Hell Dragon plunging down.

Then it twisted, coiling, tearing, screeching out of tune, and ripping into pieces as it fell toward the earth. . . .

Beside me, Purlis's scream matched that of the drache, and I turned my head as he lit like a torch. A fiery shape burned against his leg, sending up a stink of melting plastic and steel as the bone he'd given up returned and sank into the body of his prosthesis, melding to him, knitting back in place now that there was no place else for it to reside. The fire of the Dragão do Inferno blossomed bright, consuming him from the inside out. Another horrifying scream came from the darkness beyond the stones as the scorched debris of the Hell Dragon rained to Earth in cinders and ash.

Against the fire I could see two black figures locked in struggle. The larger had taken hold of the smaller's head and driven the other to his knees. A flickering ember flared nearby and illuminated them for a moment, and I could see blood coursing down Rui's face from his eyes, ears, nose, and mouth as Carlos leaned forward as if to whisper to him. As the ember died, I saw the gleam of Carlos's sharp white teeth and then more blood as the vampire ripped his old student's throat open.

I closed my eyes and turned my head against the ground, letting go of everything, not sure exactly why I wasn't dead. What had gone wrong that seemed to have gone right instead?

The blazing light within me died out and the feel of cold steel and hot iron faded, leaving only the throbbing and stinging of torn flesh and shattered bone behind. It felt worse than amputating my fingertip had and I was glad I was too tired to look to see what had happened to my left leg. It didn't feel right—it felt torn and hollow, the joints ripped apart and twisted, but not the way it had when I'd broken it as a kid or when I'd ripped up my knee a few years ago. I didn't know if the bone I'd tried to give up was there or not. It had left—I was sure—but I wasn't sure it had come back and it shouldn't have. . . . I felt worn too thin to puzzle it out and I didn't care.

I felt Quinton lift me into his arms and start running.

I raised my head off his shoulder. "Did we live?"

"For now, but you won't last a lot longer if I don't get you to a hospital quick."

"Oh," I said, feeling light-headed. Blood loss—it was almost familiar now.

Darkness loomed ahead, taking shape like a storm cloud becoming flesh. The light of the fires all around us cast moving light on Carlos's face, streaked with blood and ash.

"Give her to me," he ordered.

Trembling, Quinton did and Carlos stooped to sit on the ground with me leaning against his side and my legs laid across his lap. "That was foolish, Blaine. You keep leaving parts of yourself in strange places." I could feel his hands stroking down my ruptured leg. It felt cool and wonderful, and I sighed, going limp against him.

Quinton's voice seemed to come from a distance. "Is she . . . ?"

"Dying is not dead. Yet. Be patient," Carlos counseled him.

I decided the conversation wasn't real and responded to Carlos's first words to me in a whisper, because it was all I could manage, "Seemed like a good idea . . ."

"Why did you choose to do this?"

"There wasn't one I could take. Mine wasn't a key. I had to swap. The only one that I could move was Purlis's. I didn't want it . . . but it didn't come anyway."

"Three positions, only two bones. The spell sent the bone back to its original owner as I told you it would. Yours became part of the drache, but it broke the song and now the bone is burned to ash. I can't restore it."

"That's all right," I said, feeling much too woozy to stay awake. "Just want to sleep."

"No," Quinton said in an urgent whisper.

"Quiet," Carlos whispered back. Then he returned his attention to me. "I can save you, but . . . this is too close to blood kindred and I may not be able to stop the process. You would become like me."

"No," I said. "Rather die than be you."

Carlos's laughter was the last thing I heard as I fell unconscious.

EPILOGUE

I woke in another white bed that smelled of bleach and laundry starch. No light fell through the window and the roiling nausea of vampire made Carlos's appearance at the foot of the bed no surprise at all. Quinton was next to the bed, sleeping in the least comfortable-looking chair I'd seen in a long time. I could hear other people sleeping in the room, glimpse the nighttime glow of their auras, but no one stirred.

Carlos raised his finger to his lips, but I'd had no intention of waking anyone. He came to the head of the bed on the other side from Quinton. "Listen well," he said, his voice not even loud enough to be a whisper, more a sound that only played in the shell of my ear. "Between us, Quinton and I have disposed of loose ends while you slept. Some explanation about terrorists has been made and the wreckage is being restored, the cholera cleaned away. The mages are dead, the spies dispersed, the Ghost Division is no more, and you, Harper Blaine, were never here. Only a couple with the improbable names of Kit and Helena Smith—tell your spouse-in-soul that he has a puckish humor and terrible taste in noms de guerre."

I nodded. "I know."

"Quinton knows the details of how, and as soon as you wish to leave this place, you can resume your life—lives—in Seattle. Or not, as you please."

I watched him as he fell silent, looking from me to Quinton with a thoughtful expression. After several minutes he added, "Your leg, I fear, I couldn't save, nor the fingertip you lost. There may be something others can do, but this is beyond my abilities."

"I can live without them."

"You may not dance again and it pains me to imagine it."

"I can dance in my mind all I want. Besides, I did enough dancing to last a lifetime. Now I need the rest of my lifetime to live."

"With him?"

"With no one else."

"Good. Perhaps I shall see you again, then."

"You're not returning to Seattle?"

"Not for the foreseeable future. Cameron no longer needs me and I wish to use your gift more fully."

"I thought that was gone. . . . You died. And I still don't understand what happened there. I felt you die—but I never felt Rui or Purlis, or so many of the others. . . ."

"Some of those deaths I took from you, but as for the last, you were too close to death yourself to feel them. As for me, the appearance of my death was greatly exaggerated. I am a necromancer and difficult to kill with death still wet on my hands. Even my own death. I realized, in the moment, that my seeming to die would solve certain problems. I turned back to tell you, but circumstances made it impossible. I regretted that, but I knew you would continue with the plan as best you could and I would join you when I woke. It was Saint Jerome's Day, and I've always been born on that date.

"As to the gift, I don't refer to the blood you lent me. I will be eternally grateful to you for the days I spent in the sun, but I meant the curiosity, the desire to know. That I wish to honor. I will pursue it, but not in Seattle. Not for a while. Life, even mine, is transient. All bones are dust in time and I shall not further waste my hours in the sun."

He bent close to me. "It would have been my honor to have you as blood kindred, but it would have withered you. Few have the fortitude to choose as you did. You are the most remarkable individual I have had the pleasure of knowing." He kissed my forehead and rose, stepping back into shadow and walking away in silence.

"I was kind of fond of you, too," I whispered to the empty darkness.

"Hmm?" Quinton stirred and sat up in his chair, blinking at me. "Hey," he said.

"Hey, yourself," I replied.

"I thought I heard you talking to someone. . . ."

"Carlos. But he left. Mysterious Stranger and all that."

"He does favor a dramatic entrance."

"And exit. He said he's staying here awhile."

"Yeah, I thought he might."

"You guys still talking behind my back?"

"All the time."

"I'll have to catch up. How's the family doing? Your sister and the kids, mom, all that . . ."

"They're good. I'm still working on getting my mom back into the normal world—Dad's death is making it easier and harder—but everyone else is moving forward. Sam's here, and Ben and Mara—they're with the kids at the guesthouse."

"Not the Casa Ribeira," I said.

"No. I'm not sure I'd ever want to see that place again. But on the family front, Piet is flying back from the Azores today, so the family will be together again by tonight. Soraia apparently is still having trouble, but she's doing better than we could have expected. I think that's because of Mara. And you were right on that score—she's the perfect person to help my niece. Mara says Soraia is a witch, and not just any kind but some sort of special witch. I didn't get it, but you might. Sam's a little freaked, but she's getting over it. And the funny thing is Mara says this type of witch is a once-in-seven-generations thing, so . . . somewhere in our family or Piet Rebelo's, there's a sort of super witch. I think it's kind of cool."

"I'd rather she were just an ordinary girl. It's easier."

"I know."

"And why does she call you 'Tio Pássaro'?"

Quinton blushed. "It means 'Uncle Bird.' You know—Jay . . . Bird."

"Oh. That's cute."

Silence fell again and we both sweated it out. He glanced away and then back, his eyes not meeting mine. "So . . . the leg . . ."

"I know. Carlos said he couldn't save it."

"Maybe not, but Sam says she knows a surgeon who might. She's bullying the hell out of your doctors to get this guy out here to look at you, but it still might not . . ."

"Doesn't matter. I'll be all right. I danced a lifetime's worth. I can spend the rest of my life just walking—or not. With you."

"Uh . . . is that . . . ? There was this question I asked you and you never answered. I mean, things were hectic, I know, but I meant it. I still do. I always will."

I looked at him through the dimness of the hospital room lit with a single night-light, through years in hell, through life and death and back again, through monsters and ghosts and despair and everything between where we were and what we wanted to be.

"Yes," I said.

AUTHOR'S NOTE

I had originally planned to go to Portugal for a month and do research in person, but a lot of things happened that forced me to cancel the trip, so this whole book was written using online sources and picking people's brains. I also cooked and ate a lot of Portuguese food and drank a lot of Portuguese wine—as research! I'm pretty sure I made mistakes and I apologize for anything (and everything) I screwed up.

And if you're thinking, "Why Portugal, Kat?" I blame Carlos. I've always had a strange affection for Portugal even without having been there, and, of course, Carlos is Portuguese. Since this book leans heavily on Carlos's backstory, there was nowhere else to set it (and I'd already set it up in the previous book).

Portugal has an interesting history and I'd already used the Lisbon Earthquake of 1755 as a historical reference point in the series. It's still one of the most devastating natural disasters in recorded history—a magnitude 9 earthquake that wiped out the whole city of Lisbon, took down most of Casablanca, toppled church towers in Seville, and was followed by a tsunami (some reports claim two) and a fire that raged for ten days. Many historians and economists feel it was the beginning of the end for Portugal as a world power—at the time, Portugal was the undisputed ruler of the seas.

In the sixteenth through eighteenth centuries, if you didn't have a Portuguese chart and navigator on board, the chances of your ship returning home from a transatlantic voyage were small. And you're going to say, "Yeah, well, what about the English?" The English had access to Portuguese charts because they had a treaty with Portugal— the longest still-standing political alliance in Western Europe. It started when a group of English crusaders stopped in Portugal in 1147 to break the Siege of Lisbon, and it became an official relation- ship with the Treaty of Windsor in 1386 when the first Duke of Lancaster married his daughter Philippa to John I of Portugal. It was an uneasy relationship once England became Protestant, but it stuck and was still in effect during the Second World War—which was one of many reasons Portugal remained neutral during that war. It's still in effect today and it's the reason that Britain first became involved in the Peninsular Wars against Napoleon, but that's another story.

When Carlos talked about the families that were wiped out after the Tavora Affair (the supposed plot to kill the king of Portugal and replace him with the Duke of Aveiro in 1758), you might have no- ticed the name "Lencestre." That was the Portuguese spelling of the family name of the Duke of Aveiro, who was accused and later ex- ecuted as one of the conspirators in the Tavora Affair, along with the Count of Alvor and his wife, the Marchioness Leonor of Tavora, and the Count of Atouguia. And yes, that was the same Lancaster family that established the long-reigning Plantagenet dynasty of England that started with Edward III and continued through Eliz- abeth I. The duke was a direct descendant of the kings of Portugal and England. It took some serious confidence and a lot of gall for the

Marquis of Pombal to point a finger at three of the most important and ancient noble houses of Portugal and say, "They tried to kill the king" and then have all the men killed—most of the women and children were spared by the intervention of the queen of Portugal and the crown princess. Things didn't go so well for the Tavora family, which was wiped out completely and its estates in Lisbon torn down, plowed under, and the earth salted. There's still a memorial obelisk at the location in the Belém district with an inscription that reads:

> *In this place were razed to the ground and salted the houses of José Mascarenhas, stripped of the honours of Duque de Aveiro and others, convicted by sentence proclaimed in the Supreme Court of Inconfidences on 12 January 1759. Brought to Justice as one of the leaders of the most barbarous and execrable upheaval that, on the night of 3 September 1758, was committed against the most royal and sacred person of the Lord Joseph I. On this infamous land nothing may be built for all time.*

Of course, the obelisk is now lost in a sea of twentieth-century housing and used as a pissoir. But in spite of the housing crisis, Pombal really did have the brass balls to take out three of the most influential noble families in Portugal—only two of the ancient families survived: the de Melo family (funny that . . .) and the Bragança family (directly descended from the ruling family of Portugal by—surprise!—a bastard son).

Every biographical article I was able to find about Sebastião José de Carvalho e Melo, the first Marquis of Pombal, mentions his distrust and dislike of the ancient nobility of Portugal and most speculate that the Tavora Affair was a convenient excuse for him to take them down. While he did a lot of great things for the country during his tenure as secretary of state (a post we'd now equate with prime minister), and he was probably a genius, he was universally acknowledged as a cold-blooded intellectual, an ambitious politician, a hard-ass, and a right bastard (but not an illegitimate one). He did attend the venerable University of Coimbra and he was distantly related to the noble Ataíde family—his father, a member of the landed gentry, was Manuel de Carvalho e Ataíde. Any living descendants of the first Marquis of Pombal may wish to argue with me, but the historic record is fairly clear—he was a great man, but not a nice one (although I doubt he ever threw anyone out a window).

And speaking of bastards, while it's true that Europe—and Portugal in particular—had a history of acknowledging the illegitimate sons of influential families, there's no evidence that there ever was anyone like Carlos in the Ataíde family. The Count of Atouguia may have had a few by-blows—it was quite common—but to the best of my knowledge, none of them were necromancers. I'd picked Carlos's family name out of a hat back in an earlier book and, when I mixed the name with the earthquake and what happened later, I found myself with a really interesting backstory. Sometimes I have writer serendipity and this was one instance of random information coming together to make my life both harder and more interesting. The House of Atouguia became extinct with the execution of the eleventh count, but the family name, Ataíde, remained. I apologize to any living descendants for sticking them with a monster in their midst.

Portugal has a history of conflict with Spain and, of course, there were also the Napoleonic Wars and several civil wars with which to haunt the landscape. The country really does have Europe's highest number of ossuaries and they are unusual in that they are small but frequent. There are certainly more famous collections of bones—the spooky and bizarre Sedlec chapel in the Czech Republic being one of the most famous—but nowhere else will you see one used as a garden shed or plunked down in a seawall facing a popular tourist beach. I didn't have the room to write these particular ossuaries in, but they do exist in the Algarve, the southern coastal area of Portugal.

I had to resort to Panaramio, Google Maps, and Google Earth frequently and to translated blogs by Portuguese residents and English-language tourists passing through to get background, flavor, and the relationship of buildings and streets and even the general layout of areas like the ruins of the Carmo Convent—I looked for *hours* to find that side door.

I found the "Little Sawtooth Dolmen" through a blog called The Little Black Pig. I never did figure out the name of the woman who compiled it, but her excited discovery of the standing stones in a field near Monforte sent me all over the Web looking for more information until I finally found the name—in Portuguese—attached to someone else's photo. The stones do appear to change character drastically, depending on the lighting. I saw several photos online that were obviously the same stones, but strikingly different depending on the angle of the sun at the time. The legend of the Devil's Pool, however, I made up.

I also made up the fairy tale of the ghost bone, because, oddly, the Portuguese do not have a lot of ghost stories. I really needed a creepy tale to support the little magical detail upon which so much hinges, and I drew on the Baba Yaga stories to come up with one. Coca, however, is the real deal. There is an annual festival in Monção, Portugal, where a papier-mâché dragon, operated by several people inside, battles a knight on horseback. Coco/Coca is also a legendary "boogeyman" throughout Portugal, described as an evil ghost sporting a pumpkin head. It's that creature that was the subject of the seventeenth-century rhyme Sam says she sings to Martim. It's also the origin of the word "coconut."

My friend Jane Haddam sent me a lot of information about her tour of the Capela dos Ossos in Évora that didn't make it into the book, but her thoughts on the medieval nature of the cult of bones and her notes on the form of Catholicism in Portugal, as well as the practice of crawling to the shrine of Fátima, the angle of the roads in Lisbon, and the insanity of the city's drivers, did. I also got some excellent help from Reverend Richenda Fairhurst about the memorial day of Saint Jerome and saints' days in general, as well as the difference between a "feast" and a "memorial," which was very helpful. The doll hospital in Lisbon I found for myself. And I found the information about shipping bodies on the National Funeral Directors Association's Web site—who knew there was a special box?

I had to fake it with a lot of information, since I was writing as fast as I could and quite a few things got cut from the initial draft— like the history of Lisbon during the Second World War, references to the film *Casablanca*, the writers and publishers of *Crimespree* as incidental characters, and the revelation of Quinton's favorite superhero. I didn't remember to ask my mother-in-law about field amputations while she was visiting for Christmas, and ended up relying on the story my dad had told me about accidentally cutting off his own fingertip when he was a young man working in a factory in Oklahoma City for the instance of Harper losing hers. Gruesome, but survivable. And I relied heavily on Google Translate and some other online references for my initial translations of the Portuguese, since I dropped out of Portuguese language class to look after my mom and a dog. The translations were cleaned up later by a friendly expert to whom I owe anonymous thanks.

Carlos makes two Mark Twain references in this book—his quote to Maggie Griffin is from *The Mysterious Stranger*, and Twain was incorrectly reported to have said, "The reports of my death have been greatly exaggerated." I couldn't resist, since Samuel Clemens was my great, great uncle and I'm a huge book geek. I'm also very glad my friends at the Seattle Mystery Bookshop recommended *A Small Death in Lisbon* by Robert Wilson, *The Lisbon Crossing* by Tom Gabbay, and *Five Passengers from Lisbon* by Mignon G. Eberhart for local color and top-notch writing. Wilson's book in particular was a great help in getting a better idea of the terrain and weather in Alentejo. Neil Lochery's nonfiction book *Lisbon: War in the Shadows of the City of Light, 1939–1945* was also of help with political and social reference, and *Lonely Planet Portugal* had a lot of useful details about getting around and where to stay and what each area was like. I also read many online pages about Portugal from the CIA's *The World Factbook* as well as terrible translations of city information guides for Carcavelos, Monforte, Campo Maior, Évora, Lisbon, and Vila Viçosa. And I spent a ridiculous amount of time culling the Internet for the worst possible news stories to come out of Europe from 2012 through early 2014 as background for the activities of the Ghost Division. Ugh. Truth is not only stranger than fiction; it's more depressing.

Casa Ribeira and the Vale de Oliveiras are fictitious, but there are real *turihabs* in that part of Alentejo, facing tiny rivers that feed into the headwaters of the Tagus near the Spanish border. By all accounts it's a hot, dry area of rolling hills covered in cork oaks, olives, vineyards, wheat fields, and marble quarries that, to my California-girl brain, sounded a lot like the high chaparral and high desert on the extreme eastern edge of my home state. I hope I got that right.

I apologize to the residents of Monforte and its surrounding area for fictionally setting their town on fire.

On a different note, my friend Maggie Griffin asked to be in the book and after reading the first draft she said, "I love it, but people will think you hate me!" So let me reassure anyone who thinks otherwise that I am very fond of Maggie and deeply in her debt for letting me turn her into the most evil mage in history. Yes, Maggie, Carlos has your heart, but you have a little piece of mine.

I've tried to catch all the mistakes and clean up the messes, but I'm sure I didn't catch them all. Any errors remaining are all mine and any resemblance to actual people, living or dead, is unintentional (except where they said, "Sure, why not?").

And now we're done. This is the last Greywalker novel, at least for a while. It's been a hell of a ride and I hope I haven't left you too upset. Sorry about the leg, but I leave it up to you and your imagination to fill in the blanks as to what Harper and Quinton got up to next (until I can come back to this bit of my writerverse). Thanks for coming along on these adventures with me. I hope I'll see all of you on whatever creative journey I take next.

If you would like photo links or more information about the locations and research I did for this book, I'll be posting some on my Web site: katrichardson.com.